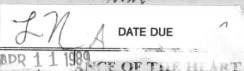
ANCE OF THE HEART

"You were disappointed in me for wanting to retire, weren't you?" Charles sounded oddly calm, as if he had at last come to terms with the injuries and self-doubts that had plagued him.

"It is unsettling, *du vrai*, to discover that a god is only human, after all," Thérèse answered softly.

"Or that he has failings and fears and can become discouraged? And what now, my Thérèse? Have you accepted the all-too-mortal side of your god?"

"Before, you were not a real person."

"And now?"

The words were barely audible, a mere whisper, and she felt him grow tense, as if her answer mattered deeply. He drew closer and his hand caught her chin, compelling her to look up into his rugged face.

All caution, all rational thought faded away. It didn't matter that she barely knew him, that this was Charles Marcombe, the man—not *Le Maniganceur,* the dream. Nor did it matter that he might be using her to placate his pride, to prove to himself—and to her—that his particular brand of derring-do suited her taste. Because it did, very much so. At this moment she cared for nothing beyond the gently enticing pressure of his mouth and the warmth and strength of the arms that encircled her. . . .

An Intriguing Desire

JANICE BENNETT

18226

ZEBRA BOOKS
KENSINGTON PUBLISHING CORP.

For Rob

ZEBRA BOOKS

are published by

Kensington Publishing Corp.
475 Park Avenue South
New York, NY 10016

First printing: February, 1989

Printed in the United States of America

Chapter One

Chassen, opening the massive oaken front door of
Ranleigh, suffered a mild spasm. The petite young
woman before him might be quality by her dress and
features, but in his seventeen years of experience as
butler to Sir Roderick Marcombe, never had he known a
lady to arrive on the doorstep of a bachelor establishment,
bag and baggage in hand, without even the vestige of an
abigail or chaperone in sight. Chassen drew his portly
figure up to its full five-feet-five and stared down his
beaked nose at her.

"Yes, miss?" His tone, cold and repellent, made it
abundantly clear what he thought of such ramshackle,
not to say wanton, behavior.

She faced him squarely, a fighting spirit lighting her
huge green eyes. She remained undaunted by the fact that
he towered over her. "I wish to see Monsieur Marcombe,
s'il vous plaît."

French, was she? Chassen sniffed, but otherwise did
not betray his outrage at such a brazen request. He knew
how to deal with brass-faced hussies of this stamp. And
deal with her he would.

"Sir Roderick is not at home to visitors." With the
slightest inclination of his head, which a more proper
visitor would have recognized as a dismissal, he started to

shut the door.

She blocked it neatly with the bandbox she held, forcing him to stop. Her eyes flashed with indignation at this Turkish treatment.

"If you please, mademoiselle?" Chassen stood his ground.

"I do not please. I find you most rude. It is not *Signeur* Roderick I must see, but Monsieur Charles Marcombe. Have the goodness to take me to him, *toute à l'heure.*"

"Is Mr. Charles expecting you?" He looked straight ahead, thus addressing the upper rim of her satin-lined high poke bonnet.

She flushed a delicate peach. "It is most urgent that I speak with him, and without delay."

"Mr. Charles is entertaining. It would be more convenient if you returned at another time."

"Or not at all?" A sudden flash of amusement danced in her sparkling, humorous eyes. "But no, m'sieur. I will wait. You will take me to a drawing room and tell him I am here, *eh, bien?*"

Before the discomfited butler quite knew what happened, she abandoned the rest of her luggage and swept past him into the sunlit hall. She looked about with lively interest, then turned to him, tilting her head to one side.

"I will not take him long from his friends. It is only for a moment that I must see him. But I cannot—and will not—go until I have spoken with him."

Chassen knew an uneasy moment. She could be no more than a designing opportunist. Yet she had both poise and assurance as well as beauty, and her manners, though determined, did not spring from the gutter. He enjoyed the confidence of his employer and was well aware of Mr. Charles's secret activities on the Continent for the past five years, undermining the efforts of that upstart Napoleon Bonaparte. On the whole, he decided, it behooved him to move with caution.

"If you will come this way, mademoiselle?" Resigned,

6

he took her bandbox and led the way across the marble mosaic floor. Their footsteps echoed throughout the cavernous Great Hall.

Rather than escort her to one of the elegantly appointed front salons, he took her to the back of the rambling old manor, to a small sitting room that adjoined Sir Roderick's library. There he ascertained her name and, with the grudging information that he would seek out Mr. Charles, left her without so much as an offer to bring refreshment.

Locating Mr. Charles would be no problem. Informing Mr. Charles of his dubious visitor without betraying her unorthodox presence to such a high stickler for proprieties as Sir Roderick or to that bacon-brained Captain Jonathon Edelston, both of whom were with him, would be another matter. Mulling over this problem, he made his way to the stables where he knew the gentlemen would be found.

As he entered the cobbled yard, Sir Roderick Marcombe, his wiry frame still agile in spite of his advancing years, swung up onto the back of a massive red roan. The stallion's arched neck and backward pointing ears betrayed its uneasy temperament, but Sir Roderick had no difficulty bringing him under control. He brought his mount forward to join a tall, fair man who already sat astride a large black gelding.

Captain Edelston cast an uneasy glance at the sidling roan and moved the black several paces away. From this safer vantage point, he eyed it with considerable respect as it played off its tricks in a vain attempt to unseat Sir Roderick. Half-afraid that the black might try to follow suit, he settled his shallow curly beaver more securely over his short blond hair. Satisfied it would stay put, he turned to address his friend Charles, who stood near the long line of boxed stalls.

"Are you sure you won't come with us in your curricle, Charlie?" Lines of concern marred the classical perfection of Captain Edelston's handsome features. "We'll stick to the roads for you."

Charles Marcombe shifted his grip on his cane to a more comfortable position. "No." The word came out short, more curt than he'd intended, and with a conscious effort he relaxed the tension in his left arm, which rested in a sling. "I already received a lecture from Dr. Bancroft this morning, thank you," he added with an attempt at his usual humor. "Enjoy your ride and don't worry about me. I'll go and make myself agreeable to your wife."

Jonathon Edelston grinned. "That's the ticket. You have Elizabeth brew up one of her possets. She'll have you right as rain in no time!"

With a firm smile on his lips, Charles watched as his grandfather and best friend rode out of the yard, bent on an inspection of the home farm. He turned, leaning heavily on his cane, and started for the house. If only he could ride, or even drive. . . . Another day of enforced inactivity stretched out before him, empty and meaningless . . . just like so many yesterdays. And just like a never-ending parade of tomorrows, as far as he could see into the future.

He had taken no more than five steps when Chassen swept up to him, bowed, and offered his arm for support. Charles stiffened, galled by the constant reminders of his injuries meted out to him by a flock of well-intentioned but misguided servitors.

"I don't need your help!" Again, his words came out sharp, making him sound like a sulky, petulant child. Realizing this, he bestowed a rueful, apologetic smile on the butler. "I can get around quite well on my own."

"Of course you can, sir. And may I say how glad we all are at your improvement?" Chassen permitted himself a prim smile. As proud as his grandfather, was Mr. Charles, and taking his convalescence hard. "A person has called to see you."

"A person?" That appellation jerked Charles out of his remaining depression. A slow grin of appreciation for the butler's turn of phrase altered his drawn expression to one of decided charm. "No, really? What sort of 'person'?"

"A young female, I fear, sir. She calls herself Thérèse de Bourgerre."

"Thérèse!" Charles's brow snapped down, puckering the recent scar that ran diagonally across his forehead from under his thickly curling brown hair to the outer corner of his left eye. "What the devil . . . is she all right?" He started forward as quickly as his stiff leg would permit.

"Yes, sir." Chassen blinked, startled by his tone. "I have placed her in Sir Roderick's sitting room. If you would like—"

"Is there anyone with her?" Charles broke in as they left the cobbled yard and started up the neatly raked gravel drive.

"No, sir. She came to the front door quite alone. And with several bandboxes and a portmanteau." To his credit, there was but the slightest trace of disapproval in the butler's voice.

"She what?" A gleam of amusement lit Charles's brown eyes. "Of all the hairbrained females! No wonder you called her a 'person'! Where are her things?"

"I have left them on the porch, sir. I did not know how long she would remain."

"Get them inside and out of sight. No, wait . . . it's pretty late, she'll probably have to spend the night before she goes on. Have a bedchamber prepared for her—well removed from any of those currently occupied. I don't want her presence known."

Chassen accorded this outrageous request the stiffest of bows. "Very good, sir. I will speak with Mrs. Abbott, since the bedchambers are rightly the housekeeper's province."

"Do as you like," Charles told him, grinning at his butler's having washed his hands of so unsavory an affair. "Just see that Mademoiselle de Bourgerre's things are safely out of the way before anyone sees them. And . . . oh, my God!" His expression became almost comical. "I was forgetting Elizabeth! Is she . . . ?"

"Mrs. Edelston is in the rose garden, sir—reading, I believe." An appropriate occupation for a lady, Chassen felt. He had always approved of the demure and proper Elizabeth Edelston, even when she was still Miss Westerly and served as chaperone and companion to Mr. Charles's younger sister Celia. You'd never find *her* arriving at a gentleman's estate with all her baggage!

Charles nodded, relieved; knowing Elizabeth, she'd read contentedly for hours, lost in the poetry she adored. They entered the house by a side door and he turned to Chassen. "Bring some refreshments, please."

"Yes, sir." After assuring himself that the gentleman would accept no assistance, the butler hurried off to the kitchens to arrange for a tray.

Charles limped across the Great Hall and his uneven steps slowed as he made his way down the corridor that led to Sir Roderick's sitting room. Thérèse . . . it had been almost six weeks since he'd last seen her, since he'd last heard her soft, enticing laugh or that lovely, melodic voice raised in song . . . An unfamiliar, uncomfortable sensation touched him and refused to be dismissed. What would be her reaction . . . ?

Damn it! Why should he feel nervous, of all things? She knew how badly he'd been injured—she'd been there, been the one to nurse him through the first few days when they thought he might not live! She'd seen his gashes and wounds!

Still, he came to a stop just outside the door. She'd been there when his injuries were fresh, when she still saw him as a figure of romance, surrounded by that dashing, heroic image that had been his. She'd been his lady in distress and he her knight in shining armor . . . he'd swept her from the very jaws of death and been wounded for her sake. . . .

Damn her, and damn all romantic fantasies! This was the reality, where the dragon got in a few good blows and left the knight a crumpled, rusty heap, unable to fight again. It would have been better had the lady stayed away. At least then, her illusions could have been preserved and the knight might have lived on in her memory, untarnished and brave, ready to face a hundred more dragons for the sake of her eyes . . . her beautiful green eyes. . . .

But now she would see the battered wreck that remained. What would be her reaction upon discovering how little of that romantic aura remained beneath his scars and bandages? Must he endure seeing the worship that had once shown in those wonderful eyes turn to revulsion—or worse, to pity? With his defenses rising like the hackles on a dog, he squared his shoulders and entered the sitting room.

She stood at the far end, near the hearth, peering into a gilt-edged mirror as she tried to restore a semblance of order to the guinea-gold tresses that curled about her face and shoulders. Her discarded bonnet lay on a nearby occasional table and she had tossed her light pelisse across the back of a chair. She turned as the door closed with a soft click and her lovely countenance flushed with joy.

She was even more beautiful—and desirable—than he remembered. A pang of longing swept through him, painful in its intensity. How could he have forgotten those delicate eyebrows, that upturned little nose, the fiery, impassioned spirit that glowed in her eyes? And that mouth made for kissing . . . why, in spite of his injuries, had he never gotten around to doing just that? The strength of his regret left him surprised and depressed.

"Mon Maniganceur!" The name by which she first knew him sprang to her lips. Light, eager steps carried her across the room and into his embrace. She raised a face filled with adoration to gaze up into his eyes, and she examined his scarred and lined face. She stepped back and her brow wrinkled in concern.

That familiar door of cold pride closed over his tangled emotions. There it was—the recoiling, the shock, the horror, even the undisguised pity . . . everything he had

11

dreaded to see! Was he doomed to this, to being nothing more than an object of solicitude? He should have kissed her while he could, while she might have welcomed it! But he'd had to be the gentleman. There would be no pretty girls eager for his company now. He set her firmly aside.

"Well, *ma Thérèse?*" He came further into the room, trying very hard not to make much use of his cane. "To what do I owe the honor of this visit? You really shouldn't have come, you know. It was quite reprehensible. You've scandalized the poor butler."

She ignored his words. Her large eyes, filled with dismay, moved from his sling to the cane and back to his marred face. "But they told me you were not injured severely, that you would recover!"

He gave a short, derisive laugh. "Oh, I have. And I'll heal—in time. Did you expect miracles?" With a peculiar grim satisfaction, he watched her delicate color rise.

"*Mais non!* Not miracles. But . . ." Her voice trailed off.

His left hand clenched, but still he could not quite close it or make the fingers meet. With care not to put any more stress on his right leg, he lowered himself into a chair. "I am sorry you have had to see me like this." To his surprise (and somewhat to his annoyance), his sincerity sounded in his words. "Now tell me, what has brought you out of hiding?"

She perched on the edge of the seat opposite and leaned forward, apparently accepting his unwillingness to talk about himself. "I have read something in the paper that troubles me. I thought to go to Milord Pembroke, but you were closer."

"I see." So much for his vanity! It had not been her onetime infatuation or even any desire to find out how he went on that drew her! She came only on business concerning the secret missions they had undertaken in France. It was just as well . . . she'd have been sadly disappointed had she come for his sake, and that he could not have borne.

He shifted in the chair in a fruitless attempt to ease the discomfort in his shoulders. "You'd best go on to London and speak to Pembroke about whatever it is. I'm no longer involved in the work." He kept his voice calm, making a simple statement of fact.

"But Milord Pembroke, he knows only the British agents, *n-est-ce pas?* The information that I need concerns a friend, a Frenchman."

"Indeed?" Charles fought off the impulse to snap at her. Her concern was now for others and not for him at all! "I fear I don't know any of your friends," he finished coldly.

"But it is of much importance!"

She broke off as Chassen entered the room, bearing a tray on which rested a decanter of madeira, a pitcher of lemonade, and a plate containing a variety of cakes. Confused by his attitude and his apparent reluctance to help, she picked up a macaroon and bit into it as Charles poured her a glass of the rich wine.

Her gaze came to rest on him and her heart swelled, forcing a lump into her throat. She was completely over that ridiculous infatuation, of course, but the sight of him again, after all these weeks . . . She had adored him, from the moment she first saw his laughing face peering through the bars of her prison cell in that gaol in Paris. And now . . . Betraying tears filled her eyes and she blinked them away before he should notice. To see the great *Maniganceur* scarred and broken like this—it was as painful as if his wounds had become her own.

She'd barely known him, yet he'd symbolized for her everything that was good about their dangerous work. He'd been so dashing and brave, so carefree. . . .

She peeked at him again as he concentrated on holding the wineglass in his injured hand while he poured. A casual observer might be excused for thinking him a Corinthian, for his tall, muscular build and impeccable riding dress epitomized the athletic perfection of a sportsman. But for Charles there had been no hunting box in Leicestershire, no playing at single sticks at Gentleman Jackson's Saloon. At an age when other young bucks of society sought to make a name for themselves in curricle races or by popping in a flush hit over Jackson's guard, Charles had sought to lose his identity, becoming the most capable of the British agents who lived a precarious and dangerous existence in France.

He looked up as he handed her the glass and she averted her eyes from the deep, angry gash across the face that had once glowed with eagerness, and with a laughing, daring disregard for danger. A wave of almost unbearable compassion washed over her. She longed to kiss that thin, disfiguring reddened line, to smooth away the pain and misery of the last few weeks, but guessed that any gesture of sympathy would only wound his pride.

"Since you're here, you might as well tell me what this is all about." He sat back in his chair with his own glass clasped in his good hand. He took a sip of wine and his cool eyes rested on her, enigmatic, veiled, revealing nothing of the thoughts and memories that must run rampant in his mind.

It was as if he had slammed a door in her face. Thérèse tried hard not to let it hurt, but to her dismay it did. Did she pity him? He would hardly thank her for that! But to see him broken like this . . . she almost wished she had not come.

She raised her large eyes to his and realized he awaited her answer. Concentrating her thoughts on her errand instead of upon the shattered picture he made, she clasped her hands. "It is that I fear there is someone in grave trouble. And me, I cannot sit by and do nothing."

He gave a short laugh for once devoid of mirth. "So you plan to go dashing headlong off to help, do you? How typically impulsive of you, to race off into danger without thinking!" And he could envy her the ability to do just that.

She blinked at his tone. "But of course I must help!"

14

"Of all the foolish, ill-judged starts . . . !" Frustration at his own helplessness caused his brow to furrow down hard and that simple action sent a spasm of pain flickering across his face. The bloody track forged across his forehead by a spent bullet might have healed to a scar, but much discomfort remained. With a visible effort he brought it under control.

"I think you forget your own position," he said. "When last I saw you, your fellow countrymen were quite eager to either capture or kill you. Unless I was mistaken?"

She flushed. It had been she they were after, that night in Brighton. . . . She shuddered at the memory of the horror when several French agents ambushed her as she left a concert. She turned her attention to the cake dish to hide the tears that again filled her eyes. Charles, hiding on a rooftop to protect her, had been the one hit, not she. But even with a bullet in his ribs and that gash across his face, he'd escaped. Somehow, he had made it through the back alleys and over the housetops to lower himself by rope to reach a window of her house—and torn the muscles in his shoulder and arm in the process.

"I'm not in any position to protect you at the moment." Charles, his voice a shade too casual, broke into her thoughts. "So you will remain in hiding until Lord Pembroke says it is safe."

"*Mais oui.* I have done nothing that I should not, all these weeks," she assured him. "But I can no longer remain idle—you know I cannot—if my friend is in trouble. This I cannot ignore!" She ended on a note of passionate entreaty.

"Who is it?" His voice held an undercurrent of irritation. Thérèse might appear petite and fragile, but she possessed a will of iron and a temper and courage to match. It had gotten her into trouble before, and he could see no reason why it wouldn't again.

"He . . ."

"*He.*" Charles repeated the word. So she had come to

15

him about another man. The lovely, bewitching Thérèse. He had been a fool to hope . . . He stared at the dark red liquid in the cut-crystal glass he held and took another sip. The rim of the base clinked as he set it down on the table a trifle too hard.

"It is the Chevalier de Lebouchon. I knew him in Paris, and nothing would induce him to leave France. He had so great a fear for his family, for they are of the old nobility, as are mine. Only his position of trust with Napoleon has kept them safe so far, but that could change at any time, for you must know his uncle speaks freely against the new regime! The Chevalier would not so put them into danger."

"And has he?" Charles sorted through her speech and found no clue as to what had occurred.

"Mais oui! He has left France and is here, in England! I read his name in the paper when he attended a party in Brighton. Something must have happened, or he would never have left France, *cela va sans dire!* I am sure that he needs help."

A skeptical frown set a deeper crease in Charles's brow. "And just what are you planning to do?"

She hesitated. "First, to ask if you knew him—or knew of him."

He considered. "I heard the name, of course. And you say he was one of Napoleon's aides?"

Thérèse nodded. "That is what he pretended to be. *Mais quant à moi,* I often thought otherwise."

"Why?"

The sudden sharp inflection in his voice did not escape her. "The Chevalier, he was not exactly a friend—at least, at first. He attended my card parties in Paris and he spoke perhaps too freely before me, but that was my job, *c'est entendu,* to induce Napoleon's confidants into indiscretion—to tell me things."

She broke off, uncertain how to explain the impression he had made on her. She had sensed an excitement, a

16

fascination about him that owed only a little to his rakish charm. "He—he was possessed of a manner quite carefree, and he hid his concern for his aristocratic parents."

"How did they survive the bloody revolution?"

Thérèse shrugged her shoulders. "He did not say. *Peut-être*, like mine, they fled the country before it was too late. They could have gone back when they thought it safe. *Vraiment*, many did. But his concern, this he permitted me to glimpse, upon occasion, perhaps because my family remained in Italy. This gave us a common bond, *voyons*, for we both understood what it is like to live in exile."

"And that made you think he was a friend?" Doubt resounded in his voice.

She shook her head. *"Mais non.* But the Chevalier alone of my acquaintances in France dared to visit me in prison after I was captured. This was a very brave thing, *enfin*, to visit one branded a spy. And often, he said he refused to believe such lies about me."

She leaned forward, eager to make Charles understand her determination to help. "When I was cold, hungry, and frightened, he smuggled little luxuries to me. He brought food, a shawl, and once a book. And he promised to use what influence he possessed to see that I was given a fair trial, that they not make of me an example."

"He might have been trying to trick you into a confession, or to betray your associates."

Thérèse straightened up and thrust out her chin in anger. *"Au contraire!* It has occurred to me that he already knew who they were! Who else could have gotten word of my predicament to Lord Ryde, who made the arrangement with you for my rescue?"

"The agent you were supposed to meet the night you were captured! What if de Lebouchon is here only to lure you out of hiding?"

"Oh, *imbecile!*" She set her glass down with a clatter. "You, of all people—to suggest I do nothing because of a little danger!"

"Lord, Thérèse, *t'es folle!* You've nothing to prove now. And if he wants help, he must be capable of contacting our people and getting it for himself. Or do you just want to see him again?" An odd, curious expression crossed his scarred face. "Were you in love with the man?"

"In love? The idea, *c'est ridicule!* He is a friend, and if he is in trouble now, I must help him! Do you not see? If he helped me, then I might be responsible for the trouble that caused him to flee France! His current difficulties, they may be my fault!"

Charles shook his head and his lips tightened. "So you came all this way just on an uneasy suspicion, did you? Why didn't you just send a letter to Pembroke and ask him to look into the matter?"

"Milord Pembroke is a very busy man." She did not meet Charles's piercing gaze. "He does nothing unless he believes it is an emergency of national importance. A feeling of unease about an old friend?" She shrugged. "He would do nothing, *enfin.* But you, you will help?"

"What on earth do you expect me to do? Make a daring rescue attempt to save him from a round of boring parties in Brighton? Even if I wanted to, I'm hardly in shape to go dancing over the rooftops right now!"

"Oh, but you are being absurd! Of course I do not expect any such thing. I only wished you to tell me if you knew that he worked for the British, as I did, and perhaps to use your influence with Milord Pembroke." She took a long, ragged breath, bringing her ready temper back under control. "But you will do nothing. *Eh bien*, I have wasted your time." She rose.

"Thérèse! For heaven's sake, sit down! Haven't you thought this through? Consider for a minute! If you're so worried about his safety, the last thing you'd want to do would be to draw attention to him. To have a pack of British agents descending on him might put him in a bad position."

"Yes, I quite see that." Her tone was too demure, too compliant.

He glared at her in seething impotence. "I'm through with it all, Thérèse. Don't you understand?" He picked up his glass and twirled the stem between frustrated fingers. "I've chased my last French agent!"

"*Vraiment?*" She regarded him through narrowed, suspicious eyes. "*Le Maniganceur,* the Intriguer, to give up his dangerous life? It does not seem possible!"

"Well, it is." He slammed the glass back down. "I've washed my hands of the whole business, and I suggest you do the same. We've done our share in this damnable war—more, in fact! There's nothing more I *can* do. From now on I'm going to devote myself to this place." He stared out the window that offered a delightful vista of a corner of the rose garden and the neatly scythed lawn that sloped down a gentle hillside to an ornamental pond. Beyond, in the distance, lay the outbuildings of the home farm. "It's amazing how much I don't know about crops and planting and tenants. And I intend to learn."

"*Du vrai?*" Somehow she could not believe it. Certainly, this Ranleigh of his grandfather's was beautiful, but how could a mere estate satisfy a dashing spirit that reveled in the dangerous life of an agent? "You will turn your back on everything you have done for the past five years?"

"I already have. As far as I'm concerned, none of it ever happened." His voice was tight and he kept his face turned toward the window.

She tilted her head to one side. "Me, I cannot believe you. Do you tell me this nonsense to make me believe you will do nothing, while *en vérité* you plan to go into danger alone, without help?"

His jaw tightened and an angry light burned in his dark eyes. "I'm hardly in condition to do anything so foolhardy, am I? I meant what I said. I'm done with it."

The bitterness in his voice made her bite her lip. He

meant what he said! The great *Maniganceur*, conquered at last—and by his own doing, every bit as much as by the French bullets that had pierced him. He had given up, withdrawn into a self-pitying shell.

She swallowed to force down a lump in her throat. *Le Maniganceur*... For the first time she knew that her infatuation had not faded at all. It was there, stronger than ever, and she longed once again to see the object of her adulation. But there was no trace. . . .

She blinked back the tears that forced their way into her eyes. This man, this Charles Marcombe who sat before her, hunched in his chair, glowering, defensive, angry—and defeated—bore no resemblance to the dashing, daring man she had idolized. No wonder her heart had not stirred while they spoke! He was not the same person at all! She had only pity for this shell that remained—though she almost could hate him for casting out her hero. A grieving filled her for the man who was no more.

The sound of footsteps approaching down the corridor reached them, breaking into Thérèse's thoughts. She started and her gaze flew to the door, but the steps went past to the library beyond.

"My grandfather." Charles pulled his cane into position and stood. "It is growing late. Will you spend the night?"

"*Merci*. It—it is most kind of you." She felt dazed, stunned by her loss. She was in the presence of a stranger who bore only a vague physical resemblance to the man who had filled her dreams. And that man was beyond her reach, lost to her forever, dead. . . .

"It will be best for you to stay here. I don't want to be responsible for you in some strange inn, without a capable guard to keep you safe. The only problem is that we have guests staying at the moment, and I can't have you seen."

"One grows accustomed to hiding." With difficulty, she kept her tone controlled and light. Even his voice was not the same, for it lacked the deep, resonant tones that had filled her with his boundless energy and confidence. She managed a wan smile. "And I shall leave early in the morning so that no one will see me."

He nodded. "Excuse me, then. My grandfather should be told. I'll see that your room is made ready, then arrange to get you up to it." Without another glance at her, he limped his way to the door.

Thérèse leaned back in her chair and closed her eyes as the door shut behind him. Never had she thought to see him like this. . . .

She blocked the thought from her mind. *Le Maniganceur* would remain a wonderful, exciting memory for her, but he was gone, he was no more. He had died that night in Brighton. She had to face that fact, and she would have to face this problem on her own, without his aid. And face it she would. She would go to London and demand Lord Pembroke's assistance. And then, if he refused. . . .

A slow, determined glow lit her eyes. If he refused, she was a capable, trained agent. She would emerge from hiding and investigate this on her own, without his or anyone else's help! She needed to know that she labored in a difficult but worthwhile effort. She was barely seven-and-twenty and full of energy, and she knew herself to have a quick intelligence. She had to be doing something —anything—or . . . She shivered. *Or she would wind up like this Charles Marcombe, broken not only in body, but in spirit as well.*

She forced from her mind the image thus conjured up. She needed to be involved, and not even returning to the stage to continue her curtailed career as an opera singer was sufficient. After weeks of enforced boredom and inactivity, she welcomed the chance to aid a friend.

And at this moment, it did not seem so terrible a thing to face a little bit of danger.

Chapter Two

Charles came out of Sir Roderick's bookroom and closed the door firmly behind him. The old gentleman had not been pleased, but at least he had raised no objection to permitting Thérèse de Bourgerre to remain beneath his roof. They had no other choice, after all. As Charles had pointed out to his grandfather, he might have retired from the work, but he was still responsible for Thérèse. She had come to him for help, and even if he could do nothing else, he could at least make sure that she was safe for one night. Tomorrow she would be gone, on her way to London.

It hardly seemed worth the effort of keeping her safe for the next twelve hours if she was going to rush headlong into danger as soon as she left! If he were really to fulfill his obligation to her, he would get her to abandon this birdwitted notion of going in person to aid the Chevalier de Lebouchon. Well, he would talk to her again, and do what he could as soon as he got her safely upstairs and hidden in a room somewhere.

But first, he must make sure that Jonathon and Elizabeth Edelston were both out of the house. After a quick survey of the front salons, he spotted them through a window, seated on the bench at the center of the rose garden, hands clasped, completely engrossed in one another. For once, her book of poetry lay abandoned. They should be occupied for some time to come, Charles noted with satisfaction. But the knowledge also disturbed him.

It seemed odd to have Jonathon, his cohort in all his boyhood escapades, caught in the toils of a woman. He himself had never experienced the least desire to become a tenant for life with any woman—not that there'd been any lack of petticoat adventures in his past. A reminiscent smile tugged at his lips as the images of a couple of high fliers—real chippers, those two—rose in his mind. Jonny had called him incorrigible when he'd thrown out lures to a Cyprian currently living under the protection of a marquis. He'd enjoyed a very delightful connection with that little barque of frailty. But it had been brief, like all of his affairs. And now every one was in the past.

Before, his women had bored him after a very short time. And now . . . now it was all too late.

He forced his attention back to the one woman he found more exasperating than boring. He still had to turn her mind from this de Lebouchon business. Why couldn't a man retire in the peace he deserved? Damn Thérèse for raking up painful memories—and a longing for action that would be better left safely buried!

He would have to induce her to stay, to keep her safely out of trouble until he could contact Pembroke. But would she be willing? The idea appealed to him, for she was lovely and entertaining, possessed of wit and charm. . . . But what if she could not bear to remain in the presence of such a wreck as himself? At whatever cost to his pride, he must, for duty's sake, make the suggestion.

He found her sitting where he'd left her, sipping her wine and staring out the window. She looked up and his shaky confidence sank to a new and crushing depth. No spark of interest or admiration shone in her lovely eyes—only pity. His jaw clenched in chagrin. Pity—that most loathsome of all emotions. How he hated it!

Deep within, a spark of his old fighting spirit rebelled. It smoldered and took hold until it burned faint but steady. He would drive that pity from her! By the time she left

Ranleigh, he swore, her pity would be replaced by admiration and respect!

He came into the room. "Our guests are busy outside. Let me take you to your bedchamber."

She stood and set down her glass. "If it is more convenient for you, perhaps your butler . . . ?"

Charles stiffened. Did she think him helpless? Well, she would find she was mistaken! And to begin, she would discover he still could be every bit as charming as ever.

He managed an intriguing smile. "It will be my pleasure to escort you." He took her hand and raised her fingers briefly to his lips. "It has been so long since I have entertained so charming a visitor, I fear I forget my manners."

He led her into the hall, where Chassen waited to take them upstairs to the chamber prepared by Mrs. Abbott. Thérèse remained at his side, slowing her steps to match his. He forced down the desire to tell her not to be so condescending and instead, as a sop to his pride, leaned a little less on his cane. To his surprise, he discovered he really did not need it so much.

They proceeded along a maze of corridors and short flights of steps to a large, airy chamber overlooking the back of the house. Thérèse's portmanteau stood in one corner with her bandboxes, which had been unpacked. A maid, who was arranging brushes and combs on a dresser, bobbed a quick curtsy and returned to her work.

Chassen gave a discreet cough. "I trust everything is as you would wish, sir?"

"Yes, thank you . . . you may go. You, too, Mary. Mademoiselle will ring if she needs anything."

He crossed the room and stared out the window, across the lawn to the spinney beyond. When the two servants left the room, he turned back to face Thérèse.

"Now, promise me, Thérèse, you will abandon this idea of going to visit the Chevalier." He leaned back so that he half-sat against the wide sill. "Remember, he can ask our

24

people for help if he needs it."

"*Oui*, m'sieur." She accompanied her answer with a coy glance. She moved farther into the room, removed the reticule that dangled from her wrist, and tossed it onto a lattice-backed chair.

She made no attempt to argue, and that bothered him more than any protests could have. Perfectly well did he know that in Thérèse he beheld a smoldering coal about to burst into flame. If, as he strongly suspected, her desire to help de Lebouchon sprang from boredom at her long weeks of enforced solitude and inactivity, she was more than capable of dashing headlong off to Brighton in an instant, without perfectly thinking things through and with no regard for her own safety. That he must prevent.

He leaned back and rested his shoulders against the mullioned panes. "I'll write to Pembroke myself and have him send someone discreet down to Brighton to investigate the situation. Will that satisfy you?"

"*Merci*. Milord Pembroke, he will listen to you."

"Then that's settled." He let out a long sigh of relief, but to his consternation found he still was not content. Her concern for this Chevalier de Lebouchon irritated him. He pulled his cane into position, brought himself erect, and held out his good hand. She seemed to hesitate, then went to him and took it. His fingers closed over hers.

"Our guests will be leaving tomorrow. Why don't you stay here for a couple of days, until we get an answer from Pembroke?"

She dropped her eyes and tried to withdraw her hand, but found he held it in a firm but gentle clasp. Something inside her—the remnants of that foolish but powerful infatuation, perhaps?—soared. But this was no longer the same man. . . .

"It—it would be pleasant, to have company again."

His lips curved into an expressive smile that turned her heart.

"Ours was a lonely job."

25

She nodded. He released her and she stepped beside him to stare out the window. "It has been long since I could talk to someone without a guard upon my tongue every moment!"

A sudden chuckle shook his broad shoulders. For a moment he seemed a shadow of his other self. . . . She turned to look at him in time to see him wince, and the illusion evaporated. He shifted his stiff arm in the sling and moved the knot that pressed into the back of his neck.

"I know what you mean." He kept his face devoid of expression. He could not let her see how his weakness infuriated him. He eased into a chair. "It was fun, though, wasn't it? And exciting. But now you're bored, aren't you?"

"A little, perhaps." She gave him a rueful smile. He managed a grin, and it transformed his countenance into a semblance of the daredevilry that had captured her heart.

"But your remaining in hiding is for your own good, you know. Or did you prefer it in that French gaol of yours?" His deep laughter rumbled forth unexpectedly, surprising them both. "Lord, Thérèse, do you remember that night I first saw you? You were curled up on a pallet in that dungeon reading a book, for all the world as if you were in a sitting room."

The book that de Lebouchon had smuggled in to her. She put the thought from her mind, for suddenly she found a more pressing need to encourage Charles in this vein, to help him throw off the mantle of defeat, to restore to him the soul of *Le Maniganceur*. Perhaps her *beau idéal* was not dead, after all, but only buried, waiting to reemerge. She discovered in herself a very great desire to cheer him, to rekindle the energy that had once been his.

The warmth that flickered through her was surprising. It seemed her infatuation lingered—or did it grow, exposed once again to the faint lights that danced anew in brown eyes that only half an hour before had been blank and lifeless?

26

She looked away, disturbed. "You were not the only one to see me in that gaol. But you did what no one else could. You rescued me."

"And got wounded for my efforts," he reminded her dryly. "I have not forgotten that I had to abandon you and let Harding and Wiggins bring you safe to England—without my help!"

"I do not forget your—your great bravery! And what a romantic figure you were!" She fluttered her long lashes, bent on teasing him. "Almost as soon as I met you, you freed me from that gaol, and then we were barely a few miles from Paris when you were shot by that soldier, yet still you delivered me safe to the couriers before you faded away into the night." She dropped her eyes as sincerity banished her joking mood. "I feared I would never see you again."

"And instead, I turn up in your house in Brighton a few weeks later only to bleed all over the carpet." His chuckle caused his voice to quaver in a fascinating manner.

"I—I knew you, then, so very little." She looked back up into the ruggedly handsome face with the long, deep scar that marred his high forehead. She had idolized her *Maniganceur*, unable to resist his daring and bravery, the courage that drove him on to complete his assignments over staggering odds. And if he were to be restored to life once again . . . ? She swallowed and found it strangely difficult to breathe.

"Ma Thérèse?" Hesitant, as if half-expecting rejection, he took a step closer and reached out to touch her cheek. "Does the battered shell of the man repel you?"

"No!" Impulsively, she grasped his hand and pressed it against her cheek, eager to reassure him and trembling from she knew not what.

His deep brown eyes glowed with a warmth kindled deep within him. *"Ma Thérèse,"* he whispered, her name soft as a caress. He released her hand only to slip his good arm about her waist, drawing her to him and lifting her so that the toes of her kid walking boots barely touched the ground.

For Thérèse the earth stood still. Everything faded from her mind but this man, his nearness, the memories of her fear and anguish for him, the infatuation that swept through her once again as powerful as the first time she'd gazed into his laughing eyes. Nervous yet eager, she lifted her face to meet his lips as they descended in a gentle, tentative touch.

A firm rap sounded on the door and he released her abruptly. She stepped back and stared up into his dark eyes. For one brief moment his longing and his miserable uncertainty were there, clear to be seen, leaving her shaken. Then his face went blank, as if he'd slammed a door on his innermost thoughts and firmly closed her out.

"My guests will have returned to the house. If you will excuse me?"

The door shut behind him and she sank down into a chair. What had just passed between them, and why had she been so willing? Charles . . . *Le Maniganceur*. . . . For a moment they had seemed one and the same, more real in their combination than either had ever been alone. . . .

But that tortured, uncertain look in his eyes . . . it returned to haunt her. That had nothing to do with her supremely confident *Maniganceur*. The fact disturbed her. Charles Marcombe was only a shadow, a pale imitation of the great *Maniganceur*, who was no more. She had been taken in, but only for a moment. The side of him that she had worshiped no longer existed.

But why had he kissed her? Certainly not out of love! The infatuation had all been one-sided. From *Le Maniganceur* she might have expected it, but not from Charles Marcombe. To her, they now always would—always must, for the sake of her heart—be two different people. And so, if he had not kissed her out of caring . . .

Perhaps he sought to distract her from her purpose, to engage her in elegant dalliance in order to keep her out of trouble. He might well have guessed she had not abandoned her intention of going to the aid of the Chevalier de Lebouchon. She bit her lip at this recollection of her duty.

Why could she not be content to let someone else handle it? She had done her share toward returning peace to Europe, and so had *Le Maniganceur*. She should not judge Charles weak for renouncing that name of honor. He was right to put the past behind him!

But still, she did not trust Pembroke to take her worry seriously. She must see to this one last problem . . . and then, she realized, she hoped there would be others.

She returned to the window, where she stood staring blindly out toward the spinney. She wanted to return to her old life, to the thrill of activity, that sense of fulfillment. And *Le Maniganceur*—he would want that also. The *Maniganceur* she had known would never retire to the peace of a country estate. That was what would always separate her idol from Charles Marcombe. Charles was through with danger and now found all the challenge he could face in Ranleigh's thousand acres.

She would not have minded the assistance of the great *Maniganceur* on this little venture. All she planned to do was to call on an old acquaintance and assure herself that nothing was wrong. What could be dangerous about that? She would concoct some story to tell Charles, slip quietly away to London to tell Lord Pembroke what she planned, then be off to Brighton. She could be back at Ranleigh in less than a se'nnight, and then . . . well, she owed it to the memory of *Le Maniganceur* to try and cheer Charles Marcombe.

She glanced at the clock on the mantel. If Sir Roderick kept country hours, it would soon be time for dinner. Someone would bring her a tray, she supposed. With a sigh she prepared to settle down for a boring evening. Perhaps she could ring for that maid—Mary?—and send her to the library for a book. Charles would be busy with his guests late into the night and would probably not be able to visit her again until morning.

And when he came, she had best have her story ready to convince him to let her leave for a week. With half her mind still trying to hit on a scheme, she rang for Mary and set about removing her traveling gown. The stage she had taken from the tiny village where she had spent the last five weeks had been filthy, packed with farmers and even a selection of squawking chickens confined in a basket. And then a laborer in a buckboard wagon filled with fertilizer had taken her up for the last few miles to Ranleigh. She regarded her gown with a wrinkled nose. She doubted if even the most efficient of abigails would be able to clean away the odor that lingered.

When Mary at last arrived, a small brindle cat padded in her wake. It entered the apartment and went at once to sniff out the strange belongings.

"Do you dislike cats, ma'mselle?" Mary regarded her anxiously. "If you do, I'll throw Jasper out."

"*Non*, let him stay." She held out her hand and called softly. Jasper regarded her with large, yellow eyes, twitched his tail, and continued his investigations.

Mary picked up a gown of rose crepe that she had unpacked earlier. With inexpert fingers she tossed it over Thérèse's head and tried to shake out the narrow skirts.

"I am so sorry it took me so long to answer your call, ma'mselle. Such a stir as everyone is in below stairs! To have two sets of guests! Why, Cook hardly knows what to do!"

"Please, you must not go to any trouble for me!" Thérèse exclaimed. She straightened the skirt and held the bodice so that the maid could more easily fasten the tiny buttons at the back of the low scooped neck. "Do *Signeur* Roderick and M. Charles not entertain much?"

"Oh, no, ma'mselle! Not even when Miss Celia lived here. Lady Ryde, I should say." She pressed Thérèse into a chair before the dressing table so that she could comb out her hair. "And only imagine, it is her former companion who has come to visit!"

"Her . . . do you mean Mademoiselle Westerly?" Thérèse turned to face Mary, her eyes wide with surprised pleasure.

"Yes, ma'mselle, though to be sure, she is Mrs. Edelston now. Turn around, do, ma'mselle. And Captain Edelston is with her, of course," she added.

"*Voyons*, I know them!" Thérèse cried, delighted. "But of course, Monsieur Charles, he does not know this! I will be quite safe with them! *Tiens*, I should so much enjoy seeing them again! I shall go down!"

"Are you sure, ma'mselle?" Mary looked worried. "I have me orders to bring you your dinner here."

"It is only because they do not know! Me, I am quite safe with my so dear friends. Oh, I have seen no one for so very long!"

Mary was not proof against the wistfulness in the lovely voice, and she quickly set about dressing the profuse golden ringlets. Jasper, having satisfied himself that the room was devoid of mice, settled himself in Thérèse's lap. Giving his fur a perfunctory smoothing with his rough tongue, he gave a cavernous yawn and settled down to sleep.

When at last a rose satin riband had been threaded through her curls, Thérèse sprang to her feet, dislodging the indignant cat. It stalked majestically off to her bed and made itself comfortable on the dressing gown of yellow gauze that rested there.

Thérèse hurried from the room and almost ran through the twisting corridors that isolated her from the rest of the household. When she reached the picture gallery, she paused to compose herself, found the excitement bubbling within her would not be contained, and hurried on, her steps light and almost flying.

In the Great Hall she hesitated for a moment. Only one door stood ajar, and this seemed to indicate that the diners would gather there. She crossed to it and peeped in.

Red satin hangings and a profuse amount of gold trim decorated the large, comfortable salon. A long sofa and several chairs, all of the same brilliant hue, were gathered at the near end in a companionable circle near the massive hearth. No one had yet come downstairs.

She went in and took a seat. A glance at the mantel clock told her that it was ten minutes before six. The others would be down soon, and she found she could hardly wait.

Less than five minutes passed before the door opened. Sir Roderick, precise to a pin in a coat of mulberry velvet and satin knee breeches, entered the room and stopped. He drew his tall, wiry frame up to its full height, raised his quizzing glass, and regarded her through it. He allowed it to drop and came forward.

"Mademoiselle de Bourgerre? It is some time, I believe, since we last met." He did not sound pleased to renew the acquaintance.

Out of deference to his age, she rose and extended her hand. He took it in a firm grasp, but released it almost at once.

"My grandson has explained your presence to me. I understood you were to dine in your room."

"But it is most safe for me to be here!" she declared, bestowing her most winning smile upon him.

A muscle twitched at the corner of his mouth. "Safe for whom?"

"Why, for me, *sans doute!* I know these guests, Captain and Madame Edelston. They are good people, *du vrai.* They would not betray my presence here. And I do so want to see them again."

Sir Roderick's lined face took on a gentler expression. "I am sorry, my dear. You must understand that it is not your safety that concerns me at the moment."

Thérèse blinked, puzzled by his attitude. "But no one has followed me here! *Voyons,* there will be no attack on this house because of me!"

"You misunderstand, my dear. I . . ." The door opened

behind him and he swung around as his grandson came in. Sir Roderick's brow furrowed in displeasure.

"Thérèse, what are you doing here?" Charles looked from her to Sir Roderick, sensing the tension on his grandfather's part. "Go up at once, and use the back stairs. Our guests will be down any minute!"

"But Charles, I tell your grandfather they are not a danger to me!"

He glanced at Sir Roderick's grim face. "We are responsible for you, Thérèse. We don't want to take any chances." He took her arm and led her gently but inexorably through the doorway—only to collide with Jonathon and Elizabeth just over the threshold.

Jonathon Edelston blinked at the sight of her, then a look of startled recognition lit his vacuous blue eyes. A flush of pleasure colored his classically handsome countenance to the roots of his modishly curled blond hair. "Mademoiselle de Bourgerre! I'd no idea you were here."

Elizabeth held out her hand. "How delightful to see you again. And quite recovered from those dreadful happenings in Brighton."

Thérèse clasped his hand between hers and smiled warmly. "It is *so* good to see a friend! And you look so very well!" She regarded with approval the simple but becoming dinner gown of celestial blue crepe, a color that set off Elizabeth's fair coloring to perfection. Never would the woman have dared to wear such a beautiful dress during her days as chaperone and companion to Charles's sister Celia.

"But why didn't you tell us she was here, Charlie?" Jonathon turned his suddenly affronted gaze on his friend. "Don't you trust us?"

"It's not that, Jonny. She only just arrived."

"Well, you might at least have let us know you was expecting her. Or . . ." He broke off and cast a delighted, speculative glance at Thérèse. "Or were you waiting until you got things settled between you?"

Charles stiffened. "It is no such thing. Mademoiselle de Bourgerre is traveling to London to see one of the government officials. And since there are few places where she can be safe, she is staying here for the night."

"Well, I just thought . . ."

"I am glad that you did," Elizabeth stepped in neatly to fill the embarrassing pause created by her husband. "A terrible thing it would be if old friends could not meet, upon occasion. How fortunate you chose to travel today! We would have been very sorry to have missed you."

Thérèse smiled her gratitude. If it wasn't just like Jonathon Edelston to misinterpret her reason for being there—and to assume that Charles considered making her an offer! The very thought was absurd! But apparently Captain Edelston had a history of jumping to wrong conclusions. It was he, after all, who had told Celia Marcombe that her brother had deserted the Navy, when in reality he had slipped away to become a spy!

"Shall we join my grandfather?" Charles, recognizing defeat but still looking harassed, ushered the party into the salon where Sir Roderick waited.

The elderly gentleman resigned himself to the situation. He raised no further protest to Thérèse's inclusion at the dinner table, and he himself rang for Chassen to request that another cover be laid. He sat silent throughout most of the protracted meal and when he raised his eyes from his plate, it was only to regard Thérèse with a thoughtful, frowning expression.

She was not unaware of his scrutiny and found it unnerving. What lay behind his antagonism? When last they had met, he'd been quite charming and pleasant. But now he seemed worried, as if he resented her presence! Had she committed some dreadful social solecism by arriving at his house uninvited? Or did it go deeper than that? Did he fear she might lure Charles back into a life of danger?

Dinner at last came to an end. Jonathon settled back, prepared to remain at the table over wine, but Sir Roderick seemed loath to break up the party. When Elizabeth and Thérèse rose, he suggested that the gentlemen accompany the ladies.

As soon as they adjourned to the drawing room, Sir Roderick rang for cards and tables to be set up. Elizabeth retired to the sofa with her embroidery, leaving the others to make up a table of whist. Thérèse, though she would have preferred piquet, took her place dutifully and soon had the satisfaction of seeing the elderly man relax in one of his favorite pastimes. More than once he complimented her on her play, and by the time the tea tray arrived they had once more established cordial relations.

This lasted until she rose to retire. Sir Roderick accompanied her out into the hall to where candles had been placed on a table at the foot of the great staircase. He stopped her as she started to light one.

"If you will spare me a few moments?" He led the way to his library.

With a growing sense of unease, Thérèse followed. Sir Roderick closed the door behind them and gestured for her to be seated. He took several restless steps about the room, then came to a stop before her.

"I would not have you think me inhospitable, but I have a very great request to make of you."

Thérèse tilted her head up, bracing herself for whatever would follow. "Yes, m'sieur?"

"I believe my grandson has asked you to remain for a few days. This is not easy for me to ask, Mademoiselle de Bourgerre, but I would like you to turn down his invitation."

She swallowed and tried very hard not to let her hurt show. *"Vraiment?"*

"It is nothing personal, mademoiselle." He clasped his hands behind his back. "I spoke of safety earlier. It is my grandson's safety that concerns me."

"But me, I would do nothing to harm him!" she exclaimed, bewildered.

"Not intentionally, of course. But just your presence here may do him harm. No, let me finish." He held up a hand to silence her protest. "I know, perhaps even better than you, how much he enjoyed his dangerous life. But he is no longer physically able to take such risks."

"And you fear I will reawaken memories and longings to take up such a life once again, *n'est-ce pas?*"

He nodded. "He has made the sensible decision to remain here. I want nothing to change that."

Her lips twisted into a sad smile. "But there is little chance of that! His injuries, they were severe, *du vrai*, but they have gone deeper than the merely physical. He does not desire to return to the old ways."

"His sense of duty goes deeper than you seem to realize. He has asked you to stay in order to keep you out of trouble. He fears that if you leave now, you will go into danger. Whatever his personal wishes or sentiments might be, you were once his responsibility, and he takes that seriously."

So she had been right. She fought back the humiliation. That whole scene in her room this afternoon, it had been nothing more than an act. Even his kiss—he sought only to lure her into an elegant flirtation so that he would not have to be troubled with going to her rescue again. He cared nothing for her!

"The only way to relieve him of his sense of obligation is for you to ignore his request and go. I hope you understand."

She roused from her thoughts to realize that he spoke to her. "Yes, m'sieur, I believe I do."

"I am glad. Now, I think it will be best if you leave first thing in the morning, without seeing him again. I will convey your apologies to him after you have gone."

Leave? Without seeing Charles, all that remained of her *Maniganceur*, one last time? The very idea tore at her. But knowing what he really thought of her, that he regarded her only as a burden . . . no, Sir Roderick was right. She could not remain, could not bear to face him again.

She rose and he possessed himself of her hand. "I must thank you, mademoiselle. And truly, this is for the best."

She nodded, not able to trust herself to speak, and hurried from the room.

She reached the solitude of her bedchamber without encountering anyone. For several moments she stood in the middle of the room, her hands clenched, her eyes closed tight as she fought back the tears that threatened to escape down her cheeks. Why should it matter to her? *Le Maniganceur* was dead! She repeated it over and over. *Le Maniganceur* was dead. Only a very different man remained, one that she hardly knew! Yet still . . .

The cat blinked sleepily from the depths of her now-wrinkled dressing gown. It yawned and stretched, arching its back. Jumping to the ground, it went to rub against her ankles.

She scooped up the purring animal and sank down onto her bed. It was time she buried her disturbing memories, along with *Le Maniganceur*. Let this Charles Marcombe who remained have his peace and comfort! She did not need him and his condescending attitude! He could retire into obscurity, for all she cared.

And for herself—she still had work to do, a cause to serve. Her way might hold pitfalls and hazards, but she would follow it to its end. She swallowed hard. If only she knew where that end might be.

She rose and set aside Jasper, who was forced to take a thorough bath to smooth down the fur ruffled by her agitated hands. She climbed into bed and tried to concentrate on the tall, rakish figure of the Chevalier de Lebouchon, but Charles's brooding, pain-filled eyes kept intruding. Jasper joined her and she stroked him as she willed herself not to cry. So much was gone forever. . . .

Chapter Three

Charles set his coffee cup down with a clatter and stared at Chassen in disbelief. "What do you mean, she has gone?"

The butler regarded the perplexed and chagrined face of his employer's grandson and assumed the expression of a stuffed trout. "As I said, sir. Ma'mselle de Bourgerre departed nearly two hours ago. Sir Roderick's own barouche carried her to the village."

"And why was I not informed?" Charles came to his feet, but his growing alarm overshadowed the fact that he had not needed recourse to his cane. "Did no one do anything to stop her?"

"I was not under orders to do so, sir. It would have been the height of impropriety, and far beyond the scope of my duties, to hinder one of your guests from taking her leave, if that was her wish."

Charles sank back into his chair, pale beneath the deep bronze of his skin. "Was anyone with her?"

"No, sir. She was alone."

At least she hadn't been taken by force! He let out a deep sigh of relief. But why . . . ? "Did she receive any messages? Anything that might make her leave unexpectedly?" He grasped at this as a drowning man might reach for a floating fragment of wood.

"Not to my knowledge, sir." The butler waited with

stoic resignation for the burst of temper in which, in his experience, gentlemen of the *Haut Ton* usually indulged themselves when their wishes were thwarted.

It was not forthcoming. Charles picked up his coffee cup and stared bleakly at the clouded swirls in the light brown liquid. She had gone of her own will. Thérèse, so delicate and so fragile, yet so very brave . . . but not brave enough to bear the sight of the broken wreck that had once been her *Maniganceur*. It must have shattered her romantic fantasies to discover that her golden idol had feet of clay.

Blindly he swept out of the room. Damn the cane, damn the sling, and damn those scars! And damn Thérèse, into the bargain! What right had she to come here, so full of life and health and vigor, and look upon him with piteous contempt? What had she seen when she looked at him? A broken shell? A helpless wreck where once a powerful man had been?

And what had she thought when he kissed her? Had she been insulted? Or just repelled? Had she run, unable to face him again, afraid he might subject her to another such unbearable caress?

He stopped and found his disconsolate steps had taken him to the stables. A fitting place for a country squire, which was what he was reduced to being! Not for him the mad adventures, the stirring events that took place on the Continent! Not for him the excitement and daring that meant the joy of life, the love of a beautiful and vibrant woman! Not for him, a companion like Thérèse, whose melodic laughter stirred his very soul.

Le Maniganceur was dead, and a very great part of him had died along with his other self.

Le Maniganceur was dead. The same realization haunted Thérèse as she huddled further into her corner of the stage. Hour after lonely hour passed as the carriage jostled and lurched along. Every country track and rutted, muddy lane appeared to be on the route.

She pulled her pelissse tighter despite the warmth of the approaching evening. The stage was crowded, the passengers pressed close together in an unwanted intimacy. The farmer seated across the swaying vehicle took a disconcerting interest in her that left her color heightened the one time she accidentally met his eyes. At her side, and no less comforting, sat a very prim and sour-faced spinster of indeterminate years who, after casting one measuring glance at Thérèse's fair loveliness and modish bonnet, sniffed and pointedly turned her head.

Thérèse stared out the window. The rolling green hills and spinneys passed unnoticed; all she could see was her present emptiness. *Le Managanceur* was gone—she had to face the fact. It was useless to expect this Charles Marcombe to act, to think like, to be her hero.

He was gone. . . . The words repeated themselves over and over with the rhythmic pounding of the horses' hooves. He was gone . . . stinging tears of grief forced their way into her eyes, and her heart ached with the pain of her loss. He was gone. . . . She tried to put the thought from her mind but failed. *He was gone. . . .*

But she was being a fool! She probably mourned a man who had no existence except in her wistful imagination! He had embodied her every desire. He had been the epitome of the perfect man: with a tall, muscular build; striking, rough-hewn features; and a deep laugh that sent shivering thrills racing through her. And he had been brave and reckless, a knight in shining armor who had swept her off her feet and to safety. What relation did such a man have to reality? None whatsoever! No man could be so exactly the answer to a woman's dreams.

She had never really known her *Maniganceur* after all. He might well have been no more than one of his own clever disguises. Their time together had been so brief, so chaotic, so fraught with drama—it was no wonder she had filled in the missing details of her memories with a free and romantic flair! She had created an ideal that no man could hope to live up to! It had been only a matter of time before she came face to face with the inadequate reality of her foolish imaginings.

But now it was time to put such nonsense behind her. As far as she was concerned, the episode was closed. *Le Maniganceur* was no more than the sweet memory of a dream. She had other, more pressing—more important!— business than the little-known Charles Marcombe to consider. She must go at once to see Lord Pembroke, travel to Brighton to speak with de Lebouchon, and then . . . what?

Suddenly the bleakness of her future closed about her. She would have to go back into hiding, back to the little cottage in that tiny village where she never saw anyone and never went anywhere. How much harder that would be, after her brief taste of freedom! All those grand thoughts she had of returning to her work, of once again pursuing adventure. It was nothing but wishful thinking! She could never return to France. Her usefulness to the British government was over.

And Brighton, was even that city safe for her? Would Lord Pembroke let her go, or would he send someone else on this errand? Would she be ordered back into igno-minious shelter, like a frightened rabbit diving for its burrow?

It was after ten o'clock that night before the stagecoach at last bounced its way over the cobbled streets of London and was reined to a halt. Thérèse and her fellow passengers stepped out into the yard of an inn that teemed with activity. Passengers for a departing coach mingled with vendors and ostlers in a noisy, neverending parade.

She stretched to ease her stiff muscles, glad that the interminable ride was over. Ranleigh might be situated a mere seventy-five miles north of London, but the route had been distressfully circuitous. She was tired; for a

41

reason she refused to consider, she had not slept the night before.

And what was she to do now? This advanced hour was hardly suitable for a visit to the man who was in charge of the British agents. Lord Pembroke would not be in his office in Whitehall and she did not know his direction.

Uncertain, she glanced toward the severe woman who had sat beside her, but that lady was busy directing two youths in the collection of her luggage. Thérèse raised a tentative hand and at once another lad came running to her assistance.

There was little she could do this night other than arrange for a bed. Even the effort of requesting a dinner seemed too much for her. The lad, after subjecting her to an assessing look, took charge, with the result that she shortly found herself standing inside the inn with her luggage at her feet. With amazing rapidity she was led upstairs to a small, quiet room overlooking the back. A chambermaid produced a can of steaming water and Thérèse was able to collapse in a chair by a fire with a cup of hot broth.

Exhaustion undermined her determination not to let her thoughts return to *Le Maniganceur*. She fought this by the simple expedient of focusing them on Charles instead. But as this led, not unnaturally, to considering his unexpected and highly improper conduct in kissing her, it did little to help ease her into much needed sleep. His behavior had been shocking, his motive suspect, and she had never been so deeply shaken by an experience before in the whole of her highly eventful life!

She climbed between sheets, blew out her candle, and curled up, only to stare out into the darkened room. She would have liked to see him again . . . but this was for the best. It was impossible for her to remain beneath his roof after he'd kissed her, after he'd insulted her by suggesting that a flirtation would make her forget the obligation she owed a friend. . . .

Tomorrow, she thought hazily as she drifted off, would be soon enough to deal with her problems.

These arrived to haunt her sooner than she could wish. After breakfasting in the morning, she asked that her bags be brought down and prepared to pay her shot. This, she discovered to her dismay, took the majority of the money that remained in her reticule. Her allowance from the government while she remained in hiding had been small, but then she had needed very little, until now. . . . She would have to request help in Whitehall to go even as far as Brighton—which meant that if Lord Pembroke did not approve, she was helpless to assist the Chevalier de Lebouchon.

To be without money—it was intolerable! What she really needed right now was a singing engagement to relieve her current difficulties. If only she could go back on the stage! An operatic soprano of her experience and talent commanded a comfortable fee. But until she was free of all danger, she had no choice but to rely on the generosity of Lord Pembroke, even to pay for her return journey to that little village. The situation could not please her. Since she'd sung in her first opera at the age of sixteen, she'd never been a burden to anyone—until now.

Her sense of discomfort grew as she perched on the edge of a straight-backed chair in the antechamber before that great man's office. She had been to this suite of rooms once, more than five years before, when, with her friend Lord Ryde at her side, she had offered her services to the British government. Then she had been welcomed warmly and with expressions of gratitude. But now, when she was little more than a burden upon everyone, what would be her reception?

The door opened and a stocky man of slightly less than medium height emerged. He stopped at the sight of her and a broad smile broke across his normally staid face.

"Ma'mselle de Bourgerre!" He came forward, his hand extended. "Whatever brings you to London?"

"M'sieur Harding!" She sprang to her feet and hurried to meet her former bodyguard. She clasped his hand between hers and clung to it for a moment. "How very good it is to see you."

"Did you come here alone?" He glanced about the room, his expression dubious. "Are you sure that's wise, ma'mselle?"

She forced a smile, encountered a brooding, almost uncanny understanding of her current unimportance in his hazel eyes, and dropped her gaze. "I do not have a guard, now. I hope there is no longer the need."

"And so do I, but that's as may be."

He did not sound convinced, and though she knew it was foolish, his concern warmed and comforted her.

"Well, now, have you heard from Lord Ryde? How do he and his lady go on?" He took her elbow and led her back to her chair. "Just the wife for him, that Miss Marcombe."

"They wrote from Italy only a week ago. I believe the letter came by way of the Navy."

Harding gave a short laugh. "Just like his lordship to occupy himself with government work on his wedding trip."

"I believe the new Lady Ryde would be most disappointed if he did not. She is, after all, the sister of *Le Maniganceur*." She broke off, biting her lip. Of *Le Maniganceur*, as he once had been. But now, broken and defeated, he was no more, and the Charles Marcombe who remained turned his back on the work and walked away, leaving it to others.

"And have you heard from Mr. Marcombe?"

She glanced up to find Harding's eyes resting on her face. *"Oui.* I have just come from Ranleigh."

"Better, is he? Lord, that night we found him in your house . . ." He shook his head. "For a bit, there, I didn't think he'd pull through."

"He says he is finished with the work, that he wishes to do nothing but manage his grandfather's estate now." With care she kept her voice level, as if the matter meant nothing to her.

"Finished!" Harding blinked. "The great *Le Maniganceur*, the Intriguer, to turn his back on it all? But he thrived on that danger!"

"But he did it for five long years." She shrugged. "A man grows weary, *n'est-ce pas?*"

"It doesn't seem possible." He fell silent, staring at the hands he clasped in his lap. "He was pretty badly injured, though, wasn't he? I suppose a man can be wounded just so many times before he stops bouncing back as readily."

"That is very true." Somehow, that had a more comforting sound to it than to say he had lost his nerve.

A slight, elegant gentleman of advancing years came out of the inner office. He smiled in apparent pleasure as he saw his visitor.

"Mademoiselle de Bourgerre. I am sorry to have kept you waiting. Pray, come in."

Thérèse stood. "*Au revoir*, Monsieur Harding. And *merci.*"

He nodded. "I will see you again, ma'mselle."

The words were a promise which gave her a measure of courage. She turned and, with the feeling that she was leaving one of the few friends she possessed, she entered Lord Pembroke's comfortably appointed apartment.

Shelves of books lined one wall and a selection of hunting prints hung upon another. The impression was that of a stately home, rather than a government office. The purpose, as she well knew, was to set visitors at ease. For her it failed.

"Now, mademoiselle." Lord Pembroke closed the door and went to hold a chair for her. "What may I do for you?"

She sat down and removed her kid gloves while he resumed his position behind the great walnut writing desk. Facing him squarely, she plunged right in.

"*S'il vous plaît*, milord, I find myself in some difficulty, *enfin.*"

Lord Pembroke rested his elbows on the cluttered

45

surface of his desk, tented his fingertips, and regarded her through narrowed eyes. "I have not heard that there has been trouble."

"*Mais non*—that is, not for me, but for a friend. It is the Chevalier de Lebouchon." Quickly she related her concern.

Lord Pembroke drew in a deep breath and exhaled slowly. "I was aware that he was in England, of course. But he has made no effort to contact our people. In fact, far from seeming in need of help, he has been going about in society quite openly."

"So you knew he was here?" She tilted her head to one side and frowned. "You did not seek to question him?"

"We have kept an eye on him, but there was no need for even that." Pembroke leaned back in his chair and bestowed a condescending smile upon her. "He is of no importance, only another member of the *ancien régime* who could not bear Napoleon's new order. He is not in danger, nor is he a spy. And he was not in a position to know anything that could help us. Does that satisfy you, mademoiselle?"

It didn't, but she found herself unable to think of a persuasive argument. De Lebouchon might be exactly what Pembroke thought, but still—doubts and worries clouded her mind.

"Well, then, that's settled." Lord Pembroke smiled. "Is that the only reason you came? Is there anything else we can do for you? You've been living up north somewhere, haven't you? Very pleasant, to be out of London in the summer."

Thérèse shook her head. "I am sorry, Milord Pembroke. I cannot be easy about the Chevalier. Please, I wish to go to Brighton."

"Excellent idea." He nodded his approval. "You were there before, were you not? Do you have friends there?"

She blinked. "You do not mind? I had thought . . ."

Lord Pembroke shifted in his chair and a slight frown

lined his angular countenance. From the depths of his immaculate coat of blue superfine, he drew an elegantly enameled snuffbox. He opened it with an expert flick of his thumb and helped himself to a pinch. When he finished, he raised his eyes to her once again.

"I have been giving your problem some consideration of late, mademoiselle. It is my opinion—and that of others involved in your affairs—that it is time you resumed a more normal life. As long as you remain in hiding, the French will believe you are still important to all of us. Therefore, the safest thing for you to do will be to appear openly in society once again."

"Openly . . . *merci*, milord." She barely got the words out. Was it over, all the danger, the waiting, the hiding? It didn't seem possible! But in all these weeks, not a single hint of trouble reached her. No suspicious strangers lurked in the village . . . no sinister faces peered into her cottage windows. And why should they? Lord Pembroke was right! She had already told the British everything she knew. Surely by now there must be more important things for French agents to do than seek vengeance.

She was free! Her spirits soared. She could do as she liked, fill her life with enough activity to drive *Le Maniganceur* from her memory. She could go anywhere, do anything. . . .

"There—there is a slight problem. Money, I have none—for now. So I must sing again. But until then . . ." She broke off, hating the necessity to make such a request.

"Of course, of course." He smiled, as if relieved at her reception of his decision. "You will need some funds to tide you over." He drew a sizable wad of flimsies from a drawer and handed them over without bothering to count out any amount.

Thérèse hesitated, then accepted the bills, shocked by what seemed to her a vast sum. But there would be so many expenses just to live until she could obtain a singing engagement and earn her own way. She tucked her bankroll into her reticule and found that Lord Pembroke had already stood.

"Well, my dear, if ever you need anything again, please be sure to call upon us. And thank you once more for all you have done."

Somehow, she was back in the antechamber with the door closed firmly behind her. So that was that. She felt dazed, a trifle lost, as if the door had closed on five years of her life instead of on a brief, fifteen-minute interview.

She took an uncertain step forward. It was all over now. The government had washed their hands of her and she was on her own. It was time to get on with her life once again, to build a future out of the odds and ends that remained of her past.

But first, there was the Chevalier de Lebouchon. . . .

"Is everything settled, ma'mselle?" Harding rose from his chair.

She jumped, for in her preoccupation she had not realized there was anyone in the antechamber. "You—you are still here?"

"Just wanted to make sure you were all right."

"How very kind of you!"

At the warmth of her words, bright, easy color tinged Harding's sandy complexion, making him appear much younger than his one-and-forty years. He grinned in embarrassment, which lessened the lines of concern that habitually marked his face.

"Not at all, ma'mselle."

"It seems that I must not hide anymore. Milord Pembroke, he says I am free and may do as I wish."

He frowned. "Is that so? Well, I'm glad to hear it, of course."

His skeptical tone did not escape her and she regarded him through narrowed eyes. Was her former bodyguard, who had gone through so much with her, not so confident in her safety as were his superiors? The thought was unsettling, but she forced herself to dismiss it as nonsense.

It had to be! She could not remain in hiding forever, with nothing to occupy her mind but memories and dreams of a hero who did not really exist.

Harding gave a slight cough. "Where are you going now, ma'mselle?"

At that, Thérèse hesitated. "There is something I wish to do in Brighton, but then . . ."

"Brighton, is it?" His frown deepened. "Look, I've got a few arrangements to make this morning, but after that, I think I can get free for a day or two. I'll take you down there myself and get you settled. Will that be all right?"

"But—but I cannot ask you to go to such trouble!"

"No trouble at all. The least we can do. Now . . ." He broke off and chewed on his lower lip. "Where are you staying?"

"I stopped at a coaching inn last night, but . . ."

"Can you go back? Fine, then I'll meet you there in about two hours."

She found it oddly comforting to know that someone still took an interest in her—even if it was not completely sanctioned by the government. And she would be glad if he could make a few arrangements for her. Lodgings in Brighton, even this late in the summer, were almost impossible to obtain. From what she remembered of William Harding, he could find her a room.

He went into the hall and signaled a clerk to help with her luggage. In a surprisingly short time they were outside in the street. Harding flagged down a hackney and had her bandboxes and portmanteau strapped on.

"In two hours, ma'mselle." Giving the name of her inn to the jarvey, he stood back and watched as the carriage carried her away.

Thérèse sank back against the squabs, still barely able to believe that she was free. She would travel to Brighton as soon as arrangements could be made. Then she would return to London and visit the manager of the opera house. It might be only early August, but she would have to let the operatic world know that she'd returned. She had a strong suspicion that Pembroke's money would not last her as long as she might require, until the little season brought the polite world back to London, eager for the sort of entertainment she could provide.

Less than twenty minutes later, they pulled into the yard at the inn where she had stayed the night before. The proprietor escorted her upstairs to a large front bed-chamber. The noise of bustling activity drifted up from below. She requested tea, and in a very short time a parlor maid tapped on her door, bearing a tray loaded not only with a steaming pot but also an array of biscuits.

When Harding finally appeared almost three hours later, Thérèse had just sat down to a light luncheon that had been brought to her room. With him came a respectable if stern-faced abigail. He introduced the middle-aged woman as Symmons, who bobbed her new mistress a curtsy.

"She'll look after you very well," Harding promised. "Now, were you wishful of going to Brighton today?"

"Today? Oh, *oui, m'sieur, s'il vous plaît!*"

He nodded. "The carriage is outside—best get under way at once."

The journey was by far the most comfortable she'd undertaken in the last few days. They did not speak much, but it was a companionable silence rather than one of strain. Harding and Symmons made every provision for her comfort, suggesting at each stop that they step down to stretch their legs and offering to procure refreshments for her.

Shortly after nine o'clock that night, the carriage entered the outskirts of Brighton and turned off New Road onto the red glazed brick paving of the Steine. In only a few minutes, they drew into the yard of the Castle Inn. Harding jumped down, helped her to alight, and ushered her inside.

To her mixed pleasure and surprise, the proprietor

recognized her on sight. Nothing, that worthy declared, could exceed his delight and gratification at having so famous and talented a lady staying beneath his roof. She was to order everything exactly as she wished, he asserted, and come to him at once if she required anything more. It was his pleasure—nay, his honor!—to serve her.

If only others—naming no names—would think of her in this way, rather than regarding her as a burden that must be coerced into remaining in hiding! But those thoughts took her nowhere, so she firmly evicted Charles from her mind. He belonged to the past, and as soon as she had seen the Chevalier, she would concentrate on her future. London might not be in need of an operatic soprano at the moment, but Brighton was a different matter. She would call upon those delightful elderly sisters, Miss Draycott and Mrs. Andover, who together managed the local musical society, and she would resume her career here under their auspices.

Filled with plans, she followed Harding to the room that he and the proprietor of the Castle Inn magically conjured for her. To what lengths they had been forced to go to obtain it, Thérèse did not ask. She could only be flattered that they had gone to such effort for her.

Symmons looked about the chamber and went immediately to work, with the result that when Thérèse was ready to retire, all her clothing had been neatly placed in the cupboards, her combs and brushes laid out on the bureau, and her dressing gown draped across the bed.

After an early night, she rose in the morning feeling much refreshed and ready to face the world. Not even the knowledge that Harding had returned to London an hour before, conveyed to her by Symmons, daunted her. She breakfasted on rolls and chocolate and stared out the window over the familiar city. It felt good to be back.

She finished the light meal, donned a freshly pressed walking gown of sky blue Circassian cloth, and with her fluffy golden curls smoothed neatly beneath a chip straw

51

bonnet, set forth to discover the whereabouts of the Chevalier.

Here the proprietor was unable to help her. The Chevalier did not stay at the Castle Inn. She hesitated to try the Old Ship, for she knew the world would look askance on a lady asking at inns after a gentleman. Still, she must find him. She could not put her past—and memories of *Le Maniganceur*—behind her until she completed this one last task.

She strolled out of the inn lost in thought. Brighton was not so large a town that a Frenchman could long stay hidden. He moved about in society, he . . . he loved music! That had been what had brought him to her card parties in Paris in the first place! And if he had so much as hinted at this liking, the Draycott sisters would have enlisted him into the ranks of their musical society.

Her spirits lifted and she turned down the Steine to the Marine Parade where the ladies resided. As she neared the ocean, a salty breeze ruffled her curls and the tangy spray filled her lungs. Waves rolled gently up the beach to the delighted screams of several children who played at the water's edge under the strict eye of a governess.

Halfway along the street she paused. Across from her, tall and silent, its windows curtained, stood the house in which she had stayed only six short weeks before. It seemed empty, which was unusual at this time of year. Houses were always fully booked in Brighton. She could remember the trouble Lord Ryde had had in obtaining the place for her.

An odd, whining cry broke across her thoughts and she looked up to see a beggar dressed in the most shocking rags shuffling along the street. He seemed rather solidly built, but his body was so badly stooped it was impossible to be certain. He glanced at her, then lowered his face back into his tattered scarf. A little flop-eared mongrel, its ribs sticking out dreadfully through its straggly, mud-plastered beige coat, slunk along at his heels. It carried one foreleg raised, not stepping on it.

Thérèse could not remain unmoved. Had she still been down to her last few coins, she would have given the man something. But several of Lord Pembroke's banknotes rested in her reticule. Two of these she pressed into the man's hand and, waving aside his mumbled thanks, she sank down to one knee and called gently to the dog. It hesitated, almost cowering, as it regarded her warily.

Thérèse took a cautious step forward and, when the mongrel didn't run away, tried another. Its one front leg was badly swollen. As she drew nearer, the little animal growled at her, then submitted to her gentle touch as she picked it up.

A barouche turned down the street in their direction. The beggar threw an assessing look over his shoulder at it and hurried across the pavement to the sand. In moments he disappeared among the bathing machines. The mongrel's scrawny body tensed, but it made no move to follow the man. Thérèse murmured soothing words as the carriage slowed, then came to a stop. Two ladies occupied the back seat and both leaned forward eagerly.

"Mademoiselle de Bourgerre? Oh, how delightful! We never thought to see you back in Brighton so soon!"

"Mademoiselle Draycott! And Madame Andover!" Thérèse transferred the dog to one arm and stepped forward to clasp their hands. "I was on my way to visit you!"

"Have you been in town long?" Mrs. Andover leaned eagerly across her sister.

"I have arrived only last night."

"Have you found a house, yet? No? Then you shall stay with us until you do. No, my dear, we will not permit you to argue." Miss Draycott held up a hand to silence Thérèse's protest. "We will be delighted to have you, and your little dog as well."

Thérèse was about to deny ownership, but something in the dog's pitiful expression touched her. They were both alone, outcasts. They would stick together.

"You must come to us this afternoon," Mrs. Andover decided, apparently taking her silence for assent. "We shall send the barouche for you at two. Will that be all right?"

"It is most kind." She smiled warmly at the two elderly ladies. "I shall like it of all things."

Indeed, it seemed the best solution. Except for Harding's concern, she had been cut off by the government, and until she could get work, her funds were limited. And best of all, they would be friends who would prevent her from dwelling on her tarnished idol, who had proved himself made of dross instead of gold. It was time she made a life for herself in this strange country and forgot about him— and the rest of that portion of her life. But first . . .

"I wondered if you could help me. I believe an old friend is staying in Brighton. The Chevalier de Lebouchon."

"Oh!" Mrs. Andover's hand darted to cover her mouth. "That poor man!"

"The most terrible thing!" Miss Draycott nodded in emphatic agreement.

A cold icicle of fear stabbed through Thérèse. She was too late, . . . Lord Pembroke had been wrong, terribly, disastrously wrong. . . . Armand de Lebouchon, who had been so kind to her . . .

"What—what happened?" The question caught in her throat. "Please, I—I must know."

Mrs. Andover took Thérèse's hand and gave it a sustaining squeeze. "I am so sorry, if he is a friend. But you see, he has been shot!"

Chapter Four

"A man, being shot in Brighton!" Miss Draycott shook her head. "Why, it is not as if this were London, or Finchley Common. Such a thing is unheard of here!"

Thérèse fought down an almost hysterical urge to laugh. Unheard of, perhaps, but not unknown. All too vividly the image of *Le Maniganceur,* collapsed on her floor, rose in her mind, followed by an engulfing wave of dizziness. Did she bring disaster to all she knew? But *Le Maniganceur,* even the Chevalier, they chose their own paths. *Le Maniganceur,* at least, knew the danger. But Armand de Lebouchon? Was this all because of her?

". . . for another two days, at least." Miss Draycott shook her head.

"I—I am sorry." Thérèse emerged from her horror-filled thoughts as she realized Miss Draycott still addressed her. "I did not hear. What is another two days?"

"Why, that the Chevalier will be confined to his bed! It only occurred just two nights ago, you must know. A trifling wound, the doctor assures everyone, but so shocking!"

"Then—then he is . . ." She broke off as relief washed over. He was not dead—not even badly wounded! She must go to him, and upon the instant. . . .

What a fool she was being! If his danger sprang from his

involvement with her, then the last thing she should do would be to go to him until he was better and able to defend himself. In the meantime. . . . In the meantime, she would make her presence in Brighton known, draw attention away from him and focus it on herself.

With firm resolve, she fought down her fear. She owed this to Armand de Lebouchon, if only for the comfort he had given her while she awaited execution in that Paris dungeon. And if he had indeed helped in her escape, then she owed him her life. She would not permit concern for her own safety to interfere with her duty. She was forewarned. She would be careful.

After telling the Draycott sisters where she stayed and promising once more that she would be ready for their carriage at two, she took her leave of the ladies. She had plans to make. She must get a message to William Harding and then arrange for a very well-publicized resumption of her singing career. Before the day was over, she determined, there would be few people in Brighton who did not know that Thérèse de Bourgerre was back!

The flop-eared little mongrel whimpered in her arms, and Thérèse, with a soothing apology, relaxed her hold on it. Whatever else she intended to do, the first order of business must be to care for this poor animal.

She carried it back to the Castle Inn. To her surprise Symmons accepted the inclusion into their entourage of such a disreputable-looking dog without a word of protest. In fact, her abigail displayed unusual knowledge in the treatment of the gashed and swollen leg, enough so that Thérèse began to wonder where—and why—Harding had procured her services.

After sending to the kitchens for basins, hot water, and strips of lint, Symmons examined the leg and, with the help of a surgical knife she produced from a small leather case, removed a deeply embedded splinter. The wound was then washed, dusted with basilicum powder, and safely bandaged.

Thérèse sat back on her heels beside the misbegotten

creature as it lapped at a bowl of warm milk and finely chopped meat scraps. Her eyes, though, rested on her abigail, who busily washed and dried her knife.

"You have unusual talents for a lady's maid, *enfin*," Thérèse remarked.

"My brother is valet to a doctor," came the calm reply.

Thérèse let it drop. Monsieur Harding, as usual, was proving most efficient in securing her well-being. The only question that bothered her was whether or not he had cause for placing a woman with medical training to guard her. Considering the fate of the Chevalier de Lebouchon, it seemed disturbingly likely that he had.

When Thérèse, followed by Symmons carrying her dressing case, came down the stairs of the Castle Inn later that afternoon, she found Miss Draycott and Mrs. Andover in the lobby with the proprietor. All three turned toward her in such a conspiratorial manner that she hesitated and clutched at the railing in sudden nervousness. Gathering her courage, she descended the last few steps.

"There you are, my dear." Mrs. Andover came forward. "We have hit upon the most delightful scheme—providing you are willing, of course."

"And what is this?" Thérèse managed a smile, though she hugged the little dog tighter against herself, as if for protection.

"Why, a concert! Quite informal, of course, to be held here, at this inn. We have been dying to hear you sing again, you must know. And this will provide you with a more intimate setting than in one of those vast, draughty halls. Since this time your visit does not have to be secret, we thought, perhaps . . ." Mrs. Andover let the hopeful note in her voice end her sentence.

"But this is *merveilleuse!*" Thérèse let out the breath she had caught. They might have read her mind! Already her plans were being put into action—though she experienced the disconcerting sensation that she was swept along with events, rather than being in control.

Mr. Livesey, the proprietor, stepped forward. "The ballroom is available next Thursday. And you may use it for practice any morning."

"Thursday!" Thérèse stared at him, startled. That gave her so little time to rehearse! And she would need an accompanist. . . .

"We are already planning a little recital," Sophie Andover explained.

"So do not fear you will be the sole performer!" Miss Draycott chimed in. "Such a burden as that would be."

"We will make the announcement at once." Mr. Livesey beamed at them all, and somehow the matter was settled. He escorted them outside to the waiting barouche, all the while rattling off innumerable plans for the event that would relaunch a career too long set aside.

In this, he was amply aided by both Mrs. Andover and Amanda Draycott. The two ladies continued to discuss details until their carriage pulled up before their house on the Marine Parade and Thérèse was able to escape to the room already prepared for her arrival.

The next few days flew by in a frantic whirl. Aware of how very long it had been since the last time she'd sung in public, Thérèse put in innumerable hours of practice, both at her hostesses' pianoforte and at the Castle Inn. The little dog, christened Aimée, curled at her feet during these sessions, her disreputably pugged nose resting on her paws and her huge, pansy-brown eyes resting soulfully on her adopted mistress.

A bath and thorough brushing, both over her vociferous protests, had done Aimée's appearance a world of good. With food and care, her leg improved rapidly as well. By the second morning, she was able to hobble on her injured leg about Thérèse's chamber. Symmons replaced the dressing and pronounced that the wound was making satisfactory progress.

"And you might take her for short walks, ma'mselle," the abigail decreed. "The exercise will do you both good."

Thérèse bent to stroke Aimée's back. "Will you like that, *ma petite?*" For an answer she received an enthusiastic licking of her fingers.

The prospect of exercise in the fresh air could not but please Thérèse. It had been quickly brought home to her that she could not venture far from her little pet. Aimée whined constantly when they were separated, disrupting the entire household, only quieting when she heard her mistress's light steps as Thérèse hurried to discover the cause of all the fuss.

Between the walks and her singing, Thérèse had little time to indulge in memories of *Le Maniganceur* or fears for the Chevalier. Every moment seemed packed with activity, and it was only when she at last sought her couch that her mind was free to wander. But fatigue overcame her tendency to lie awake, lost in fruitless speculation and worry, and somehow the time slipped past.

On the morning of the fourth day, as Thérèse prepared to set out for her walk with Aimée, the parlor maid tapped on her door with the news that visitors had arrived and that the Draycott sisters wished her to join them. Abandoning the bonnet and straightening her fluffy golden curls as best she could, she hurried down to the front salon. The little mongrel padded in her wake.

She entered the room and stopped short. Beside Miss Draycott on the sofa sat an elderly gentleman whose erect posture and keen eye belied the infirmity of his spare frame, but she barely glanced at him. A fair gentleman of stocky build, somewhat above average height, sat across the fireplace from Mrs. Andover. The studied casualness of his posture, the elegance of his attire, and his seductive, almost calculating smile betrayed a rake of no little experience.

Thérèse stared at him for a disbelieving moment. "Chevalier!" Her heart soaring in relief at this proof that he was indeed all right, she rushed forward, her hands outstretched.

Her dog hung back, almost cowering against the door. Thérèse turned from her greeting as the little mongrel whined pitifully and began to scratch at the panel as if seeking escape.

"How odd!" Miss Draycott exclaimed. "Should it be taken for a walk, Thérèse?"

The Chevalier rose and grasped Thérèse's hands in a warm, sustaining clasp, claiming her attention. *"Ma chère Thérèse!"* A gleam of suppressed pleasure lit a countenance distinguished by five-and-thirty years of riotous living, rather than by classical bone structure. The result was intriguing. "Such a surprise, to learn that you are not only in Brighton, but also to sing. How I look forward to this!"

Concern for her old friend supplanted her surprise at her pet's peculiar behavior. She raised anxious eyes to search the Chevalier's face. New lines etched his high brow, but no trace of strain or fear lurked in the depths of his piercing blue eyes. Only pleasure—or was it triumph? How she longed to know what had occurred, what brought him out of France, who had shot him! But they could not speak openly before the others, and the delay vexed her.

Aimée slunk forward, growling softly all the while, and resumed her favorite hiding place beneath Thérèse's flounced skirts. Thérèse silenced her with a quick word and returned her attention to the Chevalier. He held her gaze as he raised her fingers to his lips. His blue eyes contained a wealth of meaning as he retained his hold a fraction longer than necessary.

"I was so sorry to hear of your injury." She pressed his hands to let him know that she suspected he was in danger.

"But it is as nothing." He returned the pressure before releasing her. "Footpads, nothing more."

"Bold rascals!" The elderly man thumped his cane on the floor. "Things are coming to a pretty pass when a man can't even walk home from a party without being attacked by ruffians!"

"Thérèse, I do not believe you have met General Somerset." Miss Draycott directed her attention to the other man.

Thérèse turned from the Chevalier as the General eased himself to his feet. "It is a pleasure, *m'sieur*."

He gave a short bark of a laugh. "Glad to be able to bring a couple of old friends together. Must be lonesome, being expatriated from your own country like this."

"The General has so kindly presented me to Mrs. Andover and Miss Draycott, whom I have known only by reputation." The Chevalier bowed toward the ladies. "When I learned that you stayed with them, I was forced to call upon an acquaintance of my father's and beg him to perform the introduction so that I might call."

Thérèse, no stranger to the art of dalliance, could not but be aware that a certain measuring speculation lay behind the warmth in the Chevalier's voice and the gleam in his eyes. Anyone observing them would be left in no doubt that he sought to initiate a flirtation. Did he think they needed this explanation for private conversations? If so, that must mean trouble. A fluttering of nerves danced through her stomach.

"Thérèse." Sophie Andover watched the couple with lively interest. "The General is quite looking forward to the concert. Is it not exciting to be singing again? And when it is over, we shall hold a reception here. It is time you were properly launched into society."

"That will be of all things the most delightful!" Politeness dictated her answer. But she must be glad of this turn of events. It would not serve to sit at home every evening, lost in memories and fantasies of a man who was no more than a dream. She forced *Le Maniganceur* to the back of her mind, but it proved a struggle as he seemed disinclined to remain there. But she still had this matter of the Chevalier with which to deal.

"I am so very busy, you see." She turned to de Lebouchon with a coy smile. "I must practice and practice at the Castle Inn every forenoon, and walk my little dog after breakfast and in the late afternoon.'' As she leaned down to pat Aimée, she glanced up sideways to make sure the Chevalier had noted the places and times he could find her for private conversation. His nod, though almost imperceptible, reassured her.

When the gentlemen at last took their leave, Thérèse felt certain the Chevalier did not at the moment fear danger. Nor did he make any move to warn her against thrusting herself into the public eye by singing at the concert. Relieved of that concern, she set forth for a rehearsal session at the Castle Inn with the members of a string quartet.

When she returned several hours later, it was to find the house in chaos. Everything must be got into readiness for the reception, Sophie Andover informed her. And as long as she was back, Amanda Draycott suggested, she might see to the ordering of flowers for the decoration of the rooms. As this entailed going down to the kitchens to discover how many vases and huge pots must be obtained, then discovering the availability of various types of blossoms at this time of year, Thérèse found herself fully occupied for the remainder of the day.

Shortly after breakfast the following morning, though, she slipped away through all the commotion, bent on a gentle stroll with Aimée as far as the Steine and back. They had not taken many steps along the street when a man's voice hailed them and she turned to see the Chevalier de Lebouchon hurrying across from the walkway by the sea.

Aimée whimpered and retreated beneath Thérèse's sprigged muslin skirts, where she stood shivering. Perplexed, Thérèse started forward. The mongrel hung back, then scurried along to keep hidden in the flounced hem as her mistress continued walking.

''Mademoiselle!'' The Chevalier bowed in an exaggerated manner. ''What a fortunate man I am! But a few moments later and I would have missed you, and then I would have been inconsolable."

She could not help but smile at his nonsense, but the seriousness of her concerns sobered her at once. "I am so glad to be able to talk with you at last."

"May I escort you on your walk? It will look less singular than if we stand here in the street."

His smile, charming as ever, reassured her further. "My little Aimée cannot yet go far. Perhaps down to the ocean?"

The Chevalier glanced toward her feet, but could catch no more than a glimpse of the shaggy beige animal. "Such a very small dog," he declared. "One might almost not even know she is there." He was rewarded for this notice with a growl.

They strolled a short distance until they found a bench. Thérèse seated herself and the Chevalier settled at her side. Aimée remained close against Thérèse's ankles, standing stiff and alert rather than trying to chase the gulls that swooped low over the beach, as was her wont. It was almost as if she knew—and didn't like—de Lebouchon! But that was absurd!

Thérèse cast a quick glance about to assure herself that no one could overhear. Even so, she spoke rapidly in French. "Tell me what has occurred! Why have you come out of France, and who shot at you? I have been most concerned!" She turned toward him and gripped the hand he held toward her.

"I am ashamed that I have caused you worry. *Ma chère Thérèse*, there was no need, I promise you. Much my family could tolerate, but not Napoleon's marriage to Marie Louise. To establish a dynasty! He is a hypocrite, for it is against everything that horrible revolution stood for! If we need an emperor once more, then let us have a Bourbon."

"Where have they gone, your family?"

"Into Italy. They will be safe enough there."

"And you?"

63

A smile played about the corners of his mouth. "I found Italy to be boring. And then I thought of England, which I had visited so very long ago. And I thought of the most beautiful singer in all of Europe. So what could I do but come?"

Warm color tinged her cheeks. Always his compliments were effusive, but now they seemed even more so. "Have you not approached the British government?"

"There is nothing I could tell them." He shook his head. "No, my position was not one of confidences. I was a mere figurehead, a member of the *ancien régime*. My presence gave them respectability, but they did not honor me with their trust."

"Yet someone tried to shoot you!" Did she doubt him? She could have been wrong, but she had thought him someone of importance to Napoleon.

He laughed with real amusement. *"Ma Thérèse,* you cannot conceive how embarrassing this is for me. In all honesty, it was naught but a footpad! I struggled and he took fright and used his pistol. But he had no nerves, and little experience, I should think. The shot went wide and merely grazed my arm. Had the doctors not insisted on cupping me, the incident could have been forgotten at once."

Thérèse blinked. *"Vraiment?* A footpad?"

He nodded. "To my shame. You would think if I must be shot, it might at least be by the French, for deserting them. But you see how unimportant I am. Not even do they honor me by sending an assassin!" His eyes opened wide and a humorous glint lit their pale depths. "This is what you thought? *Ma Thérèse,* you really thought this? But why?"

"It—it was a chance. Footpads, I believe, do not often carry pistols."

He possessed himself of her hands once again. *"Ma chèrie,* how delightful of you to worry so for me! But I am in no danger, I assure you. And I am glad to see that you

64

are not, either."

"No." She stopped. She had never actually told him the truth about her work in Paris. It would be best not to speak of it now, to let that knowledge—and the last five years of her life, along with her dreams of the incomparable *Le Maniganceur*—fade into the shadows of forgotten memory.

"And what do you mean to do now? Sing in this country?"

His voice recalled her wandering thoughts. *"Oui.* I suppose I shall go to London and join the Opera, but I prefer it here in Brighton. And you?"

"I shall enjoy myself." He smiled in a very intriguing manner. "After years of worry, I believe I deserve some fun. London can be a city almost as gay as Paris before the revolution. And if I may have your company upon occasion, what greater joy can a man ask?"

His manner seemed disturbingly possessive of her. Perhaps it was understandable, old friends meeting again after many dangers and hardships, but it made her uncomfortable. She stood abruptly.

"I must return. Already I shall be late for the final rehearsal, and the concert is tomorrow night."

He escorted her back to the house, but excused himself from coming in, saying that the ladies must be quite busy with the preparations for the reception.

"Tiens, it is most true," Thérèse agreed. "Everywhere there are people in a hurry and exclaiming because everything is not just *so."*

He laughed. "Then I shall not add to the clutter. Until tomorrow, mademoiselle." He kissed her hand, swept her a magnificent bow, and strolled off down the street, leaving her staring after him in brooding silence.

At least there was no longer any need to worry about him—or so he thought. She could only hope he was right. If so, she could at last put it all behind her and start a new life. One could not live on memories or dreams; they always proved so empty in the end. She needed something tangible, something real, activity and purpose. And at the moment, to get to her rehearsal! Glad to have something constructive to do, she let herself into the hall.

As she started for the stairs, Amanda Draycott emerged from the front salon.

"Ah, my dear, you are back. Was that not the Chevalier I just glimpsed?"

"I encountered him just outside and he accompanied me on my walk."

"How very kind of him! Most truly the gentleman, I believe." The lady regarded her protégée with a speculative gleam in her eyes. "I am glad you are back. Everything is in chaos, for the cook tells me that she cannot obtain lobsters. And in Brighton, at that! Tell me, do you like rennish cremes?"

After assuring her hostess that she liked them of all things, she escaped on the plea that the string quartet would already be waiting for her. She arrived at the Castle Inn only a few minutes behind the others, and rehearsing left her little time to think of anything but the fast-approaching peformance. She returned home late that afternoon tired but satisfied that the program would go smoothly.

Preparations for the "little" reception threatened to occupy all of the next day. An army of heretofore unglimpsed servants appeared as if by magic from below stairs and furniture was moved, chandeliers were washed and polished, and flowers were set about until the rooms were almost unrecognizable. Thérèse, already tense with nerves over the evening's concert, found the atmosphere unbearable.

As soon as she could slip away, she hurried upstairs to fetch her bonnet and escape with Aimée for a walk. But as she came back down, a knock sounded on the front door. The butler, who had been overseeing two footmen in the placement of a settee, straightened his coat and with stately steps made his way to the hall. He opened the door to admit William Harding.

Surprised, Thérèse hurried forward. "Monsieur Harding! I thought you had returned to London! But how delightful!"

He took the hand she held out to him and his sandy complexion flushed slightly under the warmth of her greeting. "Just came to tell you that you can move back into your old house any time now."

"My—oh, Monsieur Harding!" She clasped her hands in delight. "But how . . . ?"

"Compliments of the government, until the end of the year. Lord Ryde had taken a lease on it for you."

"May I go there now?"

"That you may. You'll have most of the same staff as before, ma'mselle, and everything should be arranged to your satisfaction. If anything occurs, tell Bradley, the butler, and he'll send for me at once."

"You are most kind!"

He waved that aside. "I hear you're singing tonight."

She nodded. "It is time to put the past behind, *n'est-ce pas?*"

He nodded but did not appear convinced. "I wish I could stay for it. But I've got an appointment in Whitehall this afternoon and I must keep it."

Her disappointment surprised her. Surely she did not fear for her safety! It would just be nice to have a friend, a well-wisher, in the audience. With sincere regret she saw him to the door, then hurried at once to tell the Draycott sisters about her house.

"How wonderful for you, my dear!" Sophie Andover took her hands and squeezed them. "Though we'll be sorry to see you go."

"But to be sure, you will only be four doors down from us, so you will be nearby for frequent visits," Amanda Draycott pointed out.

With Aimée at her heels, Thérèse went at once to view

67

the house. The door was opened to her by the familiar Bradley, who welcomed her back with apparent pleasure.

"And the footman will go for your belongings at once," he informed her as he relieved her of her shawl.

She stood in the hallway, looking about, as Bradley disappeared into the nether regions of the house. It felt so very strange to be back. Memories flooded over her, images of little happenings, of the very few visitors she had dared receive, of *Le Maniganceur.* . . .

Slowly, as if drawn against her will, she mounted the staircase to the topmost floor and opened the door to the small bedchamber where she had found him that terrible night, collapsed on the floor in a pool of blood, nigh on dead. . . . She had known him only by his *nom de guerre*, and he had epitomized everything dashing and brave, honorable and romantic. He had filled her dreams, both waking and sleeping. . . . Something moist slipped down her cheeks and she drew a handkerchief from her reticule to wipe away the tears.

Emptiness engulfed her, mingling with loss and grief, and she fought against it. Charles still lived. Only her idolized *Maniganceur* had died in the reality of the man behind the disguise. Forcing her unwanted loneliness to the back of her mind, she made her way down to her own bedchamber. Symmons, she discovered to her surprise, was already there, unpacking her dressing case. She was home—such as it was.

She still had the concert and the reception to get through that night. That should be enough to keep her busy. Her mind threatened to relive every recollection, every fantasy she had created about *Le Maniganceur.* And on the morrow, she would begin to build new—and happier— memories in this house. She was done with living the life of a recluse. She would entertain, she would hold dinner parties and *soirées*, she would become a hostess of note, perhaps become famous for serving the best refreshments in Brighton! Anything to fill her days and nights, to keep her shattered dreams at bay.

She spent the day reorganizing the furniture and making plans until Symmons almost ordered her to her room to rest. But as the minutes ticked by, bringing her performance irrevocably closer, her buried fears began to resurface. It only Harding had been able to remain!

By the hour appointed to leave for the Castle Inn, Thérèse had reached an advanced state of nerves. Yet somehow, when she at last descended the stairs, she bore the outward appearance of calm confidence. She delayed their departure so that they arrived at the inn barely before the time specified.

The Draycott sisters, in a flutter of excitement, met her in the hall, kissed her cheek, wished her well, and departed to take their seats in the front row. Thérèse remained behind the curtain that had been arranged near the raised dais. Not far away, Symmons stood holding Aimée.

One of the members of the string quartet made a joking comment, but Thérèse barely heard it. The concert didn't matter to them. It was just another performance. But for her it meant coming out of hiding. The long weeks of caution were over. Yet still, a little voice inside her whispered: "What if it were not safe?" If any danger still lurked, she openly invited it to attack.

By now, anyone living in the vicinity of Brighton must know that Thérèse de Bourgerre would be singing at the Castle Inn tonight. And this time, if anyone chose to kill her, there would be no British agents hovering nearby to protect her. This time she was on her own, exposed and vulnerable.

For better or for worse, she had made her choice. Relegating her fears to the back of her mind and summoning every ounce of courage she possessed, she stepped out onto the stage. The first violinist winked at her, raised his bow, and struck the opening note.

It was surprisingly easy. Instinct and training took over, the hours of rehearsal paid off. Everything vanished from her mind except the music, the words, the feelings and sensations created by the composer. Nothing mattered but the performance, and piece after piece, she put her heart into it.

At last, the final, pure note of the aria died away into the far reaches of the great ballroom. A moment of silence followed, then there came a thunderous applause. Thérèse opened her eyes, blinked back tears of exhaustion and emotion, and dropped into a deep curtsy.

It was over! No French agents had fired at her, no disasters had occurred. She rose, curtsied again, then made a dignified exit from the stage. Why did it all seem so much more draining than ever before? Never could she recall longing so for her portion of a program to come to an end! And never had she experienced such relief just to be done.

Symmons met her at the edge of the curtain and led her to a seat. Aimée pulled free of the woman's hold and leaped to her mistress's lap. Thérèse cradled the furry body close with one arm as she accepted the cool drink of fruit juice mixed with water that her abigail handed her.

"That was beautiful, ma'mselle." Symmons took the empty glass from her hand and set it on the table.

"*Merci.*" She smiled at the woman in genuine gratitude.

"It will be best if you slip out now. The carriage is waiting in the back to take us to Mrs. Andover's." She helped Thérèse to her feet and draped a shawl about her shoulders. "No point in asking for trouble, I always say."

Thérèse smiled, but did as she was told. Now that the performance was over, it was easy to label her earlier fears as simple nerves, similar to those she experienced before every singing engagement. It was time to put the past behind her. Harding and Symmons might still have their doubts, but there was no need.

They emerged through a back door of the inn. The carriage stood near at hand, and Thérèse bit her lip. The last time she had gone through a back door after a concert in Brighton, French agents had started shooting and

70

That was over, and she would prove it to herself here and now. With deliberately slowed steps, she walked across to the carriage. No sounds of gunshots met her straining ears, no bullets whistled through the air. It was indeed over.

The ride to her hostess's home took only a few minutes. The coachman let her out at the front steps, waited until the butler admitted her, then drove back to the inn to pick up Mrs. Andover and Miss Draycott.

Exhaustion swept over her as she seated herself in the front drawing room. She realized her relief at being done with it all. But it was more than an ending; it was the beginning of her new life. She bent down to rub Aimée's head as the little dog curled on the floor at her feet and panted in contentment. What would this new life hold?

She had only minutes in which to ponder the question. A rumbling of carriage wheels sounded in the street without and she barely had time to compose her face into a polite mask before the first of the guests were ushered in. She came forward, murmured her greetings, and wished frantically that her hostesses would arrive.

With relief she spotted Sophie Andover entering with a small group of friends. The Chevalier de Lebouchon followed in their wake. It seemed odd to see him, as if he were out of place. She sought the elusive sensation, then realized what it was. The Chevalier belonged to the past. This was the future. It did not seem right that the two should overlap.

"My love, it was marvelous!" Mrs. Andover hurried up to her and clasped her hands. "Everyone is saying so. You are the most complete success!"

"It is quite true, my dear." Miss Draycott, beaming, joined them. "It could not have been better. Every bit of it was perfection."

"And you see how everyone is so eager to meet you!" Mrs. Andover nodded with enthusiasm. "My love, our

71

drawing rooms are filled to overflowing! Our reception is a triumph!"

Aimée growled and retreated a step as the Chevalier moved to Thérèse's side. He raised her hand to his lips. "How could it be otherwise? The polite world is anxious to meet the so very famous Thérèse de Bourgerre."

She smiled, but it was more mechanical than sincere. She moved away, but the Chevalier followed as though he sought to keep an eye on her. It disturbed her, for his presence, as flattering as it might be, served as a constant reminder of the part of her life that now lay behind her. He conjured up memories of her work in Paris, of her danger and fear . . . and the phantom of her beloved *Maniganceur*.

At last the guests began to take their leave and Thérèse was able to seek out her hostesses to thank them for all they had done.

"But of course, my love, you must be exhausted." Sophie Andover clasped her hand. "And you have your own home to go to."

"Do not let us keep you. You must be longing for your bed," Amanda Draycott chimed in.

"Permit me to escort you to your door." The Chevalier, who had never strayed far from her side, stepped forward.

"Merci." She said her good-byes and they departed.

As they stepped out into the street, a covered carriage pulled away from the curb and started toward them. The Chevalier gripped her arm. Startled, she looked from his grim face to the approaching vehicle. A thrill of fear raced through her.

The door opened behind them and several laughing people emerged from the house. The carriage drove past without so much as a check and the Chevalier's grip on her tightened, then relaxed. In silence they walked the short distance up the Marine Parade. He said nothing of what had occurred—if indeed anything had.

It was her imagination, creating danger from nothing! That, and the Chevalier's unexpected reaction. Did he fear for her? Had he not told her the full truth about the footpad? But his injury had not been severe—he had shown no sign of his arm hurting, and it did not seem to hinder him in the least.

She had gone through too much this night, facing both her fears and an audience. But she had done it, overcome her first obstacle, and tomorrow she would set about making plans to fill her life and vanquish her memories once and for all.

As they reached the steps to her house, de Lebouchon raised her fingers to his lips once again. "A delightful evening, mademoiselle. You will permit me to call upon you tomorrow, to see how you go on in this new home of yours?"

"But of course." She could hardly say no, though she found herself wanting to. It must be that he represented the past that she so wanted to escape.

Bradley opened the door and she hurried inside. He bolted it, checked to make sure that she wanted nothing, then bade her goodnight. Silence, broken only by the butler's footsteps as he retreated downstairs, engulfed the house.

Thérèse shivered. She was alone. The servants were all in their quarters by now. Only Symmons would still be about, upstairs, waiting to help her to bed . . . and the disreputable little Aimée, who rubbed against her ankle.

She stepped forward to the foot of the stairs, where a candle stood beside a low-burning lamp. She reached for it and froze as a soft thud sounded from the drawing room behind her. Aimée stiffened, her hackles rose, and a low growl started in her throat.

It was nothing! It couldn't be anything! Forcing her hand not to tremble, she lit the candle and turned toward the darkened room. She managed three shaky steps toward it, then stopped short, a scream tearing from her throat as a shadowy, misshapen figure rose up as if from nowhere and loomed over her.

Chapter Five

The candle dropped from Thérèse's nerveless fingers. It went out, plunging her back into blackness. A second scream welled in her throat.

"Don't set up such a screech, Thérèse!" An all-too-familiar voice hushed her. "I thought you'd have been trained better than that!"

"Charles?" Her heart stopped, then beat faster in giddy elation. Weak with shock and reaction, she sank into a chair and stared at him in disbelief. Her eyes adjusted to the darkness of the room and she could make out his silhouette more clearly. His left arm, resting in a sling, had given him that unearthly appearance.

Aimée ventured from her hiding place within the double flounce of Thérèse's sarcenet undergown. For once she neither barked nor snarled, but regarded the intruder with her head cocked. Charles bent down and she bundled up to him, her tongue lolling from the side of her mouth. He stroked her long, floppy ears, and her eager tongue went to work on his hand.

"*Voilà tout*, observe my protector," murmured Thérèse.

Charles glanced up at her. "Which one of us are you referring to?"

His tone was dry, but she detected a note of lurking humor which surprised her. Had he improved so much in the short week since last time she saw him? Could he now view his condition with that ever-ready sense of the ridiculous that had previously characterized him? But if his spirits were so improved, he might be led into attempting actions of which he was physically not yet capable. His bearing, even his voice, indicated he had already overtaxed his strength just by coming to Brighton.

Having made a slave for life of Aimée, Charles crossed over to the table, drew a pocket luminary from his coat, and lit a couple of candles. The flickering glow illuminated his immediate surroundings while the rest of the room retreated into deeper shadows. He turned back to Thérèse, pale and very concerned.

"Are you all right? When I heard you were actually going to sing in public . . . ! What ever possessed you? Are you trying to get yourself killed?"

She rose to her feet. "But of course not! I am in no danger." She kept her voice soothing. "It is you who are foolish, *enfin*, to have put yourself to the strain of so long a journey."

"I'm not an invalid!" He sank onto the sofa. His words might deny it, but the strain showed clearly on his lined face. She crossed over and sank down at his side.

"It was good of you to come, *mais je vous assure*, it was most unnecessary. Monsieur Harding, he has seen to my needs. And *quant à moi*, I am quite safe."

He took a deep breath and his shoulders straightened a fraction as if with stiffening pride. "I am glad you have no need of me."

"Your retirement, it is quite safe." She tried to smile, to make it a joke.

He did not seem to appreciate it. He ran an exasperated hand through his tousled dark curls. Abruptly, he asked: "Why did you leave Ranleigh like that? I thought you

75

were going to stay for a few days!"

"I—I thought it was for the best." She could not tell him the truth, that his grandfather had requested that she leave to prevent precisely this sort of occurrence. How angry the elderly gentleman must be with her for causing Charles to go to so much effort!

"The best! You could not even wait to say good-bye?"

She stared at him in surprised comprehension. "You were worried, *enfin!* You thought, *peut-être*, I was taken by force?"

"Worried! Good God, madam, what did you expect?"

"Oh, *mon pauvre* Charles! I am so sorry! I did not think . . ."

"No, you do not think!" He stood, his bronzed complexion flushed with an anger generated from his relief at finding her unharmed. "Sometimes you act like you've got more hair than wit! You go rushing off with never a thought for the consequences. . . ." With obvious effort, he controlled his emotions. "And it was unnecessary, wasn't it? Your Chevalier seems to be all right."

She nodded. "It is a great relief, *bien sûr.*"

He took several pacing steps about the room with scarcely a limp and came to a stop in front of her again. He stared down, his eyes dark and brooding. "Do you really trust him, Thérèse?"

She bit her lip. If she told him the truth, that the man made her uneasy, what would he do? Stay to defend her? Strain his already damaged muscles beyond their endurance? She could not let that happen!

"Of course he is to be trusted, *sans doute!* Your government and Lord Pembroke, they say I am now safe."

"They do, do they? I doubt they realized you were going to announce your whereabouts quite so loudly. Are you sure you wouldn't like someone to stay here for a few days and keep an eye on things?"

Indeed she would, but she could not permit him to do it!

Not for anything would she risk his health! Not now, when she could glimpse his other self beginning to stir once more. She shook her head. "I—I am quite all right."

"Perhaps I'll stay. The sea air might do me good."

But only if he took things easy, as he was supposed to! If he stayed, she would not put it beyond him to break into the Chevalier's lodgings to learn more of the man. And who knew what other foolhardy escapade he might undertake? And if real danger sprang up . . . She shuddered at the vision of Charles trying to enact the role of *Le Maniganceur* when neither his strength nor his spirit were capable of so demanding a task. He would be killed, and it would be all her fault for ever having gone to Ranleigh! Sir Roderick had been right, it was *she* who was the real threat to his safety!

She had to prevent it! She had to get him to leave, to go back to where he was safe and could continue to recuperate in peace. She could not bear to be the cause of any more suffering on his part. Yet she knew his determination of old, he would not easily be shifted from performing what he felt to be his duty. Her only hope of getting him to withdraw would be to infuriate him, to make him leave of his own accord. . . . She bit her lip. His pride was his most vulnerable point.

"There is no need of your—your swashbuckling derring-do," she blurted out. "Me, I can manage very well!"

He stiffened and she saw surprise, hurt, and chagrin cross his expressive countenance. If only those hateful words did not have to be said! But it was for his own good, it really was! She had to stand firm in this seeming cruelty.

The fingers of his right hand clenched convulsively, and when he spoke, his voice was filled with an anger that failed to disguise his injured pride. "Do you think I enjoy haring about after a silly peagoose like you who likes to throw herself into danger?"

His response was so strong as she had hoped—and feared. It would not take much more. . . . She firmed her wavering resolve and threw more fuel onto his sparking temper. "So it is a peagoose that I am? It is not I who dance about on the rooftops dodging bullets or dangle beneath windows on ropes!"

"No, you just get yourself captured!"

"Well, it shall not happen here! I have no need of any flashy and most unnecessary displays of heroism!"

"Perhaps you think yourself capable of handling your affairs on your own?"

"Mais, oui! Cela va sans dire!" She brought up her chin in defiance.

"Very well, you may do so!" He swept her a mocking bow. "I shall not bother you further, you have my word!" He picked up his hat from the occasional table and stormed out of the room. A moment later she heard the latch on the front door click.

"Mon Charles, I am sorry!" The words escaped her in a quavering whisper. It had been agony to say those shocking things to him, but she had to free him of any sense of obligation toward her! He could not, weak as he was, try to resume the role of her savior and protector. This had been the only way. . . . He would wash his hands of her now, return to Ranleigh, and be safe.

Tears trembled on her lashes and spilled over, running unheeded down her cheeks. He was gone, and he would not come back. She had seen to that. . . . With shaking hands she sought the snuffer and extinguished the candles he had lighted. He was gone. . . .

She turned from the darkened room and made her slow way up the steps to her bed chamber. Aimée bounded at her heels.

Why did he have to come, at all? To rake up the smoldering embers of her memories, of her infatuation with *Le Maniganceur*? She wiped the tears from her cheeks with trembling fingers. There, in the darkness, it was as if she saw him again for the first time. Her beloved *Le Maniganceur*, brought back to life . . .

Only he hadn't been. *Le Maniganceur* had existed only in her dreams, and she could not let this Charles destroy himself in attempts to resurrect her idealized hero. She had done the right thing by driving him away! The hurt and pain in his eyes might wrench her heart, but in the long run, it was for the best . . . there had been no other way.

Perhaps later, when his wounds were no more than a memory and his strength and laughter returned, she would see him again, have the chance to get to know him . . . or had she done her job too thoroughly? She had struck at his most vulnerable point, his pride. And he had been hurt, deeply hurt.

His pride. His sister Celia called it the curse of the Marcombe family, and she had not been joking. Well, Charles would no longer risk himself for her; she would not see him again. He had stated that fact quite clearly, and she had no cause to doubt his word.

So much for her past! She curled up in the great bed and hugged Aimée's warm, furry body. It was time to stop thinking of what was no more and concentrate on the wonderful future she must build for herself. But for some reason, she found it very difficult to focus her thoughts and instead sought oblivion in sleep.

In the morning, she rose heavy-eyed and with a dull throb that seemed to penetrate every part of her head. Breakfast held no appeal, and after sipping a cup of chocolate, she yielded to Aimée's coquettish overtures and took her delighted pet for a walk.

The stroll along the Marine Parade did them both good and went a long way to buoying Thérèse's sagging spirits. The sooner she filled her home with happy memories, the better it would be. She must give a party as soon as she could organize it. And between the comfortable honorarium she had received for her part in the concert and Lord Pembroke's parting gift, which she would not now have to spend on her housing, she need have no qualms about arranging the best.

With this in mind, she visited the Draycott sisters to borrow an invitation list, then headed home. She would begin at once! But to her consternation, Charles's presence lingered in the drawing room, angry and hurt, refusing to be ousted, not letting her work. In desperation she fled to the front salon where she at last was able to set about writing and directing her notes.

She had not gotten very far with these when her first visitor arrived. The Chevalier de Lebouchon stepped over the threshold and looked about in approval.

"Ma chère mademoiselle, it is delightful! The perfect setting for you! It is a lovely room, so full of the sun." A warm smile of pleasure lit his face.

She forced her lips to curve upward as she went to take his hand. "Some refreshment, m'sieur? Perhaps some wine?" He agreed, and she poured a glass from the decanter that stood on the occasional table.

He took it with a bow of thanks. "Mademoiselle, you make the most delightful hostess."

His words—indeed his whole attitude—seemed bent on flattering her. She might as well play along. Perhaps she could derive some amusement from an elegant flirtation—and at the very least, it might serve to divert her from the stricken and angry look on Charles's face. . . .

She gestured for the Chevalier to be seated and resumed her own place beside the small writing desk. "What may I do for you, m'sieur?"

A soft growl sounded from the depths of her flounced muslin skirts as Aimée backed away to press against her ankles. What ailed the little dog? She was afraid of Armand de Lebouchon almost as if she knew him. But the idea was absurd! Thérèse reached down to stroke her pet and a rough little tongue licked her hand.

"I have come to beg the pleasure of your company on a drive this afternoon." Idly, he swung his quizzing glass at the end of its long riband. "Such a beautiful day, is it not? It seems a pity to remain within doors."

"Very true, but I fear I must." She shook her head with feigned regret. "Perhaps another time?"

He gave an exaggerated sigh. "I am desolate. But of a certainty, I am at your disposal whenever you should wish an outing." He peered at the notes that lay scattered across the table. "Or is there something I might do to help you?"

"Have you a taste for finesse in refreshments?" She tilted her head and regarded him with a measure of speculation.

"Mademoiselle, you could not have applied to a person more perfectly suited to the task." He made an expansive gesture with his wineglass. "I am entirely at your disposal. What is it that you wish?"

"I am determined to earn for myself the reputation of setting the most unique table in all of Brighton."

His eyes gleamed. "To be the hostess most envied? You shall do it to admiration. For this, you shall need menus and recipes. . . ." He broke off, lost in thought.

"That is exactly what I need. Tell me, m'sieur, do you have any suggestions?"

"I shall seek out the most adventurous and adept of the local chefs and caterers. You must not send to London!" He shook his head for emphasis. "Ah, that it is ineligible to order from Paris! The delicacies we had there! Even in that great city, *ma Thérèse*, your refreshments were always a delight. Of a certainty, we must find a French chef."

She encouraged him in this vein, diverted by his enthusiasm. To hear him talk, it would seem that the Chevalier had few interests in life other than food. This suited her quite well for the moment, and she listened to his discourse on the various methods he had encountered of preparing lobsters and crabs.

"But I waste our time." He rose at last, took her hand, and raised it to his lips. *"Au revoir,* mademoiselle. I go to find for your party a chef worthy of the title." With a great flourish, he bowed himself out.

She still smiled as the door closed behind him. He behaved very much in the grand manner, as he had in Paris. Apparently he did not miss his homeland, and she could only be glad. He was what the English would call an "amusing rattle," and that exactly suited her needs at the moment.

By the following day, the Chevalier proved his abilities in regard to the task she had set him. He returned with not one but three cooks, all French, and menu suggestions that would have put the staff at Prinny's Pavilion to shame. The result was a dinner menu that ran the gamut from oysters floating in cream and stuffed partridges baked in wine sauce to a pastry boat made of spun sugar and filled with an assortment of tartlets and sweetmeats. In all, Thérèse selected over twenty unusual and exceptional dishes to set before her nineteen chosen guests.

"Assuredly, this will establish you in the eyes of all Brighton!" de Lebouchon declared as he read over the final selections.

"Then I shall have you to thank. And m'sieur," she turned to one of the chefs. "If you can have the first of the wines delivered this afternoon, it may rest for two days before being served."

The rest of that day and most of the next two were devoted to preparations for the party. It had been a very long time since she'd entertained members of the fashionable world. For the past few years, her only guests had been Napoleon's officers and their consorts, her only purpose to learn their secrets. But now she wished to entertain in the grand style, to create a dinner party that would be unforgettable, to secure for herself a place in the elite ranks of society hostesses.

The only time she spared from her efforts she devoted to Aimée. The little dog improved daily, and Thérèse gradually increased the distance of their walks as Aimée's leg healed and her limp all but disappeared. Aimée put on weight and her shaggy beige fur took on a silky sheen. Her huge, pansy-brown eyes glowed with a new vigor.

Thérèse relegated Charles to the back of her mind. It had been better to wound his pride than to allow him to injure himself further. He would recover from the insult of her words—and perhaps one day she would forgive herself for saying them. In desperation she kept herself so busy with her preparations that she did not have time to think.

On the night of the party, her townhouse blazed with the light of over two hundred candles. Freshly cut flowers floated in huge glass bowls, and a string quartet played softly in the long drawing room. Thérèse, resplendent in a half-robe of Pomono green silk over a white sarcenet underslip, stood near the door to receive her guests. Aimée huddled in her flounced skirts, nervous as the carriages began to pull up before the door.

The first to arrive were the Draycott sisters, escorted regally by General Somerset. They had barely time to greet their hostess and exclaim over the decor when the next arrivals were announced and claimed Thérèse's attention.

The Chevalier was one of the last to put in an appearance. He paused just over the threshold as if struck by admiration, then came quickly forward to take her hand.

"Exquisite, mademoiselle. Truly, you have made of this a work of art."

Thérèse looked about her rooms, which were now comfortably crowded with the elite of the *beau monde*. How *Le Maniganceur* would have enjoyed her triumph. . . .

She had little time to dwell on him or regret his absence. Bradley entered the salon and solemnly announced that dinner was served. Thérèse turned at once from de

Lebouchon and arranged partners for her guests. Then, with General Somerset as her own escort, she led the way into the dining room, where candles and flowers again provided the decorations. Strains of Mozart drifted in from the drawing room next door.

The footmen carried in the first course of oysters in cream, tender pigeons stuffed with crab, several vegetables, and a delicately seasoned clear broth. After sampling several of the dishes, Thérèse knew the reputation of her dinners to be secure; every morsel was delectable. She looked down the table to where the Chevalier sat beside Sophie Andover. His laughing eyes met hers and acknowledged her unspoken thanks.

When the ladies finally left the gentlemen to their port, brandy, and snuff, a mood of mellow satisfaction reigned. With General Somerset overseeing the men among her guests, Thérèse led the women back into the drawing room. The musicians took a break to partake of their own supper and while the ladies talked, Thérèse signaled for the card tables to be brought in and fresh decks arranged.

The men did not linger over their wine. They soon entered the drawing room, and for several minutes Thérèse busied herself with matching skills and tastes for the various card games. At last she stood back, certain that everyone enjoyed themselves.

"But you do not play." The Chevalier moved to her side, smiling. "Surely you have earned the right to a game. What shall it be? Piquet?" He took her arm and drew her toward an empty table.

She hesitated, signaled for Bradley to serve the champagne, then gave in. She would like to relax, and all seemed to go very well, her guests more than content. She took a seat and felt Aimée settle on the floor at her feet, still hidden beneath her skirts.

De Lebouchon opened the pack and began to shuffle the deck. He looked up, met her gaze, and an odd excitement lit his blue eyes. "What stakes, mademoiselle?"

"Whatever you care," came her reckless response.

The lines about his mouth deepened. "But the possibilities you open to me are endless," he murmured. "And so intriguing! A man less honorable might be tempted to take advantage of so tempting an offer."

Warm color tinged her cheeks, and he laughed softly. "Do not worry, mademoiselle. Tonight, and for you, I am a gentleman."

A lighthearted flirtation was exactly what she needed to rid her thoughts of the drama of her encounter with Charles. She felt not the least *tendre* for de Lebouchon, but she liked him well enough, so long as his mood stayed teasing and he did not cast those searching glances at her.

With their stakes set at pennies on the point, she need not worry overly much about the cards she held. Instead she kept an eye on her guests, watching in case anyone tired of his diversions.

De Lebouchon let out an exaggerated sigh. "I see I must wait until you are no longer a hostess. It is too cruel, mademoiselle." He leaned forward, his murmured words for her ears alone. "I come only to see you, and you must concern yourself with everyone but me." His hand covered hers for the briefest of moments before he collected the cards and shuffled them again.

She made a joking rejoinder as she stood to relinquish her place to General Somerset, but his comment and action startled her. This went beyond the friendliness that had always existed between them. It made her uncomfortable and very much aware that she did not return his regard.

As the hour grew more advanced, her guests reluctantly began to depart. De Lebouchon, a glass of champagne in his hand, stood near her side, listening to the expressions of thanks and declarations that this had been the most delightful of evenings. Very much as if he had been the host! But he had contributed to the success of the evening, and in an extremely important way, which perhaps gave him the excuse, if not the right, to behave in this proprietary manner. She should not have enlisted his aid in so casual and open a way. She would know better in the future.

As she mounted the stairs to her chamber, his behavior continued to bother her. He had been at her side most of the evening, calmly assuming chores more appropriate to the host. And that role she had delegated to General Somerset for the evening. If she were not more careful, her name would soon be linked with de Lebouchon's in the vilest gossip.

The situation still occupied her mind as she took Aimée for a long walk the following morning. The only solution that occurred to her was to keep the Chevalier at a distance. She had had her fill of being the subject of gossip in her old life, where her success as a spy depended on it. She was through with that and wanted no vicious tongues at work on her now. When next she saw de Lebouchon, she would gently hint him away.

She had her opportunity only moments later. As she approached her house, she looked up and saw him just mounting the steps. He paused as he saw her, then hurried across the street to her side. Aimée retreated growling.

"Mademoiselle." He raised her fingertips to his lips and gave her hand a caressing squeeze before releasing it. "I have come to congratulate you upon a most delightful party. You have established yourself as a hostess of note. Hereafter, invitations to your parties will be greatly sought after."

"*Merci, m'sieur.*" She drew away slightly. She had no desire to offend him, but neither did she wish to encourage him. He entertained her, but she felt nothing more than amusement at his mannerisms. Indeed, if she examined her feelings, she could not particularly discover whether

86

she truly did like him or if she merely felt gratitude for the companionship and support he offered during those turbulent days in Paris. The realization startled her.

"Now you must excuse me." She gave him an apologetic smile. "I have promised to work out a concert program for Miss Draycott, and she is most anxious to have it back this morning."

"Then I shall not detain you." He bowed in good-natured acquiescence, but a slight frown creased his brow. *"Votre serviteur, mademoiselle."*

She entered the house, put off her bonnet, and found to her dismay that it was not the Chevalier, but a very different man who troubled her solitude and crept about the fringes of her thoughts. Her dreams of *Le Maniganceur* had been laid to rest! Why could they not remain decently buried and forgotten?

It must be only the difficulty of adjusting to her new life. As soon as she settled in, she would forget him, for she would be too busy—and too happy—to dwell on mere shadows of the past. After all, he would spare few thoughts, even angry ones, for her.

With this intention in mind, she threw herself into the planning of the musical society's next concert. She would sing, of course, but they must round out the evening to present, in the best possible way, two very talented young musicians. She bent her mind to pacing the program, but try as she might, she could not prevent her mind from wandering to its forbidden topic.

For the next two days, she saw nothing of the Chevalier. She went about under the aegis of the Draycott sisters, filling every hour with activities in a vain attempt to block her dreams from her mind. She extended her walks, taking Aimée farther and farther afield, until one afternoon she found herself on the Steine facing the Pavilion.

She stood for a long moment lost in contemplation of Prinny's garish "farmhouse," over which workers swarmed like bees about a hive. A pang of bittersweet memory assailed her. It was here that she had gone to testify before the government officials, here that she had told them of *Le Maniganceur*'s bravery. And all the while he sat near, struggling to stay erect in his chair, to prevent his strength from fading, his terrible wounds so new. . . .

She turned away abruptly and retraced her steps. It had been foolish to come here, to stir so many memories that were best left alone. She quickened her pace in an attempt to escape, and the mongrel trotted along at her side without protest.

Back at the house, she wandered from room to room, restless. At last she settled down in the front salon to stare blindly at the morning paper. She was shaken from her reverie a short time later by the arrival of William Harding.

She set the unread sheets aside at once and forced a bright smile to her lips as he made a courteous bow. "How delightful to see you, Monsieur Harding! And what brings you back to Brighton?"

"You," he said shortly. He started toward the chair she offered but did not seat himself. Instead, he stood uneasily staring out the window. At last he said, "I would appreciate it, ma'mselle, if you was a little more on your guard."

"On my guard? How do you mean?" She turned to follow his gaze as if she feared to see some menacing figure lurking about on the street.

"Nothing definite." He frowned with the effort of finding words to explain his meaning. "You go about too freely for my taste, is all."

"But do you have cause to worry?" She regarded him with considerable concern.

He shook his head. "That's just it, ma'mselle. There's nothing tangible. I haven't seen anyone mysterious, nor have we gotten word someone's looking for you. I just have this feeling." He ran a roughened hand through his sandy brown locks. "I don't put much store by feelings," he admitted ruefully. "I'd lecture any assistant of mine who came out with such a farradiddle of nonsense. But there it is . . . things just don't feel right."

She nodded. "It is only habit. I, too, have foolish worries. But indeed, they have turned out to be nothing. One grows accustomed to being careful, and when there is no longer need, to return to a normal life seems foolhardy and reckless."

"I still don't like it." He turned an almost mulish countenance toward her.

That brought a genuine smile to her lips for the first time in several days. "It is because you have so great a sense of duty. It is very kind of you, but as you see, I have been here now almost two weeks, and nothing has happened."

"I know. I'd just feel better if there could be someone here keeping an eye on you all the time."

She flushed, remembering Charles's generous offer. "But there is such a one! You see, I am not without a guard." She gestured to Aimée, who lay curled at her feet, her large eyes resting on the visitor.

Harding smiled. "Well, I suppose without official authority, that's the best we can hope for. And we're not likely to get more reinforcements, since no one seems to be paying attention to you anymore. I only hope your little dog is never called upon to protect you."

After assuring himself that she needed nothing, he took his leave. Thérèse remained where he had left her for a very long time, lost in thought. Did she indeed need a guard? But even if she did, she could not have permitted Charles, in his weakened condition, to perform that role! It would have been tantamount to killing him if any danger did strike!

Harding was wrong. She did not need to hide, but to go about more. She needed more memories, happier ones, anything that might serve to divert her mind from *Le Maniganceur*. She needed the admiration of a handsome gentleman, preferably fair in coloring, to replace the image of a rugged, bronzed countenance with devils of laughter dancing in dark, mysterious eyes.

As she sat there brooding, Bradley entered to announce another visitor. She looked up to see the blond, rakish Chevalier de Lebouchon. He might have come in answer to her thoughts! Aimée, with only a soft growl, withdrew to beneath the muslin flounce of Thérèse's round gown.

De Lebouchon came quickly into the room and possessed himself of her hand. "Mademoiselle, are you not well?" His earnest blue eyes searched her face.

"Only tired." With an effort she pulled herself together and banished her wisteful memories of *Le Maniganceur*. "How do you go on? I have not seen you for the past couple of days."

"Alas, no. I have been out of town." His eyes gleamed with a suppressed excitement. "But I have returned in time for a most enjoyable evening—if you will accompany me?"

She managed an almost convincing smile. "*Voyons,* this sounds most exciting. Where is it that you go?"

"There is to be a public ball at the Castle Inn tomorrow night. Not as select as a private gathering, of course, but I am led to understand that such an event here in Brighton is quite unexceptionable. Will you do me the honor of attending under my escort?"

This was exactly what she needed! The Chevalier could be counted upon to flatter her and do all in his power to assure her enjoyment of the event. She need not fear being accosted by half-sprung bucks bent on dalliance. She could relax and enjoy the laughter and the dancing.

"It will be of all things the most delightful." And she would make sure that it was.

He stood, clasped her hand, and raised her fingers to his

lips. His eyes sparkled with anticipation. "You must excuse me. I go now to see to the hiring of a carriage suitable to carry you to the event."

She saw him to the door. Then, in an effort to keep her thoughts from drifting back to the intrusive Charles Marcombe, she devoted herself to the matter of her appearance. Her wardrobe consisted almost exclusively of gowns ordered for her by Lord Ryde, who had seen to her housing and protection when she first came safely out of France. His knowledge of feminine attire was extensive, as had been his use of the government funds placed at his disposal for this purpose. The result was that she possessed a particularly beautiful ballgown that she had never had occasion to wear.

When the Chevalier called for her at nine the following night, she awaited him in an alluring confection of silvered silk with huge puffed sleeves caught and tied in three bands, a low rounded neckline with a lace edging, and a three-quarter-length apron of matching lace. Artificial roses in the same silk nestled in her golden curls.

De Lebouchon stopped to gaze at her. "Mademoiselle," he murmured as he came forward and reverently kissed her fingers. "Your beauty is unsurpassed!"

It was a promising start to the evening. He led her outside and she found that he had obtained an elegant closed carriage suitable for a comfortable journey of many miles, instead of just around the corner and down the street.

He laughed. "For you, *ma chère* Mademoiselle de Bourgerre, nothing is too good. But you must promise me," he added as he handed her into the vehicle, "that you will save for me a quadrille. I have longed to dance the so elegant steps with you."

To this she agreed, and the ride passed quickly with his eager, almost excited, chatter. It seemed as if he were bent on charming her this night and she encouraged him in his light-hearted vein.

The ballroom in which she had sung only a week before was completely transformed. Gone were the rows of chairs and subdued lighting. Now the chandeliers blazed with hundreds of candles that glinted off the jewels of the beautifully gowned ladies.

With her fingers resting lightly on the Chevalier's arm, she allowed him to lead her about the room. To her surprise, he did not seem the least bit interested in finding seats. Instead, he sought out every one of their acquaintances to exchange merry greetings. Then, before any of the gentlemen had a chance to bespeak a dance with Thérèse, he bestowed a possessive smile on her and guided her away to speak to others.

Never had she realized she knew so many people. And what was de Lebouchon's purpose? To hint away the several gentlemen who admired her? To establish himself as her chief suitor? Rather than being flattered by his attitude, it began to irritate her. But she shrank from causing a scene in so public a place. When the orchestra at last struck up the first country dance, she turned to her companion and tried to draw her hand away.

"But *ma Thérèse*, may I not have this dance?"

It was her opinion he had monopolized far too much of her time already. But she had no other partner; he had seen to that. Giving in with a good grace was her best choice, so she followed him into a set that formed near them.

The movement of the dance separated them frequently, but his eyes remained on her with a penetrating look that left her uneasy. It was as if he sought to tell the polite world that he had claimed her. That played no part in her plans for a busy social life, and so he would shortly learn!

As the dance ended, an officer in scarlet regimentals who had been in their set begged for her hand in the round dance that would follow. Relieved to escape the Chevalier, she accepted with alacrity. As she went through the steps, she looked quickly around for de Lebouchon. To her dismay, he stood just beyond the dance floor, alone, watching her, almost like a dog guarding its bone.

He strode up to her the moment the music stopped, bowed stiffly to the officer, and allowed Thérèse barely time to thank that gentleman before drawing her away. As soon as they were clear of the other dancers, she turned on him, controlling her volatile temper with difficulty.

"M'sieur, it is not seemly that you should spend so much time at my side. 'Sitting in my pocket' is what these English would say. You make of us both a scandal!"

He clasped her hand between his own. "Forgive me, *ma Thérèse*. It is your beauty that overwhelms me." He raised her fingers to his lips and released her. "I shall try to behave as you would wish."

"*Merci.*" She looked away, embarrassed, not caring for such attentions. She much preferred the casual acquaintance, the occasional serious talks they had enjoyed in Paris.

For the remainder of the evening he stayed just enough detached from her so that she could not call him to book for impropriety. They danced the quadrille together, but when he begged for her to join him in the boulanger, she was able to turn him down.

"It would be the height of impropriety to stand up with you more than twice," she informed him.

"These so proper English." De Lebouchon hesitated. "Would you think me uncivil if I told you I grow tired?"

"*Mais non!*" she exclaimed, instantly contrite. Had she offended him? Or did he take ill? She searched his face and decided that he looked strained, not at all his usual, joking self.

"Should you mind if we leave early? I do not wish to curtail your enjoyment, but . . ." He raised a hand to cover his eyes for a brief moment.

"Of a certainty we may leave. Would you care to go

now? There will always be other balls."

"*Merci.* You are most kind. Then excuse me and I shall send for the carriage."

She fetched her shawl, then joined him in the lobby. He stood very close beside her, towering above her—but she was of so slight a build that almost anyone seemed large and overpowering in comparison.

"It is terrible of me to spirit you away like this." He leaned down to whisper the words in her ear.

"But it is as nothing. *Tiens,* do not concern yourself." She laid her hand on his arm and her soft, earnest tone matched his.

"*Ma Thérèse,* you have no idea how great a help you are to me this night." His voice quivered as if with laughter. "Do you enjoy being so great a success?"

She returned no answer. A success? Socially, she supposed she was well on her way to having everything she had ever wanted. Now, if only she could be happy . . .

The closed carriage pulled up before the door and he handed her into it. She sank down onto the cushioned seat, barely noticing that he seated himself opposite instead of beside her. Why did she feel only vast waves of melancholy?

She had everything except the one thing she wanted, the only thing that mattered—her dreams. *Le Maniganceur* was gone, and in his place stood a very poor imitation. She went through the motions of life, but without him it all lacked meaning. She had buoyed herself with her determination to help de Lebouchon, but it had proved unnecessary. He needed no assistance, she no longer stood in any danger . . . and life was dreadfully flat.

The lurching of the carriage as the horses broke into a canter at last penetrated her thoughts and she looked out the window. They were no longer on the cobbled roads of Brighton, but driving at breakneck pace along a dark, tree-lined road lit only by the moon and the stars. Startled, she looked across at her companion.

"But, Chevalier, where is this that we are? Where do we go?"

"Just a little journey." He leaned back against the squabs, smiling, rocking easily with the swaying of the coach.

Something about his manner brought her instantly alert. "If you please, m'sieur, I wish for you to take me home upon the instant!"

His smile deepened. "I am taking you home, *Mademoiselle Thérèse de Bourgerre*. Back where you belong—to France."

France . . . panicked, she lunged for the door with the hazy idea of calling to the coachman. De Lebouchon caught her arm and jerked her back onto the seat.

With firm resolve, she quelled her internal shaking. "For a moment, you—you startled me, *enfin*." She forced a laugh. "But I am in no mood for such a jest, m'sieur. You will take me home, *s'il vous plaît*."

"I fear this is no joke, *ma Thérèse*."

The deadly sincerity in his tone sent a cold shiver through her. "But this is of a foolishness! Do you think that no one will notice if I do not return home?"

"But no one will think it the least bit odd that we have gone off together. At your so delightful dinner party, if you will remember, you made no secret of the fact that I had played an important role. And this night you have helped me to show the whole of the so foolish *beau monde* that there is an attraction of great strength between us."

"But . . ." Real fear gripped her and she fought against its paralyzing effects.

"No more protests, if you please, mademoiselle. I grow weary of them." His smile never wavered as he drew a pistol from the capacious pocket of his coat and pointed it directly at her heart.

Chapter Six

At ten o'clock the following morning, William Harding strode up the Marine Parade toward the house occupied by Mademoiselle de Bourgerre. Two voices raised in heated argument reached him, and he became aware of an altercation between a maid and a groom taking place on a doorstep . . . Thérèse's doorstep. A deep sense of foreboding filled him and he broke into a run.

Symmons looked up as he reached the bottom step. "Oh, Mr. Harding, I'm so glad you've come! The most terrible thing! Ma'mselle didn't return home last night after a ball, and now this servant of the Chevalier de Lebouchon's has come to collect her baggage!"

"What is this about?" Harding snapped the question at the hapless lad.

"Gone off together, they 'ave, sir," the groom asserted.

Symmons shook her head. "Ma'mselle would do no such thing! Not without telling me, she wouldn't. Now you tell Mr. Harding what's toward if you know what's good for you, my lad!"

The groom shook his head. "I 'as me orders, and that's all I knows."

"Where are you to take Ma'mselle's things?" Harding regarded him with a compelling eye as he fought down a cold stab of fear for Thérèse. Not for a moment did he believe she would go haring off like that! Even if she did wish to go off with some man—which he did not for a moment believe—she wouldn't just flee like this without leaving word that everything was all right. Another young woman, perhaps, but not Thérèse de Bourgerre!

"It's nothing to make such a fuss about," the boy assured him, dismayed by the commotion his simple request had caused. "It's only . . ."

He was interrupted as the door, which stood slightly ajar, was thrust open and the little mongrel bounded out onto the porch, whining and yipping. She rubbed up against Symmons' legs, shivering, and the abigail stooped down and picked her up.

"See, Mr. Harding! Ma'mselle would never go off and leave her little Aimée!"

Cold certainty clutched at Harding as he slowly nodded in agreement. "Where were they going?" He turned back to the boy. "Quickly, lad!"

The groom shook his head. "Dunno, sir. I was to 'ave 'er things conveyed to 'is 'ouse. Said she wouldn't be needin' nothin' while they was away, but that everythin' was to be there waitin' for 'er when they got back."

"What's his address?"

Harding wrote this down, then stared off into space. Would it do him any good to go there? If de Lebouchon was indeed a French agent, he would hardly leave the particulars of his travel plans with his servants. And if he wasn't—no, he would only waste time on such a visit. He had to take action, and fast!

"Please, Mr. Harding, what are we to do?" Symmons still hugged the dog.

"Find her, of course! Bradley!" He called the butler through the doorway. "Keep this fellow here and find out everything you can. And go to de Lebouchon's house, personally, and ask when he's expected back." He turned and strode off, muttering a string of violent oaths under his breath. Despite all his efforts, Thérèse had been recaptured by the French. Of that he had no doubt. *Damn* Pembroke, for not authorizing more precautions!

And what should he do now? His brain seethed as he almost ran back up the Marine Parade and onto the Steine. He had ridden in last night, leaving his mount stabled at the Castle Inn, so his horse must be rested by now. And it was only a five-mile ride out to Hastings, Lord Ryde's estate. He desperately needed to consult with someone in authority. His best hope would be if Lord Ryde had returned from his wedding trip.

While his horse was saddled and brought around, he paced in restless circles about the length of the yard. No sooner did the ostler lead the animal up than he leaped into the saddle, dug his heels in, and bounded out toward the street. Here, traffic forced him to proceed with caution, and he ground his teeth in impatience until he reached the New Road and could give his mount its head. He urged it along as fast as he could make it go.

Less than half an hour later, he reined in as he reached the main gate of Hastings. At first he allowed himself to hope that the empty appearance was due to the only partially finished renovations, but as he neared the house itself, he acknowledged with dismay that it looked closed up. Still, he jumped down, ran up to the door, and pounded on the oaken panels with his fist until the outraged butler opened it.

"Why, Mr. Harding!" Gosson blinked in amazement. "His lordship has not yet returned!"

"When will he be back?"

"Well, really, sir, I could not take it upon myself to say. He . . ."

"Soon?"

Something of the anxiety in Harding's manner finally touched the butler. "No, sir. We do not expect his lordship and Lady Ryde back for some time yet."

"Damn! Thank you, Gosson." Balked, Harding returned to his horse, who had taken the opportunity to stray onto the newly reseeded lawn by way of a freshly weeded flower bed. Collecting the bridle, Harding swung back into the saddle. He would have to go to London, which would mean a considerable delay. And what was happening to Mademoiselle de Bourgerre during all this time? She had been in de Lebouchon's hands since some time the night before!

Then followed the wildest ride he had ever undertaken. Five times he stopped for fresh mounts, and each time he chafed at the delay. Despite all efforts, he could not hope to reach London before five o'clock at the earliest. And what had become of Thérèse? Did that de Lebouchon fellow have her out of England? Was she even now in France, being escorted back to Paris under armed guard? Or had she simply been killed? The possibilities haunted him mile after endless mile.

He made a last change at the King's Head in Croyden, and as he raced along Streatham Common toward Brixton, he began to consider alternate courses of action. What if Lord Pembroke were not in his office in Whitehall? It did not take Harding long to dismiss the possibility of presenting his story to anyone else. He would have to track him down, wherever he had gone.

At last he reached the outskirts of the metropolis, where the increased traffic forced him to slow his breakneck pace. With a sigh of relief, he urged his blowing mount across Westminster Bridge, then made the turning onto the street that led to the Whitehall complex.

Drawing up before the building, he leaped to the ground and tossed his bridle toward a startled lad who chanced to be walking by. He ran up the steps, crossed the lobby, and bounded up the inner staircase that led to the wing where Pembroke had his office.

He threw open the door, startling the mild-looking clerk and causing him to splatter ink from the quill he had just dipped. The little man peered at him reproachfully through wire-rimmed spectacles.

"Where's Pembroke?" Harding gasped as he tried to recapture his breath.

The clerk clicked his tongue in disapproval. "Really, Mr. Harding, that is hardly the . . ."

"Tell me, Willits, where is he?"

"In a meeting. No, really, Mr. Harding," he protested as Harding thrust past the desk and made for the inner office. "You must not disturb him!"

Harding paid him no heed. Pushing open the door, he burst in on the five gentlemen who sat around a long table at the far end of Pembroke's office. All eyes turned on him, and he flushed hotly as he recognized several of the most prominent members of His Majesty's Government. Only the urgency of his errand kept him from stammering an apology and retreating.

Lord Pembroke rose slowly, leveling a haughty stare at the intruder. "What is the meaning of this?"

"If you please, my lord, a word with you in private. It's of considerable urgency."

"Very well." Pembroke excused himself and led the way through a doorway into a small chamber. Harding followed.

"What is this about?" Pembroke closed the door firmly and turned his frowning gaze on Harding.

"It's Ma'mselle de Bourgerre, my lord. She's been captured by a French agent."

Pembroke half-sat on the arm of a comfortable chair and drew a silver snuffbox from his coat pocket. "What happened?" While he helped himself to a pinch, Harding gave him the bare facts of the story.

"We'll need to do something at once, if we're to save her, my lord." He finished the tale and fixed his earnest

100

hazel eyes on his superior's face.

Pembroke brushed the remaining flecks of tobacco from his fingertips. "Why are you so certain she was taken by force? You know as well as I do, there's no proof this Chevalier de Lebouchon is an agent. We investigated him pretty thoroughly when he first turned up in England."

"Which didn't happen until after ma'mselle went into hiding."

Pembroke looked up and met Harding's earnest, worried gaze. "It would not be the first time a lady has run off with an intriguing gentleman."

"But there's her little dog, my lord. She'd never go off and leave the animal."

Pembroke shruged. "You said it barked at de Lebouchon? Then he would hardly want it along for a tryst with the lady. To have it forever growling every time he approached her would not be—er—conducive to a romantic atmosphere."

Harding shook his head. "She's not gone willingly, my lord, on that I'll stake my life. Why wouldn't she tell Symmons? Ma'mselle is no fool, she knows we'd worry."

"It might have been a hasty, impulsive decision." Pembroke shook his head. "We don't have any agents to spare on what will in all probability turn out to be a wild goose chase. Until there's proof she was abducted, and has not just gone off with the fellow as his groom says, we can do nothing."

Harding took a rapid turn about the room, seething with frustration. "You don't want to help her!" He spun about to face Pembroke.

His lordship folded his arms. "There are other matters just now," he admitted. "Very pressing ones, in fact, that occupy my mind—all our minds. You seem to forget that the war continues and Bonaparte makes new plans. Mademoiselle de Bourgerre has played her role."

"You're abandoning her, and after all the trouble and

101

danger she went through for us!" Fury at such a betrayal sent caution to the winds. "Good God, Pembroke, just think of all the information she got for you! Where would your damned war effort be now if she hadn't been risking her life for the past five years?"

Pembroke ran a hand through his thinning gray locks. "I meant what I said about agents. We have far too few. It would be a job for *Le Maniganceur*, I suppose, if he weren't out of the picture. Well, you'll have to handle this one yourself."

"Myself?" Harding felt his heart sink.

"I can spare you two men," Pembroke admitted grudgingly. "They're new recruits, just finished their training. They can use the experience."

Harding groaned inwardly. If that dire warning meant what he feared it did, he would be in a worse position than if he went on his own. The last thing he needed was to play nursemaid to a couple of johnny raws.

While he awaited their arrival, he paced the ante-chamber, wondering what he could expect by way of monetary support and advice. If only Ryde had been at home! But there was no use repining over something that couldn't be helped. Like it or not, he was on his own.

His first look at his new assistants confirmed his worst fears. Althorp, an eager young lad of barely twenty, bore a reckless air, seeming only too anxious to have a shot at dealing with French agents. His lean, wiry muscles gave him an athletic appearance. He might prove of use, Harding decided—but only if his fiery nature could be controlled.

That would not be his trouble with Bosworth, who appeared in every way to be his companion's opposite. Short and stocky, he might have been any age between forty and fifty. His ruminative aspect and bovine expression might hide a keen intelligence, but somehow Harding doubted it. Whatever had possessed such a man to swear his services to his country so late in life remained a mystery.

After performing the brief introduction and ordering the two men to obey Harding implicitly, Pembroke returned to his own concerns. Washing his hands of them, Harding guessed shrewdly, and eyed his new recruits with disfavor.

"When will we be starting, sir?" Althorp asked. "*Allons à France!*" he added, thus proving both his eagerness to visit the country and his mastery of the language.

Bosworth pulled a pipe from his pocket and began to fill it with slow, deliberate movements. "Maybe you could tell us a bit more about this first, sir. Don't want to go rushing into something we don't understand." He turned a disapproving eye on Althorp.

"So what is there to discuss?" Althorp took several quick steps about the room. "If this Chevalier has her, he'll have taken her back to France! So we follow and rescue her!"

Harding closed his eyes. "It's not quite so easy as that. Where do you think she will be?"

"In Paris! Where else?" Althorp regarded him with disapproval. All this talking merely slowed down the action he craved.

"Paris is a large city," Harding pointed out.

"The gaol! Or don't you know where that is?" The minimal amount of patience possessed by Althorp appeared to be reaching the breaking point.

"Ma'mselle has already been rescued from their gaol once. I do not believe they would risk lodging her there a second time."

Bosworth nodded. "No telling what them Frenchies will do."

Althorp showed a somewhat chastened mien. "What do you suggest, sir?"

That question had haunted Harding. He knew himself

to be a good, reliable agent, but like most men he had his limits. His strong point lay in carrying out orders in a capable, efficient manner—not in formulating plans. If Thérèse were to be saved, they must recruit a leader for this effort. And aside from Lord Ryde, he knew of only one man both experienced and brilliant enough to find Thérèse once she had been taken by the enemy.

"First," Harding said slowly, "we are going to consult *Le Maniganceur*."

"That's the ticket." Bosworth nodded his approval of his new commander. "Let's talk to someone who knows what's what."

Althorp looked up in reverence at the name. "Do you know who he is, sir?"

"That I do, and you may be very sure we can count on him for some help, even if he has retired."

The hour was too far advanced that night to do more than commandeer a carriage for the following morning. But with first light, Harding and his two companions set forth on the seventy-five-mile journey to Ranleigh. It was not an easy step for Harding to take, for it meant revealing Charles Marcombe's secret identity to the inept duo who were otherwise his only hope in this endeavor. Under the circumstances it could not be helped. Every moment he delayed might put Thérèse de Bourgerre into further danger. And *Le Maniganceur*, despite Thérèse's assurances that he had turned his back on the work, was bound to be anxious to play a role in this rescue. From what he remembered of the man, nothing held him down.

The afternoon faded into evening as the carriage turned up the neatly raked gravel drive at Ranleigh and proceeded between the pruned hedges of hawthorn. Harding, who had never before visited the estate, found himself considerably impressed by the simple elegance that characterized both the house and extensive grounds. Everything bespoke loving care, with no expense spared. He would not be the least bit surprised if *Le Maniganceur* did indeed choose to retire to this place, as rumor claimed. Heaven knew, the man had certainly earned a peaceful life in such a beautiful setting.

The carriage rolled to a halt on the circular drive and Harding jumped down, glad to stretch his legs after the many stiffening miles of jolting along the post road. As he looked about, Charles Marcombe's tall figure came striding toward them up the long expanse of scythed lawn.

As he neared the drive, Charles paused and regarded with frowning scrutiny Bosworth and Althorp, who had climbed down and now stood beside Harding. The latter, at least, he recognized. Something had happened. . . . A surge of energy swept through him, a readiness for battle that bordered on elation at the prospect of action. But all that was past. . . . Still, he came forward quickly, his movements once again as controlled and graceful as a cat's.

"Harding." He took the man's hand in a firm grip. "What's toward?"

Harding experienced a wave of relief. Intelligence gleamed in the other man's brown eyes and his instant recognition and acceptance of trouble made everything so much simpler. Harding subjected him to a quick, considering gaze and decided he looked restored to health, though somewhat drawn.

"I need your help, sir. For Ma'mselle de Bourgerre."

Charles folded his arms, easing the left one with care. A carefully blank expression settled over his features like a rigid impenetrable mask. "In case no one told you, I've retired."

"That's as may be, sir, but I wouldn't have come if it weren't necessary. I need your help. And so does ma'mselle."

"I'll wager she never asked for it," Charles said.

"She would if she could, sir, of that I've no doubts. The

105

devil's in it that she's not able. But I ask for it."

Charles stiffened and shot him a penetrating look. "Not able, is she? You'd best tell me the whole. Come inside."

He led the way across the Great Hall and down the corridor to the library. Bosworth and Althorp looked about at the shelves filled with books that lined the walls and the elegant appointments and comfortable furnishings with which the apartment was abundantly supplied. Charles gestured for his visitors to take seats and they did so with care, as if afraid to mar the perfection of the room. On a table near the hearth rested a decanter of excellent madeira and several glasses; Charles filled these and handed them around.

"Explain. And make it short. I want to know what's been going on since I saw her last week." He seated himself in an upholstered arm chair, leaned back and regarded Harding through narrowed eyes.

"She's been taken by a French agent, sir."

"De Lebouchon?" Charles shot the question at him.

Harding nodded, marveling at the man's quickness of wit. More than ever he was convinced he had done the right thing in coming to *Le Maniganceur*. As quickly as he could, he conveyed everything he knew about it.

Charles drew his snuffbox from his pocket and helped himself to a pinch. "Are you quite certain that Thérèse did not go with him willingly?" With apparent interest he studied the enameled depiction on the box of Zeus, in the form of a bull, bearing off Europa. "She has been acquainted with him for some time, and I'm sure she made it as clear to you as she did to me that she was concerned about him. What could be more natural than for two expatriated countrymen to find solace together? They certainly seemed on friendly terms last time I saw her."

"I can't believe it, sir. She never would have gone off like that."

Young Althrop, who had been staring in awe at the

great *Maniganceur*, paid no heed to Harding's words. "You think this is all a hum, sir?" He shook his head, abashed at having been so ready to make a great deal out of nothing and disappointed at not getting to instantly set forth on a dangerous mission to France. But he accepted Charles's ruling upon the subject. He would agree unquestioningly with anything his idol said and dismiss the whole venture, albeit reluctantly, as nothing more than unreasoned panic.

Bosworth stared stolidly ahead. "The dog," he pronounced in measured tones.

Althorp's head came up as he saw the possibility of tackling those damned Frenchies revive. "It does seem an odd start for a female to rush off without so much as a nightdress on a tryst of that nature," he ventured, pointing out what seemed to him to be another pertinent objection.

Charles looked across at him, his eyes little more than steely slits. "Mademoiselle de Bourgerre is a lady, and I will thank you to remember that. There is no question of her slipping off on a tryst."

Althorp appeared suitably abashed. "But I thought you said . . . ?" He broke off under the thunderous glare directed at him by Charles.

"There are any number of reasons why she might have gone with him willingly, and not one of them dishonorable! Mademoiselle has a great sense of loyalty to her friends and considerable experience in her work! Far more than some people I could name."

"But she can't have gone off on an assignment!" Harding objected. "Lord Pembroke must have known, if that were the case! Nor she wouldn't go without leaving some sort of message for Symmons, sir. Ma'mselle knew we was worried about her. Even if it were naught but a harmless outing, as it were, she'd make sure we knew what she was up to."

Charles straightened up a fraction, his expression more

alert as a tense energy almost radiated from him. "She trusted de Lebouchon. Could he not have convinced her he worked for our government?"

"Whether he did or not, she's still in his hands, sir."

That was the one inescapable fact. And even if Thérèse had trusted de Lebouchon, Charles most assuredly did not. But he had retired, he was no longer fit for the work. Yet Thérèse needed his help. . . . What could he do? His injuries might have healed so that only the scars showed, but would his muscles respond to his needs? Would he be able to pull off one last daring rescue, or would he fail Thérèse—and all of them—at the crucial moment?

The door opened and Sir Roderick stopped on the threshold. His old eyes moved from one to the other of the strangers seated in his bookroom and finally came to rest on his grandson. He took a deep breath and straightened his stooping shoulders.

"What has happened?" Tension filled Sir Roderick's voice and his gaze never wavered from Charles. As he listened to the explanation, his head came up and his chin thrust out in a belligerent, defiant attitude. "Damn the woman!" he breathed. His gaze swept over the other three men and came to rest on Harding. "And what are you planning?"

"To go to France, sir," Harding responded. "With only Bosworth and Althorp, if need be. We'll get Ma'mselle de Bourgerre back."

"Don't be absurd!" Charles glanced at his grandfather, then back at Harding. "You haven't the least notion of where to begin! You'll get nowhere, except perhaps captured yourselves."

"Well, he can count on me to do all I can!" Althrop, his expression zestful in the extreme, seconded his commander's decision.

Sir Roderick regarded him through frowning eyes. "Suicide," he pronounced with feeling.

"Aye." Bosworth nodded agreement, but accompanied

the monosyllable with a fatalistic shrug. "But orders is orders."

"You're a pack of fools!" Sir Roderick glared at them. "Charles, you will not go with them. They can go and get themselves shot if they want, but there's no need for you to do so."

"I was rather hoping he might care to join us, sir." Harding faced up to the elderly tyrant.

"Charles?" Sir Roderick turned on him.

Charles looked from one to the other, then slowly shook his head. "I'd only get in your way." His clouded eyes held Harding's for a long moment. "I'm no longer the man you remember. I'd let you down just when you counted most on me. I can't be sure. . . ." He stood abruptly and left the room. The door slammed hard behind him.

"I'm sorry." Sir Roderick addressed himself to Harding. "His injuries were more severe than you seem to realize. His reactions are slowed and his muscles have weakened. He's wise not to try and live up to his own legend."

Harding nodded and came to his feet. The others did the same. "Very well, sir. Sorry to have disturbed you."

Disheartened, Harding started for the door. He had been deserted by the man he'd regarded as his last hope! Without the help of *Le Maniganceur*, the mission had very little chance of success. But the British government owed it to Thérèse de Bourgerre to rescue her if it was humanly possible, so he had to try. He only wished it had not all come down to him.

With dragging steps, he led his two assistants outside to the waiting carriage, at a loss as to what to do next. Never had he imagined that Charles Marcombe would refuse to help. Where was that daring, devil-may-care attitude that characterized *Le Maniganceur*? For a moment he thought he had glimpsed it. But it was gone, set aside as if it had been nothing more than another of his masterful disguises.

It didn't seem possible. He certainly hadn't believed

Thérèse when she'd told him of this change in Charles Marcombe. He didn't really know if he believed it now, even with the evidence so forcibly thrust upon him.

Bosworth gave a deprecatory cough. "Will we be spending the night nearby? Or will we be stopping to bait at an inn? A close-by inn?" His tone held a vast amount of hope.

Harding drew his watch from his coat pocket. It was growing late and he, too, would like to have his dinner. He could not remember ever feeling so beaten down and discouraged. It was almost as if he'd failed even before making an attempt to begin!

. "Dinner!" Althorp's voice dripped scorn. "All you can think of is trivialities. We should concern ourselves with starting for the coast at once! How are we to get to France?"

Bosworth considered the matter. "It won't do to take a packet," he decided.

"The packets aren't running!" his exasperated cohort informed him. "Do we take a smuggler's craft?"

"Now, where would we be finding one of them?" Bosworth asked, his curiosity aroused. "Do you think they carry brandy with them on all their trips?"

"Let's just get started!" Harding shoved Bosworth toward the carriage. Althorp followed more willingly. Harding climbed in after them and reached back to close the door. But he never did so.

Charles appeared in the doorway, his shoulders squared, his head held high, a new determination in his bearing. He briskly descended the shallow flight of steps to the drive and signaled to the coachman who had just climbed onto the box.

"Wait!" he shouted.

Chapter Seven

Charles blamed it on boredom. There could be absolutely no other excuse for deciding to take on so foolhardy a mission. After all, he did not really care a whit what became of Thérèse. He'd washed his hands of her affairs, and his duty, as far as she was concerned, had ended. The possibility that he still sulked from her cutting words never crossed his mind.

But most important to the decision, he assured himself, was the fact that he had never been able to tolerate inactivity. With his wounds healed and his strength beginning to return, the days stretched out long and dull before him. The lure of the hunt that Harding dangled tantalizingly before him proved too irresistible to ignore.

He caught up with them just as they climbed into their carriage. Harding, about to close the door, let out a deep sigh and jumped back down.

"Thank you, sir." Harding caught his hand in a firm grip.

Charles returned the pressure and found himself strangely glad he'd prevented them from leaving. "If this is a suicide mission, we might as well all be in it together."

"Are you sure, sir?"

Charles shrugged. "I can think of worse ways to die.

111

From boredom, for example. I'll warn you, though—I meant what I said. I'm likely to let you down."

"That you won't, sir. Not with ma'mselle depending on you."

Charles's smile became a bit lopsided. "At least I won't be able to indulge in any of that 'swashbuckling derring-do' that she so deplores."

Harding threw him a sidelong glance, but forbore to comment.

"I'm accustomed to working on my own," Charles added, almost as if speaking to himself, "but I'm out of practice and my reactions just aren't what I'd like. It will be a good idea to have others to back me up for a change, to lend some assistance." His dubious gaze came to rest on Althorp and Bosworth.

"You'd best spend the night here." He signaled to a footman who stood by the door, and the lad came running to fetch the baggage. "We'll start for Brighton at dawn."

"Brighton?" Althorp jumped down from the carriage. "But Mademoiselle de Bourgerre will be nowhere near there now! That Chevalier has a two-day start on us!"

"We have no guarantee he'll be taking her to Paris. For all we know, they may not even have left the country." Charles led the way into the house and sent the startled butler for the housekeeper, to arrange for their unexpected visitors. He ushered them into the bookroom once more, where the brindle cat lay sleeping atop a pile of papers on the desk.

Charles closed the door, then stood staring at its dark-paneled surface. "We have no guarantee they'll keep her alive." He turned to face the other three, his expression grim. "She is of no use to them, and it is too late to prevent her from talking to us. The only reason they'd take her is for revenge, and they could kill her just as easily—more so, in fact—in England." He drew a deep breath and forced himself to continue. "Why should they go to the trouble of

112

taking her to Paris first?"

"What do you suggest?" Bosworth sat down on the edge of a chair, accepting with a philosophical shrug this change in leaders.

Charles crossed to the desk chair and perched on the edge of it. The cat Jasper blinked at him through sleepy eyes, rolled over, and eased himself onto the newly provided lap. Absently Charles stroked the soft fur. "We'll start in Brighton and pick up their trail. Then we follow wherever it leads."

Harding studied the toes of his boots. "You don't really think she's dead, do you?" He raised his gaze to meet Charles's.

Charles hesitated, then shook his head. "Not really, not yet. It's a possibility, but it seems to me it would have been easier just to shoot her . . . unless he took her away to some deserted spot to do it." He leaned back and closed his eyes as his hands cradled the contented cat. "No," he said at last, "there's no reason to go to so much trouble. They've taken her for some purpose."

"And there's still the chance it's naught but a hum, and they're off at some house party in the country, when all's said and done," Althorp threw in cheerfully in an attempt to dispel the emotionally charged atmosphere.

Bosworth nodded. "Caution, that's the ticket. Take things slow."

"If we take things slow," Althorp responded, "we'll never find Mademoiselle de Bourgerre!"

"And what if you go rushing off to Paree, while they've gone to Marseilles, or some other such town?" Bosworth demanded, warming up for an argument.

Harding closed his eyes for a moment. Leaving his cohorts to argue to their hearts' content, he turned to Charles. "How are we to proceed?" he asked.

"By asking questions." A hint of the old excitement crept into his eyes. He stroked Jasper until the feline purred. "And now, I suggest we find your rooms so you can prepare for dinner. And I must go in search of my grandfather."

Sir Roderick, not much to Charles's surprise, was not pleased by the news that he had the honor of entertaining three of His Majesty's agents for the night. He regarded his grandson through tired eyes and his erect posture drooped perceptibly.

"And I suppose you will be going with them when they leave?"

"Yes, sir."

Sir Roderick closed his eyes. "I should have known I couldn't prevent it. It's not in you to exchange a life of active service for that of learning estate management."

"It will be, sir. This is just one job, unfinished business. When we have her safe, I'll come back."

"And I suppose you expect me to be pleased about your undertaking a mysterious journey of unspecified duration to an unnamed destination?"

Charles could not help but smile. "Not really, sir."

Sir Roderick sank back in his chair. "I'll not hide from you how it's not what I like. Nor that I gave Mademoiselle de Bourgerre the hint not to involve you when she was here."

"Did you, sir?" Charles's eyes narrowed.

"A great lot of good it did me." Sir Roderick snorted. He eyed his only grandson and a gleam of pride sparked in the depths of his old eyes. He clasped Charles's arm. "Take care of yourself."

"You may be sure of that, sir. I'll be back as soon as I can. For the fall harvest, if not before."

Charles spent considerable time that evening preparing for the expedition, with the result that he added a small dressing case and two bandboxes to the pile of luggage to be carried down to the waiting carriage before first light the next morning.

His companions awoke in dark rooms to trays of chocolate and rolls and the information that they'd depart within the half-hour. Bosworth, who regarded anything less than a red beefsteak and a tankard of ale for breakfast as paltry, grumbled somewhat, but after being promised that a basket would be prepared and sent along with them, he cheered up enough to set about dressing. Just short of the appointed hour they all gathered in the hall.

The journey was for the most part accomplished in silence. There seemed very little to say, for nothing could be decided until after their initial discoveries in Brighton. Charles sat staring out the carriage window, a faraway expression in his eyes.

The same thoughts haunted him mile after mile, seldom varying, getting him nowhere. What was happening to Thérèse? Had she been killed? But she couldn't have been . . . he wouldn't believe it! No one so full of life and laughter could be dead! But how could it profit the French to keep her alive? It was more likely she *had* been killed . . . which brought him back to where he'd begun.

Shortly before ten o'clock that night, having traveled at a remarkable pace, with frequent changes of horses, the carriage turned off the New Road and proceeded along the Steine until they reached the Pavilion. They turned in at the Castle Inn, where Charles announced his intention to put up for as long as necessary.

Harding looked at him in surprise. "Would it not be easier for you to stay in Ma'mselle's house on the Marine Parade?"

Charles shook his head. "It would make us too conspicuous. We'll visit there, of course, but until we know what we're up against, we'd best take every precaution." With a concerted effort he mastered the impulse to go to her house at once, to be among her things. He could not let such foolish sentimentality for a woman who'd scorned his help interfere with his good judgment.

Damn her, anyway! This was her own fault! If she'd not insulted him, but let him remain to keep an eye on her as he had suggested, this would never have happened.

They entered the inn and found they were in luck: the crowds that flocked to the resort during the summer months had begun to depart for their country residences and two rooms were now available. Charles took these for his party. Althorp and Bosworth, in agreement for once, went off to investigate what was to be found in the kitchens at so late an hour, leaving Harding to follow Charles up to the room they would share.

Charles, though tired, set to work at once. There was not a moment to lose if they were to have any hope of tracing her. Even as it was, the chances were slim that they could pick up the trail. Thrusting this defeatist thought from his mind, he concentrated on the job at hand.

While Harding sat in a chair, watching with fascinated eyes, Charles opened up his dressing case, drew out a collection of bottles and jars, and set about altering his appearance. Harding had heard that *Le Maniganceur* was a genius of disguises, but to actually watch him was an education of sorts.

After a few minutes Charles stopped. "You'll have to go downstairs."

"Why?" Harding dearly would have loved to master a few of the techniques he observed. How could a nose so patrician and straight as Charles's suddenly appear thick and crooked, just by the application of a soft, pliable substance and a little paint?

"I don't like an audience." Firmly Charles sent him from the room. He had enough occupying his mind without adding other distractions.

Half an hour later, a man bearing every appearance of an unliveried footman came down the stairs of the inn. The clerk on duty in the lobby barely spared him a glance before returning to some papers he sorted. Servants entrusted with messages were a common sight . . . this one might be unusually tall, but nothing in his demeanor gave the least hint that he was anything other than he seemed.

As he reached the lobby, Althorp and Bosworth emerged from the dining room, where they'd just finished a very satisfying meal consisting of a saddle of mutton, roasted potatoes, and a rather tasty venison pie. They glanced at him, but paid him no heed as they headed out the door for a short walk to stretch their cramped legs before seeking their beds.

Harding, who sat restlessly leafing through a newspaper, glanced up, then returned to his reading. Suddenly his eyes widened and he almost threw the pages aside in his haste to catch Charles, who followed Althorp and Bosworth outside.

"Sir!" He caught Charles's arm.

"Kindly do not make me conspicuous." Charles fixed him with a reproachful eye. "And while I'm gone, please make arrangements for a boat to be ready—just in case of an emergency. A smuggler's craft should do."

Harding breathed a sigh of relief. This was precisely the sort of task at which he excelled. "And where might you be off to, sir?"

"Just asking a few questions." Charles gave him an enigmatic smile and slipped away into the night.

Harding stared after him, but already Charles had disappeared. He shook his head in admiration . . . now *there* was a man who knew his trade. He'd not like to come up against him, not by a long shot. Looking about, he spotted his assistants.

"Hoy! You two!" His call was soft, but it carried. As they joined him, he cast a quick, appraising glance at their raiment. Plain enough for their destination.

"Well, come on then, lads, we're off to make the rounds of the fishermen's taverns."

A short while later Charles strolled into one of the

taverns patronized by domestic servants. He sauntered among the tables, ordered a tankard of ale, and soon fell into conversation with a retired butler who prided himself on his knowledge of the local clientele. After standing him a drink, Charles gleaned enough information to make a shrewd guess as to where de Lebouchon's servants might be found. Satisfied, he paid the barman and took his leave.

He had his first lead! A surge of elation swept through him. Before this night was over, he vowed he would know a great deal about the Chevalier de Lebouchon's movements! And when he caught up with him. . . .

Following his best instincts, his next stop was a modest-looking establishment facing onto a back road and bearing the sign of the Cat and Fiddle. Procuring a tankard for himself, he leaned against the bar in a fairly central position. His sharp eyes searched out possible contacts. It was not long before his attention was caught by a conversation between a couple of young footmen.

"'Opped it, 'e did, without any warnin'!" one lad declared in disgust.

"Those Frenchies are a bad lot, Alf. Me, I never work for 'em." His companion smiled in a vastly superior manner.

Alf glared back. "'Ow was I to know, Bert? Claimed 'e was a chevalay, 'e did, then what does 'e do but sack the entire staff without botherin' to give a one of us references! Just up and left the 'ouse." He shook his head in disgust.

With a laugh for his friend's misfortune, Bert stood and strolled off. Charles waited a minute, then went to the table.

"'Appened to me of a once, it did." Charles's expression one of complete sympathy, he drew out the vacated chair and sat down. "'Ere, what're you drinkin'? Let me get you a Blue Ruin, lad. I know what it's like, 'avin' an employer lope off on yer like that. Makes yer feel real low, it does."

"Aye," Alf agreed with feeling. He swallowed the cheap gin as soon as the barman set it down, and Charles signaled for more. After the second shot, the young man leaned forward in a confidential manner, his elbows on the table and his hands propping up his chin.

"Was yours a damned Frenchy, too?" With an effort, Alf focused his blearing gaze on Charles.

Charles nodded. "That 'e was. And never again, lad, never again. Came to England to catch an 'eiress, 'e did, only none would 'ave 'im. Ran 'imself into debt, livin' so 'igh an' fancy, then just loped off, leavin' us without no word whether or not 'e was a-comin' back. Not that we ever thought 'e would, o'course."

Alf nodded in vigorous agreement. "Not this feller, neither. Chevalyay de Lebouchon! Bet 'e made up that title! No gen'leman would behave scaly like 'e done. An' 'e didn't even 'ave the bailiffs after 'im, least not that we knows of—yet. Jus' took a fancy to some female and ran off with 'er."

Charles gritted his teeth. "Wonder where they went to? You'd think with a fine 'ouse 'ere in Brighton, 'e'd a-kept 'er right 'ere."

Alf gave him a sly wink. "That Chevalyay, 'e weren't all that 'e seemed, leastways, that's what *we* all thought. Mysterious comin's an' goin's, there was, comin's an' goin's . . . and all the time. Never knew who we might run inter on the stairs late at night. Nor we didn't like 'im, neither. 'Is manners was all polished an' fancy-like, but jus' between you an' me, there weren't much to make a mort like that singer fall 'ead over 'eels for 'im."

"Is that what she did?" Only by exercising considerable effort did Charles keep his tone casual.

"Seemin' like. They loped off t'gether from a ball. I'll tell yer what we reckon, though." Alf gave him a wink. "We reckon 'e abducted 'er."

Charles drained his glass. "What makes yer say that?"

"This other Frenchy. At the 'ouse the 'ole day afore de Lebouchon loped off. Somethin' sinister there," Alf assured Charles. "Didn't like 'im. Neither of 'em."

Charles, who had never actually met the Chevalier, found that he shared this feeling. Even if she'd gone with him willingly, it must've been a carefully laid trap. In spite of her training and all her worldly wisdom, she had far too affectionate a nature and at times little more sense than a newborn babe. And from what he'd glimpsed of de Lebouchon, he'd seemed a handsome man, free of scars and bitterness. . . .

That got him nowhere! He could not let his feelings get in the way of his work . . . there was too much at stake! The thought of the impulsive Thérèse in de Lebouchon's betraying hands filled him with a cold hatred as solid and uncompromising as a rod of iron.

"Yer know what?" Alf leaned forward in a conspiratorial manner. "Wouldn' be surprised to find out that chevalyay was a French spy!"

Charles was inclined to share this opinion. He set his empty glass down too hard. "Where do you think they went off to? France?"

"If I 'ad the least idea, I'd be after 'em in a flash, I would. An' so would the rest o' the staff. 'Adn't paid me for more'n a fortnight, 'e 'adn't."

"Didn't give you no clues, then? Yer didn't 'ear 'im order no carriage, not give no instruction?"

The footman shook his head. "Nothin'. Even Wiscombe, what served as 'is valet, never 'ad no inklin' o' what was afoot. Gave us all the evenin' off, 'e did, on account o' 'e was takin' the lady to a ball."

So there was no more to be learned here. But he'd heard a couple of things that were useful. No doubt remained in his mind as to de Lebouchon's intentions—or Thérèse's danger.

After standing Alf one last drink, Charles took his leave. He still had to discover something of de Lebouchon's activities for that night. Somewhere there had to be a clue as to where he might be taking Thérèse. He needed more information before he could commit himself to any course of action. He could not afford to make a mistake.

He returned to the Castle Inn and a short while later came down the stairs in the guise of a groom. As he crossed the lobby the clerk looked up and almost gasped.

"Here, you! The back door, if you please!"

"Beg yer pardon, sir." Charles touched the lock of unnaturally light hair that artlessly curled down his forehead. "Me master wanted me upstairs fer orders."

"Well, go out through the taproom, then, not here." The clerk fixed an uncompromising eye on him and watched until Charles disappeared through the appropriate doorway.

Despite the lateness of the hour, there was a fair amount of activity in the stableyard of the inn. An ostler leaned against an empty carriage, chewing on a bit of straw while two grooms led away the pair that had been between the shafts. A barouche pulled in, a tiger jumped down from behind, and the owner's personal groom hurried forward to take charge.

Charles slouched over to the ostler and stood with his shoulders drooped and his hands thrust in his pockets, watching as the matched bays were unharnessed. "Good job, working for gentry what will pay yer," he said at last.

The ostler removed the straw. "Aye," he agreed.

"Don't you never go working for no Frenchy." Charles kicked at the cobbled stones with the toe of a dusty boot. "'Ired me services, 'e did, then loped off without payin'."

A coachman overheard him and strolled forward, a broad grin on his face. "Let that be a lesson to you, me bucko. Always demand payment in advance. That's how I deals with Frenchies."

"'Ave yer seen a tallish, stocky 'un around 'ere, 'bout thirty-five or so, with yeller 'air an' blue eyes? Talks real flash, with only a slight accent, an' dresses 'isself up like a gen'leman? Gunna catch up with 'im, I am, and collect what 'e owes me!"

The coachman shook his head. "You'll have a hard time catching that one. Hey, Joe!" He signaled to a man who had just entered the yard. "Got someone here interested in that Frenchy o' yours!"

The man Joe strolled over and joined them. The coachman said, "'E owes this fellow some money. You drove him off just a couple o' nights ago, didn't you? Him and a lady?"

"Aye, that I did. Very pretty, she was, too." Joe gave Charles a knowing wink. "Took 'em to a snug harbor a little ways away, and your Frenchy carried the lady off to a boat."

"Carried?" Charles made a disgusted face.

"Asleep. Leastways, that's what 'e said."

The leer that accompanied this comment made Charles long to hit the man. He controlled the impulse with difficulty. "Which 'arbor? An' where was they a'headin'?"

He named a small inlet only a few miles from Brighton. "And yer can forget yer money from that one." Joe shook his head. "No idea where they was off to, nor do I care." He patted his pocket in a sigificant manner. "I got me money, and that's all I cares about."

Charles hunched an angry shoulder. "Guess I'll jus' 'ave ter ferget about mine," he said, and strolled off.

As soon as he was outside the yard, he quickened his pace, dropping the stooping shuffle of his disguise. Thérèse's being taken to a boat could mean only one thing: de Lebouchon had taken her to France. But why? She should have been safe! There should have been no further interest in her, on the part of either the British or the French! But it also meant that she was alive—at least for the moment. Hope combined with his anxiety, driving him on.

His next stop was her house on the Marine Parade, where he sent the sleepy-eyed butler to fetch Symmons. He paced about the elegant drawing room as he waited, trying very hard not to notice little ornaments that he remembered. On one wall hung an etching he had given her. Why did the sight of it cause a stab of pain to shoot through him? Thérèse was resourceful. She would be all right until he could reach her. She had to be!

The door burst open and the abigail, wrapped in a dressing gown, ran in. At her heels came the fluffy-haired mongrel, who bounded up to Charles and greeted him like a long-lost friend, despite the groom's disguise. Charles stooped down and stroked Aimée as she let out a series of soft, frantic yips.

"Oh, Mr. Marcombe, is that really you? I'm so glad someone has come! I'm worried about Ma'mselle. And so is her little Aimée." She sank down onto a sofa and Charles took a chair. The little dog scrambled up into his lap and huddled against him.

"What were you able to learn from de Lebouchon's butler?" His restless hands continued to stroke the animal.

"Nothing. Oh, it is quite terrible! His valet found a note requesting that the house be shut up and the servants turned off, that he was not returning. Oh, sir, I know she's in danger! No matter what anyone says, she'd never have gone with him willingly! I know it!"

He nodded. "Tell Pembroke we're off to France as soon as the tide turns."

"Oh, thank you, sir!"

Charles stood. "Just you take care of this." He handed over the dog.

He let himself out, but as he started down the stairs, Aimée squirmed free of Symmons' hold, jumped to the ground, and darted after him. Firmly, Charles ordered the little dog back, but it refused to leave his side. With a sigh, Charles picked it up and once again returned it to the charge of the abigail. While she held it tight, he hurried off. The last thing he needed on this desperate journey was a flop-eared mongrel!

He strode quickly up the Marine Parade and turned onto the Steine. Once, he thought he heard someone following him, a stealthy sound, but when he turned it was only a cat darting up a tree. Returning his mind to the more pressing matter of getting his companions organized and off on their journey, he returned to the inn.

He slipped in by way of the taproom and made it up the stairs without being seen by the watchful and disapproving desk clerk. Letting himself silently into his room, he found Bosworth stretched out on one of the beds, fully dressed except for his boots. Althorp and Harding sat on the other bed, a deck of cards spread between them. Their baggage, newly repacked, stood in a pile in the center of the floor.

Harding nodded a greeting. "Got a boat waiting, sir."

Charles nodded. "Fine. We sail with the tide."

Bosworth sat up and stretched. "Sail?" Even in the dim light of the room, he could be seen to pale perceptibly.

Althorp scooped up the cards and grinned, his eyes gleaming with excitement. "Just give us a minute to fetch the right clothes, sir."

In less than an hour, they stood on the dock with the cumbersome packs and bedrolls they had been able to obtain on such short notice and at so ineligible an hour. Before them stood the small and highly suspect yawl procured for this voyage. The crew of three carried the baggage aboard and stowed it safely below deck.

Althorp touched Charles's sleeve. "I think it's a smuggler's boat, sir." He kept his voice to a whisper as he eyed the men askance.

"I'm damned sure it is. Whatever you do, don't say anything about it!"

Bosworth regarded them stolidly. "Hope they know what they're doing," was all he said.

The tide was turning. When the last of their packs was off the dock, Charles herded his assistants onto the ship. The crew silently manned their posts and the boat eased away from the dock.

"France!" Althorp came up beside Charles, his eyes ablaze with excitement.

"Aye, you'll see your fill of it before long." Harding settled in the stern, his expression unusually grim.

Bosworth groaned. They had only just cast off, but already he suffered from *mal de mer*. Charles kept his reflections on the subject of his assistants to himself.

And as for his reflections on Thérèse . . . he would find her, that he vowed. But what would she have to say when she saw him? At least she wouldn't pity him now, in spite of the scars that remained! But gratitude . . . that wasn't what he wanted from her either. Restless, he strode to the prow of the ship and stared ahead into the darkness.

Soon the lights of Brighton faded into the gathering fog that filled the wide expanse of the Channel. Wavelets lapped at the hull, and the chill salt spray stung Charles's face. Still, he remained where he was, gazing ahead, as if willing the French coastline to come into sight. Yet they were still hours away. And Thérèse . . .

A sharp scratching sounded below deck, repeated a moment later. One of the crew threw open the hatch, but before he could climb down, a little dog scrambled out onto the deck, looked around, and ran straight toward Charles. It was a little mongrel.

"What the—" Harding broke off, staring at Aimée in amazement.

"She must have followed me." Ruefully, Charles scooped her up and allowed her to lick his face. Well, he had thought he was being followed!

"But what are we going to do with her?" Harding demanded. "We can't turn back, the tide's against us!"

Charles rubbed Aimée's head. He found her presence oddly comforting, as if she were a tie to Thérèse. "No," he said slowly. "It's too late to turn back now. I guess she'll just have to come with us."

Chapter Eight

The first pale streaks of dawn had not yet begun to lighten the eastern sky when the yawl slipped silently into a tiny bay along the northwest coast of France. Beyond the pier that stretched out into the black water lay a collection of rough wooden shacks shrouded in darkness.

"Doesn't look like they get many travelers through here." Harding peered through the predawn mist at the little he could make out of the sandy beach.

"Not officially, at least. It's a smuggler's port." Charles signaled to the captain of the ship, and they held a low-voiced conversation. He turned back to Harding. "It's most made up of small farms and a few shops."

"I suppose you know your way around?" Harding regarded him with sardonic eyes.

Charles smiled. "As a matter of fact, I do—rather well."

The crew of their yawl lowered a small rowboat into the water and Charles went to help load their baggage. He sent Harding and Althorp to shore with it and watched as they disappeared into the darkness. The minutes crept by. Finally the little boat appeared once again and Althorp brought it alongside. This time, Charles, Bosworth, Althorp, and Aimée were ferried to the shore by one of the crewmen.

As soon as the prow touched sand, Charles, carrying

the dog, jumped out into the shallow water. The others followed and they stood in silence and watched the rowboat return to the yawl. In a very short time, the ship set to, turned about, and made for the open waves.

Charles checked the pack he carried on his back with his free hand and began to wade through the cold water toward shore. There they found Harding, who had already divided the remainder of their provisions into four piles. Charles set Aimée down and dropped his pack to the wet sand. While the little mongrel ran about among the wavelets, sniffing intently, he began to stow his portion of the supplies. The others did the same.

"What now?" Harding sat back and peered up the beach into total darkness.

"We made very good time. The wind was with us, which was more than we could hope for. That means we should be able to get what we need and be on our way before anyone finds out we're here."

"To Paris?" Althorp jumped eagerly to his feet, anxious to get started.

"To Paris." And to Thérèse, too, Charles prayed. If she was not there . . . He swallowed hard and hoisted his pack again, refusing to consider the possibility. She *would* be there. She *had* to be. "Let's get started."

Bosworth looked about suspiciously. He might once again be on dry land, but his stomach and legs still felt as if the water rolled about beneath him. He started up the beach.

"This way." To everyone's surprise, Charles scooped up Aimée and led the way back toward the ocean. Aware that they didn't follow, he looked over his shoulder and a reluctant grin eased the tension in his face. "If we walk in the shallow water, we won't leave any footprints," he explained.

In this manner they worked their way along the bay until they reached a tiny inlet where a stream ended its course. He turned up this and waded along the sandy bed through a thicket of trees. A cottage lay off to their right. Scrambling up the bank, Charles gestured for his companions to remain in the shrubs while he looked about.

Moving with extreme caution so as not to dislodge so much as a twig, he crept up to the two-room shack and peered in through a window—and suffered a nasty setback. The cottage was deserted. He swore softly under his breath. He had expected to find help there, as he often had before, in the form of French country clothes and horses. One did not roam the French countryside in garments of obviously British cut.

Well, he would have to help himself to what he could. He made his way around to the other side, where a dilapidated barn stood. Inside this unlikely looking shelter he found several horses, kept by the cottage's owner for the express needs of such nocturnal visitors as might wish to procure land transportation without being seen by anyone in authority. Only the briefest of messages, left in the usual spot, was necessary to explain who had taken them.

Charles looked the animals over and selected enough for his party. At least the problem of their transportation was settled. But their clothing was another matter. Again, he wished the cottage's owner might have been home, but that couldn't be helped.

Leaving Bosworth and Althorp to saddle their appropriated mounts, Charles took Harding with him on a short journey of exploration. They had not taken many steps when Aimée bounded up beside them with a soft yip, and Charles was forced to take her back and hand her over to Bosworth. They started out again, but only minutes later she was back. Recognizing that she was not about to let him out of her sight, he gave in and permitted her to go along.

It was eerie in the almost complete darkness, for the moon had already set, thick clouds covered the stars, and a low-lying mist rose from the ocean. Walking proved hazardous, and several times they tripped over rocks and fallen branches. Colliding with a large stone, Charles swore softly. His shoulder muscles hurt abominably from the tearing they had suffered barely two months before. Hefting his pack all over France was not going to do him any good.

After peering over several stone walls into cottage yards, they finally spotted that for which they were looking— something flapping in the breeze. Charles crept closer, then signaled Harding to join him.

"A clothesline!" he called softly. Together they scrambled over the fence.

"Rather like buying ready-made clothes in Cranbourne Alley," Harding whispered. "You just poke around and make your selection!"

After considerable sorting, they picked out a shepherd's smock. Harding wanted to find another, but Charles stopped him.

"No more than one or two items from one place," he directed.

They repeated the process until they had three smocks and a tunic and four loose-sleeved peasant shirts and breeches. Charles had just begun to examine neckcloths when Aimée suddenly stiffened, her hackles rising. She gave a low growl.

That was enough for Charles. Scooping her up, he dived for the wall and scrambled over. Harding stared at him in surprise, then heard the barking of dogs coming closer and closer as they bore down on him. He, too, dived for the stone wall, barely reaching the top as the first of three ferocious hounds snapped at his heels.

Charles, who had landed somewhat unceremoniously on the other side, got up and dusted off the knees of his buckskin breeches. "That was close! Let's get back to the others before anyone comes to investigate."

Harding made no objection. With the dogs barking

furiously at their retreating backs, the two men raced along the dirt cart track in the direction from which they had come. Aimée ran at their heels.

At the cottage they found Althorp and Bosworth ready for them with the horses saddled and waiting. Their selections of clothes, made rather at random, proved somewhat less than perfect. Charles was by far too tall, and none of the breeches they had obtained would fit. With a philosophical shrug, he kept his buckskins, though he exchanged the rest of his garments. Bosworth also had difficulties, though his was a problem of girth. For him, a loose shirt and a change of neckcloths had to suffice.

Ready at last, they again shouldered their packs and led their mounts out of the barn. Charles conscientiously bolted the door. They swung up into their saddles, and avoiding the narrow road, started across country. Aimée kept pace beside them.

Harding urged his horse alongside Charles, who led the way. "Excuse me, sir, but how are we going to manage without French coin?"

"I suppose we'll find out." Charles grinned suddenly. The journey under way at last, he felt the old, familiar energy and excitement fill him. His worry and fear for Thérèse's safety remained, but they were easier to control, now that he had something positive to do. He threw a look brimful of devilish laughter at the concerned Harding and urged his horse into a trot. The first light of dawn crept over the horizon and he wanted to be away from the village before anyone was up and about to see them.

He kept his little troop going as rapidly as he could, bent on putting as much distance between them and the coast as possible before they were observed. Mile after mile slipped past and still he pressed on. Was it their safety that drove him on, or Thérèse's? Would they arrive in time to save her?

Not until the sun climbed high in the sky did he allow a

stop for a hasty meal. In the relative safety of a thicket, they drew up their tired horses and dismounted.

Harding brought bread, cheese, and ale from the top of his pack. "How far do you think we've come?"

"Not far enough. We've got a good hundred miles to cover." Charles lay back in the tall, prickly grass, willing the knots out of his stiff, aching muscles.

"We are making for Paris, are we not?" Althorp leaned back against a tree and took a large bite of cheese. He regarded Charles with wide, eager eyes.

Charles nodded. "It's the most likely goal, at least to begin with. She was imprisoned there before, though."

"Makes a habit of it, does she?" Bosworth finished his first slab of bread and reached for another.

"I hope so. God knows where else they may have taken her."

Packing up all traces of their meal, they mounted once more and left the shelter of the thicket. Progress was necessarily slow, for they rode across fields whenever possible to avoid the roads, where they would be likely to encounter curious people. They stopped to rest and to water the animals frequently, for there would be no changes on this journey.

As the morning faded toward afternoon, Charles noted that Aimée no longer ran abreast with him, but lagged behind, limping slightly. He was all too well aware of how troublesome an old injury could be on a desperate ride such as this. He stopped, picked her up, and held her before him on his horse as they continued.

It was a ridiculous move to bring her, he knew. Whatever had possessed him? He could easily have sent her back with the smugglers. His arm closed more tightly about Aimée at the thought. The answer was not so very far to seek. The disreputable little mongrel was his only tie to Thérèse, and he wouldn't abandon it.

As they began to look for a safe spot to rest for a bit in the late afternoon, Charles suddenly pulled up short and gestured the others to silence. He led them deep into a grove of evergreen trees, where he dismounted and crawled back to a sheltered place from which he had a view out. In a moment Althorp joined him.

Below the hillock on which they lay, in a shallow valley formed by the rolling terrain, and headed directly in their direction, came what appeared to be an entire cavalry squadron. That would mean approximately 140 men. . . . As they moved closer, Charles made out their dark green uniforms with the orange trim that identified their regiment. Black busbies with brilliant red plumes rested on their heads.

Althorp swallowed hard. "Who—what are they?"

Charles almost smiled. Being inexperienced and eager was one thing. To come this close to the enemy, all of whom were armed with curved sabers, with many carrying carbines as well, was a very different matter.

"They're *chasseurs à cheval*—light cavalry. The plumes and red epaulets mean they're the elite troops."

"Oh." The information did not seem to make Althorp feel any better. "Where do you think they're going?"

"I've no idea. But I can't say I like seeing an entire squadron headed in this direction. I wonder what we would have seen if we had come by way of Le Havre."

"What do you mean?"

To Charles's amazement, he saw that Althorp actually had no idea. Really, he would have to speak to Pembroke about the training his agents received. Someone ought to explain the basic facts of life and geography to them.

"Napoleon might be building up troops for an invasion of England," he said, and saw the color drain from Althorp's face. "If we had adequate agents in this area, we would know for certain—and someone would have warned us."

As they watched, the French troops left the road and started across the fields toward a thicket of trees about a half-mile from the one where Charles's little band hid.

132

Althorp inched farther forward, peering at them.

"What are they doing?"

"Probably looking for a spot to set up camp for the night. In case you haven't heard it, there's a fast-running stream that would provide fresh water just down there."

Althorp turned to look and listen, chagrined at not having noticed this before.

Behind them, twigs snapped and brush rustled as one of the horses stamped uneasily. The animal pricked up its ears and started to whinny, but Harding clapped a firm hand over its nostrils, silencing it. At a signal from Charles, Harding and Bosworth led the animals farther back.

The parade of soldiers seemed endless, and they all passed uncomfortably near. Still, they continued to pass and did not come up the hillock. From his coat pocket Charles drew out a quill, ink, and paper and took some quick notes on the number of cannon and supply wagons that followed in the tail.

Charles's horse, for the moment unattended as Harding concentrated on his own, whinnied loudly. One of the mounted officers looked up, stared hard in their direction, and rode toward them until he was so close they could see his face. He leaned forward in his saddle and peered into the dense underbrush. Charles and his companions held their breaths.

Another officer hailed the first and he turned to shout a response. After one more searching scrutiny of the shrubbery, he wheeled his horse about and cantered down the hill. In a moment he rejoined the line of cavalry.

Bosworth leaned against a tree, weak with reaction. Althorp, though, recovered from his initial nervousness. His eyes shone with excitement at so near an encounter— and at escaping undetected and unscathed. This sign was not lost on Charles, who noted it with dismay. Excitement in the face of danger often led to rectklessness.

They settled down to wait until the troops would be

busy with unsaddling and tending their mounts . . . but not for too long, Charles directed. Once his men were settled, that officer might well take a walk to do some further investigating, and Charles did not want to take that chance.

As soon as he felt it was safe, he signaled the others to begin moving once more. They circled wide around the French encampment, going well out of their way, then came back on course. Clear of this hazard and once more on their way, Charles breathed more easily.

Not many more miles farther along, the wide expanses of pastures and fields gave way to smaller farms, neatly laid out. After another quarter-hour, they approached the outskirts of a village. Farmers came in from the fields, carrying hoes and rakes over their shoulders. At the sight of the strangers, they stopped and stared at them with suspicion.

"Wish we had captured us some French uniforms," Harding murmured to Charles.

Charles shook his head. "Then we'd most likely have been caught as deserters. And probably shot."

One farmer, bolder than the others, stepped forward and hailed them. "We don't get many travelers through here," he called in accents more guttural than Harding remembered having encountered in the French language.

"Don't you count the Army?" Charles's own tone matched the farmer's almost exactly, and Harding directed an appraising look at him.

The other man gave a short laugh. "Commandeered most of the village horses, they did. We can do without that kind of traveler."

No wonder the farmers eyed them—or rather, their four mounts. To avoid further questions and subsequent suspicions, Charles led them out of the field and back to the road, which now seemed the safer route for them to follow for a spell.

Far too soon the gathering dusk made the uneven

surface of the road a dangerous footing for their tired mounts. All were tired and hungry, and at last Charles reluctantly agreed to look for a safe place to camp.

He chafed at this—at any!—delay, but could not help but acknowledge that his strength was not yet all he could wish. Had his injuries not completely healed, or did he just grow older and less resilient? It was a vexing, not to say downright unsettling, problem. He needed his strength and abilities now more than ever. He could not let Thérèse down!

Leaving the road, he again led his band through the fields until they found a hollow with a stream deep in a thicket that seemed a safe refuge for the night. They tended their mounts, lit a small campfire for warmth against the chill evening air, and ate most of the remaining bread and cheese. As the flames burned low, they settled down to try and sleep.

It seemed to Charles that he'd barely closed his eyes when a sudden yelping bark brought him up onto one elbow. Aimée stood beside him, her body quivering, a low growl sounding in her throat. He rolled to a crouch, straining his ears to catch any threatening sound.

It came, louder and closer than he'd have liked. A volley of barking broke out as a pack of hungry dogs answered Aimée's challenge. They bounded into the clearing, aiming with unerring accuracy at their packs, into which they tore with long, vicious, and very capable teeth.

The horses nearest the dogs lunged in fear, rearing and pulling against the long ropes that tethered them to the trees. A branch broke with a wrenching crack and the horse tied to it broke into a panicked gallop. The length of wood dragged behind, terrifying the animal even more.

Althorp pulled a gun from beneath his blanket and leaped to his feet. By the smoldering coals of the fire, the dark forms of the dogs could just be distinguished as they fought over the right to savage the packs. He raised the pistol and took careful aim.

He never fired. Charles dived at him and knocked his hand aside, then silenced his protests with a gesture.

"We don't know how close we are to any farms!"

"But those dogs! They're already made enough noise to wake anybody!" Despite his protests, Althorp allowed his arm to drop.

"That's a natural noise." Charles kept his voice low, but his tone was urgent enough to make the other man pay heed. "A gunshot would bring anybody within hearing distance down on us in minutes, and undoubtedly armed with anything they can find!"

As he spoke, he looked about and found the remaining wood from their evening fire. Wincing as the bare sole of his foot encountered a sharp rock, he muttered something under his breath and stepped more carefully. He tossed the kindling onto the coals and fanned them into a dancing flame. Grabbing up a branch, he lit it, then advanced on the dogs as he swung it wide before himself. Harding followed suit at once, and in moments they were joined by Althorp and Bosworth. The dogs backed off snarling, then turned tail and ran.

Charles waited, but they showed no signs of returning. At last he dropped his burning branch into the fire and went to soothe the remaining horses. When their trembling stopped and they lowered their heads, once more calm, Charles went back to his blanket and sat down.

"What about the other horse, sir?" Harding remained by the animals.

Charles shook his head. "There's nothing we can do in the dark. We'll look for it in the morning." And they had better find it! At the moment, they were one horse short, and that would prove a severe handicap with probably close to fifty miles still to travel. He could only hope it had not run too far or hurt itself in its panic.

"Why did the dogs attack us?" Althorp dropped down beside Charles. Harding continued to stand guard.

"I'm getting old and careless." Charles was silent a

moment as he glowered into the flames. "I never should have done anything so clumsy. It was our food, of course. The smell brought them, and now we've lost most of it. *Damn!* I'm no raw recruit to make such mistakes!"

Bosworth picked up the torn packs and carried them to the fire to examine them. Bread crumbs and shredded paper wrappings from the cheese were all that remained of their meager food supply. He tossed them aside in disgust.

"Now what?" He looked at Charles with much the mien of a hopeful puppy who expected instant solutions to all its problems.

"Now we try to get what sleep we can. Tomorrow is going to be one hell of a day." He lay back on his folded coat, pulled the blanket over himself and determinedly shut his eyes. Dear God, was this how he set about saving Thérèse? By making one mistake after another?

As soon as a lightening of the clearing announced the approach of dawn, Charles rose and pulled on his boots. Armed with a rope, he set off with Althorp and Harding, leaving Bosworth to do what he could with the remains of their packs.

Tracking the horse proved easier than they'd expected. They had only to follow the ragged path created by the dragging of the thick branch. Fortunately, this had come free after about half a mile, and they found the horse grazing not much farther on. While Charles, talking in a soothing manner, approached the animal, Althorp and Harding looked about.

"Here, you were right," Althorp called softly as Charles caught the dangling end of tether and gently drew in the horse.

"About what?" Charles led the now-placid animal up to the others.

"There's a farm, back the way we came, on the other side of the hill. They'd have been bound to hear a gunshot."

Harding regarded the neat, two-story building with concern. Beyond it lay a low barn and an outbuilding. "I

137

wonder if they've seen us."

Charles shook his head. "There's no one moving about."

"Maybe there's no one there." Althorp shaded his eyes against the rising sun to look more closely. "And if there isn't, maybe we can bother a few hens for some breakfast." Before Charles could stop him, he started off at a run, bent on exploration of the outbuilding.

Harding sighed. "I'd best go keep an eye on him, sir."

Charles left him to it and returned to their camp, where he found that Bosworth had made a creditable job of tying up the loose ends of the packs. Together they saddled the horses, then mounted and rode up the slope toward the house. There was no one in sight.

"Where the devil have they gotten off to?" Charles muttered.

"I'll check." Bosworth swung down from his horse and hurried toward the barn, dragging both his own mount and Althorp's behind.

Charles almost shouted at him to come back, but stopped himself just in time. Just because they didn't see anyone did not mean there was no one about. He settled down, his expression one of exasperation.

A minute later Harding appeared from the outbuilding. "It's a larder, sir," he called, keeping his voice low as he ran up.

Charles nodded, not displeased to see the small wheel of cheese Harding held out to him. He stuffed it into his pack. "We are allowing hunger to overrule caution. Let's get moving. Where's Althorp?"

His question was answered a moment later. Althorp appeared from the barn, raised his hat, from which several brown eggs protruded, and headed toward the house.

"Good God," Charles sighed. "What is he up to now?"

As Charles watched in disbelief, Althorp set down his hat, slipped up to a window, worked it open, and climbed inside. "Get him out of there!" The command, though softly spoken, was no less urgent. Harding almost saluted before running to retrieve his cohort.

Before he had taken three steps, Bosworth emerged from the barn, dropped his horses' reins, and ran to the window. From it, Althorp handed out a pie and two large loaves of bread, which Bosworth received in grateful hands. The horses started wandering, and Harding veered off to intercept them.

And then the dogs arrived, barking loud enough to wake the countryside and bearing down on the hapless Bosworth. Aimée, who had remained until now by Charles's mount, let out a wild yip and darted into the fray. Startled, Bosworth dropped the food and ran, but the dogs were on his heels. Charles kicked his startled horse and they lunged forward, getting between the fleeing Bosworth and his furious canine pursuers. The horse reared to avoid stepping on the dogs and Bosworth took the opportunity to scramble into the saddle of the riderless horse Charles led.

Harding, the reins in his hands, swept down and salvaged the food. As he turned toward the kitchen where Althorp could be glimpsed, a hefty farm wife in a billowing flannel nightdress of a brilliant red entered the room and shouted at Althorp, who made a flying dive out the window. He landed rolling, missed the dogs by inches, leaped to his feet, and dashed for the horse that Harding held out for him. In moments all four raced for the lane with Aimée dashing along behind.

They did not slacken their pace for several wild, desperate miles. When at last they pulled up to rest their blown mounts and share their stolen meal, Charles's shoulders were shaking with ill-concealed mirth. Harding fixed him with a reproving eye.

"Discipline is what we're needing, sir."

That proved too much for Charles's sense of the ridiculous. He almost collapsed. "Discipline doesn't come close, my dear Harding. What you lot need is a hefty dose of sanity! Never, in all my life, have I seen anything like you three dashing about that farmyard, begging to get caught!"

Althorp broke off a piece of their pilfered bread. "At least we're eating, sir." He looked affronted. "You didn't say as we *weren't* to get food, after all."

Charles swung down from his horse. "Good God, do you mean you'd jump off a cliff if I *didn't* tell you not to? I think I aged five years this morning. You are never to do anything like that again! Is that understood?" His voice took on an edge of command that defied disobedience.

Bosworth regarded Charles with dismay. When he spoke, his tone held no argument, merely curiosity. "But how are we to eat, then?"

Charles buried his face in his horse's steaming neck, torn between the desires to laugh and cry. What had he ever done to deserve this comedy act that masqueraded as a set of British agents? With all the patience he could muster, he regarded his assistants.

"From now on, all forays will be carried out *only* after you consult me. And with luck, which we have been stretching with a vengeance of late, we won't need to do any more. We should reach Paris tonight."

Their luck held. The remainder of the day passed without any of the incidents that had thus far enlivened their journey, and just as dusk began to fall, they rode sedately through the western gate of the capital city. No one paid them any heed, though they all felt very conspicuous, tired, and filthy. Althorp and Bosworth tried hard not to look about, for the babble of strange voices around them brought it home that they were on foreign territory—and one with which their government was at war. If they were captured now, there was no question but that they would be shot as spies.

Charles, without so much as a moment's hesitation, led the way through a maze of side streets. They stopped in the yard of a rough-looking tavern where they handed over their spent horses to the ostler who hurried forward. A quick word from Charles in flawless French satisfied the lad, and he signaled to a companion to help him.

They entered the dimly lit taproom and Charles made his way to a table in the far corner, in the inglenook of a cavernous hearth. Harding drew out a chair and seated himself beside Charles.

"We have no money," he muttered in his quite capable French. He looked about uneasily.

Althorp leaned forward and cast an eager glance about the large room, his eyes wide. For once his enthusiasm appeared to be decently in check. Bosworth sat quietly, studying his folded hands.

"How much of the language can they speak?" Charles asked suddenly, noting the extreme nervousness of his other two companions.

"Oh, Althorp should be all right."

"And Bosworth?"

"Just a few phrases, sir." Harding tried an apologetic smile that failed miserably.

Charles closed his eyes. "Then for God's sake, let us do all the talking."

A dark-eyed girl with black curls cropped short about her neck, much in the manner of a boy, approached their table and looked them over with little interest. "What do you want?" she asked.

"Champagne." Charles leaned back in the chair, his laughing gaze resting on her rather plain face. Her eyes opened wide as they rested on him and he grinned.

"This way." She jerked her head toward a closed door and they followed. As soon as they were all inside, she closed it, turned back to Charles, and threw herself into his arms with a little sob.

Chapter Nine

Thérèse stood at the narrow stone window staring out over the fields of waving golden wheat. As prisons went, it was a definite improvement over the damp, cold gaol she had occupied only a few months before. The elegant, comfortable apartment in which she was locked stood four stories up in a very beautiful—and apparently impregnable—chateau.

She had no idea where she was, except that it was somewhere in France. She had been unconscious most of the time, since shortly after de Lebouchon drew his pistol in the carriage. She had panicked and lunged for the door, and that was all she remembered. The painful raised lump on the back of her head was the only clue to how he had dealt with the situation. She remembered regaining consciousness, but it had all been so hazy. . . . She'd been in a bare room, unbelievably thirsty, and someone had held a cup to her lips. . . . He must have drugged her, for daylight and darkness, waking and sleeping blended together in a hazy blur.

She rather thought it had been dark when they carried her into the chateau, but it might only have been the drugs dimming her vision, or even a blindfold. When she finally awakened, it was morning. Her head ached abominably but her mind no longer felt like so much cotton wool. Bits of memory drifted back, enough so that she could piece together the rest of her story. The only question that remained to haunt her was *why*.

She had no opportunity to ask. During the next two days, she saw only the servant who carried in her meals and the soldier, dressed in the white-and-blue uniform of the *Garde Impériale*, who stood at the door with a gun in his hand and a sword at his belt. Neither spoke so much as a single word, and she eventually abandoned her attempts to pry answers from them.

Why had de Lebouchon not simply shot her? It made no sense. She must have been brought here for a purpose, but she had no idea what it might be. There was a stillness about the chateau, a patience about the two people she'd seen, as if everything waited on something—or someone.

A quavering sigh escaped her and she rested her head against the stone window embrasure. She, it seemed, had no choice but to wait as well. Her general living conditions might be greatly improved over her last prison, but her chances of escaping without the help of the British government were every bit as slim as they had been then. This time there was no Lord Ryde to interest himself in her and orchestrate events. This time there would be no *Maniganceur* to come creeping through the cells in the dark of night to whisk her to safety. He was gone, dying like a phantom in the light of reality, and the Charles Marcombe who remained had washed his hands of her.

Resolutely she wiped a tear from her cheek. If only there was something she could do, or plans for escape that could occupy her mind . . . But there was nothing. She was helpless. She must wait and see what happened. And she must not under any circumstance indulge herself in wistful thoughts of a nonexistent *Maniganceur*.

A clicking, grating sound reached her and she spun about as the key turned in her door. It swung open with a creaking protest and the Chevalier de Lebouchon stepped into the room. Behind him the guard swung the heavy oak panel closed and the key again scraped in the lock.

She swallowed hard. Not for a moment would she allow him to see her fear. She turned to face him and silently commanded her inward shaking to cease.

"So, I am to have a visitor? *Quel honneur!*" She leaned back against the cold stones and folded her arms as she eyed him haughtily.

Her sarcasm did not discompose him in the least. He smiled with a pale imitation of his earlier charm and seated himself in the most comfortable chair that her spacious apartment offered.

"How do you go on?" he asked with all the air of one making polite small talk.

"*Tant pis, tant mieux.*" She crossed to a chair and seated herself with much the air of a queen she'd once portrayed in an opera. "What would you?" She forced a false smile to her lips that matched his own.

"I must see that you are entertained more regally."

She inclined her head in acknowledgment. Whether her act was meant to disconcert him or to fool herself into a courage and composure she was far from feeling, she did not try to fathom. Not by a single sign would she indicate that he held the upper hand, that his very presence set her trembling with fear.

"What may I do for you this morning?" With care, she adopted the manner of a gracious hostess.

"Only talk to me, *ma chère*. You have much to say, I am certain, that will be of the greatest interest."

"Now, that I cannot believe." She forced her lashes to flutter in a flirtatious manner, but from beneath them she directed at him a searching scrutiny as she sought to understand his motives—and protect herself.

"We shall see. I must say, it is much easier to converse with you without that abominable little dog."

"It is very true. She tried so very hard to warn me against you, did she not? I should have paid her heed."

"You should, indeed. And to think I worried that she

144

would give me away by recognizing me!"

"Recognizing you?" Thérèse tilted her head, regarding him in perplexity. "But how should my little Aimée . . ."

He laughed softly. "She served her purpose. When first you saw me, your concern was only for her. You did not look closely at that beggar, did you, *ma chère?*"

"The beggar . . ." Realization of her own gullibility left her shaken. She had never looked at the man, only the poor, injured dog! "But—but why the disguise?"

"I wished to keep an eye on your old house so that I would know when you reappeared. When news of my arrival in Brighton did not bring you out of hiding, I circulated the story—all pretense, I might add—that I had been shot. I was quite certain you'd come rushing to my aid. I could hardly be seen wandering about Brighton when I was supposed to be lying abed. But enough of these pleasantries! Tell me, have you ever met Sir Arthur Wellsley? Ah, I should say the newly created Viscount Wellington, should I not?"

Thérèse blinked at him, bewildered. Was this just a social ploy? Did he seek to throw her off balance by the unexpected question? But an alertness underlay his seeming blasé attitude, warning her of danger.

"*Mais non.* How could I have? I believe he is a great admirer of beautiful ladies, but not, I think, of singers." She bestowed an apologetic smile on him to disguise the whirling of her thoughts. Why did he ask that?

De Lebouchon stood. "Then you cannot help me."

"I am desolated, m'sieur." She rose also and offered her hand. "Do come again, perhaps for tea? You shall find me always at home. *J'y suis et j'y reste.*"

He raised her fingers to his lips. "It is very true, *ma chère.* Here you will indeed stay." He strode to the door, rapped sharply on it, responded to the guard's query, and was released from the room.

Thérèse sank back into her chair, her carefully culti-vated sang-froid deserting her. How could she have been such a fool, never to have guessed about that beggar! She was too soft-hearted for her own good, to have been concerned only for the dog!

- But that was a past mistake. Now she must concentrate on not making any more mistakes. And to begin with, what had de Lebouchon really wanted? Information about Wellsley—or rather, Wellington? It was true that he had recently taken command of the British forces in Portugal, but what had that to do with her, or with any of the work she had done in the past?

About an hour later, two guards entered her room. Her gaze fell on the pistol that one of the men pointed at her. Her mouth went dry and her stomach seemed to turn over. Were they through with her? Had that one question been it? Had she outlived her usefulness?

A fragment of reason struggled through the fear that engulfed her. There was no need for de Lebouchon to have gone to so much trouble in bringing her here just to ask her about Viscount Wellington! There must be more they wanted to know. It was not likely she would be killed out of hand—at least, not yet.

The guard gestured with the gun that she should accompany them. She stiffened her resolve. With one soldier in the lead and the man with the pistol behind, they escorted her down a long corridor to a flight of stone steps. Farther along, she thought she glimpsed another stairway, perhaps for the servants. She would keep it in mind—and could only hope she'd have a chance to put the information to good use.

At the second landing they traversed another corridor until they reached a wide, oaken stairway that curved gracefully down into a huge hall. Here, oak paneling overlay the gray stones, and hung on the walls were massive tapestries about twenty feet wide and ten feet long. Their footsteps echoed hollowly as they crossed the marble floor. If they had selected these surroundings for the sole purpose of intimidating her, they'd succeeded admirably. She swallowed and found her throat uncomfortably dry. She felt very insignificant and very, very much alone.

At the far end of the Great Hall, they turned down a corridor, then almost at once stopped before a door. The first guard opened it, moved aside, and indicated that she was to enter. She hesitated only long enough to force her escaping courage back into line, then stepped into the elegant drawing room. The door closed behind her with an uncompromising thud.

There was only one occupant in the room. He sat against the opposite wall, his gray head bowed dejectedly, his clasped hands resting on the table before him. Thérèse took a tentative step closer. He was silhouetted against the light that flooded in from the open draperies, but she would almost swear. . . .

"M'sieur?" She moved closer, staring in disbelief. "Milord Pembroke?" Had they taken him prisoner as well? If so, the French would soon know the identity of every British agent working in France, the nature of their work, and even their contacts! A sense of horror filled her, followed at once by a wave of compassion. She hurried forward to sink down at his side.

"Milord, are you well? Have you been hurt?"

He raised his head. She stared in shocked realization into the eyes of a complete stranger. Gasping, she leaped to her feet and took a faltering step backward as the truth dawned on her: someone had created a cunning likeness, good enough to fool anyone at even a short distance. She peered closely, barely able to discern the lines of stage paint that so perfectly disguised this man.

The door opened behind her and she spun about to face de Lebouchon. He looked from one to the other and seemed satisfied.

"Are you having a pleasant reunion with Lord Pembroke?" He came forward to stand at her side.

"With whom?" She made her expression into one of

polite confusion.

The false Lord Pembroke smiled. "She was completely taken in—at first. Now all we must do is discover what gave me away." He rose, came around the table, and perched on its edge with one foot swinging. He addressed Thérèse in flawless, unaccented English. "You are to tell us everything you can remember of Lord Pembroke. You may begin with his mannerisms, any style of dress, his patterns of speech . . . anything about him that will assist us in this impersonation."

"Why?" She looked from one to the other. What plan had they concocted?

The false Lord Pembroke drew a snuffbox from his pocket and helped himself to an infinitesimal pinch of snuff. He offered the box to de Lebouchon, who waved it away. Still holding it in his hand, he raised his gaze to Thérèse. "Lord Pembroke controls the British spies. Is it so unexpected that we would wish to know more of him?"

"I am sorry, I cannot help you."

"Cannot or will not?" The man shook his head. "My dear Mademoiselle de Bourgerre, must we remind you that you are, after all, French? Your loyalty should lie with the new régime." He replaced the box in his pocket and leaned forward in earnest entreaty. "Napoleon is creating a new nobility, a new order. He is very generous to those who help him. He would even be prepared to overlook certain past . . . shall we say, indiscretions?"

De Lebouchon possessed himself of one of her cold hands. "Listen to him, *ma chère Thérèse*. We have friends in positions of great influence with our emperor. Your family need not remain as outcasts in Italy. And when Napoleon wins, as eventually he will, you will not want to be on the losing side."

The other man nodded. "Even England, as great as she believes she is, will fall. Who will help you, then? These people who have failed to protect you, who have cast you aside when your usefulness to them ended? France, your motherland, will not treat you thus!"

She hesitated, as if thinking over what he said, while her chaotic thoughts whirled. How could her fellow countrymen have allowed themselves to be deluded by this Corsican upstart Napoleon? The French, who had known the glory of Louis XIV! Did they truly expect her to help this regime that so brutally murdered so many of her relatives? Her own hope, all along, had been to bring this hateful war to an end as quickly as possible. And for that purpose she had been willing to serve the British.

Her eyes strayed from one to the other of the men as she tried to determine the true intentions behind their entreating words. Could she play along, pretend to help until she found an opportunity—and the courage—for escape?

"We can make your stay with us pleasant, or very uncomfortable." De Lebouchon glanced at the false Pembroke, who nodded. He turned back to Thérèse. "We will leave you alone to think it over. I am sure you will see reason."

She kept her eyes downcast until the two men left the room. As soon as the lock clicked into position, she ran to the door and listened . . . not a single sound penetrated the heavy panel. Relieved, she hurried to the window and pushed on it. It would not budge. Biting her lower lip, she cast a frantic eye around the edge of the glass. A heavy bolt fastened by a lock held the casement structure. It would not be opened easily.

Unless . . . hope surged through her. She could always break it. But first . . . she stood on tiptoe to peer out, then sank back, momentarily defeated. Even if she managed to break the pane and slip out, an armed guard stood on the terrace facing the window. It seemed that de Lebouchon and his friends took no chances. These were formidable opponents. She sank down into a chair, terribly aware of her own inadequacy in this situation.

What would *Le Maniganceur* do? Her dashing, brave

149

hero, whose deep laugh rang forth when he faced danger, whose dark eyes danced and sparkled with his energy and daring? He would not cower here, broken and afraid! He would set his lively mind to work on how to best turn the situation to the advantage of the British! After all, it mattered less that she escape than that the French learn nothing from her—or perhaps even be fooled by her.

She clenched her hands together. If only *Le Maniganceur* could be here! Just the sight of him would give her courage. And how desperately she longed to see him, just once more . . .

By the time the two men returned, Thérèse had overcome her sense of defeat. It was what they wanted her to feel, after all, and she would not be so obliging as to succumb to it! But there was no need to let them know that.

As they entered the room, she composed her features into an expression of complete dejection. She did not look up, but kept her blank gaze focused on the empty hearth. Her shoulders drooped dispiritedly and the eyes she raised to them were tired, devoid of their usual fire. De Lebouchon regarded her for a moment and smiled.

"What have you decided, mademoiselle?" He drew a chair up opposite and sat down.

She returned her gaze to the hearth. "There is little I can tell you that will help." The words came out barely above a whisper. "I knew Pembroke almost not at all."

"Try." The false Pembroke returned to his position by the table and leaned against it.

"I met him only twice, and did not pay much attention to him on either occasion." She raised her eyes, met de Lebouchon's searching gaze, and lowered them again. "He is, I believe, very particular about his dress. Both times I saw him, his neckcloth was tied in the same manner: the *Trone d'Amour*. And his mannerisms, the ways that he moved, were those of a dandy."

The false Pembroke glanced at de Lebouchon. "Is

this so?"

The Chevalier let out a deep sigh. "*Ma Thérèse*, you disappoint me. You do not speak the truth. His manners, I have been told," he added to his companion, "are more those of a soldier than a dandy. It would seem that she hopes to mislead us."

The other man strolled over to tower over Thérèse. In spite of her determination to remain calm, she shrank back. It took a massive summoning of will-power for her to prevent herself from trembling as his icy gaze swept over her.

"You do not wish to help, mademoiselle?" He shrugged. "It does not really matter, you know, whether you do so willingly or under persuasion. For help us you will, in the end. It would have been more pleasant if it had been your choice, but we are not without means of convincing you. Perhaps a day or two without food will encourage you to turn from your traitorous ways."

He summoned the guards and Thérèse was escorted back to her room. Alone, she went to the window and stood looking out, trying to sort through the meager scraps of information she had gathered. The almost exact duplicate they had created of Lord Pembroke had left her shaken. Did they intend to infiltrate Whitehall? And if that succeeded, even if the man only gained just a few hours alone with the records of the British spies, how much would the French learn?

Morning wore on into afternoon, and as her first pangs of hunger struck, she realized these men intended to carry out their threat. No lunch was forthcoming, and as evening turned into night, she accepted the fact that dinner would not come, either. By now she was terribly hungry but this petty form of punishment angered her. They treated her as if she were a disobedient child!

She sat at her window and stared out at the starlit sky, fuming. If only Lord Pembroke had taken her concerns more seriously . . . Or if only she had not trusted the

Chevalier and tried to use him to help drive her bittersweet memories of *Le Maniganceur* from her mind . . . Perhaps if Sir Roderick had permitted her to return to Ranleigh after a brief visit to de Lebouchon in Brighton . . .

But it was no use repining. She had given her word to Sir Roderick, and he had every right to protect his grandson. Charles Marcombe was not *Le Maniganceur* of her dreams. No man was. She had created him, basing her phantom only loosely upon a real person. It was not Charles's fault that he did not live up to her delusions.

She stood abruptly. Enough of this wallowing in self-pity. It profited nothing! It was up to her to save herself, for no one else would bother. She was on her own—she was not important to the British anymore.

A slight smile eased the deep creases that lined her brow. In effect, it was she who must save them this time. She must warn them of this plot to infiltrate Whitehall—and who knew what else. But before she could do that, she had to get herself out of this chateau.

She closed her eyes, buoying herself to action. She had absolutely no intention of sitting here tamely, being starved like a naughty child. There might not be a dashing *Le Maniganceur* this time, but that was not going to stop her. She would save herself.

Once again she examined the window, and her spirits suffered a severe setback. She was a full four stories above the ground. . . . But there was a moat just below her window! If she could lower herself far enough, the drop into the water would not hurt her. She tried very hard not to think how dirty the water must be.

She returned her attention to the room, a plan forming in her ever-fertile mind. Both bedding and curtains were available for an enterprising prisoner to use. It seemed odd that her captors hadn't thought of that. Surely, with a bit of ingenuity, she could create a rope to let herself down far enough to drop safely into the moat.

Putting her plan into action was not quite so easy as

dreaming it up. For one thing, she had nothing with which to cut the heavy fabrics. For another, she had never needed to tie really strong knots, and was not at all sure any she tried would support her weight. But she was not about to let minor details like that stop her when it was her life—and possibly that of a great number of British agents—at stake. Giving the problem due consideration, she began on her sheets, which she could tear without too much trouble.

It took a little over half an hour, but she succeeded in tearing these into long, wide strips. Next came the laborious job of tying them together. She eyed the result of the first two knots dubiously. Discretion being the better part of valor, she decided to test her creation. Tying one end to the bedpost, she pulled on her makeshift rope with all her strength. The knots held.

In relief, she leaned back, unwittingly putting most of her slight weight on her rope. It was enough. The strips of sheet slipped and separated, and she fell backward on the floor.

She got up slowly, brushed herself off, and regarded the loose strips with loathing. If only she had studied knot tying as well as singing! Well, there was no time like the present to learn.

On her fourth attempt, she managed to devise a knot that held, and she began adding more pieces. At last all the strips of sheet were fastened together. She laid these out on the floor, estimated the length, and found it sadly lacking. There could not be much more than twenty feet, which would take her no more than two stories down. The drop to the moat, which might be shallow for all she knew, was still too far.

She'd been putting off the inevitable, but could do so no longer. Standing on a chair, she managed to unhook the heavy hangings from one side of the bed. But try as she might, she was unable to rip the thick fabric. Depressed and momentarily defeated, she sat down in a chair to think.

Light flooded the room when at last she raised her heavy eyelids once more. She'd fallen asleep! She sank her head into her cupped hands and groaned in disgust. She'd wasted the night, and to make matters worse, she was twice as hungry as before!

She had no idea what time it was, but the sun was well up in the sky. Hastily she made up her bed and hid her rope. Tonight the coverlet, heavy as it was, must join the sheets . . . and somehow the curtains as well. If only she had a knife to start the tear! But she would manage anyway. She had to. And then her only worry would be whether or not she was strong enough to make the descent safely. She might put up a brave front, but she grew weaker from not eating.

The door opened abruptly and two guards came in. One grasped her by the arm and led her forcibly along the hall, down the long series of steps, and back to the drawing room she had seen the day before.

This time a slender man of advancing years sat behind the table. She was pressed into a chair before him, met his eyes, and experienced the unsettling sensation that he saw directly into her mind and would know if she lied. She swallowed hard and prepared to bluff it out.

He leaned back in his chair and toyed with a quill that he clasped lightly between the fingers of both hands. His piercing eyes never left her face. "You will tell me," he directed, "the names and appearances of everyone with whom you spoke in the British Government."

"Do you not want to know what information I passed on?"

"That is no longer of any importance. It would concern old matters. No, we are only interested in the officials themselves."

She shook her head. "I cannot remember."

"Really, my dear, is that wise? I would not care to see so lovely a lady harmed. And just think of the rewards if you

154

were to join us."

Thérèse lowered her head and kept it down, refusing to answer. She paid no heed either to the string of gentle enticements or the stern and perilous threats that followed. She roused only when the rough hands of the guard grasped her by the arm and pulled her to her feet for the return to her room.

She took three steps into this apartment and stopped dead. The Chevalier de Lebouchon sat in the chair by the window, her makeshift rope in his hands.

He looked up and smiled at her. "Very clever. Very clever, indeed. It is most unfortunate that you won't get the opportunity to finish it. As you see, the bedding and curtains have been removed from your chamber. I do apologize for the inconvenience, but really, my dear, you have no one but yourself to blame. You must not be so stubborn."

She sank into the nearest chair, too weak and discouraged to remain on her feet. Well over twenty-four hours had passed since she'd last eaten, and then it had been no more than a roll. She hung her head, dejected, as she tried to think what she could say to appease them without endangering the British cause.

The door opened, but she did not turn until she heard a clinking noise and smelled the delicious aroma of food. She looked about to see the tray which a guard had just set on a table. The cover sat beside it and those wondrous smells continued to waft toward her. Without realizing she moved, she sat up, staring at the appetizing contents of the plate with wide eyes.

De Lebouchon sauntered across the room and leaned negligently against the doorjamb. "If you want to eat, you must tell us what we want to know. We will begin with Lord Pembroke."

"No." She shook her head firmly, but an idea began to form. The door to freedom stood open, just beyond the Chevalier. She would pretend she was too weak from hunger to put up a fight, find something that would serve as a weapon, and give it all she had.

De Lebouchon remained, waiting. As hour after hour passed, she slumped further down in her chair, allowing her hand to dangle, limp. The food on the table grew cold. As dinnertime approached, her weakness became less and less of an act, but still she never completely relaxed. Out of the corner of her eye she watched the anticipation grow in de Lebouchon's expressive countenance as he regarded her. He believed her ready to break. If she told him something outlandish enough, he just might believe her. Yet still she waited, watching, biding her time every bit as much as did de Lebouchon.

A new guard appeared bearing a fresh tray. Picking up the cold plate, he left the room. De Lebouchon lifted the lid and sniffed the heavenly aroma, then held up the plate for Thérèse's inspection. Slices of chicken covered in sauce, new potatoes, and peas met her longing gaze. A satisfied, confident smile played about the Chevalier's lips and she longed to slap it away. Now, she decided, was the time. She dropped her face into her hands and artistically set her shoulders shaking.

"Well, Thérèse?" His voice was gentle, persuasive.

"He—he has a snuffbox. Lord Pembroke. He toys with it when he is nervous and thinking. On both occasions that I saw him he held it, gestured with it, always waving it but never opening it. It—it is a round enamel box, set with a table-cut emerald." She hung her head and it took disturbingly little effort to bring the tears slipping freely down her cheeks.

"*Ma chère Thérèse.* It was not so very difficult after all, was it?" He strode up to her and held out the plate.

She grasped it quickly, in case he planned to pull it away, but apparently he had believed her lies. With trembling hands, she set the plate in her lap and picked up the fork. It was an effort not to eat everything before her as rapidly as possible, but that would not serve her purpose.

Instead, she pretended to be too weak to eat more than a few mouthfuls.

"And now, *ma chère*, I must leave you." He bowed mockingly before her.

"Please—please, leave the tray." She clutched the plate.

He smiled. "But of course. You will want more, later, when you are stronger." With that, he left her, closing and locking the door behind him.

She was alone at last! She let out a deep sigh and returned her attention to her much-longed-for dinner. Slowly but steadily she ate every morsel and had the satisfaction of feeling her strength begin to return. When she finished, she set down the plate and concentrated on perfecting her plan.

The guard would come to take away her tray. She looked about. A small occasional table stood in the corner, the only heavy but liftable object the room possessed. She picked it up, hefting it carefully, then stood beside the door. She would have only one chance and she had better not ruin it.

She had only a few minutes to wait. The key grated in the lock, the door opened, and the guard entered the room. With every ounce of her strength, she swung the table. The man dropped hard and she set the table aside as a wave of nausea engulfed her at what she had done. But she had no time for repinings now!

Turning, she fled down the corridor to the back stair she had glimpsed previously, praying it would lead to the kitchens. One, two, then three flights passed and she was almost safe. She bounded around the last landing and down the steps, then pulled up short.

At the base stood de Lebouchon, a pistol in his hand. He did not appear pleased.

"Really," he drawled, "if you are not going to cooperate, you will soon become too much trouble to keep alive."

Chapter Ten

Charles pulled up a chair and signaled for Harding and the others to do the same. Aimée settled at his feet and her small, turned-up nose came to rest on his boots. The dark-eyed girl with the short, unruly mop of curls stood before them and regarded the exhausted and dirty men with interest.

"So, you return to us. *Eh, bien*, what is it, now?" She eyed the little flop-eared mongrel with curiosity and disapproval.

Charles lounged back as if completely at his ease. No trace of the urgency that drove him showed in his beguiling smile. "Ever direct, are you not, Margit? Tell me what has been happening in Paris."

She hesitated and a guarded expression crept into her eyes. "Oh, much that you might find of interest. Do you wish rooms? Or have you stopped by only to chat of old times?"

"They're safe, and they know who I am. Now cut line, Margit, and give me the news."

She turned a searching gaze on the other three, then gave a shrug of resignation. "As you wish." She straddled a chair much in the manner of a boy and rested her arms along the low back. "There is something of a very great importance that goes on, but we have not been able to find

158

out what it is."

Charles straightened up a bit and frowned. "What sort of thing? An invasion of England?" His thoughts flew to the squadron of the *chasseurs à cheval* that they had seen headed toward the coast.

Margit shook her head. *"Non.* Me, I do not think it involves a build-up of the military."

Harding folded his arms across his chest as he eyed her with distaste. In his opinion, a girl should act like a girl, not have the manners of an unkempt youth. "What would a mere chit know about the likes of that?" he muttered to Charles in English, his tone filled with scorn.

Margit, who'd learned that language at the hands of Charles, possessed a vocabulary as rich as it was varied, and inappropriate to a young female. She turned her affronted gaze upon Harding, but found herself at a loss. Some women might have known precisely how to give him a set-down designed to make him see the error of his narrow-minded thinking, but Margit lacked this skill, or any semblance of subtlety.

"Imbecile." She turned a cold shoulder on him and addressed herself once again to Charles. "It is something of so great a secret that the Army does not seem to know."

"So Napoleon has something afoot." Charles pursed his lips. Did it have anything to do with the capturing of Thérèse? He couldn't see the connection . . . but still, it would probably bear looking into.

Aimée raised her head and gave a soft whine, as if sensing his tension and alertness. He leaned down and stroked her back until she dropped her nose to his boots.

Margit tilted her head to one side. "Monsieur Fouche might be involved."

At that, Charles's eyebrows flew up. "An internal matter, then? What does our beloved Minister of Police have in mind? And is it with or without his emperor's knowledge?"

"With, I believe. The men he sees, they are all of

great importance.''

''If the girl's to be believed, it looks like we came after one problem only to find another.'' Harding glanced at Margit and his lips tightened in disapproval at the unkempt picture she made.

''Of course I am to be believed!'' She straightened her shoulders and her chin came up in defiance. ''*Voyons*, me, I know what I say.''

''What sort of problem?'' Bosworth, who had been unable to follow the rapid French of Charles and Margit, leaned forward in mild interest at Harding's words in English. ''What's going on?''

Neither Harding nor Charles appeared to hear. Althorp explained as much as his schoolboy French had been able to follow. When he finished, Bosworth nodded.

''More trouble.'' That stolid individual seemed to accept the situation with unshakable placidity.

Margit glanced at the two men as they conversed comfortably in English, then returned her attention to Charles. ''Now that *Le Maniganceur* is here, we shall discover all, and soon.''

''Actually, I'm here on another matter.'' Still, as long as he was here, he might as well look into this matter as well. He never could resist a challenge—or the hint of a mystery. What had happened to the reluctance with which he had set off on this trip? For once he'd thought himself satisfied to extricate Thérèse from whatever trouble she'd gotten into, return to England, and wash his hands of the whole business. But it seemed he'd been wrong: if there was something afoot, *Le Maniganceur* could not just meekly walk away.

''You have come for a purpose.'' Margit nodded, pleased to have her suspicions confirmed. ''Tell me.''

''Begging your pardon, sir,'' Harding protested. ''But is it safe to talk so freely in front of her? She's just a chit, when all's said and done, and half-boy at that, by the looks of her!''

Margit's volatile temper flared. "Me, I am now eighteen. And since I was six I have done this work."

"Why?" Harding ignored her and to her growing fury addressed the question to Charles. "What makes her help the British?"

"I am half-gypsy," Margit responded before Charles could speak.

Charles nodded. "That's still a criminal offense in France. If the details of her background were known for certain, her family would be hounded out of Paris—if they were lucky. Hunting gypsies like wild game used to be a favorite sport around here."

Harding shook his head. "Gypsies are a careless lot, sir. Wouldn't trust them an inch."

"I have proved to *Le Maniganceur* on many occasions what I am worth. Have you done the same?" Her dark eyes burned as she spat the question at him.

"I think we'd best go to our rooms and get cleaned up." Prudently Charles interrupted what bade fair to become a violent argument. "Margit, we are starving. Can you get us some dinner? And some for little Aimée, here? We'll be ready for it in half an hour."

"But of course. Come with me." Pointedly ignoring Harding, she led the way back through the crowded taproom and up the stairs.

With the mongrel padding along after them, they traversed a series of halls that twisted and meandered up and down flights of two or three steps, passed through a door, and at last reached a quiet corridor. Charles looked into one of the rooms opening off this and dropped his maltreated pack on the floor. Aimée followed him in.

Margit jerked her head toward the other doors. "You may use any of these. No one will disturb you. I am the only one who comes up." With that she excused herself and went to see to the preparation of a hearty meal for them.

Harding entered the room next to the one Charles had

taken and glanced about. A narrow bed stood against one wall and a jug and basin stood in the corner. As far as he was concerned, the room was perfect—or would be, once that jug was filled with hot water.

It arrived a few minutes later. He'd barely set his pack on a chair and begun to sort through the few belongings he'd brought with him in search of a razor when a solid rap sounded on his door. He opened it to see a steaming pitcher on the floorboards before each room and Margit's ragged back disappearing toward the main corridor.

As soon as he'd done what he could to make himself more presentable, he went to Charles's room, knocked, and entered in response to the call. Aimée lay curled at the foot of the narrow bed, snoring softly. Charles stood before his basin, razor in hand, peering into the cracked mirror. Harding sat on the only chair the tiny chamber offered.

"Can we trust the people at this tavern?"

Charles nodded. "With our lives."

"It seems we are."

Charles chuckled at his companion's dry comment. "We'll be quite safe with them. And Margit is a jewel."

Harding snorted. "An uncut diamond? She's more a boy!"

"It's kept her alive. Half the time she's disguised as one." He set down the razor and rinsed his face. Harding tossed him a towel and he rubbed vigorously. "She's never had the leisure to become a simpering miss—nor even to learn any airs," he said as he emerged. "It's not much of a life for a girl, but it's all she's ever known. She's got courage." He hung the towel to dry and pulled on a fresh but creased shirt.

Harding shook his head. "Can't say I like any of this, sir. What do you think this trouble is that she spoke of?"

But to this Charles had no answer. Before they could discuss the problem, they were interrupted by the arrival of Althorp and Bosworth, both considerably cleaned up from their unorthodox journey through the French countryside. Charles awakened the little dog, locked both his room and the door to the outer passage, and led the way downstairs to the dimly lit taproom.

A fire burned in a cavernous hearth at one end of the long room. Numerous tables crowded the area and the benches and chairs were filled by members of the lower orders of Paris society. The deep, harsh voices of men resounded in the room, though occasionally a shrill and unrefined female voice added a higher note.

Charles and his party wended their way through the crowd until they reached an empty table. Aimée scuttled under this, then drew close to Charles's feet, as if seeking protection from so many strangers.

No sooner had they seated themselves than Margit appeared, bearing wooden bowls and a kettle of steaming chowder. As she ladled out the servings, she regarded each of the members of the party through curious eyes. Charles she knew of old, and his presence filled her with both confidence and relief. Whatever was afoot, he could be counted upon to get to the bottom of it.

The man Bosworth, though, perplexed her. He hardly seemed the sort of companion that *Le Maniganceur* would recruit. His interest appeared limited to his dinner! But never would she question any decision made by the man she'd idolized for so many years.

She poured an overflowing ladle of the thick soup into Althorp's bowl. He glanced up, a broad grin on his handsome face, and gave her a wink. Now, why would he do that? From the top of his light brown curls to the bottom of his dirt-streaked Hessian boots, every part of him seemed to bespeak youth and energy. Reckless, she decided . . . that sort held no appeal for her.

Her gaze moved on to Harding. His frowning eyes remained on his bowl as she filled it. He had made his disapproval of her very clear, and that rankled. But still, *Le Maniganceur* both trusted and depended on him. That gave her pause. His attitude might be unreasonable where she was concerned, but in every other respect he seemed to be a man of worth, both solid and cautious. For the first time in her very young life, she felt a stirring of interest in a man. She would like to know him better, she decided.

"Would you care for some bread? I made it myself only this afternoon." She tried to flutter her eyelashes at him to attract his attention, imitating a certain woman of questionable morals who served in the taproom. She lacked the art; Harding barely spared her a glance.

"We'd love some." Althorp smiled at her, phrasing his answer in stilted French.

Margit hurried away downstairs. That man Harding, he did not even notice her except to express disapproval! She cast an appraising eye over her shabby attire and the short, solid build it concealed. Her appearance befitted a serving wench in a low tavern. For the first time it bothered her. Harding, she supposed, would prefer a voluptuous creature like that Jeanette in the taproom, who knew all too well how to entice a man. Perhaps she would spend some time studying Jeanette's methods.

She reached the kitchen and loaded a tray with two loaves of the fresh bread, a leg of mutton, and several chickens. These she carried back and arranged on the table. She brushed against Harding's arm and he looked up, scowled, and returned his attention to his meal. Margit fumed.

She turned an inquiring glance on each one of them, with the pointed exception of Harding. "Do you require anything else?" Only Althorp and Charles bothered to answer.

"This is just what we needed," Althorp assured her.

"Try the bread, Harding." Charles grinned at his friend. "You'll have to acknowledge that Margit is a first-rate cook."

Warm, unexpected color flooded Margit's cheeks. So, *Le Maniganceur* noticed her interest in this man Harding and found it *fort amusant*, did he? She spun about with a flounce and stalked back to the kitchen.

Charles watched her go, and a reminiscent smile played about his lips. Had it been only a few short years ago that she'd been a child playing in the streets? It seemed that his little half-boy had begun to blossom into a woman. What she needed was some guidance and a few lessons. His smile faded. What chance did she have here, in a place like this tavern? What sort of men would she meet? She would have been better off if she could remain a boy!

Unless . . . He threw a glance brimful of speculation at Harding. He seemed a confirmed bachelor, certainly not a man to be caught in the snares of a temptress. But what of the clumsy, unpolished attempts of a gangly yearling more adept at the arts of espionage than those of love? They were similar in many ways, both intensely loyal and both stubborn to the point of hard-headedness. He found he wished Margit every success—though he feared her assault against Harding's defenses would be to no avail.

And thinking of loyal and stubborn females . . . he stared down at his plate without seeing the thick slices of mutton. Where was Thérèse? Or more important, *how* was she? It was time he found out.

Without staying to finish his meal, he carried Aimée to the kitchens and handed her over to the care of Margit. Leaving his companions in the taproom, he retired to his bedchamber and locked the door. He pulled the chest of drawers out into the room, pressed a knothole in the wall, and drew open a secret cupboard. He made a selection from the several garments that hung on pegs.

As the hour approached eleven, an old, stooping man with a beaked nose descended the stairs of the inn. Margit looked up, nodded, and smiled at this ancient, who was a familiar though long absent sight. Paying him no further heed, she continued delivering tankards of ale to the inn's patrons.

Aimée, who lay in a corner near the kitchen, spotted him

as, leaning heavily on a cane, he made his way toward the door. With a short yip of pleasure and her tail wagging at speed, she bundled up to him and fell into step at his side. She showed every sign of accompanying him on whatever excursion he had in mind.

Margit hurried over and caught the little dog in her arms. "I am sorry, m'sieur. I thought her secured."

"Put her in my room." His words were barely above a whisper, but Margit heard him and nodded.

Free of his determined shadow, Charles limped his way out the door. He stopped just outside and breathed deeply of the cool night air; his nose wrinkled at the smells of the Paris back streets that assailed his nostrils. The luxurious life at Ranleigh had definitely spoiled him.

And Thérèse . . . wherever she was in this great, dirty city, he could be sure she was not being spoiled. He would find her. He swore it to himself, making it a vow, and was startled by the vehemence of his determination.

Making a great show of relying on his cane, he turned his tottering steps up the street. He made several turns and proceeded up more than one dark, unsavory alley before he reached a tavern with the sign of a sleeping cat hanging above the door. He entered and made his way to a seat in the far corner.

With a tankard of ale on the table before him, he leaned his stool back so that he rested against the wall. From the depths of a cavernous coat pocket, he pulled out a very distinctive curved pipe which he filled and lighted with care. Settling back to smoke this, he waited, watching people arrive and leave through amazingly sharp eyes.

A quarter of an hour passed, and a middle-aged farmer rose from a nearby table and strolled over to join him. Charles nodded as the man sat down.

"Been awhile," the newcomer commented.

Charles nodded and drew on his pipe.

"Something big is going on." The farmer kept his voice low.

Again, Charles merely nodded. This was the second hint he'd received, and his interest grew. "Any ideas?"

The farmer shook his head. "No one can find out."

Charles set aside his pipe and took a long drink from the tankard. As intriguing as another problem might be, his primary concern was to find Thérèse, and that must come first.

"Heard anything of interest from the prison?" He picked up his pipe and appeared to concentrate on this.

"What you need is to talk to our man inside the gaol."

Charles nodded and received directions on how to find this individual. He finished his tankard, knocked the still smoldering tobacco from his pipe and restored it to his pocket, then nodded to the farmer. With the help of his cane, he stood and made his way slowly out to the street.

The tavern he sought was not far away. He paused in its doorway, then began to weave among the tables. At last he spotted a rather nondescript man seated alone, smoking a pipe identical to the one that rested in his own pocket. Charles settled down at a table near him.

"Excuse me." He leaned across. "Do you have any tobacco to spare?" He drew out the identifying pipe and let the man have a clear view of it.

The gaoler brought out a small leather pouch. Charles pressed some of the aromatic mixture into his pipe. When he had it drawing, he tied the little bag closed and handed it back.

"What can I do for you?" The gaoler glanced casually around to assure himself that no one paid them any heed.

"I'm looking for a woman who may be a new prisoner at the gaol. A rather beautiful, blond lady. She was there before, for a couple of months."

They fell silent for several minutes while the gaoler concentrated on blowing a few shaky smoke rings. "That singer? De Bourgerre, wasn't that her name? I remember her."

With a determined effort, Charles kept his voice calm.

"Is she there?"

The man shook his head. "I'd have recognized her."

Charles's mouth felt oddly dry. Had she been killed? A rage welled within him and he struggled to control it. If they had harmed her . . . he would personally take this de Lebouchon and each of his cohorts apart, piece by piece, and know a savage joy in the process! He rather thought he would do so, anyway, even if he found her safe. What he would do to her for causing him this worry, he was not at all sure. But he was not about to give her up for dead yet!

The gaoler exhaled a perfect ring of smoke and nodded in satisfaction at this feat. "There's another place she might have been taken."

"Where?" The eagerness with which he jumped at this proffered crumb startled him. He was losing his objectivity—another effect of that damnable Thérèse. He grew careless in his concern for her, and that would only lead to his being captured as well. A fine lot of good that would do them all!

"A house on the Rue St. Honoré. The home of Colonel Mercier of the *Garde Impériale*. I know of at least one prisoner who was taken there before." He exhaled another smoke ring. "And if you like, I will ask questions—oh, so very casually—about where someone might be taken for interrogation. Will this help?"

"It will."

With that, Charles took his leave and made his way back to the tavern. He could not be easy, for the feeling haunted him that he had not yet done enough. Would that exasperating female still be alive? And why did it matter so much to him? It went far beyond any sense of duty, but when he tried to explore the subject further, he came up against the stone wall of his pride. She'd made her opinion of him abundantly clear when he saw her in Brighton. He would prove her wrong by saving her, but after that, he would have nothing further to do with her.

But why was saving her necessary? Why had the French recaptured her? Try as he might, he could think of no reason why they should have gone to any pains over Thérèse. The most reasonable thing would have been for de Lebouchon to carry her away into the depths of a forest and shoot her. Yet he had gone to the trouble and danger of hiring a carriage and then taking her to sea. Which must mean that they needed her alive. Unless . . .

Impotent fury and frustration filled him, leaving him seething. What if their destination had not been Paris? What if de Lebouchon only carried her far enough into the channel to dump her quietly overboard where her body would not be found? What if, after all this, she was indeed dead? But that was something he would not—could not!—permit himself to believe.

More by instinct than by design, he found himself once more before the tavern owned by Margit's uncle. Most of the downstairs lights were extinguished, a sure sign of the lateness of the hour. He let himself in, made his way to his room, and began to remove the numerous layers that made up his disguise.

As he climbed into bed, a sharp rap sounded on his door. Ever alert, he drew a pistol from beneath his pillow and held it at the ready as he slid back the bolt. The landlord stood on the threshold with little Aimée grasped firmly in his powerful hands. She let out a peremptory yip and squirmed to be free.

"Sorry to disturb you, m'sieur, but the dog, it will give no one any peace! Always it is underfoot."

Charles received the delighted mongrel into his arms. She reached up to try and lick his face and he set her down on the bed.

"I'm sorry. I thought she was to be brought up here."

"She was, m'sieur. But she would bark so! Margit thought it best to take her back downstairs."

Charles thanked the man, then closed and bolted the door behind him. For good measure, he wedged the room's one chair beneath the knob. This accomplished to his satisfaction, he regarded the panting, shivering little animal with disfavor. Under his disapproving eye, she curled up on his blanket with all the air of one settling in for the night. She let out a contented sigh.

"Never has it been my misfortune to travel with anyone as useless as you," he informed her. "Do you have the least idea how much trouble you are?"

Aimée stirred herself enough to thump her tail in pleasure at being restored to him and he shook his head. "Just like a female," he muttered. Climbing back into his bed, he blew out the candle and tried to get comfortable for what remained of the night.

He did not find it easy to sleep. Visions of Thérèse in danger, locked in a dark, dank dungeon, haunted him. All women were nothing but a pack of trouble! Slamming his fist into his pillow, he rolled over and tried to capture elusive slumber.

When the first thin rays of the sun seeped into his room, he rolled over and stretched, thus dislodging the sleeping Aimée from her position near his feet. Nothing would be gained by lying abed, no matter how tired or unrested he felt, so he rose and pulled on his clothes. Listening at the other three doors assured him that his associates still slept, so he went down for breakfast with only the little dog for company.

A sleepy-eyed Margit, broom in hand, wandered into the taproom as he sat down. She drew him a tankard of ale and set it before him. "You are up early."

Charles nodded and glared at the amber liquid. He might be up, but he did nothing to help Thérèse! He would have to gain entrance to that house on the Rue St. Honoré. . . . Aimée whined, recalling his attention.

Charles looked about and spotted Margit sweeping the floor. "Can you have the dog taken for a walk?"

She collected the unprotesting Aimée and carried her out to the kitchens. She reappeared alone a few minutes later and went straight to Charles.

"This has just been delivered for you." She held out a sealed note. He took it and she went back to her broom.

He tore the message open and scanned the scribbled page. It was from the gaoler, very brief, but to Charles extremely interesting. There were two places, he read, where many important men had been gathering of late. A chateau on the road to Versailles, and a house along the Seine. This last place, the note said, had been the site of high-level meetings for the past two weeks.

A surge of elation swept through Charles. That house on the Seine held out real promise! To him, it seemed exactly the sort of place where Thérèse might have been taken. She could be smuggled in and out with ease, and anyone interested in questioning her would not have to travel far. He folded the sheet and tapped it rhythmically against the edge of the table while plans blossomed in his mind.

He looked up as footsteps approached and he nodded an absent greeting when William Harding took the seat beside him.

"Morning, sir." Harding rested his elbows on the table and dropped his chin into his cupped hands.

Charles glanced at him. "You look uncommonly grim this morning." Now that he had a clear goal in view and real hope surging through him, devils began to dance in his eyes.

Harding looked about for Margit, who appeared almost at once with a tankard for him. Her sweeping forgotten, she headed off to the kitchen to obtain a sustaining breakfast.

"It's Bosworth and Althorp, sir."

"Good God—tell me the worst. Have they been taken up by the watch?"

Harding awarded the sally a perfunctory smile. "It might well happen. They're likely to become bored if they just sit about this inn."

"So let's have them help out around here." Charles looked up as the subjects of their conversation strolled into the room. "Althorp, you and Bosworth are to lend a hand in the kitchens today. I need Margit to help me."

Althorp blanched. "The—the kitchens?" He threw a beseeching glance at Harding, who made no attempt to hide his smile.

Bosworth sat down and nodded. "Might get to know the cook. Always helps, if you want a good meal."

With Margit at his side, Charles set forth in less than half an hour to explore both banks of the Seine near the house in question. Dark clouds hovered on the horizon, threatening a storm in the not-too-distant future. Margit muttered the hope that it would hold off until they finished, but Charles paid it no heed.

They spent considerable time in their reconnoitering, strolling through the streets and even climbing down to the river. The house in question backed up against this, thus providing a watery avenue of approach—or retreat. At last, sure of his territory, his plan formed, Charles led the way back to the inn to begin preparations.

This time, he pressed his three companions into service. They might be skeptical of the unusual roles he demanded that they perform, but no one questioned his authority or even the sanity of so daring a plan.

The approaching storm brought an early dusk, which suited Charles quite well. As soon as it was dark enough for their movements to be obscured he donned the disguise of a tinker and led his three followers toward the house. Harding, he ordered, would watch the front; Althorp, inwardly quaking, prepared to create a diversion; while Bosworth, already turning somewhat green, set forth to row a boat along the Seine.

With the members of his party safely at their posts, Charles turned his attention to the scullery entrance of the house. He hefted a tinker's wooden yoke over his shoulders and started forward with the hastily assembled collection of copper wares dangling and clanking about him. He knocked on the door and shortly found himself within a large, homey kitchen, displaying his supposed merchandise. He could only hope that Althorp would begin his part, for his knowledge of cookware was not extensive.

It seemed an eternity while the cook and his assistants examined the pots and asked questions. What took Althorp so long? Had he not been able to obtain access to any of the windows? If he didn't make his move soon, Charles would be forced to take matters into his own hands.

A quick survey of the scrupulously tidy kitchen warned him he would find little there with which to create a sufficient diversion to allow him to slip upstairs. Unless he could start a fire. . . . He began to inch his way toward the blazing hearth.

A commotion of scraping chairs sounded from the servants' hall next door and a woman screamed. Several voices rose at once.

"A man! At the window, peering in! There!" Another scream followed.

Charles looked through the open doorway and saw a hideously flattened face pressed against the glass. As a sturdy footman lunged toward the window, Althorp scrambled upward toward the next floor. His boots scraped along the stones seeking toeholds in the masonry, and in moments he vanished from sight. The footman threw open the casement and Althorp gave a soft shout, as if warning someone above him that they had been discovered. His hold, precarious at best, slipped, and he lost his grip. He turned and dived into the cold, murky waters of the Seine. When he surfaced, he struck out for Bosworth's boat.

"Housebreakers!" a kitchen maid screamed.

"And it sounds like there's at least one of them already in the house!" The butler signaled to his underlings to set off in pursuit.

In the resulting confusion, Charles tossed his collection of pots aside and ran after the servants, up the inner stairs to the hallway above. He looked quickly about. Thérèse, if she were indeed here at all, was not held below in the basements . . . of that he was certain. That left somewhere up here, and probably on an upper story. He headed at once for the stairs to the next floor.

After a quick reconnoitering of the upper levels, he came to the reluctant conclusion that Thérèse was not being held in this house. Disappointed out of all proportion, he made his way cautiously down the back steps. He would have to reenter the kitchen premises very carefully unless he wanted to be taken for a thief. He reached the lower hallway without being seen and started down a corridor.

The muted murmur of voices reached him through a closed door and he started past as silently as he could. Suddenly he pulled up short, for the name of Wellington, quite unmistakable, reached him.

He pressed gently against the dark wood panel, but it remained tightly closed. Stooping down, he placed his ear against the keyhole. The conversation continued in low, rapid tones, but one other name stood out, repeated over and over. Torres Vedras. Wellington and Torres Vedras. Charles searched his memory. Was that not a village just north of Lisbon? And Wellington, he knew, had recently been sent to Portugal to take over command of the Peninsular forces. If only he could hear what was being planned!

As he again bent to listen, the sound of footsteps running up the stairs from the basement caught his attention. He dived into an open room across the hall just as the butler, pistol in hand, burst through the servants' door.

Chapter Eleven

The butler's footsteps thundered past the room in which Charles hid. That had been close! Charles opened the door a crack and peered out, only to shut it again at once. Two footmen, less swift of foot than their leader, burst through the servants' entrance, panting in not very hot pursuit. They, too, disappeared up the hall.

Charles waited, but stillness engulfed the lower regions of the house. And while he just sat there, being hunted by butlers in the wrong house, what was happening to Thérèse? He wasted time, precious time, perhaps Thérèse's last few hours. . . .

Venturing out of his hiding place, he crept along the corridor and peered down the kitchen stair. All seemed safe. The sooner he escaped from here and set about doing something useful for a change, such as finding Thérèse, the better! He descended, careful to make no noise.

He stepped into the spacious kitchens and stopped short. A scullery maid stood at the large wooden table, sorting carrots, onions, and potatoes. She looked up eagerly.

"Did they find him? To think of someone being in the house . . . !" The girl gave an expressive shudder.

"Not yet." Charles leaned negligently against the edge of the table as if he were not seething with impatience to leave. He directed a particularly charming smile at the maid. "Thought I caught a glimpse of him once, and went dashing all over the house. I was probably chasing a footman the whole time."

The girl giggled and eyed him with speculative interest. His tinker disguise was not unappealing. "You're new, aren't you? I don't remember seeing you before. Now, the old tinker!" She rolled her eyes heavenward and shook her head, giving Charles to understand that he himself was a distinct improvement.

He gave her a knowing wink and straightened up. "I suppose I'd best be on my way. No hope of getting your cook to buy any pots tonight, not after this dust-up."

She shook her head. "All he'll talk about are those housebreakers. Here, why don't you come back tomorrow?"

"Maybe I will. Where are my things?" He looked about, spotted the wooden yoke with its collection of copper wares, and hoisted it onto his shoulders.

"Until tomorrow." The maid slipped past him and opened the door. She bestowed her most enticing smile upon him as he went out then with reluctance locked up behind him.

He hurried up the area steps. Once on the street, he quickened his pace and his swinging steps set the cookware clanking about him. He rounded the corner and almost collided with Harding. Charles swung back, steadied the swinging pots, and Harding caught at the heavy yoke.

"How did it go? Did you find any trace of her?"

"No." Charles shook his head, his expression grim. "She's not being kept there. But I did hear something interesting . . . something to do with Wellington and Torres Vedras."

"What?" Harding almost ran to keep up with Charles's long-legged stride.

At that, a muscle at the corner of his mouth gave a reluctant twitch. "I couldn't find out. I had a near run-in with a butler."

Harding forbore to ask. Very little about this rescue mission made much sense. Why should it start now? "What do we do next?"

"Colonel Mercier's house, I believe. I just want to change disguises."

When they got back to the inn, they found Bosworth and Althorp there before them, lounging in the taproom with large tankards of ale before them and their booted feet extended to the fire. Althorp, his light brown hair still damp from his swim in the river, looked up as they approached and sprang to his feet.

"Did you find the lady, sir?"

Charles shook his head. "No. But you did an excellent job. The staff was in complete confusion and I had a free hand."

Althorp beamed. "Then it was worth getting a little wet."

Margit appeared at their sides and handed each of the new arrivals a tankard. Charles took a long swallow and then set it down.

"Where's Aimée?" He looked about as if expecting the disreputable little dog to come running out from the shadows and make a beeline for his side.

"In the kitchen. Our cook, he has given her a bone, and she seems content."

Charles nodded. "Harding, will you two keep an eye on her? I'm going back out."

Without giving the man a chance to object, he headed toward the stairs. He wanted to be at the house on the Rue St. Honoré before ten o'clock, and that did not give him much time to alter his appearance again.

Just over a half-hour later, a blind beggar made his careful way down the inn stairs and on outside. He

177

clutched a small tin cup in one gnarled hand and swung a long stick before him with the other. As he emerged onto the street, a drizzling rain began to fall. The drops came harder and faster until they drenched his patched and ragged clothing. His old, drooping shoulders began to shiver in the cool night air.

It was only partially an act. Charles's thin garments provided little protection as the hovering storm gained enthusiasm. A wind joined in and began to whip rain against his face, almost blinding him. It was not a good night to be out, but that would not matter in the least if only he could find Thérèse. . . . At the moment his hopes were not high—he'd already had a trying evening dodging butlers and footmen.

He turned onto the Rue St. Honoré and began to seek out the correct address. As he strolled past it, he studied the facade with care. In the next doorway he paused for shelter and prepared to wait, maintaining his fiction of blind begging while watching the house of Colonel Mercier. Traffic on the street proved light, and there was little for him to do as the minutes ticked by except to think of Thérèse. . . .

Half an hour melted into an hour, and still nothing untoward occurred. For all he knew, the house he watched might be empty this night. Or prisoners might abound on the upper floors. There was no way he could tell without gaining entrance! No one chose this night to pay a visit.

Another half hour slipped past, and the rain let up to become a light drizzle. Charles regarded the dark sky through baleful eyes and began to feel that he'd wasted the evening. Was he losing his touch? To make two wrong guesses in one night! And why must this happen to him now, when this job meant more to him than any other he had ever undertaken?

Or was that the reason? He huddled in his wet rags and tried to turn his thoughts elsewhere. He could just imagine Althorp and Bosworth, snug and dry in the tavern, enjoying a peaceful evening.

He would have done better to coerce another entrance, as he had at the house on the Seine. At least he knew for certain that Thérèse was not there. But here, he learned nothing!

And where was she? In some dank dungeon? Alone and friendless, terrified for her life? Where were the cunning and wiles of the great *Maniganceur*, now that she needed them?

A coin dropped into his cup and he started. Mumbling a *"Merci,"* he swore under his breath and called himself several choice names, of which fool was the least. He had allowed himself to become totally taken up in his worry for Thérèse! Damn her! Must she interfere with his work, make him useless and careless, when his sole concern should—must!—be to help her?

At least the night was not a total waste, he told himself with heavy sarcasm. He had earned a franc. But during the almost two hours that he had been there, not one single person had either gone into or come out of this house. Disgusted, he decided to wait one last half-hour.

Fifteen minutes proved enough. The door to Mercier's house opened and Charles, instantly alert, left his shelter and stumbled uncertainly toward the two men who emerged, chanting his beggar's cry. The men stopped on the street. Neither paid him the least heed.

"Remember," a short, dark-haired man said. "De Lebouchon will be waiting at the chateau. Make sure that Fouche is told."

Charles kept going, never ceasing his muttered pleas for francs. So, the Minister of Police and de Lebouchon were to be together at this chateau? Which chateau? He rather thought he could wager a guess. And if de Lebouchon was there, it was very likely that Thérèse would be as well.

His spirits soared as he continued on his way. There was

no need to remain out in this damnable weather now. His luck had finally come through! If Thérèse was alive—which she was, she had to be!—he would find her on the morrow. M. Fouche and the Chevalier de Lebouchon would not be the only gentlemen to visit the chateau.

But it would take careful planning. If Thérèse was there, it would be reasonable to assume she was carefully guarded. He could not just walk in, knock on her door, and lead her out the front entrance. He was going to need help. His ever inventive mind went instantly to work.

At the inn, he found his companions, along with Margit and Aimée, gathered in his room. A large bowl of punch sat on the dresser and it was obvious that everyone had spent a comfortable evening. As he entered, Aimée let out a yip of welcome and jumped up to greet him.

Margit stood. "You are wet." Her tone was resigned. *"Voilà tout,* I will dry your things."

Charles took off his disreputable coat and handed it to her. Next, he pulled the threadbare scarf from his head and went vigorously to work with a towel Harding tossed him. Somewhat drier, he pulled up a chair next to the small hearth and held out his hands to relieve their numbing cold. "I think I know where they're keeping Thérèse."

"When do we start?" Althorp, his blue eyes gleaming with excitement, leaned forward.

"Do you have a plan?" Harding's gaze narrowed as it rested on Charles's tired and grim face. Their escapades so far on this journey had not been up to the standards of the great *Le Maniganceur.* Where Thérèse de Bourgerre was concerned, he had realized, Charles was less than his cool, efficient self.

Charles glanced over at Margit, who hung his coat over the back of a chair near the crackling blaze. "How would you like to scrub a few floors?"

She grinned. *"Pourquoi pas?* And what will you do?

The stables?"

"Pots, I think. I want to be in the kitchen."

"And the rest of us?" Harding gestured to his two assistants.

"Someone will have to hold the horses for our escape."

He refused to discuss anything else about his plan, which in fact was not yet fully formed. The others, giving up, retired to their chambers for what remained of the night. Charles sought his own bed, but lay awake long, thinking through every part, every role that each of his helpers might play. He had performed other rescues in the past, but this one—this one just mattered more than usual. Thérèse's mocking words had stung his pride, that was all. He would prove her wrong.

He rose at an early hour, before any of the others were awake, and once again donned his disguise of the beaky-nosed old man with the pipe. As soon as people began to stir in the street, he went off to pay a visit to a certain chemist's shop where he was known of old. Without question, the proprietor gave him the powder for which he asked, then carefully measured out a dose of an unpleasant smelling liquid into a tiny glass vial. These Charles tucked safely into his coat before taking his leave.

He returned to the inn, shouted for Margit, and bounded up the stairs two at a time. Now that he had the scent, he was as eager as any hound to pursue his fox. As soon as he reached the privacy of his room, he set about removing one disguise and replacing it with another. To complete this, he needed certain items of clothing that Margit brought with her from the kitchens.

At last he stood back and regarded himself critically in the mirror. Not quite satisfied, he allowed his mouth to droop and worked to achieve a partially glazed, unfocused stare. He met Margit's eyes in the glass.

"What do you think?"

"Speak only in guttural grunts." She walked around

and inspected the ill-fitting garments of a pot boy. *"Eh, bien.* You look the perfect half-wit."

He swept her a mocking bow. *"Merci du compliment.* And you look the perfect scullion. Well, we'd best be going."

"Have you decided what to do if they will not give us work?"

Charles's smile became lopsided. "It will have to be the tinker again. Harding will bring the pots and the disguise, in case it's needed." He held the door for her, then locked it behind them. *"Mon Dieu,* what a never-ending job this is!" he added with a sudden grin.

With Aimée settled in the kitchens with a very large and tasty ham bone provided by the cook, Charles and Margit made their way out to the stable, where they found their three companions waiting with six horses. Two bore sidesaddles. Charles helped Margit onto one of these, then swung up on another horse. Bosworth took the reins of the mount meant for Thérèse.

Harding, bearing all the appearance of an affluent citizen, led the way astride a large, flashy chestnut. Althorp and Bosworth followed at a respectful distance, for all the world like servants. Margit came next, leading the horse on which Charles sat slumped, gripping the mane, his expression one of dim-witted fear. In this manner they passed through the crowded streets without arousing comment.

As soon as they had cleared the gates and gone beyond the outskirts of Paris, they paused to regroup. Around them now lay nothing but fields, free of prying eyes. Charles claimed his reins and they rode on in silence for several miles.

At last, off to the left, they glimpsed an ancient and stately chateau. Charles reined in and a rush of excitement swept through him as it did every time he prepared to walk into a lion's den. Only this time there was more at stake than his own life. Somewhere, in that great, stone house that bore more than a passing resemblance to an impregnable castle, Thérèse might well be a prisoner.

He dismounted. Margit did the same, and they handed their bridles over to Harding and Althorp. Harding hesitated, then extended his hand.

Charles gripped it. "It's going to be a long day of waiting for you."

"We'll be all right, sir. And as soon as it's dark, we'll move in and be ready. Good luck."

Charles and Margit set forth on foot. The day was hot and the walking anything but smooth, and by the time they neared the chateau, Margit limped from stepping on innumerable stones in her thin, well-worn shoes. Not a single complaint escaped her lips.

They entered the grounds through a break in the shrubbery. From this point on, they would be in clear view of the house. Charles slackened his pace, took Margit's hand, and allowed her to lead him. When they reached the servants' entrance, they looked every bit as bedraggled and desperate as they could wish.

Margit knocked and Charles hunched over and retreated a pace as if to hide behind her. The heavy door swung wide and he crouched down with a whimper. Margit patted his hand and faced the young woman who wore a mobcap.

"We need work. We are honest, *je vous assure,* and we work very hard." Margit inserted a note of desperation into her voice. "And we will do anything."

The maid eyed Charles askance. "What's wrong with him?"

"He is my brother. He may be a half-wit, but he is very good with the pots and kettles and does everything just exactly the way you tell him. Please, even if you cannot pay us, we will work just for a meal!"

The maid stepped back. "Come in. I will bring Madame Mornay, the housekeeper."

Margit coaxed Charles into the great kitchen. He held back, staring about the high-ceilinged room with large, round eyes. When Margit pressed him into a chair, he sat. His mouth hung slack and he focused his attention on a kitchen maid who kneaded bread dough.

An elderly man in the apron and cap of a cook turned to regard them. "Does he do a thorough job on the kettles?"

"Just give him a brush and you will see." Margit turned large, eager eyes on him.

"And you, do you scrub?" A gray-haired woman swept into the kitchen and looked over the prospective servants without much enthusiasm.

"Very hard, madame. My brother and I, we are very good workers."

"We could use some help, what with so many people coming this night." The maid who had let them in regarded her superior hopefully.

"It is true." The cook nodded. "There is to be a dinner, and for that there are many extra pots to be cleaned. And my helpers, there are too few."

"Where do you come from, girl?"

"Paris. We have references." She dug in her pocket and pulled out folded sheets that Charles had written just that morning. "But my brother, he is frightened by the noise of the city, so I hoped we could find work in the country. But it is all so very far to walk."

The housekeeper took the references and read them with care. When she finished she nodded. "Very well. We are shorthanded. You may stay this day and we shall see how you do."

"Oh, *merci, madame!*" Margit took off her ragged coat and helped Charles to do the same. "What shall we do first?"

Margit turned Charles over to the cook and urged her supposed brother not to be afraid of the nice man. After assuring the cook that he need only repeat his instructions twice, provided he kept them simple, she followed the maid. Charles next saw her with a large bucket of soapy water and a scrub brush, trying to remove a congealed mess from the stone paving before the oven. He had little time to spare her more than a glance, for he found himself facing the greasy, burned insides of a huge kettle.

They worked throughout the day until the other servants seemed to take their presence for granted. Charles, in particular, they tended to ignore, which suited him perfectly. He worked industriously at any task without ever speaking—and without displaying any initiative or intelligence whatsoever. The cook seemed satisfied and paid him no heed until a new task came to mind.

As evening approached, the cook summoned a large, burly footman to him. "We'll have to send up the prisoner's meal early. You'll be wanted in the dining room for serving, with so many important guests coming."

The footman shrugged. "Or I can take it up later, when they're all done."

The cook considered. "Best do it first. You go help with laying the table, now."

Charles's spirits soared. Thérèse was here—and alive! He would have her free this night. And when he did, he was not sure whether he wanted to kiss her or strangle her.

He turned his attention to the job at hand. He could not tell from the number of dishes being prepared how many guests there would be. He could only hope it was an elaborate meal for only a few. The chemist had given him a considerable amount of laudanum, but it would go only just so far. He wanted everyone asleep, not just drowsy. If only he could find a way to control the dosage and administration!

He looked about but could see no sign of Margit. Finally, he spotted her coming down the stone steps carrying her bucket and brush, her face covered with grimy

185

streaks and her short, dark hair straggling out from beneath her mobcap. Charles signaled to her and she went to where he sat on the floor with a large pot balanced between his legs as he scrubbed the inside.

"Thérèse is here," he murmured, then gave a guttural grunt as she stroked his head.

"Are you doing just as they tell you? That is good, very good. I am proud of you." She patted his arm and moved off.

He finished the pot and found that for the moment there was nothing for him to scrub. Taking the opportunity, he wandered over to where the food was being assembled on a long wooden table and peered longingly at it. From his pocket, he slipped out the bag of white powder.

A clatter from the other side of the kitchen caught everyone's attention. Margit, wailing that she was sorry, began to mop up the sloppy mess from the pail she had dropped. While all eyes were on her, Charles, undetected, poured a very generous dose of powder into the flour that the kitchen maid had measured out for a cream soup.

The cook turned back to his work and the flour—and laudanum—disappeared into the melted butter base. Charles moved on to the other end of the table where a maid whipped frosting with a wooden spoon. He made an urgent, grunting noise and gestured toward it. The maid glanced at the cook, who nodded, and she handed Charles the sugar-coated spoon. He received it with so much excitement that she giggled.

He licked it and rolled his eyes in delight. Clutching it in one hand, he patted the maid's arm in gratitude with the other. She set the bowl out of his reach and went to fetch a jug of cream. As soon as her back was turned, another generous dose of laudanum went into a second bowl of flour, destined for a pastry-wrapped ham.

That should keep the dinner guests above stairs quiet—if not actually asleep. But how to drug the staff? He shuffled away, still licking his spoon and eyeing the various dishes. Which of these were destined for the servants' hall? He made his way over to Margit and generously offered her a lick of his treat.

"Thanks for the diversion. Now try to find out what the servants will eat," he murmured.

The cook called him and he returned to his cleaning. A few minutes later, he saw Margit approach the maid, who spooned preserves over a thin layer of cake.

"It all looks so grand, doesn't it?" Margit sighed. "It makes me so very hungry, just looking at such wonderful food."

The cook permitted himself a smile at her undisguised admiration. "Don't worry. You'll eat well—and probably better than you got at that inn of yours. There's a very tasty game pie here for us. And we'll be eating before they're served upstairs."

Charles made a few quick calculations. The laudanum did not take effect at once. Drowsiness would gradually creep over the victims. That meant he could administer the dose in their meal, and they would not begin to drop off until after the dinner was well under way upstairs. And by that time, the guests should be long through with their heavily laced soup and have started on that ham. . . .

He finished polishing the bowls, set them gingerly on a table as if they were made of the finest crystal, instead of copper, and went back to watch the cook. As soon as the man began the delicate operation of rolling out a second crust, Charles sprinkled the last of the powder over the filling of the game pie and watched as it dissolved. No traces remained when the cook placed the crust over the top and crimped down the edges. An underling carried it to the huge oven.

Charles took the kettle in which the filling had cooked and set about cleaning it. This, along with various bowls and utensils, kept him occupied until the maids began laying out for their meal. When this was ready, Margit took Charles's hand and led him to the foot of the long, wooden table on which the platters had already been arranged in the middle.

Bowls of vegetable soup were handed around and Charles concentrated on this. Margit, watching his choice of food, followed suit. When the game pie was passed down to them, Charles let it sit.

"But I thought he was hungry!" the maid seated next to Margit exclaimed. "Why, the way he eyed the food, I thought he'd eat several helpings!"

Margit shook her head. "He often does this, when he has had a sweet. But don't worry, it won't make him sick. He's just not hungry now."

She toyed with her portion and took only a small bite. She disguised this by spreading it about on the plate and scattering bread crumbs over all. The others were too busy eating their own meals to pay her any heed. When it came time to clear up, Margit set another dish on top of her plate and began to help.

Charles returned to the kitchens and sat down on the floor near the fire, humming off-key to himself. The butler and footmen donned their liveried coats and went upstairs to announce dinner and begin serving. Charles threw a surreptitious glance at a clock. It was only minutes before eight. That meant he would wait until almost nine to make sure that the drug had time to take effect.

He remained where he was until summoned by the cook, and he obediently went to wash the dishes. Out of the corner of his eye, he kept watch on the members of the staff who remained below stairs. One by one, they began to yawn. The maid who sat in a rocking chair, darning an apron, lowered her needle as her head nodded forward. The hands of the clock stood at a quarter to nine.

Charles pulled off his grimy apron and signaled Margit. Together they slipped up the stone steps that led to the

Great Hall of the chateau. They reached it and stood looking around.

"Where do we begin?" Margit whispered.

"We know she's not below stairs. That would leave anywhere up here. Probably not on this floor, though."

"*Eh, bien.* I will take the next, and you the one above. *Hein?*"

They went up the main staircase. Margit turned down the hall and Charles continued up one more flight. The first door he opened confirmed that he would find mostly bedchambers. He tried room after room, and at each he drew a blank.

He turned down the last hall on his floor and opened the first door. Directly before him stood a soldier in the blue-and-white uniform of the *Garde Impériale*. The man opened his mouth to shout, but never got the chance. Charles's fist connected with his jaw and the man staggered backward. Charles followed, closing for a struggle, but a second jab neatly placed to the man's chin proved sufficient. The soldier dropped to the floor, unconscious.

Breathing heavily, and muttering at himself for his carelessness, Charles looked about for something with which to secure the soldier. The only thing that came into view was a cord that tied back the draperies at the window. He quickly detached this and bound the man's hands tightly behind him. For good measure, he drew a handkerchief from the uniform pocket and stuffed it into his mouth for a gag.

Resolving to be more careful, Charles shut the door softly behind himself and continued his inspection of the remaining rooms. No one else, it seemed, lurked on this floor. His wanderings brought him back to the main stair and he made his way up the next flight.

As he turned down the first hall he reached, a deep sigh sounded only feet away. He spun about and found himself facing Margit.

"You frightened me. I heard you on the steps." She kept her voice to a whisper.

"I'm getting clumsy. Have you gotten far?"

"*Non.* I have just begun here. You found no one below?"

A smothered laugh escaped him. "Only a soldier. That was a near miss. You go that way, and if we don't find her here, we'll try the attics."

Margit nodded. "How long will they all remain drugged?"

"It depends on how much of the laudanum they swallowed." He gave her a rueful smile. "There was no way to measure the dose, or even to be sure that they all got some of the stuff. They could be unconscious for minutes or for hours."

"Then we'd best hurry." Margit started for the front of the house, leaving Charles to cover the rear.

He crept along the hall, checking every door he passed. He reached the end, rounded a corner, and ducked back. Ahead of him, about halfway down the corridor, a uniformed guard sat slumped in a chair. Charles's pulses raced with growing certainty.

Adopting the mien of the half-wit, he shuffled toward the guard. Out of the corner of his eyes, he noted the remains of a substantial dinner lying on a tray on the floor. There was a good chance the man would be drugged, but he dared not take any chances. If, after years of caution and success, he failed Thérèse now. . . .

He reached out a tentative hand and touched the guard's arm, which hung limp. The man's only response was to draw a deep, stertorous breath and slump further sideways. Relieved on that head, Charles grasped the door handle. It was locked. The key . . . he looked about and spotted a ring hanging from the guard's belt. Kneeling at his side, Charles carefully pulled it free and began the

190

trial-and-error process of finding the right one. And a wonderful fool he would feel if Thérèse was not in this room!

The scraping of key after key in the lock penetrated the haze that surrounded Thérèse. Why did she feel so odd, as if her hands and feet were numb? They must be poisoning her! It could be the only explanation. Unless she had been drugged. Either way, she could not give in to it! She must fight, try to get away before it was too late!

Unsteady, she came to her feet, clutching the back of the chair for support. Never could she remember feeling so groggy, as if her hold on reality—or life—slipped away. And the scraping in the lock continued. Was it minutes that passed, or only seconds? She was so befuddled. . . .

But she would not give up without one last fight! She stumbled farther from the door and knocked into a light wooden chair. She grasped at it to prevent it from falling over, then continued to clutch it in her desperate hands. She could not just let someone come in and kill her. . . .

The chair, unwieldy as it was, provided a weapon—and her only chance! She dragged it toward the door, positioned herself just behind it, and with every ounce of strength she could gather, lifted it above her head.

The door swung open and Thérèse struck with all her might. But the chair was so heavy, her blow went wide, she was falling with it. . . . The room whirled about her. Dizzy, crazy, she fell but did not hit the ground. Something held her, strong arms. . . .

She forced her eyes open and stared up into the face of a man. Her blurred mind filled in the beloved features of *Le Maniganceur* and with a sob, she reached out and clutched tightly at his arm. Her fingers felt nothing. It was a trick of her drugged brain, an illusion, but he seemed so real. Then, through the fog, came his familiar voice.

"Damn it, Thérèse, quit trying to tear my arm off! Now, pull yourself together. We've got to get out of here!"

191

Half-laughing, barely conscious, she held onto him as if to a buoy in a storm-tossed sea. "Only you would ever say anything so unchivalrous when I am so desperately ill."

"You're not ill. You just had some of the laudanum."

"The—how—how do you know?" With his help, she found her footing.

Still supporting her limp figure, Charles pulled a small bottle from his pocket. "Because I put it in the food. Now drink this."

"You . . ." She blinked, trying to focus her uncooperative eyes. "I suppose this will make sense later. Of a certainty, you have a good reason for drugging me."

His deep, amused chuckle shook his broad shoulders. "Don't worry. I drugged everybody in this chateau. But I brought you something to bring you out of it. Now drink it."

But she was too weak to manage. Scooping her up into his arms, he carried her over to the bed as if he scarcely noticed her slight weight. He set her down on the edge and held her erect while his fingers fumbled with opening the tiny bottle. Placing it between her hands, he guided them to her mouth.

She swallowed, then lay back on the bed with her eyes closed. After several minutes, she felt the lethargy begin to seep away and her senses steady. Her mind, more alert, began to function again.

Cautiously, she sat up and stared at her companion in disbelief. It really was Charles under that peculiar disguise, not some drug-induced fantasy. She held out a hand toward him as joy surged through her—but then she saw the grim impatience on his face. She allowed her hand to drop as a vast emptiness replaced her elation.

"What—what are you doing here, in France?"

"Rescuing you. Are you stronger yet?"

She shook her head, dazed. What had brought him? A sense of duty? And after she had tried so hard to rid him of that! No wonder he was so angry with her. . . . But never had she been happier to see anyone!

She tried to concentrate on their immediate predicament, but it was not easy. If only the room would stop spinning so she could get a proper look at him! "What—what did you give me?"

"Only a stimulant, to counter the effects of the laudanum. It won't last long, so we'll have to move fast to get you out of here."

The door behind them swung wide and Thérèse jumped. Charles, still sitting, reached for his gun as he spun about, only to find it missing. To his relief, it was Margit who stood in the entry.

"Is this Mademoiselle de Bourgerre?" Margit looked her over critically. *"Eh, bien.* Let us go."

Charles stood, his expression dark. Margit raised a curious eyebrow.

"Is something the matter?"

"I lost my gun." His lips tightened in irritation at this further sign of carelessness in himself. "I had a bit of a struggle with a soldier one floor down. I must have dropped it."

"Vraiment?" Margit's expression was almost comical. "That is not like you."

He glared at her. "As you said, let us get out of here."

Thérèse looked from one to the other, trying to make her brain work. Something had gone wrong. . . . *Le Maniganceur,* Charles, was not yet ready for this sort of work, he had not completely recovered from his injuries. If he suffered for her sake, she would never forgive herself!

Margit slipped back into the hall to make sure their way was clear while Charles helped Thérèse to her feet. A moment later Margit reappeared, gave them a quick signal, then hurried ahead. Charles, his arm firmly about Thérèse for support, assisted her to walk.

Through the haze that still clouded her thinking, Thérèse noted how well these two worked together. There appeared to be no need for Charles to give the girl orders.

She might be short and solidly built, but a certain graceful charm marked her quick movements. In spite of her surroundings, their continuing danger, the fear of the last few days, Thérèse knew real jealousy.

They slipped down the hall and a new wave of dizziness swept over her. It would be the result of the conflicting drugs she'd been given, but that knowledge did not help her to think or move more quickly. What she really wanted was to lie down.

With an effort, she stopped, forcing herself to remember what she'd seen of the chateau's layout. Charles muttered something under his breath as he tried to pull her along.

"No, wait. That way." Thérèse gestured farther along the hall, where the back stairs stood.

Margit darted ahead, peered down the dark steps, and gestured for them to join her. With her in the lead, they made their stealthy but slow way down. Charles half-carried Thérèse, though with every step she felt her strength returning as the stimulant gained the upper hand.

Ahead of them, Margit reached the bottom landing and stopped short. Charles pushed Thérèse behind him, instantly alerted by Margit's rigid stance. Slowly he descended the last few curving steps.

Only two sconces lit the base of the stairwell. The Chevalier de Lebouchon stepped forward, and the eerie, flickering fire of the candles danced along the blade of the sword that he pointed neatly at Margit's throat. He smiled and it was not pleasant. He spared no more than a quick glance at the two women; his cold eyes narrowed as they rested on Charles.

"Monsieur." He swept a mocking bow that did not cause the point of his sword that rested against Margit's neck to waver so much as a fraction. "Unless I am much mistaken, I at last have the pleasure of meeting—and finishing—the great *Maniganceur.*"

194

Chapter Twelve

De Lebouchon's eyes gleamed in the dim light of the candles. "Swords are so civilized a weapon, do you not agree?" He came a step forward and Margit, pressed tightly against the wall, descended the last stair. He evinced no further interest in her, for his concentration rested solely upon Charles.

It seemed that he had no intention of allowing his opponent one of the rapiers he praised so highly. He advanced another step and an unpleasant smile curled his lips. The point of his blade traced small circles in the air.

Charles bent down slowly, never taking his eyes from de Lebouchon's face. He drew a small but serviceable dagger from his boot. "Run!" He hissed the order at Margit and Thérèse.

Margit obeyed at once and slipped past de Lebouchon, who did not spare her so much as a glance. Thérèse, still dizzy, looked from one to the other, torn, wanting to stay at Charles's side, yet knowing she would only be in the way. The dangerous, deadly gleam in his eyes sent her hurrying after Margit.

If she were to help Charles, she must get him a weapon more useful than that dagger. With difficulty, Thérèse forced her wavering consciousness to focus on the problem. There had been something in the Great Hall, hanging on a wall—ancient crossed swords beneath a decorative shield!

Turning, she made her shaky way in that direction. Margit ran to her side, half-supporting her, and together they reached the hall. Thérèse leaned back against the cool stone wall, trying to gather her strength. She gestured toward the weapons and Margit went to them at once.

They hung above her reach. She jumped, batting at them with her hand, and succeeded in dislodging one sword. It swung precariously and knocked into the light metal shield with a ringing clang. Thérèse stumbled to her aid as the shield teetered and came down. She leaped sideways out of the way as it fell to the stone floor with a resounding clatter.

The point of the sword remained fastened securely to the wall. Thérèse found a heavy chair and began dragging it toward the weapon. Margit joined her, and together they positioned it so that they could reach the fastening. A wave of dizziness swept over Thérèse again and she gripped the chair and waited for it to pass, leaving Margit to scramble up and pull desperately at the sword.

A door across the hall flew open and a footman, roused by the commotion, stumbled in, clutching his head. He stopped, stared at Margit balanced precariously on the chair, and came forward in a rush. Margit freed the sword, but before she could jump to safety, the man launched himself against her.

Thérèse fought the fog that clouded her mind. She had to help the girl! Frantic, she looked about. The only movable object within reach was the shield. . . . She grabbed up the ornamental device and brought it down on the footman's head.

Margit straightened up. "*Merci*. That was very neat."

"Charles." Thérèse met her eyes. "We—we must help Charles."

With the heavy sword in her hand, Margit ran back down the corridor. The men had moved away from the stairs, out into the hall, where they had more room to maneuver. Charles still held de Lebouchon at bay—but it was not by much. With every slow, circling movement, de Lebouchon came a little closer. The dagger was far too short to prove an effective weapon against the deadly rapier.

Thérèse, still holding her shield, followed Margit as quickly as her unsteady legs would carry her. As she reached the hall, Margit tossed the sword to Charles, who caught it neatly, then turned with a broad grin of anticipation to face de Lebouchon. The fight began in earnest as he lunged forward and steel clanged and slid against steel.

Thérèse leaned against the wall, dizzy, trying to focus her blurring eyes. From down the passage toward the Great Hall, she could hear the sounds of movement. Margit stood alert, her head cocked, looking in that direction. If they didn't escape quickly, they would all be captured. Thérèse could find in herself no desire to spend any more time in the chateau.

Charles parried and thrust and de Lebouchon retreated, his back to Thérèse as he concentrated on his opponent. Charles, slowly but steadily, maneuvered him into a defensive position. But they didn't have time . . . Sticking with a device that had already proved effective, Thérèse raised the shield and brought it down with a satisfying crack.

Charles stepped back as his opponent crumpled to the floor. "Coarse." He regarded the result critically. "Your method lacks finesse, Thérèse. I intended to do it more neatly, myself."

"Blood is not neat." She threw her useful shield aside. "And you were taking too long. Me, I wish to leave. Already I have stayed in this chateau too long."

"It was a move quite superb!" Margit applauded her action.

Charles drew himself up, very much on his dignity. "Do you think I am not capable of dealing with a man like de Lebouchon? Oh, I am forgetting. You dislike 'swash-buckling derring-do,' do you not?"

"But it is no such thing! I . . ."

"But Charles, listen!" Margit interrupted. "It would not have been de Lebouchon alone that you faced!" Margit's placating explanation broke off as a loud shout reached them, followed by the rapid beat of running footsteps.

It was enough for Charles. With Margit just behind him, he ran. Thérèse stumbled behind, her legs still disconcertingly numb. As they reached a corner, Charles stopped and turned back to throw a supporting arm about her. He almost dragged her along toward the kitchens. Margit led the way down the flight of stone steps she had not long ago scrubbed, and across the pantry, then through the kitchens where the servants were just beginning to wake, and out into the cool night air.

On the other side of the wooden bridge that spanned the moat, three large, dark, shadowy figures emerged from the shrubs. Thérèse drew back in alarm, but Charles dragged her forward. She stumbled and almost fell, and he once again swept her up into his arms and held her tightly against his chest as he ran. His breath brushed her forehead, hot and rapid.

The shadows cleared and separated, becoming three mounted men, each leading a riderless horse. Margit scrambled into her saddle, but Charles, still cradling Thérèse close, knew she was too weak to stay on her mount alone. He threw her up onto his horse and swung up behind.

"Change of plans! Back to the tavern!" His deep voice rang clearly over the sounds of pursuit from the chateau.

"I thought Bosworth and I were to take mademoiselle

direct to the coast!" Althorp protested. "It's not safe to take her into Paris."

Charles urged his horse forward. "She'd never make it. She's been drugged."

Thérèse clung to him, secure in the crook of the arm that held her tight. Everything spun so crazily about her, but she was free, safe—with Charles. She snuggled closer, aware only of the warmth of his body and the lurching movements of the horse that threw her against him. The last thing she remembered was burying her cold fingers within the warm hold of his hand.

She awoke a very long time later to a headache that throbbed unbearably. Something cool and moist rested on her forehead and she reached up and moved away a damp cloth. She tried opening her eyes but the darkened room spun unsteadily.

Something yipped, over and over, disturbing her. It seemed vaguely familiar, but the explanation proved beyond her still fuddled mind. Aimée . . . the little flop-eared mongrel yipped again and scrambled up on the bed, where it nuzzled her limp hand. Aimée? Thérèse stared at the dog in disbelief. Were they in Brighton? Or was this a dream?

A boy with short dark curls turned from the table where he sat as the dog continued to yip its excitement. His face seemed vaguely familiar to Thérèse, but she could not place it. Something out of another dream . . .

"Are you better?" He rose and came to the bed to lay a hand on her forehead.

She had heard that voice before, she was sure. But where, and . . . "Who . . . ?" The question formed on her lips.

"I am Margit." The boy pulled his chair over to the bedside and sat down.

Thérèse closed her eyes as bits of hazy memory reassembled into a coherent pattern. This was no boy, but a young woman—a girl—dressed as a lad. She was in

France, and . . .

"Charles!" She sat up, then clasped a hand to her aching head. Aimée pressed anxiously against her, working herself into her mistress's arms.

"Charles is out." Margit stood. "If you will be all right, I will go and bring you some food." Without waiting for an answer, she went out the door.

Thérèse sank back against the pillows, closed her eyes, and cradled Aimée. She did not open them again until the girl returned, bearing a tray piled with food from which very tempting aromas rose. Thérèse sat up and took it eagerly.

"Eh, bien. You are better." Margit regarded the ethereal creature who lay propped against the pillows. Golden blond curls fell about her shoulders and large green eyes turned to regard her. No wonder the great *Maniganceur* went to such trouble for this one. Delicacy and grace characterized her every movement. The woman was not at all like herself. Margit experienced the oddest mixture of dislike and admiration, and realized with a sense of shock that it was jealousy.

"You helped to save me. I cannot thank you enough." Thérèse held out her hand.

Margit hesitated, then took it. Her own hands seemed so large and rough in comparison.

"Where are we?" Thérèse applied herself once more to the tray.

"At my uncle's tavern, in Paris."

Thérèse's delicately arched eyebrows flew up. "Paris?" A soft laugh escaped her. "If that is not just like *Le Maniganceur,* to take me to the one place from which I must escape!"

"You are quite safe here."

"Vraiment?" Thérèse considered and a mischievous smile twitched her lips. "But of a certainty! They will look for me to escape to the coast, not to hide in Paris itself! I am

200

quite safe! Ah, but I have been kept in one room for so long. It will be good to go out!"

"Charles will not permit it."

"I will not stay in here!"

They faced one another as each measured the other's strength of will.

"*Le Maniganceur* has given me orders to lock you in here, if necessary. We will have been seen entering the gates last night. When you are not found where they expect you to be, they will look elsewhere, and of a certainty those soldiers at the gate will remember us." Margit almost bristled in her defiance.

Aimée, who had followed Margit about every bit as willingly as she had Charles, now sensed a menace to Thérèse and set up a low growl.

Thérèse silenced her. She could see no point in irritating Margit any further. She sensed antagonism on the girl's part and could not understand it. Clearly it behooved her to move with caution until she learned what had been taking place.

A brisk knock sounded on the door. Margit went to it and, after a whispered conversation, admitted William Harding. He came quickly into the room and stopped awkwardly beside the bed. His easy color tinged his sandy complexion.

Thérèse extended her hand. "*Merci*," was all she said, but there was great sincerity and warmth in her voice.

His color darkened as he raised her fingers to his lips. "I'm glad to see you safe, ma'mselle."

"It must be due to your watchfulness. I cannot tell you how grateful I am." She set the tray aside. "But please, will you not tell me what occurred after that so vile de Lebouchon abducted me?"

Harding took Margit's vacated chair and began his story. Margit retired to a corner and sat with her arms folded, her eyes never leaving his face. She did not interrupt, but when he finished, she poured him a cup of coffee from the pot on the tray and brought it to him. He took it with a brief nod of acknowledgment.

Thérèse noted the odd strain between the two, but her mind was occupied with a more pressing matter. Harding might have glossed over one part of his story, but it was obvious that Charles had been reluctant to come to her aid. But that was to be expected. He had been defeated, ready for retirement . . . and she had done her best to insult him that night in Brighton, to make certain he did not risk himself again for her sake. . . . What had happened to make him change his mind?

She turned her attention back to the two in the room. "I must truly thank both of you. I have caused so much trouble, and you have both been so very brave." Her warm smile was genuine, and both Harding and Margit looked embarrassed. "It seems I must meet these two men, Althorp and Bosworth."

Harding grinned. "I don't see any way of avoiding it."

"And where is Charles? I must thank him as well."

"He's looking into something. Ever since we arrived in Paris, we've been hearing rumors that there's something big afoot. Once he got you safely off to the coast, he was going to come back here to learn what he could."

So he was improved in soul as well as in body! If this were so, then her danger and fear had been worthwhile. It had shaken him out of that dreadful lethargy and provided him once more with a purpose. And had it brought *Le Maniganceur*, her idol, back to life?

A thrill of excitement raced through her. Her brave, dashing, wonderful *Le Maniganceur* might not be dead, after all! At last, if only he would let her, she could come to know her hero. . . .

A light tapping sounded and as Margit stood, the door opened to admit Althorp. He hesitated on the threshold as his bright blue eyes rested on the lovely Thérèse, who had sat up in the bed. With an effort, he remembered his errand.

"There's a message come for *Le Maniganceur*, Mr. Harding." He handed over the sealed note.

Harding hesitated, turning it over as if he longed to read the contents. With firm resolution, he thrust it into his pocket. "He'll be back soon."

Charles did not, in fact, put in an appearance until lunchtime, when he strolled into Thérèse's chamber. His dark hair curled back from his forehead, glistening from the water he had used to wash off a disguise. His eyes gleamed with a suppressed excitement that sent Thérèse's wayward heart skipping in sudden nerves.

All his companions were gathered in the room, partaking of a light meal off of trays. Charles lounged against the old wooden dresser.

"Where's mine? Or do I get my own?" He looked toward Margit, who jumped up at once and hurried out to bring his meal.

Thérèse set down her fork and regarded him with what she hoped was calm speculation. His energy had returned —she could feel it, as strong and tangible as if it were a physical object. And there was the humor, glinting in his dark eyes as he exchanged a joke with Althorp. And the quick, ready smile, the deep, disturbing laugh that sent a shiver through her. That dashing aura, the thinly veiled power of his graceful, controlled movements . . . a lump welled in her throat and tears stung her eyes. Had he really come back to life, her beloved *Maniganceur,* once again perfect and worthy of adulation? Or was this naught but another delusion?

And what would he say to her? He had gone to so much trouble on her behalf, and after the dreadful things she'd said that night in Brighton! What had brought him so many weary, difficult miles? The old, irresistible lure of danger? Or her?

His enigmatic eyes met hers and there was an odd, defiant light in his expression. An empty, sinking sensation gripped in her stomach. He had come to prove her words false. It was as simple as that. She had issued a challenge and he had risen to it, nothing more.

The proud, stubborn Charles Marcombe, the romantic *Maniganceur* . . . It was disturbing to see them blended together into the same man. But this was the reality, not the impossibly perfect dream she had built about his heroic image.

Harding coughed and, as they turned to look at him, he drew the note from his pocket and handed it over. Charles ripped it open and glanced over the contents.

"It is from one of my contacts, saying there will be a masked ball tonight at the home of Colonel Mercier." A gleam of anticipation replaced the brooding expression in his eyes. "Now, it may be purely innocent, or . . ."

"Colonel Mercier! But I have met him! He came to ask me questions at the chateau!"

Charles nodded absently. "Something is afoot!" His smile of enjoyment deepened. "But what could be kept so secret that I can get no wind of it?"

"Wellington and Torres Vedras." Harding shook his head. "That's not much to go on."

Thérèse looked up. "Wellington? Do you mean their plan to have someone impersonate him?"

Charles gave a short laugh. "Would that it was that! Smoking out an impostor could prove entertaining."

Thérèse's brow wrinkled. "But they do intend this."

Charles straightened up and stared at her intently. "Do you mean that?"

"*Mais oui.* I saw this man myself, and though I have never met Viscount Wellington, I suppose the disguise must be quite perfect. Almost I was taken in by their man who looked like Lord Pembroke."

"Pembroke! Good God, Thérèse, why didn't you tell me all this?"

Her ready temper flared. "As if this were all my fault! But of a certainty, I thought the great *Maniganceur* must have learned this for himself by now."

His color darkened and his lips pressed tightly together. "And what else do you see fit to keep from us?"

"It is not that at all, Charles!" She glared back. "This is the first time I have seen you! Had you not been so busy giving me drugs, I might have remembered sooner."

"Well, think now. Why are they going to impersonate Wellington? And for how long? They can't expect it to work for any length of time." He rose and took several rapid paces about the room. "At Torres Vedras." He stared hard at Thérèse without actually seeing her. "If their man could get just one hour at Wellington's headquarters . . ."

"The maps, all of his plans . . ." Harding stared at Charles in dismay.

'Lisbon." Charles swung about to face him. "With one order, he could clear the British out of Lisbon long enough for the French to take it. And without the supply line, the Peninsula effort would fall apart!" He turned back to Thérèse. "When is this to happen? And how many men is he taking?"

She shook her head. "I do not know. They only asked me questions about Wellington, which I could not answer. And there are other officials, in England, they hope to impersonate."

Charles drew in a deep breath and exhaled slowly. "It seems our work is cut out for us." He looked at the note he still held in one hand. "I wonder if I can learn any more here?"

"Why don't we just go straight to Portugal and warn Wellington?" Althorp demanded. His eyes gleamed with enthusiasm.

"What if they've already made the switch? Or what if we're wrong? So far, this is all just a guess. I'd rather be certain."

"*En effet*, you do not believe me." Thérèse directed an

injured glare at Charles.

"I would have thought someone as experienced as you would know enough to make certain before you act. What if I go haring off to Portugal while all the while they meant to cross the channel to England with their Wellington?" He had not forgotten that squadron on the road to the coast. "I think I will attend this ball."

"Might it not be a trap?" Grudgingly, Thérèse expressed her concern.

He directed a sudden, unexpected grin at her. "There is only one way to find out."

Thérèse could not be easy. Too short a time had passed since he had been so severely injured. "I—I will go with you!" As soon as she said the words, she realized that they sprang as much from her unreasonable fear for Charles as from her own restlessness.

"Don't be absurd!" Charles turned as Margit entered and he took the tray from her. He sat down on the edge of the low dresser and began to eat.

"Absurd! It is you who are absurd. A gentleman, to arrive alone at a ball without a lady? You would be quite conspicuous!"

He set down the knife with which he had cut a generous mouthful of beef and glared at her. "Do you want to be captured again?"

"But who would ever expect me to do something like that? The search must be concentrating on the route to the coast! The center of the lion's den is undoubtedly the safest place for me."

He gave her one long, comprehensive look, then pointedly turned his back on her. "Harding, will you arrange for a carriage for me? It will not do to arrive on foot. And one for Mademoiselle de Bourgerre as well. Since she is now feeling herself again, it is time to get her back to England."

Thérèse rose from the bed. "If you will not escort me to this ball, then I shall go on my own! Me, I have seen how much trouble you can get into. Someone must be there to rescue you!"

"By hitting people over the head with shields?" He shook his head. "Your approach lacks finesse."

"It is more effective than playing with swords or guns!"

"You have made your views on that subject very well known!"

She flushed. "To me it seems you have been wounded an alarming number of times of late for so capable an agent as *Le Maniganceur.*"

Charles's brow lowered. "And each time, unless I am much mistaken, it was while rescuing you!"

"Begging your pardon, sir." Harding deemed it time to intervene. "The help of a lady at the ball is a good idea. A gentleman seeking a quiet place for dalliance with a willing female might explain your presence in unusual places if you wished to search the house."

Charles glowered at Harding, but could not deny the truth of his words. Once again, he allowed Thérèse to interfere with his normally clear thinking. Her presence would be an obvious asset—but it galled him to have to admit she was right.

They set about preparations at once with an efficiency that startled Thérèse. How Charles managed to obtain suitable clothing for them both remained a mystery to her, but the ballgown Margit carried up a short time later was magnificent. She lifted the confection of delicate sky-blue silk from the bandbox and held it up against herself. It would need careful alterations to fit her petite frame, but the result would be stunning. And for her role of "willing female," as Harding had phrased it, it would be perfect. Any man could be pardoned for leading away a lady gowned in this alluring creation. Under no circumstances would she cover it with a domino.

When the dress had been taken in to her satisfaction, she and Margit turned their attention to her hair. It was not to be expected that anyone would be looking for her in Paris, but the blond curls must be hidden. Margit hurried away and did not return until shortly before they were due to depart. With her she brought a dark brown wig and some of Charles's paints and cosmetics. She went to work on Thérèse's eyebrows and lashes, and by the time they were done, no one would have suspected that Thérèse was not naturally a brunette. Next, they removed a loo mask from its stick and fitted it with string so that it could be tied, rather than held.

Pleased with the result, Thérèse wrapped herself in a cloak and went down the stairs to where Charles awaited her. He took her arm without comment and hurried her out the back to where Harding, dressed as a coachman, sat on the box of a barouche.

The short drive passed in a silence fraught with tension. Charles made no attempt to hide his displeasure at having her company foisted onto him. The knowledge that it was for the best—in spite of the danger to her—only served to worsen his temper, and he sought refuge in stony silence. Fortunately for Thérèse's growing nerves, they soon pulled up before Colonel Mercier's house.

They were met at the door by a footman and Charles produced a phony invitation. They were admitted without question. In the hall Thérèse untied the strings of her cloak and allowed it to fall into a lackey's hands, revealing her sparkling blue gown.

Charles's eyes narrowed as they rested on her full curves revealed by the clinging materials. An arrested gleam lit their dark brown depths, and it was a moment before he spoke. "At least no one will be surprised if we are seen slipping off into a quiet corner."

Thérèse's breath came more quickly. His words might be designed for the sole purpose of getting her back up, but there could be no mistaking the waves of awareness that almost shimmered through the air between them. Against her will, she felt herself drawn toward him as his smoldering gaze held hers, robbing her of all conscious thought or will.

He blinked and looked down, breaking the spell. He stepped back, his expression now sardonic. "You look every inch a *demimonde*."

Thérèse flushed, floundering from the abrupt withdrawal of the tangible emotions that had wrapped about her a moment before. "You—you selected the gown, if you will remember." She made an admirable recovery. "I must suppose your experience in that field to be greater than mine."

"I suppose it is." An unexpected half-smile lit his dark eyes. "My poor Thérèse. In spite of all your training and experience, you are really quite a little *innocente*, are you not?"

Warm color flooded her cheeks and his soft laugh of amusement at her embarrassment filled her with an exciting tingling sensation. His gaze lingered on her a moment longer before he turned away to look about the hall.

Remembering their danger, she adopted the role of clinging female and draped herself on his arm. The sensations this roused in her were disturbing in the extreme. There were tensions between them of unsettled insults and arguments. Yet there was also an attraction that was undeniable in its strength and bore no resemblance whatsoever to the worship she had felt for *Le Maniganceur*.

But now was not the time to indulge in exploring the possibilities! If she did not want to end the evening once more in French custody, she had best concentrate on the job they had come to do. Still clinging to Charles's arm, she strolled with him into the ballroom where they blended easily into the milling guests.

The orchestra struck up the opening notes of a quadrille and a man appeared before them. Bowing to Charles, he turned to Thérèse and requested the honor of the dance. His eyes roamed over her with apparent relish, and when he raised them to her face, his look spoke volumes.

She took the man's arm and threw a saucy glance over her shoulder at Charles. It would only help their charade if she established herself as an outrageous flirt. With very little effort, she soon had the man laughing and murmuring shockingly fulsome compliments and hints into her ear whenever the movements of the dance brought them close together.

As the music ended, she drew away and dismissed her admirer with a coquettish wave of her fan. She had to find Charles. . . . She spotted him across the room, making himself very agreeable to a shapely young lady. A wave of irritation swept over her, startling and unwelcome. Mastering it, she strolled over and dangled her fan invitingly toward him with such a come-hither look in her lovely green eyes that anyone could have excused him for deserting his companion and joining her.

"We are wasting time," she murmured as she fluttered the fan before her face as if to hide her blushes. A trilling laugh accompanied the words. "Or can you not resist a well-turned ankle?"

"I wish you hadn't come!" Even hushed and disguised by a smile, his tone was sharp.

"*Voyons*, you have made that very clear. But do not let me stop you from flirting." She peeped out from behind her fan, her eyes burning with her confused emotions. "I would hate to spoil your so delightful evening with work."

"Has anyone ever offered to wring your neck?" The smile that accompanied the words was dazzling.

She shook her head and gave him a not very playful rap across the knuckles with her useful fan. The orchestra struck up a waltz and Charles swept her onto the floor and into his arms. He pressed her slight body tightly against himself and she felt her heart beating fast and light at the contact. Never before had they danced, and she found the experience unsettling.

"*Mon cher* Charles." She fluttered her long lashes up at him. "I am surprised you did not leave me to the French. No one forced you to rescue me."

He drew the hand that he held in his to his lips and planted a kiss on her wrist. "*Le Maniganceur* must always do the unexpected. And you so obviously expected that I was now useless."

"But I did not—" She broke off. It *was* his pride that lay behind his antagonism. But she needed to anger him that night in Brighton, at whatever cost to herself. Yet her purpose had failed. He had become involved in the dangerous work once more anyway, and because of her. . . . She became aware of his fingers about her wrist in a painful grip.

"What 'did you not'? Did you mean to insult me further, though I did not give you the chance? Pray, don't hesitate to indulge yourself now to your heart's delight!"

"But that was not my intention!" she exclaimed, goaded by the hurt he could not disguise in his voice. "My words, I did not mean them!"

"No? You read your lines most convincingly, then."

She looked up into his angry eyes and knew she had to tell him the truth. "What I said, it was to make you go away!" Her voice, though soft, was vehement. "Already you had done too much for me. You risked your life before and I could not bear for you to do so again, when you were not yet recovered. And I had promised. . . ." She broke off once more, aghast that she had almost betrayed Sir Roderick's role in her decision to free Charles from any sense of obligation or duty to her.

"What did you promise? Or should I rather ask 'whom'?"

She could feel his tension as he nuzzled the hair

211

behind her ear with his lips. Wild, unfamiliar sensations danced through her and she fought to keep them under control. "Only myself. That I would not cause you any more suffering."

"And what of my pride? The damnable Marcombe pride." A hollow laugh escaped him. With her hand still captive in his, he brought it up to her chin and tilted her head so that he could look fully into her eyes. "It was my grandfather, was it not, who ordered you to leave Ranleigh and have nothing more to do with me? No, don't deny it . . . he all but gave himself away before I left."

"Do not be angry with him." Her fingers clutched his.

"No, how can I be? He meant it for the best. But you!" An odd expression clouded his eyes. "I thought you knew me better than that. *Le Maniganceur,* to live without excitement and danger? It would be a living death! And I very nearly succumbed to it."

"But I do *not* know you!" The words came out as a desperate cry. "I thought I did, but . . ."

His arm tightened about her waist as they continued to spin about the room. "You had only met one side of me, and one of my best disguises at that. Did the reality confuse you?"

She nodded, unable to speak.

"My poor Thérèse. It confused me as well. I think I forgot during those days in France that I was also Charles Marcombe. Perhaps we must both come to know me."

The music ended and he led her from the floor. She risked a glance up into his face and encountered a look she could not fathom. Disturbed, she glanced away and tried to concentrate on their job.

"Where do you think we should begin?"

"Have you seen anyone you recognize?" He bent down to whisper in her ear, which was at about the level of his shoulder.

She cast a casual glance about the room. *"Non.* I see no

one. *Hélas,* but everyone, they are in costume."

"Then shall we explore a little?" He gave her a slight nudge.

She broke away from him and tripped merrily from the floor, casting a coquettish glance back over her shoulder. He set off in instant pursuit. With a carefully ill-bred shriek of delight, Thérèse hurried on, weaving her way through the crowded rooms to the hilarious delight of the people she pushed past. Clear of the main assembly rooms, she headed down a hall, peeking into doorways, startled by what she observed in more than one of them. She and Charles were not the only couple bent on dalliance, she discovered. That made their subterfuge all the more convincing. Charles, laughing and calling enticements to her, took the opportunity of memorizing the layout of the rooms.

As they neared the main hall once again, a late arrival came in through the front door and handed his cape to the footman. De Lebouchon. A second footman hurried forward, bowed low, and led him up the stairs to another floor.

Thérèse waited a moment. Then, with another high-pitched giggle, she followed. Halfway up the stairs she turned, fluttered her fan at Charles, then ran ahead. As she reached the top step, the footman bowed de Lebouchon into a room partway along the hall. The lackey came back and passed her without so much as a glance and returned to his post in the hall.

Thérèse wasted no time. She darted into the room next to the one de Lebouchon had entered. Charles was behind her in a moment. A connecting door stood in the middle of the wall and Charles went to it and placed his ear against the keyhole. Thérèse hovered near.

"Mademoiselle de Bourgerre has escaped." De Lebouchon's deep voice reached them, muffled but distinct.

"Recapture her." An unknown man's voice gave the

sharp command.

A slight pause followed before de Lebouchon spoke again. His tone held a hint of apology. "She was not found anywhere on the roads leading to the coast."

"It is possible she is still in Paris."

"But that is madness!" De Lebouchon objected.

"Nevertheless. How much of our plan did you permit her to learn?"

"She saw du Lac and Brienne."

The other man swore. "She must not be allowed to warn the British. Place guards on every gate from the city and keep them there until she is captured."

"And there is *Le Maniganceur* to be dealt with." De Lebouchon's casual tone did not hide his hatred.

"Yes," the other man agreed. "It was quite clumsy of you to permit them both to escape. They must not leave Paris, if they are here."

"And Brienne?"

"He must depart for Torres Vedras at once. You will accompany him to the edge of the fortifications, then send him in alone. You know where to take your troops to wait. Lisbon should be ours within the month."

With that, the conference appeared to be over. The sounds of chairs sliding back reached them and Charles rose quickly from where he knelt. He cast a quick glance about the room, grabbed Thérèse's wrist, and pulled her over to a sofa. Before she could protest, he thrust her down and dropped on top of her with a force that drove the breath from her lungs. Gathering her into his arms, he proceeded to kiss her until she clung to him in earnest.

A clicking of the door to the hall was her only warning. She jumped, but beneath Charles's weight she could not move. Trembling, she kept her eyes closed.

"*Pardonnez-moi.* It would appear that I intrude." De Lebouchon's smooth voice sounded alarmingly near.

Chapter Thirteen

Thérèse stiffened and her hands gripped the velvet of Charles's coat. De Lebouchon . . . She drew in a deep, shaky breath. She must not panic! She must not give them away! He wasn't looking for her—he would have no reason to think she might even be here! She must stay calm. . . . She had faced danger before, many times. And this time she had *Le Maniganceur*. The thought gave her courage. She moved her head and peered out.

"Mon amour, we have company." She accompanied the husky words with a deep giggle, a tone not normally her own.

Charles gave an exasperated sigh and straightened up enough to look over his shoulder. "Be a good fellow and take yourself off." His French was flawless.

De Lebouchon studied them closely, then swept a magnificent bow. "Forgive me. Not for the world would I disturb so enjoyable an occupation."

He left them and Thérèse let out the breath she had not realized she held. Charles sat up and stared at the closed door in disbelief.

"It worked!" He shook his head. "I didn't really think it would."

Thérèse pulled herself up beside him and tried to

straighten her disheveled gown. "Has—has it?" she whispered. "Did he really leave?"

Charles crossed the room and bent down to listen at the keyhole; from the deep pocket of his coat he drew a pistol. Pulling the door open, he looked quickly about the hall: no one was there. He closed the door again and turned back to Thérèse.

"If only all our adventures proved so easy."

"*Tiens,* we have not yet escaped from this house. Or is there more that you wish to learn?"

He shook his head. "I think we heard enough." He returned to the sofa. "They are going to leave at once with this impostor of theirs. Brienne." He said the name slowly, committing it to memory. "Now, I have only to get you off my hands and I'll be free to act." Lost in thought, he stared with unseeing eyes at a large ruby ring that he wore on his middle finger.

Thérèse rose to her feet, feeling very much as if he'd slapped her. Chagrin and anger mingled within her. He had the insolence to kiss her as if she were some—some *fille de joie,* then casually speak of getting rid of her! Her slight body stiffened and a fire blazed in her large green eyes.

Charles went once more to the door, peered out, and signaled for her to join him. Bracing herself to do her job and put her personal feelings aside, she complied. He slipped one arm about her and led her out into the corridor. She went with him, enduring his embrace for the sake of their safety, but her mind seethed with indignation.

On the stairs he gave her a quick squeeze. "What's wrong? Did de Lebouchon frighten you?" His mouth brushed her ear, sending an unsettling response fluttering through her.

"Do you think I am afraid of that one?" She turned her injured gaze on him.

"Well, something has put you out of temper. Remember

216

your act or we'll be ruined."

Biting back an angry denial, she leaned against him in an amorous pose and grasped his lapel.

"That's better. Shall we go?"

Slowly, and with an occasional stop for a lingering kiss that left Thérèse disturbed and shaken, they made their way down to the hall, where Charles sent for the carriage. While they waited, he drew Thérèse back into his arms and proceeded to nuzzle her neck in a manner that left her weak and yielding, in spite of the knowledge that it was all an act. Fortunately for her equilibrium, Harding brought the barouche around in a very short time.

As soon as the coach moved forward with them inside, Charles dropped both her hand and his pretenses. She took the opportunity to slide to the farthest corner of the seat. He made no protest and she stared blindly out the window, willing her erratic senses to behave themselves. Charles was far too dangerous to allow them free rein in his vicinity!

"I should have gotten you to the coast at once!" Charles's sharp voice broke the silence.

"It was what they expected. The chances are very good we would have been caught."

"Not on the route I had planned!"

"Let it be a lesson, *enfin*, to be more careful who you drug." The warmth of his embrace and the coolness of his heart still rankled.

"If you like, I'll take you straight back to the chateau!" Tension brought an edge to his words. "Now I'll have to find some way to smuggle you out of Paris."

"*Hélas*, you do not have to do anything with me. You freed me from that chateau, *bien sûr*, but now I shall go to England on my own. You need have no worries for me."

"That's all I ever seem to have!" He glared at her, exasperated. "Perhaps I should just leave you in hiding at the tavern for a few months, until the search blows over.

I've planned enough escapes for you of late. I don't have time for another right now. I've got this Torres Vedras affair to work out."

"I did not ask you to bring me to Paris!" She flushed. "Nor to be drugged in that hateful manner! It is all your own fault!"

"Well, how else did you expect me to search that place for you? Ask permission? You're damned lucky you're not still there!"

She hunched her shoulders. "This gets us nowhere. What is our next move?"

"You are doing nothing. For once, you are simply going to stay out of trouble."

It was his turn to glower out the window. Not for the world would his pride permit him to admit it to Thérèse, but he was torn over his conflicting duties and his next course of action. He no longer felt safe entrusting her to Harding and his men. Now that the gates of Paris would be watched for her, getting her out of the city would be tricky. But neither did he want to just leave her at the tavern, where at any moment she might be discovered. He had few doubts that if the French found her again, she would be killed out of hand. She was no longer of any use to them and she knew—or could guess—too much of their plan.

But he didn't have time to take her to England himself. His first duty must be to get word to Wellington about the impersonation plot, which was already being put into action. And if he were not there before the French . . . The impostor—Brienne—would need no more than an hour to implement almost any scheme the French had concocted, to the ruination of the British endeavors in the Peninsula. There was only one way to ensure that a warning reached Wellington in time. He must go to Torres Vedras himself—and at once.

When they pulled up in back of the tavern, Charles

ordered Harding to turn the coach over to the ostlers, collect his cohorts, and bring them up for a conference. In a surprisingly short time, they all gathered in Charles's room in varying stages of eagerness to hear what had been learned at the ball. Thérèse retired to a corner where she sat huddled in her cloak with Aimée curled at her feet. As soon as they settled down, Charles informed them of his intentions.

For perhaps thirty seconds after he finished, no one said a word. At last Harding nodded. "I'll go with you."

Althorp grinned, glad that they would be taking part in so hazardous a plan. "So will I." He looked to Bosworth, who leaned back in his chair, staring in ruminative silence into the fire.

The man shrugged with fatalistic calm. "Why not?" he agreed. "We'll all go."

"Yes." Thérèse looked up and met Charles's fulminating gaze. "We will all go."

"No!" he exploded. "You've caused me enough trouble! You are staying right here, with Margit to watch over you."

"But that is not possible!" Margit, her arms folded, regarded him with placid determination. "Quant à moi, I, too, am going."

The unexpected support buoyed Thérèse's determination and she faced Charles with more confidence than she felt. "To remain in Paris is not safe, with these men looking for me. To go with you will be as good as any other plan."

"It's going to be a long, uncomfortable and difficult journey! For God's sake, be reasonable for once! It's no place for women! I'll have to travel fast to reach Torres Vedras before the French, and I won't have time to coddle you along." His glare took in both of them. "I won't have women on a trip like this!"

Thérèse, her expression mulish, met his eyes. "Eh, bien.

219

Then we follow. Though it seems to me very foolish that we should not travel together."

"You'd do it, wouldn't you? You are without doubt the most exasperating female I've ever had to deal with!" A reluctant grin suddenly lightened his grim expression and a touch of warmth crept into his dark eyes. "You're prepared to take on anything. Is there no way of making you see sense?"

"None."

He shook his head. "What a motley band we are! Very well. Torres Vedras it is. For all of us."

Harding folded his arms. "There's still one problem, sir. How are we to get ma'mselle out of Paris?"

Charles stroked his chin. "We'll have to provide a decoy." His eyes strayed to Margit.

She pursed her lips and looked at Thérèse. "We are much of a height." Her dubious gaze rested on the other's petite frame and ivory complexion. A blond wig and a free hand with the cosmetics could alter her own swarthy coloring to do the trick, but nothing could disguise her sturdy build in imitation of Thérèse's delicate fragility. Still, she was not one to give up easily.

"I will do it. *Cela va sans dire. Le Maniganceur* is not the only one who is adept at disguises."

"But it might not be safe!" Thérèse looked from one to the other, alarmed for Margit's sake by her obvious intention of impersonating her.

Margit shrugged. "Charles will devise a plan."

All eyes turned to him in expectation.

He turned his frowning scrutiny on Margit. "The disguise will be penetrated quickly enough," he said at length. "So you must have a plausible excuse for trying to alter your appearance."

"An elopement?" Thérèse suggested.

Margit laughed. "But of course! I shall elope with Monsieur Althorp, and my enraged Papa shall chase after

220

us!" She turned to Harding. "You can play the role of an outraged parent, *hein?*"

Harding straightened up, almost sputtering. "It would take some disguise to make me look like the father of as bold a piece as you!"

"Mais non. It will not serve." Thérèse shook her head firmly. "Once your papa has caught up with you, he would be expected to return you to Paris, not accompany you on your flight."

"Your brother, then!" Charles grinned at Harding's glowering stance. "And Margit can insist on you escorting them to your father's house outside of Paris to let him decide on the marriage."

"C'est magnifique!" Thérèse nodded in vigorous approval. "And Monsieur Bosworth?"

"You don't speak much French, do you?" Charles regarded the stolid individual and deep lines creased his brow. "You'll have to be their coachman. Just leave the talking to Margit and Althorp."

Harding shifted in his chair. "This is all very well, but how are we to get ma'mselle herself away?"

Charles's eyes twinkled with suppressed merriment. "She will be Margit, of course. We will drive out with a gypsy wagon."

"I thought you said it was dangerous to be a gypsy," Althorp protested.

"That's the beauty of the plan. No one will bother gypsies leaving Paris—only those entering. And no one would expect her to adopt a disguise that is bound to draw the attention of soldiers!"

"My cousins will help! They are jugglers!" Margit joined in the scheme with enthusiasm.

Charles nodded. "I'd already thought of them. If they'll ride with us, they'll make a perfect cover. Now, we'll need to obtain some supplies for the journey. Thérèse and I can purchase some at the morning markets, but we'll have to ransack the tavern for most of the things we'll need. Once we're all away from the city, we'll meet up and exchange the carriage and wagon for riding horses.''

''We'll need pack animals?'' Harding drew a notebook from his pocket and began to make rapid entries.

''A couple. We'll be conspicuous enough as it is. We'll have to stay clear of the roads, and it won't be easy to stop and buy food.''

Together, they created a list of things they would need for their headlong flight across enemy-infested territory. Each took part of the list and went off to procure what he could. Thérèse, unable to leave the tavern, was forced to wait.

As she trailed the others down the stairs and watched them depart, she had a deep sense of foreboding. What if Margit and Harding did not succeed? What if her own disguise was not good enough? This time, she was not the only one in danger. Charles—and the others—stood to be captured as well.

But Charles—*Le Maniganceur*—would bring the thing off. Just seeing him filled her with supreme confidence. She could only be glad for his devil-may-care attitude in the face of danger. Without it, she would still be in that chateau. She was grateful to him no matter how irritated she also became.

She handed Aimée to the tap keeper, who summoned an underling to take the little dog for a walk. The hour was late and few people remained at the tables. Thérèse made her way into the common room, which was empty, and sat down in a corner near the great hearth to wait. With unseeing eyes she stared into the glowing coals as the flames burned low.

She must be losing her taste for adventure. She had been quite eager, so many years ago, when she offered to spy for the British. And she had enjoyed the danger and challenge. Even during her weeks of hiding in England, she had chafed at the inactivity and had longed to return to her work. But now . . . The thrill of it had given way to nerves. She no longer saw romantic adventure, but grim reality.

Behind her, nailed boots brushed across the wooden floor and she spun about, startled. Charles stopped several feet from her, then came forward with the spring in his walk under careful control. Energy radiated from him.

"I have passed on your warning for Lord Pembroke and the other officials at Whitehall."

"*Vraiment?* Your methods, they amaze me." She looked away, vexed by the answering shiver that raced through her, leaving her nerves alive and ready for she knew not what. "Was it so easy, then, to send word to London?"

"There are ways." His lips twisted into a rueful smile. "I only wish it was so easy to warn Wellington."

"So do I."

"No one is forcing you to go," he reminded her.

She shrugged. "It is better than staying here. And to go to London . . . *Non!* It is far worse, by far, not to know what occurs."

He regarded her through narrowed eyes. "Why aren't you sleeping in a comfortable bed while you still have the chance?"

"I wait for Aimée."

He seated himself on the settle at her side and stared into the hearth. "I must be crazy, agreeing to take that damned fool dog with me across France and Spain."

"If you feel like that, why did you bring her in the first place?" She forced her temper to rise, falling back on the anger which formed her only defense against his nearness. He had made it all too clear that her presence only complicated his work.

"She brought herself." Charles turned his brooding gaze on Thérèse. "Just like a female, to thrust herself in where she is not wanted and will only be in the way."

"Then why did you come after me at all?" She gripped her hands together until they hurt.

A slow smile softened his expression as if he laughed at an inner joke. "Force of habit, I suppose. It's become a challenge to see how many times I can rescue you."

She stiffened. "I shall try not to put you to the trouble again."

"Oh, no trouble." A curious note entered his voice. He reached for a poker and stirred the embers of the fire back to flame. "But so far it has proved a rather thankless job."

His dark eyes seemed to burn as they rested on her, tantalizing, compelling—and infinitely enigmatic. She hesitated, unsure of his mood, unsure of whether he offered a truce or something more—the beginnings of friendship. She looked down, willing her erratic pulse to stop behaving in so ridiculous a manner.

"I thanked you the first time, *enfin*, and if I have not had the opportunity again, then I shall do so now. This tavern, it is a place much nicer than the chateau."

"So very formal. Have I angered you?"

"*Voyons!* We do little else with each other," came her candid answer.

He chuckled—a deep, enticing sound that sent a tremor through her. She turned to stare into the fire. Her heart seemed to behave in the same erratic pattern as the leaping flames.

"But I do so enjoy arguing with you," he murmured provocatively.

"*Vraiment?* Is this why you insult me whenever you can?"

"Insult you?" His brow snapped down. "When have I done that?"

"You have said—oh, often!—that you wished to be—to be rid of me." It hurt to say the words.

"I only meant that I would rather have you safe." He took her hand in his and gave it a comforting squeeze. "This

224

is not a job for a woman."

"It is not a job for anyone, *bien sûr*. But someone must do it."

"Duty?" He made the word a joke, but a serious note lurked just beneath the surface.

She shook her head. "It is more than that. Sometimes, *du vrai*, it is life itself. But then . . ."

"But then you see the other side? The defeat, the death?"

She nodded. "It is more than the game I used to think it. And, *quant à moi*, it is no longer only my own life that is at stake. If something goes wrong . . . Before, it did not seem so possible. But now . . . ! *Voyons*, but I have been captured not once but twice!"

"It shakes your confidence, doesn't it? The invincible agent discovers he has an Achilles heel."

She looked up and saw the self-mockery in his expression. "Perhaps it is time that we rediscovered our strengths instead of concentrating on these weaknesses."

"Perhaps it is."

He held out his hand, and after a moment's hesitation, she took it. His fingers closed firmly about hers in a warm clasp. He released her almost at once and stood.

"*Bonne nuit, mademoiselle*. I think we had best try and get some sleep. This may well prove to be a very difficult journey in many respects."

Thérèse watched his retreating figure until he disappeared in the shadows of the stairwell. What had he meant by that last comment? That they were like to be at loggerheads at every turn? It seemed very probable to her as well. She rose and went in restless search of Aimée.

It seemed to her as if she had barely drifted off to sleep when a brisk tapping on her door roused her. She opened sleepy eyes to see her room still plunged in darkness. Aimée, with a series of excited yips that indicated she knew who was without, danced playfully up to the door. Thérèse climbed from bed, drew on a dressing gown, and went to admit her visitor.

Margit entered bearing a colorful dress, a black wig, and a box containing a selection from Charles's case of theatrical makeup. "We leave within the hour," she warned, then returned to her room to don her own disguise.

Thérèse removed her nightdress, then eyed the selection of bottles with a certain amount of trepidation. Her hands shook as she picked up the cotton wool and bottle of brown liquid. Dabbing up a generous amount, she set to work staining the skin of her upper body. At last she stood back and examined herself in the cracked mirror. The result—at least by candlelight—was all she could wish. Not a trace of pale skin showed at the revealing bodice of the low-cut gown provided by Margit.

A soft tap sounded on the door as the girl returned. They eyed each other, and in spite of her fears, Thérèse smiled.

"But you look *merveilleuse*."

She hardly recognized Margit with her creamy complexion and golden ringlets hanging about her shoulders. Her gown, simple yet respectable, was a far cry from the tattered affair she'd worn in the tavern. She could be surprisingly pretty, Thérèse realized. Yet a careful scrutiny would reveal the paint and wig. Thérèse could only hope for her sake that the illusion would suffice long enough.

Margit nodded slowly as she walked around Thérèse, examining the disguise from all sides. "The soldiers, they will look at you, but they will not be seeing a British spy. Be bold and try to attract their attention."

Thérèse managed a wan smile. "I have had much experience with acting. But you? Are you sure you will be safe?"

She shrugged. "It is not a crime to dress up in pretty clothes. And *peste*, we want them to see through this paint."

226

Still, Thérèse could not be easy. The girl almost welcomed the danger, but if anything went wrong, Thérèse would not be able to forgive herself. They all took too many risks, believing—as she once had—that nothing could go wrong.

Ready at last, they descended the stairs to the back hall. Aimée danced at their feet, sensing their uneasy excitement. The men were there ahead of them, and it was obvious that they had been busy. Althorp and Bosworth carried the last of their supplies out to the waiting vehicles and Harding and Charles stood in a corner in low-voiced conversation. As the little mongrel bounded up to them, Charles turned.

Thérèse swallowed. At all times he was handsome in a dashing, rugged sort of way; in this costume of gypsy disguised as peasant, he was breathtaking. The billowing loose sleeves of his white shirt and the wide, colorful belt knotted about his waist suited him to perfection.

He subjected her to a close scrutiny and a sudden gleam lit his eyes as his gaze rested on the revealing décolletage. Much to her embarrassment, he nodded his approval.

"Let's get started." He led the way to the door.

It opened abruptly and two strange men came in, dressed in a similar manner to Charles. Margit gave a soft cry of delight, pushed forward, and embraced each in turn.

The taller of the men swung her off her feet while the other contented himself with planting a kiss on her cheek. Taking a hand of each of her cousins, she led them from the tavern.

Thérèse followed. In the dark street she could make out the outline of a job coach and crude wagon. In the back of the latter, several boxes and bundles were stacked in a haphazard manner. Everything, it seemed, was in readiness. Everything, that was, except her courage.

Charles came up behind her and she almost jumped. He

gave her an encouraging smile and handed her up onto the seat of the wagon. If only she could share his laughing confidence!

"We're off to market." Charles turned to address the others. "Wait about half an hour, then head for the southern gate."

Margit's cousins jumped up into the back of the wagon, picked up several colorful leather balls, and began to juggle. Thérèse swiveled about in her seat to watch, fascinated. They grinned at her and began to toss the balls back and forth between them.

"Pay them no attention!"

Charles's sharp order startled her and she looked at him in surprise. "But why not? They are so very good."

"You act as if you have never seen it before. By now you should have seen it so often that it bores you."

Chastened, Thérèse concentrated on the horse pulling their cart. There had been tension in Charles's voice and it frightened her, reminding her how much was at stake. She could not afford to forget her role for a moment.

They made their way through the nearly empty streets until they reached one crowded with carts, produce, and every conceivable ware. Charles tossed the reins to her, picked up a basket, and jumped down. Within moments he disappeared among the milling crowd.

Margit's cousins stood, still juggling, and climbed down to the street. They made their way to the outskirts of the market, where they kept up their act and drew a considerable amount of attention. It made Thérèse uneasy.

The minutes passed slowly and her stomach was in knots. Soldiers strolled among the shoppers and two stopped to watch the jugglers. One walked by her, casting a casual glance at the boxes in the back. He returned to the crowd and Thérèse could breathe again.

Finally, when she thought her nerves had passed the

breaking point, Charles returned. Two blankets hung over his arm and his basket overflowed with bread, cheese, and fruit. From one corner protruded several cooking utensils. They had been unable to borrow any the night before. Throwing their new acquisitions into the back of the wagon, he climbed onto the seat and took the reins from Thérèse. As he started the old horse forward, the jugglers jumped into the back, never missing so much as a single toss.

"You took forever." Thérèse sank back on the hard wooden seat and closed her eyes.

"Did you want me to rush? That would be the surest way to attract attention."

She bit back her retort. They were both on edge and angry words came far too easily to them both these days. Bickering would do no good, for now, if ever, they must work as a team.

They turned a corner and started for the gate that would lead them south from the city. From behind them came sounds of commotion, and a loud voice shouted, ordering them to stop. Thérèse peered over her shoulder and saw an officer with several mounted men giving chase.

"Halt!" The order was repeated.

Charles, his expression grim, urged the horse forward. But the streets were now filled with milling people who impeded their progress. Thérèse gripped the edges of her seat, trying to see a way through the growing crowds. They could force the horse faster—but how many people might be hurt by their wagon?

The soldiers drew closer, and for a third time the officer shouted the command to stop. Thérèse, her eyes wide with fear, looked frantically about for a way to escape. Should they jump from the cart and try to disappear in the maze of buildings and streets? But the French troops were so very near. . . .

To her horror, Charles pulled the horse to a stop. The

soldiers surrounded them, one going to the cob's head and two more dragging the jugglers from the wagon. Another grabbed Charles, and a fifth pulled Thérèse from her seat. They subjected the men to a rapid but thorough search, while the young officer, holding Thérèse by the shoulder, eyed her with a certain dubious embarrassment.

"What is the meaning of this?" Charles squared his shoulders and faced the officer with swaggering defiance.

"A gentleman's watch was stolen in the market."

"And why chase us?"

The officer's lip curled. "Gypsies are always thieves. And don't try to tell me you lot don't have gypsy blood!"

"Maybe a little, and many generations ago!" Charles's manner became conciliatory. "But we are innocent. The woman was in the cart the whole time, and my cousins juggled to entertain the crowd!"

"And you?"

"I was engaged in honest purchases. We are leaving Paris, as you can see. There were things we needed."

"You will be taken to the authorities for questioning. If what you say is true, you will be allowed to leave."

Taken to the authorities, searched, her disguise uncovered . . . An almost hysterical desire to laugh welled within Thérèse. After all their effort, they had been captured after all—but for the wrong reason!

Chapter Fourteen

Margit sat in the dilapidated traveling carriage, clutching Althorp's hand for courage. They plodded slowly through the crowded streets as Bosworth, inexperienced on the box, fumbled with the ribbons. What if they were discovered too soon? Or what if they were too late, delayed by Bosworth's ineptness? But there was not much farther to go. The gate—and the soldiers guarding it—were just ahead. Not much farther, now . . . A tiny drop of blood formed on her lip where her teeth bit it. She didn't even notice.

"Don't worry so much, Mademoiselle Margit. All will go well. It's *Le Maniganceur*'s plan." Althorp gave her hand a comforting pat.

Had she been less nervous, Margit might almost have smiled at this blind faith in their leader. But she knew how he felt. She had been involved in many such escapades before, and she infinitely preferred it when Charles was in charge. So what made this one different? Why did she lack confidence in herself? Surely not even that man Harding could blame *her* if something went wrong!

She glanced across at the pile of valises and bandboxes that were stacked on the seat opposite. "Poor little Aimée. *Peste*, do you think she is all right?" She raised her large, anxious brown eyes to look at Althorp.

"What could be wrong? Mr. Harding didn't give her very much of the drug. She'll sleep comfortably enough in that case until we're safe out of Paris. And there are holes so she can get air to breathe. As soon as we're away from the city, we can let her free."

Margit nodded, only partially reassured. Still, it was pleasant to hear supporting words rather than a command not to be such a fool, as her uncle often issued. It felt strange to have a man showing her every consideration, treating her with respect—almost as if she were important!

It must be her gown. If she were not quaking so badly in fright, she would relish wearing such a lovely dress. Few opportunities had come her way to wear anything other than the much-patched attire of a tavern wench. To dress—and be treated—as a lady was a new experience.

In all truth, she enjoyed it. Now, if only Harding might have succumbed to such an urge . . . but that was not likely. To him, she was nothing more than a gypsy serving girl, not a woman at all.

The carriage slowed further and she swallowed the lump that threatened to block her throat. All would go well . . . it had to! Althorp's grip tightened on her hand and she turned to look up into his handsome face. He forced a grin, a rather pathetic attempt which warned her that he was as nervous as she.

"Time for our act," he whispered.

The vehicle drew to a stop, the door was pulled open, and a soldier stuck his head inside. His eyes opened wide and his mouth dropped open as he took in Margit's small stature and blond curls.

"Oh, please, *monsieur,* you must not slow us down!" She gripped Althorp's arm in very real agitation as she turned her anxious gaze on the soldier.

"And where would you be going in such a hurry, *mademoiselle?*" A gleam of triumph lit his eager eyes at her obvious fright.

"We must not delay!" She looked beyond the soldier, then leaned across Althorp to peer out the other window, back the way they had come.

The soldier grinned. Without moving away from the door or taking his eyes from Margit, he signaled for his companion.

Another soldier hurried forward. "Is this her?" Eager yet disbelieving, he peered into the dark interior of the carriage, anxious to get a glimpse of their quarry.

The first soldier nodded, his grin broadening as Margit huddled against Althorp, her eyes wide with apprehension. He turned to Bosworth. "You. Come down from the box."

The meaning of this utterance was clear to Bosworth, even with his limited knowledge of French. With stolid indifference he knotted the reins and hooked them over a rod, then climbed down with slow, deliberate movements. Nothing in his demeanor indicated that he had more than a mild interest in what took place.

"And now, *mademoiselle*, you will get out, if you please."

"No! Oh, let us go, please!" She turned wild eyes to Althorp, who put a protective arm about her.

The soldier beamed in growing glee, convinced now that to him would go the honor—and reward—of capturing Thérèse de Bourgerre. He gestured to his comrade, who unhooked a horn from his belt and blew a resounding blast that carried far over the bustling noise of the great city.

Thérèse and Charles, less than a block away, heard it—and so did the officer and his men. The officer tensed, alert at once, almost incredulous. Leaving one man to guard the troupe of supposed gypsies, he signaled the others to come with him instantly. Swinging up onto their horses, they dashed for the gate while the hapless crowd in their path dived for safety.

Charles did not waste a minute. Their solitary guard stared after his departing comrades, bemused. Charles caught him neatly under the chin with a well-placed fist and the man crumpled, unconscious. Before he hit the ground, the jugglers caught him and deposited his body discreetly to one side of the road. Charles assisted Thérèse back into the wagon and they drove on—after the soldiers.

They rounded a corner and were forced to halt almost at once. Ahead of them a motley assortment of vehicles, riders, and pedestrians formed a rambling blockade, waiting their chance to pass through the gate, which itself was blocked by a dilapidated carriage surrounded by excited soldiers.

Thérèse peered ahead, trying to see what went on. She could just glimpse an officer who gripped Margit by the arm, his stance wary yet triumphant. Two soldiers held Althorp and a fourth pointed his rifle at the hapless couple. Bosworth leaned negligently against a wall a short distance away, watching with little concern.

"But this is all nonsense! You must let us go!" Margit's voice rose on a wavering note that Thérèse could detect. She clutched at the officer's hand, beseeching.

From behind them came a clatter of hooves. Thérèse turned to see a lone horseman round the corner. He raced past and bore down on the group by the carriage. The soldier with the rifle spun about to take aim at the rider.

Harding leaped down from his saddle and ran forward, his face livid with fury. "So, I have caught up with you after all!"

Another soldier ran forward and grabbed his arm, but Harding shook him off with ease. He stalked forward toward Margit, who cringed back against the officer as if seeking his protection.

"What is the meaning of this?" The officer looked down at Margit, startled by her demeanor.

"This is my sister, and she is going nowhere with—with him!" Harding glowered at Althorp.

"*Non! Mais, non!* I do not know him! Oh, please, m'sieur, let me go!" Margit spun to face the officer.

The man's eyes narrowed. "Your sister, is she?" He gave a short laugh and his gaze moved from Harding to Althorp and back, obviously trying to guess their identities. "*M'sieur*, mademoiselle is nothing like you. What is this you try to do?"

Harding shook off the soldier who once again had latched onto his arm. Striding forward, he grasped Margit's golden ringlets and pulled them from her head. Her short, dark curls fell about her ears and her face crumpled as if she were about to burst into tears.

"Ah, you are hateful!" she shouted at Harding.

"A pathetic disguise!" Harding shook the wig under the officer's nose. "She tries to escape from me, for she knows I will never permit her to marry such a wastrel as that!" He pointed an accusing finger at Althorp. "She thinks I will not recognize her, but no one but an idiot would be taken in by such a wig. She is as dark as I!"

A deep, enticing chuckle sounded beside Thérèse. Charles's shoulders shook in his enjoyment of the scene as the harassed officer's face took on a purple hue.

"But they are *merveilleuse!*" Thérèse whispered.

"Oh, of a certainty!" Charles agreed. "Harding has been wasted until now."

Harding drew a handkerchief from his pocket and attacked Margit's face, scrubbing. She cried out, but he ignored her. The officer, rigid, permitted him to proceed.

He drew back the cloth and held it up to the officer, who stared in consternation at Margit's darker complexion, which now showed from beneath the concealing paint.

Margit pulled free from the officer's suddenly limp grip and dropped to her knees before Harding, begging. "Do not stop me!"

"You'll not marry him while you are in my care!"

At that, Margit's head came up. "Then I shall return to Papa! It is not for you to decide, but for him!" She came to her feet and faced her supposed brother with defiance. "We shall go to him at once!"

Harding blustered, but at last agreed to escort the truant couple to the home of their father. Taking Margit's arm, he shoved her back into the carriage. When Althorp started to follow, Harding jerked him back and instead handed him the reins of his horse. Bosworth recognized his cue and scrambled back up onto the box as Harding climbed in after Margit. Harding shouted directions that Bosworth would be incapable of understanding, but it made no difference. The soldiers stepped back and allowed them to pass.

The line of wagons and carts began to move forward and Thérèse caught her breath. If the officer or soldiers who had stopped them looked up now . . . But only one of the gate guards paid the procession any heed. The other stood before the officer, his head lowered. The words that Thérèse overheard as they passed were enough to make her blush. They would not be anxious to raise any other fuss for a while. Their cart passed unhindered.

Still, Thérèse clenched her hands. Not until they were several miles south of Paris, with no sign of pursuit behind them, did she begin to relax. Charles drove on at the same slow, steady pace until he at last turned into a narrow lane that led to a small farm.

The traveling carriage stood in the yard with the occupants gathered about it. Margit knelt in the dirt, stroking Aimée, who still slept peacefully. She looked up, then scooped the little dog into her arms and hurried toward the cart as it approached.

Charles jumped down. "Let's get the horses and get moving."

Leaving Thérèse, Margit, and Bosworth to divide up the

baggage, he led Harding and Althorp toward the barn. An elderly man emerged from it, consulted with them briefly, and they all went inside.

"You did very well." Thérèse smiled warmly at Margit. "That officer's face! You should have heard what he said to those soldiers when you had gone!"

Margit grinned a trifle shakily. "Never have I been so afraid! Those men, they were so certain I was you. How can you bear to be hunted like that?"

"You do not permit yourself to think of it." Thérèse averted her face and busied herself with the cookware. With every ounce of determination she possessed, she willed her hands not to tremble or her shoulders shake. One might not think about it, but the fear was always there, lurking in the background, waiting for just the wrong moment to spring to the forefront with paralyzing effect.

Before they had finished with the supplies, Charles and the others reappeared with horses. In a very short time, everything was strapped to the two pack animals, the vehicles were turned over to Margit's cousins, who started back toward Paris, and Thérèse realized they were ready to depart.

Charles came up behind her as she stood beside her horse. "With your permission, *mademoiselle?*" His dark eyes danced with his eagerness to be off. He cupped his hands for her foot and tossed her lightly up into the saddle.

Margit grasped her stirrup and prepared to scramble onto her mount. To her surprise, Althorp came up to her and offered his help. Flushing softly, she glanced at Harding, but he paid her no heed; he already sat on his own horse. She accepted Althorp's assistance, he swung up into his own saddle and Harding tossed him the bridle of one of the pack animals. The entire party set off at a heady trot.

"How far will we be able to go in a day?" Harding

brought his horse up beside Charles.

"We should be able to make seventy-five to a hundred miles, barring any difficulties." He glanced up at the sun, which rose high in the sky. "A bit of a late start, I'm afraid. But with luck, we'll cover fifty miles before we have to stop for the night."

Fifty miles. He had not been joking when he said it would be a long, hard ride. Thérèse squared her shoulders and promised herself she would not let the others down.

The miles slipped past, but the scenery changed very little. They rode through concealing trees whenever they could, or through fields and pasture when no shelter was available. Low stone walls and shallow streams alike proved no obstacle to the horses, which had been chosen for their strength. The only people glimpsed were farmers, and always at a distance. Charles took no chances.

Aimée, who at first ran eagerly at the horses' feet, slowed and began to lag behind. Charles dismounted and handed the little dog to Thérèse, then climbed back onto his horse.

It was Margit who next grew weary. She who prided herself on being as tough as any man found she was barely able to keep up. She was accustomed to life in the city, at the tavern. There she could work from dawn until the early hours of the next morning; but sitting on a horse was something to which she was totally unaccustomed.

She cast a surreptitious glance at Thérèse, who rode erect in her saddle. Not one word of complaint passed her lips, though the tension about her eyes betrayed her fatigue as the day wore into late afternoon. She was so delicate, so very much a lady! Margit felt a spark of growing admiration, not untinged by envy, at her stamina.

That thought recurred after the sun had long since sunk beneath the horizon and Charles announced that the horses had taken all that they could for one day. They approached a tiny thicket from which the welcome sounds of a babbling stream could be heard. That meant fresh water, which they would not have to carry far. Margit climbed stiffly down from her saddle and led her mount the last few feet.

"But it is perfect!" Thérèse, her voice soft and lilting despite her exhaustion, looked about through the heavy dusk at their proposed campsite. "We should be quite safe here."

Charles swept her a low bow in acceptance of the compliment. "It's always best to write ahead to secure accommodations at these luxurious resorts. They tend to be so very crowded. You have no idea how many squirrels and rabbits would like to take our place." He held up peremptory hands and Thérèse, after a moment's hesitation, allowed him to clasp her slender waist and lift her to the ground.

Margit looked from one to the other and experienced a pang of jealousy. *Le Maniganceur* was such a gentleman! And Thérèse was such a lady. Even after a long day fraught with hazards and fears, she betrayed none of the fatigue or aching muscles that must assail her.

Margit directed a glance filled with longing at Harding, but his attention was absorbed in the care of the horses. Bosworth somewhat clumsily assisted him. She dragged her tired mount further into the clearing and set about the unfamiliar operation of unfastening the girth. Althorp came to her aid and Margit watched closely to see how it was done. When she looked up, she saw to her chagrin that Thérèse had removed her own saddle and even now scraped the sweat from the animal's back with a dried weed.

Charles handed his own unsaddled mount over to Althorp and went to look around. They seemed enclosed by the darkness, protected somehow, yet the night could as easily hide enemies as it did them. Thérèse watched him depart, then turned to look at Margit. "We must eat. What—what do we do?"

Margit smiled for the first time in hours. So there was

something Thérèse could not do, after all! Margit regarded the other's rueful expression and found herself liking her very much. She crossed to where Harding and Bosworth had stacked their supplies. "What did you buy?"

Thérèse began to search through the packs. After considerable rummaging, she located bread, cheese, potatoes, and vegetables, which she laid out on a blanket. The kettle, which was the only pot she could find, followed. Uncertain what to do next, she looked to Margit.

"These will do very well," the girl pronounced. "We will clean and chop the vegetables, *n'est-ce pas?*"

Thérèse regarded them with a certain amount of doubt. "If you say so."

When Charles returned with the encouraging news that the area seemed deserted, he lit a fire for them. He then picked up a bucket and went to fetch water. Thérèse watched in fascination as Margit concocted a delicious-smelling soup out of their meager provisions.

"We will have to hunt soon, unless we are able to buy meat or chickens in a market." Margit tasted the broth and added more onion.

Charles chuckled, a deep, comfortable sound. "I may already have two females and one mongrel too many in my train, but I draw the line at having chickens perched up on top of the packs."

Margit shrugged. *"Eh, bien.* Then you may snare rabbits or catch fish." She added several small dried branches to the fire, which did not quite touch the kettle suspended above it.

Thérèse, unsure of what else to do to help, turned her attention once more to the packs. From the depths of one of them she unearthed several bowls, spoons, and knives. She found cups tucked into another, which she also set out. This accomplished, she began to slice the bread.

A muffled pop came from behind her, and she jumped, spinning about to face the source. Charles stood in the glow of the firelight, a bottle of wine in one hand and a cork in the other. His smile set her heart racing.

He gathered the cups Thérèse had found and poured a small amount of the claret for each of them. "I think we've earned it, don't you? It's been a good day's ride."

"A long one," Margit agreed. She took the bottle from Charles and poured a little of the wine into her soup.

Thérèse took her cup and settled down on a fallen log to watch. Two females and one mongrel too many. Charles was right! Whatever had possessed her to come on such a difficult, dangerous journey? She would have been safe—and comfortable—at the tavern. Or she could have gone with the messenger who traveled to England with word of Lord Pembroke's impersonator. But no, she'd had to follow *Le Maniganceur* on this crazy expedition.

Aimée thrust her cold, wet nose into her hand and laid her head in her lap. Absently, Thérèse stroked those ridiculous floppy ears. What had made her come? Her only thought had been for Charles's safety, to make sure that he did not overtax his impaired strength. Or had that merely been an excuse? Had she really wanted the opportunity to come to know Charles Marcombe a little better—and to reconcile him with her fantasies of *Le Maniganceur?*

Bosworth came through the bushes from where they had tethered the horses for the night. Squatting down beside the pot, he sniffed at the contents in appreciation. He settled back, a hopeful expression on his stolid countenance as he waited for the meal.

It was not long in coming. With Althorp's help, Thérèse brought the bowls over and Margit ladled out the simmering contents of her pot. Harding passed around the bread and cheese and Charles refilled their cups with the remaining wine.

"That was excellent," Charles pronounced as he finished the simple meal.

Harding set his bowl down and regarded Margit with

a new measure of appreciation. "Very good," he corroborated.

Warm color tinged Margit's cheeks at this unexpected praise. She met Harding's appraising gaze and, embarrassed, set about clearing away the dishes. With Thérèse's help, she soon had everything washed up.

"Some music, Margit?" Charles leaned back on one elbow and stared into the fire.

She unrolled her blanket. At the center, tucked away with care, lay a violin and bow. She brought these out, returned to the fire, and began to play a country song. Thérèse listened for a moment, then joined in, her soft, clear voice blending with the instrument. Charles leaned back and shut his eyes, a contented expression on his face. The other men followed suit.

The second day proceeded much the same as the first, though they covered considerably more territory. Margit's muscles ached and it was an effort to keep her shoulders from drooping, but she kept doggedly on until darkness again forced them to stop. Once more Charles located a secluded place to make camp.

By the end of the third day, her stiffness began to wear off. She was exhausted, but her determination to make no complaint at last bore fruit. They entered the sheltered glade that would serve as camp that night, and as she unhooked her knee from the pommel, Harding appeared at her side and held a hand up to her.

Gazing down into his tired, frowning face, the normally capable Margit experienced the most unsettling flutter of nerves. It was quite an unusual experience for her, and one she found strangely pleasant. Uncertain, she put her hand in his and felt a rush of color warm her cheeks as he took it in a firm hold. He reached up, caught her about her sturdy waist, and gently pulled her free.

"Long ride today." He set her on her feet and released her.

"*Merci.*" She kept her large, dark eyes focused on the

middle button of his waistcoat, afraid to look up, yet unsure why. Never before had she encountered a man of such dependable mien, and it made her feel unaccountably vulnerable, as if all of her prior existence had been unsteady and tenuous.

"Well, best see to the horses." He took her bridle and led both their mounts away.

She watched his retreating back with wistful eyes. Nothing but a newfound camaraderie marked Harding's manner. He accepted her as a member of their team—not in the way he accepted Thérèse, with deference and respect, but as a fellow worker. It was a vast improvement over his flat disapproval of all females on this trip, and yet. . . . With stoic resignation, she ordered herself to be content and hugged to herself what little he offered.

Harding ate his stew that night with a hearty appetite, then lay back on his blanket to stare into the fire. When Margit brought out her violin, he looked up. "Why don't you play something I know? All those gypsy songs!" He shook his head. "I want to hear an old English folksong."

Margit flushed. Must he now be disagreeable, to atone for his earlier friendliness? "But they are lovely melodies!" she defended her choices. "Your English songs, they would cause us only trouble if anyone were to hear! I play my songs to keep away a chance traveler who would fear the wandering gypsies. What do you think they would do if they heard your music?"

Charles nodded. "She's right. We'd have someone notifying the nearest troops, and they'd be after us within the hour."

"I still want to hear something familiar," Harding maintained stoutly.

"Why must you dislike everything not British?" Margit demanded, bristling. She felt certain this prejudice included her.

"That's not true. Nothing can compare with French brandy!"

A deep chuckle escaped Charles, and Margit flushed. "Always, you are suspicious. And in other ways, you seem to me to be a sensible man."

He considered. "Maybe that's why," he said, unconsciously adding fuel to her smoldering irritation.

She regarded him through brooding eyes, but he paid her no further heed. Hunching her shoulders and turning her back on him, she proceeded to play her gypsy songs until the fire burned low. Tired, she put away her violin and gathered up her blanket to find a place to sleep. Althorp and Bosworth seemed to have dozed off where they lay. Harding stood and stretched.

"Why don't you try to get some sleep?" Charles suggested. "I'll take the first watch."

Harding nodded. "Wake me in a couple of hours, then." He settled back down.

"And you?" Charles turned to Thérèse who sat slightly apart from the others, staring with unseeing eyes into the dying embers.

"What of me?" She did not look up.

He crossed over and sat down at her side. "What are you thinking about?"

She managed a wan smile. "Am I to stay up and talk with you so you do not fall asleep on watch?"

"If you like. But you didn't answer my question. What are you thinking about?"

"Your grandfather," came her honest response.

He stiffened. "He is not your concern."

"But he is! If he had any idea what you have been dragged into because of me . . ."

His jaw tightened. "It is not because of you, and I'll thank you to remember that! Good God, do you think I'm fit for nothing except bear-leading a female? You thrust yourself onto me for this trip, not the other way around. And I could do far better without you!" He stood abruptly and strode with an angry, swinging stride to the edge of the clearing, where he remained.

Thérèse let out a deep sigh. They had been so comfortable together these last few days, but now she had ruined it, wounding his already-raw pride. Why must so many of their discussions end in an argument? His despicable pride! If he intended to take offense and go off every time they exchanged a few words on this journey, she strongly suspected she would hit him over the head with something long before they reached Torres Vedras.

His temper showed no improvement in the next two days. Thérèse, riding just behind him, glared at his back in frustration. *Damn* the Marcombe pride! she thought, startling herself by the intensity of her feelings. She was not one to use harsh language, even in her thoughts, but Charles could drive her to the verge of it—and beyond.

His pride made this trip more difficult than it had to be. If only she could spend her days getting to know him, finding out how much of *Le Maniganceur* was real and how much was just one of Charles's disguises! But now he had retired behind an impenetrable wall that was covered by only the thinnest veil of civility. He did not provide her with a single opportunity to break through.

They continued south, riding as hard as they could. It was the sixth day, Thérèse realized. She looked about the fertile valley as the morning mists lifted from the fields. Yet still something blurred the horizon, something purplish and jagged. . . . Mountains. Thérèse reined in her horse, staring ahead. The Pyrenees . . .

Althorp, who had been scouting ahead, rode toward them at a gallop and her thoughts fled. Wildly, he signaled for his companions to leave the road. Charles led the way into a stand of trees.

"French troops!" Althorp gasped as he rode up to them.

"Where?" Motioning for the others to remain, Charles crept forward to look out.

They had concealed themselves barely two hundred yards short of a crossroads. Already the sounds of drums, hoofbeats and many marching feet reached them. As they watched, a vanguard of officers, dressed in the white and green of the French dragoons, came into view. Behind them in seemingly endless lines stretched an entire cavalry squadron. Two full companies of infantry came next. At the rear rumbled supply fourgons and three cannon. They reached the joining of the roads and the vanguard turned onto the southern arm, taking the route that led toward the western crossing of the Pyrenees.

Charles crept back toward the others. "Looks like we'll be going cross-country for a bit." The suddenly cheerful note in his voice belied the grim set of his jaw. "We've got to get ahead of that lot."

"Where are so many men going?" Thérèse, anxious, peered out of the thicket to get a better view.

"Could they be the guard for this Wellington impostor? What was his name?" Althorp crowded forward, excited yet nervous.

"Brienne. And no." Charles shook his head. "They're not coming from Paris. But they might be backup troops. They won't be able to take Lisbon with only a few men, whatever their plan."

It occurred to Thérèse that his manner was too casual. She looked at him closely and sensed the underlying urgency behind his words. He was worried, but he would say nothing to alarm them. . . . However exasperating he might be, she could not deny his ability to lead.

As soon as their way was clear, they remounted and headed through the fields, circling a small village, trying to maintain as much speed as possible. Charles drove them on, harder than ever, and they did not stop until well after dark.

They were up again with the dawn, not letting up their frantic pace until late afternoon, when they reached the foothills of the Pyrenees. Once over these, they would be in Spain. Eager, Thérèse pressed ahead—yet still they were miles away. Dusk gathered around them when Charles at last drew in rein and signaled Althorp to scout ahead again.

"Will we be out of France tonight?" Harding rode up to join Charles.

He shook his head. "We won't be able to take the main road. Nor follow the coast. It's going to be too well watched, particularly with those troops moving this way. We'll probably have to take to the mountains and find a path across."

"But that will take time!" Thérèse protested.

"Do you have some strange fascination for French prisons?" Charles gave her a derisive look. "We'll play this one safe."

"*Eh, bien.* We have made excellent progress so far," Margit declared. "We can be cautious."

"Do you expect other troops as well?" Thérèse wondered at Charles's uneasiness.

He nodded. "I didn't like the looks of the ones we saw yesterday. Napoleon may be mounting a major campaign in Portugal, and this business with Brienne impersonating Wellington may be only a very small part of it." He took a deep breath and exhaled slowly. "We'd best waste no time reaching Torres Vedras."

Althorp returned with the unwelcome information that French troops covered the landscape beyond the first rise. Resigned, they turned from the main route and started up into the foothills in hopes of finding a not-too-difficult path through the mountains.

At last it grew too dark to make progress safe. Little shelter offered itself, but after almost an hour of steady searching they found a partially concealed alcove beneath an overhanging rock where a fire would not instantly draw attention to them. As soon as the others began making camp, Charles climbed a bit higher to get a better view. Far below, toward the coast, hundreds of flickering fires marked the position of the French.

He directed a searching gaze through the darkness, up into the hills that towered above them. The presence of so many troops below made it unlikely that any lurked in the mountains. But still . . . He made his way back down to his friends.

Thérèse looked up from the stew that she and Margit cooked over the fire. She could sense his tension. In a hushed voice she asked, "What is the matter?"

"Nothing, probably. I just want to look about a bit more. Althorp, come with me. No," he added as Harding stood. "You and Bosworth stay here."

The two men disappeared into the darkness. Thérèse met Harding's frowning gaze and bit her lip. Apparently it was not only she who was jumpy. Was it just that they were so close to escaping from France? Or the presence of the troops so very close by? Restless, she forced herself to sit down while the stew simmered.

"Margit, will you play?" She turned to the girl who stood beside the fire.

Glad to have something to do, Margit abandoned her wooden spoon in the kettle and pulled her violin from her bedroll. She began an old French song that Thérèse remembered well from her childhood. Yet tonight she felt no desire to sing. She sat tense, sensing danger, her eyes straining into the darkness, trying to discern menacing shadows from among the trees and shrubs. Aimée, ever sensitive to her mistress's moods, stood at her side with her hackles raised, oblivious to Thérèse's soothing touch.

Bosworth rose and went to stir the stew. He tasted it, returned the spoon to the pot, and stirred some more. Harding lounged back, appearing almost asleep—but the light from the fire glinted off the barrel of the pistol he kept partially concealed.

A rustling noise came from the bushes nearby. Before Thérèse could spin about, two large, rough men stepped into their clearing. *Guerrilleros.* Bandits.

Chapter Fifteen

The shaggy mongrel leaped forward with a volley of ferocious barks. Frightened for her pet, Thérèse dived after her and grasped her quivering little body in a firm hold. The sounds of the violin stopped abruptly as Margit froze.

"Keep playing." One of the *guerrilleros* waved at her with his gun. With fumbling fingers, she complied.

The other stepped forward, his pistol in hand. While he kept them under guard, the first man gestured Bosworth away from the stew pot and went to it himself. He sank down and gave it a stir with the wooden spoon.

Thérèse stood slowly and immediately both guns pointed at her. "I will get you bowls," she said, forcing her voice to stay calm.

"*Merci*." The bandit rose but kept his gun on her as she picked up the dishes and spoons.

His unpleasant smile never wavered, leaving Thérèse so unnerved that her hands shook as she ladled out the simmering stew. His cold, piercing eyes followed her, and with every ounce of resolution she possessed, she refused to betray her fear. Handing over the bowls, she stepped back to allow the two men to eat. In a very short time they tossed the empty dishes to the ground.

"And now," the first man said, "we will relieve you of

your provisions." He gave a low whistle which was followed almost at once by further thrashing in the shrubbery. But no one stepped into the clearing, and the second of the *guerrilleros* cast a rapid glance over his shoulder.

It was enough for Harding. He swung out the pistol he had kept hidden at the same time that Bosworth came up from behind the first of the bandits with a length of wood. Before that man could do more than swing his gun about, Bosworth struck. His opponent crumpled to the ground.

Harding came to his feet as the other man took a wary step backward. Nervous, the *guerrillero* pointed his pistol, then jumped as a fresh crashing came from the bushes. Althorp stepped into the clearing, supporting Charles. In the momentary confusion, Harding brought his gun down on the *guerrillero*'s head.

"Charles!" Thérèse, her face pale, darted forward to grasp his arm.

He waved her aside. "Just that shoulder again."

Althorp helped him down to the ground, and he let out a long, ragged breath.

"There's a whole camp of these *guerrilleros* just over the next rise!" Althorp kept his voice hushed, as if the dreaded bandits could hear him even at that distance. "And there were three more of them lurking in the bushes, waiting for a signal." He sat down abruptly beside Charles, still shaken by the encounter.

"We had a bit of a set-to," Charles explained with a lopsided grin.

"And you were in the middle of it, I suppose?" Thérèse knelt at his side. "*Voyons,* let me look at your arm."

"Leave it." The command was curt. "It'll do."

She rose and looked down at him in no little concern. He was too proud to admit to a weakness. For all she knew, his arm could be badly injured. She looked toward Harding for help, but he was fully occupied at the moment. With Bosworth's assistance, he dragged the fallen *guerrilleros* to the center of their clearing and bound them with the ropes that normally secured their packs. It had all happened so quickly. . . .

Charles straightened up and rose tentatively to his feet. He stood for a long minute with head lowered before he moved forward. He looked at the men, then cast a quick glance about the camp.

"Now what?" Thérèse folded her arms, pretending to no more than mild interest, as if she did not tremble from reacton. Aimée whined from within the long folds of her woolen riding skirt.

Charles glanced over his shoulder at her. "The least that useless dog of yours could do would be to fend off attackers."

"But that is unkind! Aimée . . ." Thérèse began a spirited defense, but Margit interrupted.

"If there are more of these men about, we cannot stand here and argue, as much as you might enjoy it. Me, I do not wish to be killed."

"Then let's get moving." Charles strode over to the packs and, his left arm hanging limp at his side, began thrusting things in at random.

"Tonight?" Bosworth stared after him in horror.

"We're lucky only a few of them came to scout out our fire." He fastened the first sack and began on a second. "If they don't return soon, the rest may come to see what's keeping them."

"But our supper . . ."

"Shall we just invite the rest of the *guerrilleros* over to join us?" Charles rose, and the effort sent a spasm of pain across his face.

"Monsieur Bosworth is quite right. We have already made the stew. You can eat it in the time it takes to argue about it." Thérèse strode quickly to the great pot and began to ladle out a serving. "Monsieur Harding, will you and

Althorp saddle the horses? And Margit, if you will help me with the packs?" She thrust a filled bowl at Bosworth and another at Charles. "*Voilà tout*, we shall eat in shifts and be out of here before you know it."

Charles looked down at the steaming bowl he held in his right hand and his glare relaxed into an unexpected grin. "You're a damned managing woman, Thérèse."

"*Merci, m'sieur*. Now eat. Others would like a turn."

In a very short time, Harding and Althorp reappeared with the saddled horses. While Bosworth strapped on the packs with the remaining rope, the two men took their turn eating along with Margit and Thérèse. When they had finished the meager meal, Harding doused the fire.

Charles dragged himself up into the saddle. "As quiet as you can manage, if you please," he called softly to the others. With only the light of the stars and the thin crescent moon to help them, they made their slow way through the low foothills that bordered the mountains.

They kept going for perhaps three hours, though Thérèse had no method of guessing how much distance they covered. It could not be many miles, for the footing was treacherous and the sheep track they followed wound its rambling and unhurried way around boulders and shrubs. Below them to their right, the fires that marked the location of the French troops became more scattered, then ceased altogether.

At last, as Thérèse caught herself swaying with exhaustion, Charles drew up his mount and indicated an overhanging rock off to their left. Shrubs grew thickly in the dark shadows beneath, offering shelter.

"Shall we check to see if any *guerrilleros* are at home?" Thérèse rode up beside Harding and Charles.

Harding jumped down from his saddle. "If you don't mind, sir, I'll take Althorp and scout about a bit."

Charles, his lips pressed tightly together, gave a short nod and the two men slipped away. Thérèse sprang down as lightly as she could and took the reins of Harding's horse as well as her own. Charles remained in his saddle, his back erect, but his left arm hanging still. Somehow, she would have to convince him to put it back in a sling.

He looked up and caught her watching him. He thrust out his chin in defiance.

"I must apologize for making you move tonight." His tone was antagonistic, as if he wanted to lure her into a rousing argument.

It might relieve his sense of injured pride, but she was too tired to oblige. She just shrugged in a very Gallic gesture. "These things happen, *cela va sans dire*. We should have written ahead to request our rooms."

A muscle twitched at the corner of his mouth at this masterly repetition of his own words so many nights before. Yet he held in check the impulse to laugh, as if he needed to keep his ill-temper simmering. "I warned you this would not be a comfortable journey. This isn't at all the sort of thing to which a lady is accustomed."

"No, that is very true, *bien sûr*," she agreed with complete cordiality. "It is not at all like the chateau. There, *c'est entendu*, I could be quite certain I should remain precisely where I was."

A low, reluctant chuckle escaped Charles, very much like the breaking of ice. "You are holding up remarkably well." A note of admiration warmed his voice. "Few women would have the courage to attempt such a journey."

"Or the so great stupidity to insist on going along," she agreed promptly.

"Not stupidity." Charles shook his head, smiling. "Stubbornness."

"Ah, upon that subject you are an expert." As soon as she spoke the words, she could have bitten her tongue. But to her surprise, he did not take offense. Another deep, rumbling chuckle was her only answer, for at that moment

Harding and Althorp returned to announce that all seemed safe.

The trek through the Pyrenees took two more days and resembled nothing so much as a nightmare. The going was slow, for they had to remain out of sight of the French troops who moved along the main road in a neverending line. More often than not, they were forced to dismount and lead their horses, for the footing was uncertain, with seemingly solid paths disintegrating beneath their feet and sending a shower of rocks and dirt rattling down the hillside. The nights were cold and their provisions sparse, for the bread and cheese gave out on the evening of the second day.

Nor did they dare light a fire to cook a meal, though Margit assured the company that she was well able to snare a rabbit if given the opportunity. What, precisely, she would do with it after she caught it, the tender-hearted Thérèse did not want to contemplate. She could only be glad that Charles refused the offer, saying that they had best concentrate on getting through the mountains without attracting any attention.

Then suddenly they rounded a bend to find flat land spread out ahead. The coast, with its well-traveled road, lay far off to the right. Below them, just beyond the last of the foothills, stood a small town.

"Spain," Charles announced.

Margit rode forward. "Spain," she whispered. Then, "Are we safe?"

He shook his head. "Not while there are French troops about. But at least the *guerrilleros* won't bother us with a village so close. Let's stop and have a fire in the daylight, when no one will see it."

"And supplies?" Thérèse ran through a rapid mental inventory of the foodstuffs that remained in their packs. The beans would take several hours to cook up into something edible, and rice, even seasoned by the capable

Margit, would not be overly sustaining.

Charles threw her a sympathetic smile. "Tomorrow," he promised. "We'll find shelter and camp for the night. Any objections?"

There weren't any. They found a relatively safe place near a stream that made its leisurely way through a shrub-filled ravine, and Thérèse and Margit went to work on the beans while the men tended the horses. Thérèse, casting a surreptitious glance at Charles, noted that his arm moved more easily this day. When he used it, the lines of unacknowledged pain did not form so deeply in his face.

By morning, all were eager to hurry on; just being on Spanish soil bolstered their tired spirits. And ahead lay a town where they could purchase supplies, and that meant real meals once again. This near to the border, no one would question their French notes.

After some deliberation, they at last agreed to split up as they approached the town. Over Thérèse's and Margit's objections, Charles and Harding decided to enter the town alone. The others, they declared, could ride around and meet them well to the other side.

After delivering orders for the things they wanted purchased, they allowed the two men to proceed alone. Thérèse and her companions circled through the empty fields, staying well clear of the village. At last they reached the line of trees which served as the appointed meeting place. There was no sign of Charles and Harding, so they withdrew into a thicket and dismounted to wait.

"It seems odd to be doing nothing," Thérèse remarked presently.

Althorp grinned at her. "Enjoy it while you have the chance. They'll catch up with us all too soon."

His words proved prophetic. Only moments later, two horsemen rode into view, approaching at a leisurely trot. As they neared the line of trees, they cast a quick glance around and, as no one was in sight, turned off the road.

Margit hurried forward, eager. "What have you brought?"

"Enough food to keep even Bosworth happy," Harding said.

"And what is this?" Thérèse pulled a guitar free from the pack.

Charles had the grace to look somewhat sheepish. "It didn't seem fair to leave the evening's entertainment entirely up to you two ladies."

"Do you play?" She looked at him in surprise.

"But of course he does!" Margit turned to them in delight. "My own cousins taught him!"

"I doubt I've played since then," he admitted. Uncharacteristically self-conscious, he stowed the guitar away.

They distributed the provisions among the packs and set forth once again. For the first time since beginning their journey, they risked following the road. They were far enough to the east from the main route to avoid French soldiers, Charles decided, and they had to make as much time as possible. The French who accompanied the impostor Brienne would not have to face the delays of circuitous paths or enemy troop activity.

By evening, though, they turned west to keep on course and left roads behind. The sun had long since set before a suitable camping place could be found, and for some time all were busy setting up.

At last, with the horses hobbled to graze and a chicken roasting on a spit over the fire, Thérèse sat back. Charles and Margit stood by the packs, examining his new guitar. Thérèse looked forward to hearing him play. Everything seemed so peaceful, almost like a dream. Even Charles was more relaxed, apparently having recovered from the blow to his shoulder—and his pride. It was not easy for the great *Maniganceur* to accept the new injury of his arm in a simple bout of fisticuffs with a few *guerrilleros*.

Charles began to strum his new instrument while Thérèse and Margit cleared away the remnants of their meal. Bosworth and Althorp went to their aid and washed their few dishes, and Thérèse began to prepare biscuits for the morning. Margit picked up her violin and went to join Charles. Soft strains of a gypsy love song filled the air.

After perhaps twenty minutes, Margit set down her violin and began to dance. Charles kept up a throbbing, alluring melody, and though the girl swirled in time to it, she possessed few of the gypsies' amatory wiles. What she lacked in coquettishness, though, she more than made up for in spirit. She whirled about the fire, trying her hardest to entice, but Harding, her obvious target, remained unmoved.

Thérèse watched Margit's growing frustration with understanding. When she at last was able to remove the biscuits from the stone where they baked, she walked over to her. "Margit, you must teach me!" she called.

Charles continued to strum his guitar softly, watching through half-lidded eyes as Thérèse swirled under Margit's guidance. Her supple grace held his attention, causing him to miss more than one chord as she followed Margit with quick, light steps. Harding got up abruptly and went to the packs to drag out his sleeping roll. Setting this near the fire, he lay down for the night, resolutely turning his back on the dancers.

Margit dropped the hands she had raised above her head as she spun. "Me, I am also tired. I will show you some other time." Dejected, she walked off.

Thérèse looked after her, wishing there was something she could say that would comfort the girl. With a sigh, she turned back to the others. Althorp and Bosworth went for their bedrolls.

Thérèse strolled to the edge of the clearing, tired but not yet ready for sleep. Behind her, Charles began to pick out a tune on the guitar. How odd this life of camping was, so very different from anything she had ever before experienced. It made her feel so very free.

Charles stopped playing and she looked over her shoulder. He gestured for her to join him. She hesitated, then took a seat at his side.

"We're half way to Torres Vedras."

"*Vraiment?* And we are in Spain! We should be able to move more openly, now. What a relief that will be!"

"Sorry, not yet." He shook his head. "We're still in danger and we can't forget that."

"But the Spaniards rebel against Joseph! They will not long submit to having him here."

"And who can blame them? Would you like one of Napoleon's brothers foisted onto you as your king?" He shook his head. "But unfortunately, the Spaniards' strong point lies not in their military organization, but in their *guerrilleros* tactics. They only attack stragglers and small bands and harass the enemy as best they can. And their best is quite something." His tone became grim. "They do not deal kindly with their victims."

"But surely . . ." Thérèse frowned, concerned.

"These are the descendants of the people who devised the Holy Inquisition," Charles pointed out.

Thérèse shuddered. "But we are not their enemies!"

"I'm afraid we won't get the opportunity to explain that. If you don't mind, I think we'll be careful."

She turned away to stare out through the thicket and across a plain shrouded in darkness. The pale moonlight from the vanishing crescent cast the faintest glow over the scene. She shivered.

"Afraid?" His soft voice sounded very near to her ear.

She laughed, but it was not a convincing sound. She reached over and scooped up Aimée, who lay curled near her skirts.

"Perhaps I weary of adventuring." She did not turn back to him. Her words were true, she realized. For the first time, she longed for the peaceful serenity of that little village where she had stayed in the north of England. She might grow bored, but at the moment even that sounded pleasant.

"Do you miss your singing?"

She rubbed the little dog's head. "It is a way to earn a living. Better than some, *peut-être*. Me, I do not think I would make a good governess."

His deep, responsive chuckle sent a disconcerting thrill of pleasure through her.

"No, my dear, that would not be the life for you. But I know what you mean. This is a game for young men." His hand came up to massage his shoulder that still ached.

His arm brushed hers with a gentle, almost feathery, caress. Thérèse stiffened as the oddest sensations ran riot within her. She wanted to lean back and rest her head against the broad shoulder that just touched her ear, yet if she did so . . . When he had kissed her before, it had been only part of an act, but even so, the yearnings he created in her had been frightening by their strength. If she permitted this to happen again . . .

"You were disappointed in me for wanting to retire, weren't you?" His voice sounded oddly calm, as if he had at last come to terms with the injuries and self-doubts that had plagued him.

She hesitated but, incurably honest, she could not lie. She nodded. "But it was not you that I considered, for I did not know you. To me, it seemed that *Le Maniganceur* had died and you were not at all the same person."

His hands tightened as he gave a short laugh. "The broken shell of your heroic image? My poor Thérèse! I must have been a terrible disappointment to you."

"It is unsettling, *du vrai*, to discover that a god is only human, after all."

"A god," he repeated, his voice hollow. "It seems *Le Maniganceur* developed quite a reputation for himself."

Thérèse turned, anxious to reassure him. "But it is only natural! When a man does such things that to other seem so very brave and impossible, *enfin*, he becomes a hero! They do not see that he has feelings or even any other life!"

"Or that he has failings and fears and can become discouraged? And what now, my Thérèse? Have you accepted the all-too-mortal side of your god?"

"Before, you were not a real person."

"And now?"

The words were barely above a whisper, and she felt his tension as if her answer mattered deeply. It was almost impossible to breathe. He drew closer so that his shoulder pressed against her cheek and his hand caught her chin, compelling her to look up into his rugged face.

In the darkness, she could barely see the line of scar that protruded from beneath the hair that curled low over his forehead. Her heart beat strong and erratic as the heavy stubble of his rough, unshaven chin brushed against the tip of her nose. His lips touched her eyes, closing them, then found her mouth.

All caution, all rational thought faded away. It didn't matter that she barely knew him, that this was Charles Marcombe, the man, not *Le Maniganceur*, the dream. Nor did it matter that he might only be using her to placate his pride, to prove to himself—and to her—that his particular brand of swashbuckling derring-do exactly suited her taste. Because it did, very much so. At this moment she cared for nothing beyond the gentle, enticing pressure of his mouth and the warmth and strength of the arms that encircled her. She melted into his embrace and one hand crept about his powerful shoulders.

The yelp of the indignant mongrel, which stood in imminent danger of being crushed between them, brought them apart. Charles, his large frame shaking in silent laughter, rubbed the animal's head.

"I see you are well chaperoned."

Whether it was humor or emotion that set his voice quavering, she could not be sure. She clung to the little dog while she tried to regain some measure of equilibrium.

He stood, held down a hand to help her rise, and brought her easily to her feet. "It will be another long, hard ride tomorrow. Go to bed, my Thérèse."

She did, but found it impossible to sleep. For a very long while she lay awake, reliving every breathless, enticing moment of that kiss. *Le Maniganceur* might have been a glorious dream, but Charles Marcombe . . . The mere thought of him left her tinglingly alive. He filled her with a surging joy, a sense of security, a longing to remain safe in his arms forever. Compared to the phantom, the reality of the man was far more satisfying—and exasperating. She much preferred it this way.

He had not exaggerated the difficulty of the following day. In actual fact, many long, hard days of riding followed, but Thérèse existed in a strange new world in which exhaustion and danger played little part. Her idol had been resurrected, but this time he had taken the form of a flesh-and-blood man. The bravery and undaunting courage remained, but now they blended in her eyes with his very human qualities of humor and warmth and vulnerability. She had looked up to him before; now, purely and unquestioningly, she loved him.

The realization came at the end of a particularly tiring day. The sun sank lower and lower, yet still they were unable to find a suitable camping place where they could find both water and shelter. Charles encouraged them on, though Thérèse could see the strain in his own face and the rigid set of his back that indicated pain in his shoulder and side. But rather than complain, he concentrated on rallying the others to keep on—just a little farther, just until they were safe.

His efforts paid off. As they crossed a weed-infested field, Charles, who had ridden ahead to scout out possible campsites, spotted a rickety barn more than half-collapsed. Nearby stood a covered well with a battered bucket lying beside it. The rope was gone, but he used the one that strapped his pack to his saddle. By the time the others caught up with him, he had tested the water and found it good.

He waved to them, a smile in his tired eyes. "Everything we could ask for! There's even old straw in the barn."

He strode up to where Thérèse unhooked her knee from the pommel of her saddle and held out his hands. A warm glow lit his eyes as they rested on her. She leaned toward him without hesitation and he caught her up with surprising ease and set her on the ground. His hands lingered on her slender waist.

"The end of the day." His voice caressed her.

She looked up into his brown eyes, so far above her own, and knew herself lost. Here was a man so infinitely worthy, so completely the epitome of her every secret dream. How could she help but love him?

He led her horse away with his own and left her floundering in a flood of chaotic emotions. Their mission, the war, the uncertainty and danger of this journey, everything faded before the reality of her love for Charles. But what could their future hold? How long could *Le Maniganceur* continue before a French bullet did more than wound him?

She was shaken from her thoughts by Margit, who called her to help with dinner. Together they assembled the meal, though Thérèse had no idea what they prepared. Charles came into the barn with Althorp and Harding, leading the watered horses, and she could see nothing but him.

He did not play his guitar that night, but instead lay back against a stack of old straw to ease the strain in his shoulder. Thérèse sat near him, singing softly, barely daring to raise her gaze to his face for fear he would see the love that overwhelmed her. His eyes never left her.

Margit looked from one to the other, her expression one of longing. Her gaze strayed to Harding, but he merely hunched a shoulder and turned his back. He was the first to turn in that night. The others followed shortly.

Thérèse curled into her bedroll, wrapped in a warm glow of happiness. Love for Charles filled every part of her. With her eyes closed, she could still see his special smile, just for her, that was more a caress. The strength of their attraction was undeniable, the emotion that ran between them strong and tangible. If only he would speak the words of love . . . But now, with danger on all sides, was not the time for promises or plans.

She rolled over to face the dying embers of the fire. She was rather jumping ahead. Loving Charles and sharing any sort of a life with him were two very different things. He might well have no desire for a wife. She was aware that any number of amatory intrigues lay in his past, but this was not the sort of arrangement he would offer her. He might very well offer her nothing. This traveling life they led might be conducive to romance but it had very little to do with everyday existence. He might be indulging in a mere flirtation to while away the time with never a thought that she might seriously fall under his spell.

She had more time than she could wish over the next several days to indulge in her troubled thoughts. They continued at the same quick pace for mile after endless mile, pausing only to rest their mounts, to scout ahead to make sure their way was clear, or to camp for the night. They reached a river and turned to follow it, only swerving away to avoid first Valladolid, then Salamanca. Then it was a long, dry run until they neared Ciudad Rodrigo.

They circled well around the city, then paused to rest on a slight bluff to the southwest. Charles urged his horse forward, staring intently toward the west. Harding rode up beside him.

"The Portuguese border is only hours away." Charles sat back in his saddle.

Althorp joined them. "Can we make it tonight?"

Charles shook his head. Already the sun was westering, shining in their eyes. "Tomorrow, but not tonight. We'll go as far as we can, though." He gathered his reins and they started up once more.

"Charles!" Thérèse had been looking not toward Portugal, but about their more immediate vicinity. "Over there!" She pointed off to where a narrow, rough lane wound its way toward a farm.

Charles stiffened. Three ox-driven wagons plodded along that lane, coming slowly toward them. "Baggage fourgons," he breathed.

"And French, I'd say. Look at the guards' uniforms." Harding shook his head. "I don't like the looks of that."

"There must be a supply magazine down there." A gleam of devilish enjoyment lit Charles's eyes, wiping away the fatigue. "Perhaps that huge old barn."

Thérèse felt his excitement and with a sinking sensation realized what he had in mind before he spoke. Althorp, not blessed with her perspicacity, eyed his leaders.

"What should we do?" He looked from Charles to Harding.

Charles answered, and a soft laugh shook his voice. "Burn it down, of course. What else?"

Chapter Sixteen

Harding stared at Charles open-mouthed. "You're out of your mind!"

"Of a certainty." Charles grinned back. Energy and determination radiated from him as his ever-active mind went to work on this new situation. "But I'm going to destroy that magazine."

Complete silence followed his words. Althorp swallowed hard and looked from one to the other. "I—I'll go with you, sir!"

"You're both mad!" Harding shook his head, his expression grim. He cast a swift glance at Margit, found her eyes resting on him, and turned back at once to Charles. "Well, we might as well all be mad. What do we do?"

"We'll have to wait until dark," Charles decided. He looked around, searching for a place to hide. A slight rise, covered in shrubs and trees and well above the farm, provided a perfect vantage point. They made their way there, then settled down for a much-needed rest.

Leaving his horse in the care of Bosworth, Charles inched forward through the dirt to lie on his stomach behind a bush where he could watch what went on below. "There are several guards," he called back softly at last.

"We'll have to take them out."

Harding crept up beside him and rested on his elbows. "Pistols?"

Charles shook his head. "Too noisy. I don't want a single sound made until after the place is blazing." Again, he concentrated his attention on the farm. "There's a haystack over there large enough to start a pretty good fire. We should be able to move it closer to the barn without too much trouble."

Harding let out a sigh. "You like to work, don't you, sir?"

Charles's eyes danced with his sense of purpose, and his low, infectious chuckle rumbled forth. Thérèse, who had remained with the horses, looked up at the sound. For once, she did not find it comforting. She had learned that it too often accompanied the craziest and most dangerous of his ideas.

"If something has got to be done, you might as well enjoy doing it," he told Harding.

"I suppose it is necessary to burn this place?" Thérèse crawled to their side. Aimée trotted up and lay down next to her. "We cannot just remove the guards and allow the Spanish to have it?"

"Too risky. The French could retake it easily. Located this near the border . . ." He shook his head. "It must be a major supply magazine for their troops in Portugal. With it destroyed, it will take some time to bring up more food, arms, and clothing."

"That should hamper them somewhat," Harding agreed. A measure of satisfaction sounded in his voice, a sure sign that he had become reconciled to the proposed project.

"Let's hope it at least shakes them up a bit." Charles returned his attention to the farm.

As dusk blended into night and the shadows grew dark enough to provide concealment, Charles took Althorp with him for a quick inspection of the fenced yard and barn below. Harding remained to guard Margit and Thérèse while Bosworth went to work saddling the horses, which had been allowed to graze.

Margit came up to Harding, whose rigid stance betrayed his unusual tension. Tentatively she reached out and just touched his arm. "This should not be too dangerous, should it?"

He glanced down at her, but his face was closed, revealing nothing of his thoughts. He shrugged and walked away, leaving her alone and gazing after him with sadness, a vast longing filling her soft brown eyes.

Thérèse bit her lip. She could not bear to see Margit so unhappy. And as for Harding . . . She followed him to the edge of their little hill, where he stood gazing down at the dim outline of the farm.

"You do not approve of this plan, my friend?" She laid a gentle hand on his arm.

"Oh, it's what we ought to do, all right."

"But it is dangerous?" She had little doubt of his answer. Aimée whined softly, sensing her unease.

Harding nodded, confirming her fears. "But what do you expect? This whole job is dangerous!"

The unexpected harshness of his words startled her. "But surely . . ."

He managed a rueful smile that vanished almost at once. "Oh, he'll have planned it with care, never you fear. *Le Maniganceur* is nothing if not thorough. But in a job like this . . ." He shook his head. "Nothing is ever certain. The least little mistake and you can be killed. Oh, it's all right for a man like Charles Marcombe. It's everything to him, his whole life. But for others . . . A man in this work has no right to go and get complications for himself!"

"Complications?" Thérèse prodded gently as he fell into a brooding silence.

"Friends . . . a wife." He gave a hollow laugh. "You

must have realized that from knowing Mr. Marcombe. There's no room in this sort of life for anything but your work. A man's got to be a loner. He'd be a fool to marry—or even indulge in love." He stared bleakly out over the dark landscape.

"Why should he not allow himself some happiness?" An urgency underlay her words, but whether it was for his sake or hers, she was not certain.

Harding shook his head again. "There's nothing but pain for his woman, worrying all the while he's away, just waiting for the news of his death—if it ever reaches her." He turned to Thérèse. "She could wait for years without ever knowing."

"The pain is there for the woman, whether her man acknowledges her or not." Thérèse spoke softly, almost to herself. "*Voyons*, she cannot help who she loves. It may not be wise, but it is no less real, and the pain no less as great, just because her man refuses to accept it."

Harding looked down at her, his face a mask. "She should try to find another man."

"I do not think love is like that." It was her turn to stare down at the silent farm below. "If one must do this work, is it not better to love while one can, to have at least memories, instead of only emptiness?"

Even as she spoke, her heart wrenched. Would Charles feel the same as Harding and refuse to let her stay with him? But the last couple of days they had been so close, there had been that special smile just for her, a caress in his voice. . . . Happiness enveloped her, warm and gentle as a cashmere shawl.

It slipped away a moment later. Their time together, even if he offered it to her, might be so fleeting! Could she bear the strain of Charles's constant exposure to danger? If only he would abandon his risky existence and return to the security of Ranleigh!

But she did not have the right to order the life of one so

full of energy and *joie de vivre* as Charles. Unless he made that decision himself, freely and without interference on her part, it would not be fair—or right. He must be willing to walk away, to give up the excitement. . . . Something warm and moist slipped down her cheek. She wiped away the tears with a surreptitious hand.

Charles and Althorp returned. Bosworth came up to join them and Thérèse moved away and scooped up the shaggy little mongrel. She hugged Aimée tightly, seeking comfort.

The four men held a brief discussion which involved much gesturing. At last all seemed satisfied. Leaving the pack animals tied to shrubs, Thérèse and Margit climbed into their saddles and each took the bridles of two saddled but riderless horses. Aimée stood beside them, her head tilted, alert. They watched in silence as the men slipped noiselessly on foot toward the farm.

Thérèse could make out very little in the darkness. She leaned forward, straining her eyes to catch a glimpse of the stealthy figures who'd already disappeared. Below them all remained serenely calm.

"They'll be all right." Margit stated it as fact rather than making it a question. Still, an uncertainty sounded in her voice.

"Of course they will," Thérèse agreed. "They have to be."

The chirping of crickets blended with the rustling leaves in the light breeze. All else subsided into stillness as the darkness grew more complete. Thérèse strained her ears, anxious for some sound, some sign that all went well. But it was not likely she would hear anything. Unless . . . would they hear an alarm if the French soldiers discovered Charles or any of the others? There were four of them to do the necessary work—or to make a mistake.

What if they were caught? What would happen to them? Would she and Margit hear anything if the guards dealt efficiently with the intruders without needing to summon aid? Suddenly the waiting seemed interminable!

Aimée whined softly. Thérèse jumped, then looked down into the large, soulful eyes of her pet. The little dog stood up on her hind legs and pawed at the hem of her mistress's skirt, which she could barely reach. Thérèse murmured a soothing word and Aimée subsided.

"They will be all right," Margit asserted once again.

Thérèse caught the note of anxiety. "Nothing will go wrong. They'll be back very soon." Her own voice quavered so badly that it robbed her words of their intended comfort.

Her horse took a restless step forward, and she realized she unconsciously urged it on. With difficulty she fought the impulse to go and see what happened.

"Surely they have had time to take out the guard and start the fire," Margit cried, fretting. "They've been gone for hours!"

"Not yet." Thérèse tried to smile but knew it to be a pitiful attempt. "It has not really been very long."

But it did seem like hours. Thérèse craned her neck, wishing there was something—anything—she could do besides wait.

"We should have created a diversion to draw off the guards!" she exclaimed suddenly.

"We still can!" Margit, as eager as Thérèse for action, looked up, excited. "Though perhaps Harding and Charles might not quite like it." Her enthusiasm collapsed.

Thérèse clenched her hands, setting her horse sidling uneasily. Aimée whined again. Thérèse looked back to where the two pack animals stood quietly, their heads lowered. "We—we should get them ready," she decided, unable to think of anything else.

Securing the reins she held, she dismounted. With Aimée trotting along beside her, she collected the pack animals and tied them to riderless horses, leaving Margit and herself each with four horses to control. She had barely finished when Margit let out an excited squeal.

"There! They've started the fire! Do you see?"

Thérèse spun about. A pale light flickered far below, followed by a sudden burst of red-gold flame that shot high into the sky. Their horses perked up their ears, alert and watching. Aimée let out an excited yip.

A bell clanged loudly, ringing the alarm, but the guards were too late. Already the blaze surged higher and wider as the tongues of fire devoured the dried wood of the barn. Within seconds the entire side facing them seemed to be engulfed. Thérèse scrambled back into her saddle and soothed her nervous mount as she gazed in awe at the terrifying spectacle.

The men must have prepared for the fire carefully, for the result was spectacular in the extreme. Flames shot high into the dark sky, casting a brilliant illumination on the scene of chaos as the guards ran to and fro, unprepared for such an emergency. There was little hope that any of the French supplies would survive.

But where were Charles and the others? At least a dozen dark shapes could be seen swarming about the blazing inferno, but not a single one ran from it. Had they been captured? Setting the fire had not been enough—they still had to escape!

What if they needed help? She became aware of Aimée's excited barking, but paid it no heed. What if Charles needed her . . . ? Panicking, Thérèse urged her startled horse forward. It balked, then plunged wildly. They started down the low hill, dragging the riderless animals behind.

Althorp and Harding appeared first, running as hard as they could up the dark slope. Margit rode toward them and each grabbed at the reins of their horses. Thérèse continued down, scanning the hillside, fear for Charles's safety robbing her of all caution.

Then something—no, someone!—moved below her, and the broad-shouldered figure of Charles emerged from the shrubs. Behind him, panting from exertion, stumbled Bosworth. Aimée darted toward them and her barking ceased. Thérèse let out the breath she'd not realized she held and reined in as she reached them.

Charles grasped one of the bridles she held. From head to toe he was covered with grime and soot. A long tear left the sleeve of his coat hanging and in the dim light Thérèse could see a scraped, reddened spot on his cheek. Already it looked swollen.

"What happened?" She caught his hand as he swung up onto his horse.

He gave her fingers a quick squeeze. "A little contretemps." He grinned cheerfully. "Well? What are we waiting for? Come on!"

His mount needed barely a touch to take off at a lunging gallop back up the hill. The frantic pace could not long be maintained, and they were quickly forced to slow to a trot. Away from the blaze, they could see very little; and the ground, as they remembered it, provided difficult footing for the animals. As soon as they reached a road, Charles's horse broke into a canter again and the others followed. They kept this up for almost an hour before turning off into the fields.

Charles came to a halt and stared back the way they had come. "That should be enough distance between us and that magazine. Let's camp for what's left of the night." The little mongrel, panting heavily, caught up.

While Bosworth, Althorp, and Harding saw to the horses, Thérèse drew the protesting Charles over to their packs, where she fished out their meager medical kit. He eyed it with a mixture of amusement and wariness.

"What are you planning to do? Operate? I don't want my face amputated, you know."

"Your cheek, it must be cleaned. As soon as we have heated water, I shall . . ."

"No! No fire."

Margit, who had searched out her cooking pot, set it aside with a sigh. "You have had your fill of fires for this night?"

"You might say that." He grinned, though it went a trifle lopsided at the pain from the swelling.

"Eh, bien." Thérèse shrugged. "Then I'll wash it with tepid water from a canteen." Undaunted, she made good her threat. She dabbed gently at the bloodied, scraped patch of skin and winced right along with him as it stung.

What a fool she was! Harding had spoken the truth. The terror she had experienced had little to do with the success of their mission, which had mattered very little to her. All that she cared about, all she could think of had been Charles, whether he would be captured—or killed.

Why must she love a man who constantly sought out danger? Life presented one with enough difficulties! It was senseless to seek out more. If only he would stick to his original decision and retire! How could she have ever scorned him for such an intelligent, reasonable choice? How she wished he'd never been lured into taking on one more job!

But he had, and what was worse, it had been because of her. He had tasted the excitement and challenge once again, and now he would never turn his back on it. She could see it in his eyes, that thrill of outwitting the enemy, of beating the odds, that supreme confidence and lack of concern for the inevitable consequences. It would be only a matter of time until his reflexes slowed or his uncanny luck ran out.

She blinked rapidly to force away her tears. It was her fault! How could she have done this to the man she loved? If she had not been such a fool as to let herself be captured, he might even now be sitting in a garden at his beloved

Ranleigh! Instead, not even fully recovered from his last escapade, he launched himself whole-heartedly into perhaps the most dangerous undertaking of his outrageous career.

Well, if she had caused it, she would see it through at his side. She could do no less, so it was fruitless to repine. Determined not to let him guess how deeply she was distressed, she concentrated on the job at hand. With the gentlest of touches, she patted the swelling dry and from a small jar took a fingerful of cream, which she smeared over his cheek.

"It is done. How does it feel?"

He gave a low groan for answer, but his eyes still danced. "I'm getting too old for this."

He might shake his head, but she caught the lilting note of lingering excitement in his voice. No, she could place no hope in his words.

Harding, who had strolled up to watch the treatment, snorted. "You're more fit than the rest of us."

Thérèse busied herself with putting away the emergency kit. If only he *were* done with it all! But no matter what Charles said, this *was* his life. Without it, he would be bored, empty, unfulfilled. She rammed the small medical kit back into the pack. His sister Celia had warned her, once, in tones of disgust, that he lived only for the thrill of danger.

Throughout the following day, Thérèse rode in unaccustomed silence, her heart heavy. As they finally stopped for the night, Charles came to help her from the saddle. Unable to resist the pleasure of his touch, she allowed him to lift her to the ground.

"You look sad." His voice was soft and concern set tiny wrinkles at the corners of his brown eyes. "Don't you like being in Portugal?"

"Portugal? We have made it?" She looked up, excited in spite of her inner unhappiness.

274

"Vraiment? Are we indeed?" Margit sprang down and hurried to join them.

"We should have crossed the border a couple of hours ago." He grinned as Althorp raised a desultory cheer.

"Can we now ride openly?" Thérèse looked eagerly toward Margit. "How pleasant to follow a real road instead of the uneven ground of the fields!"

"And not to seek cover at the first sign of anyone approaching!" the other girl agreed.

"To be able to have fires every night to cook real meals and keep off the chill!"

"Aye, now that would be a treat!" Bosworth declared as he strode up.

Charles shook his head, dashing their hopes. "The French are on the offensive here."

"But will not the Portuguese be friendly?" Thérèse could barely hide her disappointment.

"If they can figure out which side we're on. I'm not so sure they'll stop to ask us. And there will be plenty of French troops on the move." He handed the reins of Thérèse's horse to Althorp, who led the animal off for brushing and watering. He turned back to find the others still regarding him in dismay.

An amused smile quirked up the corners of his mouth. "Have you all forgotten why we're taking this little journey of ours? The whole purpose of having Brienne impersonate Wellington must be to help cut off the British supply route from Lisbon. That will take more than infiltrating Torres Vedras, you know. They're going to need troops, lots of them, in position near Lisbon."

With the uneasy sensation that their troubles were just beginning, Thérèse turned her attention to setting up their camp. If only they might reach an end to their dangers! But if she knew Charles, he would just look about for another situation fraught with peril that only the great *Maniganceur* could resolve. That thought did not soothe her as she vainly sought sleep as an escape from the ache that assailed her heart.

The dangers returned to haunt her sooner than she liked. Late the following morning, when they had been under way for a good three hours, they spotted French wagons—coming toward them, not heading toward Lisbon. Charles left the others in hiding in a thicket and crept forward on foot for a better look. He remained some distance from the road, but the contents of the flat carts were all too obvious. Men—and badly wounded. Frowning, he made his way back to the others.

"There's been a battle." He retrieved his reins from Harding.

"A battle?" Thérèse stared at him, her eyes wide. "But we heard nothing! Are you certain?"

"I wish I wasn't. Come on, we'd best get moving. No, wait. I'd like you to carry Aimée, to keep her from chasing rabbits and squirrels."

He handed the little dog into Thérèse's arms, then swung up onto his horse. "We'll be safe if we stay well clear of the road."

"What do you think has happened?" Harding maneuvered his mount up to Charles's side.

He shook his head. "I don't know."

"Are—are we too late?" Thérèse fought down an unreasonable and almost hysterical desire to giggle. "Have we gone through all this for nothing?"

"Well, something has happened." Charles's expression remained somber. "But whether or not it has anything to do with the Wellington and Torres Vedras business, I can't say. It might well be just a regular battle."

"Can't say I like taking the women into an area where there's fighting." Harding cast a strange glance at Margit, then looked away at once.

Margit rode in silence, staring straight ahead. Not by a single sign did she betray that she was aware of Harding's words, or indeed of his presence. Thérèse experienced a pang of sympathy. She was not the only one to love a man wedded to dangerous work. And William Harding, like Charles, was a man of determination and stubbornness beyond bearing. Never would he give in to any feelings for the swarthy half-gypsy who had more the manners and demeanor of a boy than a girl. No, the obstacles for Margit were as complete and insurmountable as those for herself and Charles.

By mid-afternoon, Althorp, who scouted ahead, spotted a straggling company of battle-weary French troops trudging their dejected way on foot toward Spain. Charles listened to his report and his frown deepened.

"It sounds as though it might have been a British victory."

"Vraiment?" Thérèse peered out through the shrubs, trying to get a glimpse of the distant road. "Perhaps there is no need for us to warn Lord Wellington?"

"On the contrary." Charles followed the direction of her gaze. "It may mean this infiltration scheme is their last hope to take Lisbon and drive the British out of the Peninsula. Which means they'll be all the more determined to make it work."

"And it will be all the harder for us to stop them." Bosworth stuck in.

"Let's get moving. I want to give them a wide berth." Charles started off in the opposite direction from the road.

"Are you sure?" Althorp stared fixedly toward the wandering army unit. "That's a cannon in their tail! Let's capture it as a present for Wellington!"

Harding closed his eyes and his shoulders shook in silent laughter. "Why not just shoot yourself? The results would be the same, and it would waste a lot less time."

Althorp directed an injured glance at him. "But we need all the cannon we can get!"

Charles shook his head. "There are about a hundred of

them . . . and four of us—six," he corrected, and threw a smiling glance at Thérèse. "What do you think that makes the odds? Even with surprise on our side?"

Althorp fell silent, considering. While this weighty mathematical problem occupied his mind, the others started off.

Throughout the day they spotted more troops, all looking exhausted, all heading toward Spain. Each time, Charles insisted that they circle around, which slowed their progress.

"I thought we had need of great speed!" Margit complained after their fourth detour.

"The French may be tired, but I'm sure they'd pull themselves together enough to shoot at you," Charles offered.

"But why should they—" Margit began, firing up.

Thérèse intervened before an argument could develop. The endless days of strain and weary traveling were beginning to show on all of them. "How much farther do you think it is to Torres Vedras?"

Charles shook his head. "I have no idea. It can't be too many miles more."

She nodded. "Then let us ride on tonight. The moon, it grows fuller. There is light and the land, it is not difficult. We will see the fires of the French camps so we can avoid them." Her suggestion satisfied everyone except Bosworth, but as no one listened to his grumblings about dinner, the matter was settled.

The progress they made during the evening encouraged them all, and they continued the next morning with the knowledge that their goal could not be too distant. Avoiding the sandy roads, they passed through the arid countryside, through scattered pines and olive trees. As the day wore on, Charles stopped to consult a map, then steered them slightly more to the northwest. He kept them going long after darkness fell; and the others, tired but resigned, made little complaint.

A line of scattered lights shining above them in the distance caught Thérèse's attention. She peered ahead to try and determine the source. "Charles!" she called softly. "What is that?"

He brought his horse to a halt. "The first line of fortifications, unless I'm much mistaken."

"Fortifications? Do you mean for Torres Vedras?"

"You mean we're almost there?" Althorp came up to join them.

Charles shook his head. "Torres Vedras is a village, well behind the lines."

"If we're close enough to see the lights, that means the French won't be far away," Harding pointed out.

"They'll probably be occupying the villages around here," Charles agreed. "And a few camps. Here's where the going really gets tricky."

"But of course." Thérèse nodded wisely. "Until now it has all been quite easy."

He grinned. "We'll get a bit closer, I think, then find a place for the night. I want to look the situation over before we go in."

Thérèse let it pass. Several half-formed cracks about why should they start being cautious now came to mind, but she was too tired to do them justice. Instead, she urged her horse after the others. Their journey was almost over.

By the time they found a place to camp, Thérèse was so tired she could scarcely keep her eyes open. Though the evening was cold, they did not risk a fire. Bread and cheese sufficed for their supper.

It seemed to her that she had barely gone to sleep when noises awakened her. Pale light illuminated their make-shift camp, filtering through the leafy branches above. It must be almost dawn. She rose up on one elbow and saw Charles kneeling beside Harding. Aimée, wagging her shaggy tail, stood between them as the two men held a low-voiced conversation. The others still slept.

"What is it?" she called softly.

Charles rose and went to her, and Aimée trotted along. "I'm just going out to look things over."

In the semidarkness she could not quite make out his expression, but his tension enveloped her, setting her nerves tingling. She reached out and grasped his hand.

"Take someone with you!"

An odd smile touched his firm lips. "Like that ridiculous mongrel of yours? Don't worry so, my Thérèse. I'll be better off alone. I can pass for a peasant. Go back to sleep."

"Sleep? You are being absurd!" She sat up. "How can I when you do so dangerous a thing?"

He smoothed a hand over her tousled blond curls. In the growing light, his brown eyes seemed to sparkle as they rested on her.

"It's been a long journey." His voice remained soft. He bent closer and his lips just brushed hers. "Have a large breakfast ready for me when I get back. I'll be hungry."

He disappeared into the hazy shadows, leaving her to stare after him, yearning. Almost, he could make her forget their danger, everything they had been through. Almost nothing mattered but the deep tremor of his voice and those dancing lights in his eyes as they gazed into hers. *Almost.*

Restless, she rose and set about making a fire to heat water and cook a meal. A chill hung about the air and she wrapped the blanket she used as a shawl tighter about herself. September had slipped away, along with the miles that separated them from Paris. It was October now, and the approaching winter made itself known. Clouds hung low overhead and the air tasted damp, as if rain threatened. She shivered.

Harding, still pulling on his jacket, came to her aid and in a short time they had a comfortable fire blazing. She held out her hands to warm them.

"Will he be all right?"

"Don't you worry about him. He's got his old flair back again, our *Maniganceur*."

"*Tiens*, that is what I fear." She stared into the flickering flames. "He does not remember how badly he was injured. What if his shoulder fails him when he needs that arm?" She turned large, distressed eyes on Harding.

"It won't. Now, he's not going far, just to take a look around in the light. He'll be back before you know it." He gave her shoulder a comforting pat.

It was some time later before Charles put in an appearance, slipping silently back into the camp while they refastened their packs. Aimée trundled up and proceeded to greet him as if he'd been absent for days rather than hours. Charles grinned at everyone, ignored their questions, and demanded his breakfast.

"Not until you tell us what you saw!" Thérèse snatched his plate away. The deep lines of strain about his eyes had not escaped her notice. His every mood affected her almost as strongly as it did him!

He sank down onto a rock. "We should be able to make it up to the walls without too much trouble. The French are pretty well scattered and staying almost a mile back."

"Then what is wrong?" Thérèse handed him the plate of eggs and cheese.

"There isn't much cover. The British will see us coming, all right, but there's a good chance they'll open fire without asking who we are."

The others exchanged uneasy glances. Charles ate in silence, then handed the empty plate to Margit.

Thérèse swallowed hard. "There is only one way to find out. Let us go!"

Her first sight of the fortifications did much to undermine her confidence. The first line made full use of the mountains. On every point that might have been passable, the British, with the aid of their Portuguese allies, had constructed abutments and walls. Well over a hundred pieces of field artillery pointed down on the terrain below.

"It's incredible!" Althorp breathed.

"They have not left a single way through, from the Tagus River to the ocean." Charles reined in at Thérèse's side. "And behind that are two more lines quite similar to this."

"It is almost one enormous, impregnable fortress." She regarded it with awe. "It is no wonder the French resort to this scheme of impersonation! No one could break through those defenses."

"Which means no one can reach Lisbon." He looked directly at her, but his eyes were frowning, unfocused. "Not even Wellington could issue an order that would allow this place to be breached. What is their man supposed to do once he gets in?"

"Perhaps just look at the British plans?" Harding did not sound as if he really believed his own suggestion.

Charles shook his head. "They've got something in mind, something that will clear a route to Lisbon. But what?" He scanned the fortress-like facade that stretched out endlessly before them, as if hoping to spot some weakness, some clue. None presented itself. With an exasperated exclamation, he urged his horse forward again. "If we wait much longer, I suppose we can just watch them put their plan into action."

"How do we get in?" Thérèse regarded the mountainous approach. "If we try to climb, will we not make of ourselves excellent targets for the French troops?"

Charles grinned back at her. "The terrain is uneven. If we follow that ravine over there, it will lead us to a low depression."

It took them almost two hours of careful maneuvering to reach the gully. Once within it, Charles led the way along the narrowing, twisting path as it wound its way first downward, then steadily up into the hills. Thérèse cast an uneasy glance behind, but discovered that after the first few turns, they were almost completely concealed behind the first outcropping of mountain. No French troops met her worried gaze, though she knew that somewhere, someone must be watching. She could only be relieved that the sun, which had passed its zenith and begun its westward descent, would shine in the eyes of any French scouts who might spot them.

Then suddenly Aimée tensed and began to growl. Around the next corner, filling the span between the higher rocky cliffs on either side, a man-made wall loomed up to block their path. Through it protruded the barrels of three cannon. And all around them, ranged along the rocky protrusions, stood perhaps twenty soldiers in Portuguese, Spanish, and British uniforms. Each held a rifle, aimed with care.

Thérèse tensed and her horse sidled, as jumpy as she. Aimée's hackles rose and her lip curled in a threatening snarl. For a long moment no one said a word as the two groups faced each other. Then Charles broke the uneasy silence.

"We have an urgent message for Lord Wellington. Can you take us to him?"

One of the Portuguese *cacadores*, an *atirador*, a sharpshooter, by the black plume in his shako, jumped to the ground before him. Aimée set up a snarling, defiant bark, but Thérèse silenced her with a sharp word as a scarlet-coated British sergeant joined the Portuguese soldier.

"Want to see Wellington, do you? I'll just bet you do." The sergeant ran a dubious eye over the six bedraggled travelers. His gaze narrowed as it rested on the two women.

Thérèse opened her mouth to speak again, then shut it firmly. All they needed now was to hear her heavy French accent. The brown-coated Portuguese soldiers looked nervous enough to fire upon them without any further ado.

"We are going to throw down our pistols," Charles told him. He gestured for his companions to do so. His own gun landed at the foot of the British sergeant.

The man signaled, and a very young infantryman scrambled down from the rocks and collected the pistols. He could be no more than eighteen, Thérèse guessed. His large eyes were wide and scared. She gave him a tentative smile.

"And now you will dismount." The sergeant stepped back, never once lowering his rifle.

Charles swung down first, followed by the others. Thérèse landed lightly on the rough ground and Aimée disappeared beneath her long riding skirt. Two more British soldiers came forward and subjected them to a rapid but thorough search. Satisfied, they stepped back.

The sergeant gestured for them to move away from their horses, which the soldiers took in charge. "Now, state your business."

"As I said, we have a message for Wellington. A very important one."

"I see. And you came through the French lines to deliver it." Now that he had these strangers unarmed, the sergeant's confidence grew.

Charles waved the indignant Harding to silence. "That's the only place we're likely to get any information of interest to Wellington." An amused smile just touched Charles's lips.

The sergeant hesitated, clearly not trusting them. Just as Thérèse felt ready to scream with impatience, the man came to a decision.

"All right, perhaps you should see him. He just might want to ask you a few things." Ordering them to follow, he led the way through the only entry, behind the first line of defense. Several soldiers accompanied them, their rifles at the ready. In the rear came more, leading their horses.

They walked in silence along rocky, uneven paths. The footing was difficult and the progress necessarily slow because of their animals. For some time they continued in this manner.

At the second line more troops awaited them, this time led by a captain. The sergeant made his report and handed them over to their new guard with much the air of a gaoler handing over his prisoners. The comparison, which Thérèse could not dismiss from her mind, left her nervous.

The first red streaks of sunset crept across the sky as they passed the third line of defense. Ahead of them, now quite close, lay the village of Torres Vedras and Wellington's headquarters. Tears of emotion stung Thérèse's eyes. They had made it! They had accomplished a very dangerous and almost impossible journey! But they still had their warning to deliver. It was not yet over.

As they neared the collection of buildings occupied by Wellington and his staff, darkness settled about them. Lanterns shone in windows, and campfires and torches lit the surrounding area. A guard stepped forward with a challenge, and the captain who commanded their escort spoke with him briefly, then led them through.

Thérèse looked about anxiously as they entered a surprisingly large house. Indoors for the first time in two-and-a-half weeks, she became very much aware of their travel-worn appearance. Stains, dirt, even tears marred their unfashionable clothing. As they stood in an entry hall surrounded by smartly turned-out officers, Thérèse realized she had never felt so wretchedly attired!

The captain, after a low-voiced consultation with a soldier, escorted them across a hall to a room where music could be heard behind a closed door. Here they were left under armed guard while he entered the dining room.

Thérèse peeked in through the open door. To her utter

amazement, a formal dinner party seemed to be under way. Ladies were present, as elegantly gowned as if they were in London. As she watched, the captain made his way to the head of the beautifully appointed table and bowed before the brown-haired, hawk-nosed man in an old blue frock coat who could be none other than Wellington himself.

She could not see his expression, but his bearing betrayed his annoyance with this interruption as he excused himself to his guests. With quick, controlled steps, he left the room and came face-to-face with his unexpected visitors. He looked them over and annoyance shone clearly in his bright blue eyes.

"Now, what is this all about?" He addressed Charles.

"I believe this had best be said in private. With your permission?"

Wellington nodded, apparently somewhat reassured by Charles's undeniably aristocratic accent. Taking him by the elbow, the commander led him a little way from the others. "Now, who are you, and what is this message you say you bring?"

"I am known to Lord Pembroke as *Le Maniganceur*." Charles paused, but saw no reaction from the great man. It was possible Wellington had never heard the name. It made what he had to relate all the more unbelievable. "I have been serving as a spy for the British in France for a number of years. About three weeks ago, I came across a plot by the French to impersonate you and infiltrate these fortifications."

Wellington folded his arms. "That is not very likely."

"In Paris, it seemed quite likely." Charles rubbed his chin. "But then we saw your lines of defense here. I'll admit, if I hadn't overheard the plans myself, I don't know if I'd believe them, either."

"You have come from Paris?" If anything, Wellington's skepticism was growing.

Charles nodded. "We've been almost three weeks on the

journey, and dodging French troops the whole time."

"You have come all this way just to warn me?"

"There didn't seem to be much choice. Their impostor, a man named Brienne, was going to leave the same day we did, and we had to get here first."

"Since I am not an impostor, it seems you have succeeded. And such an impossible journey, at that. You are to be congratulated."

"But you don't believe a word of it?" A wry smile crossed Charles's lips.

The blue eyes glinted in unexpected amusement. "Can you blame me? An impossible story, an impossible journey, an impossibly bedraggled party, complete with two women and a dog—if that's what you call that animal?"

He signaled the captain, who stepped forward smartly. "You will be escorted to a suite of rooms and I will question you further in the morning. You will not, I trust, object to a guard? Merely a formality, of course, until we have time for more discussion."

"Of course." Charles's lip tightened, but his smile never wavered.

Wellington strode back into the dining room and Charles returned to his companions. Concern creased Thérèse's brow as she touched his arm.

"What did he say? Will everything be all right now?"

"Not exactly." His broad shoulders began to shake with barely suppressed laughter at the ridiculousness of their situation. "I believe we are now under arrest for being French spies."

Chapter Seventeen

The door closed behind the guard, and Charles and his companions found themselves locked into a suite of rooms on the uppermost floor of Wellington's headquarters. Thérèse, with Aimée padding at her heels, went to the window of the sitting room and found iron bars covering the outside of the pane. The rooms might be comfortably appointed, but they were little more than a prison.

She turned back to see Margit peering into the second of the three bedrooms that opened off the sitting room. Charles came out of the third, shaking his head.

"Well, it's better than sleeping on the ground," he said. "How does it compare with your chateau?"

Thérèse met his eyes and both of them burst out laughing. Weak, she sank onto a chair and dropped her head into her hands. The others stared at her blankly and Aimée whined softly, thrusting her nose into her mistress's lap.

"Did he say something funny?" Harding looked from one to the other in mild exasperation. Charles, his shoulders quaking in mirth, could only shake his head, unable to speak.

"But—but it is *fort amusant!*" Thérèse gasped, stared at the incredulous faces about her, and went off in another peel of uncontrollable merriment.

"I am sure we could all use a good laugh," Margit informed her dryly.

With a determined effort she brought herself under control. *"Voyons,* but it—it is quite simple! First, I am captured by the French and, *voilà tout,* I am rescued by the British. Then I am again captured by the French, and *en avant,* I am again rescued by the British. And now I am captured by the British! Who shall save me this time, the French? *C'est ridicule!"*

Charles chuckled. "Oh, we'll do it ourselves. After all, it wasn't the British so much as me who keeps saving you." His eyes danced. "Never fear, my Thérèse. As always, *Le Maniganceur* is at your service." He accompanied his words with a sweeping bow.

Thérèse rose and dropped into a low curtsy in response. "We await your move with great eagerness, m'sieur."

"Indeed we do, sir." Harding, a reluctant smile in his own eyes as the absurdity of the situation struck him, turned from the window.

Althorp strolled over to join him and peered down. About twenty soldiers sat about a fire or strolled around the closed entry yard below. "No escape that way," he said with regret.

"We don't want out," Charles protested. "What we have to do is prevent someone else from getting in."

"And how are we to do that?" Margit sank into a chair near Thérèse. *"Hélas,* we are a little too 'in' ourselves."

Bosworth, who had been staring at the door, shook his head. "Do you think we can order up some dinner while we talk?"

Charles grinned. "An excellent idea."

He tried the knob, but not surprisingly found it locked. He knocked, and after a few moments the door opened. Two soldiers stood there, both with rifles at the ready. Charles raised his eyebrows in polite disapproval and drew himself up to his full, impressive height.

"At what hour is dinner served?"

His haughty tone, carefully calculated to abash the hardiest soldier, had its effect. The rifles wavered and lowered. A gleam lit Charles's eyes as he noted that he awed his uncertain gaolers.

"A clear soup, if you please, to be followed by fish. If you haven't any partridges, I suppose we can make do with a pullet or two, though we'd prefer pigeons. And see that the sauces are not heavily seasoned. And after that . . ." He turned to the others. "Any preferences?"

"But of a certainty!" Thérèse swept forward, her manner regal in the extreme. "Asparagus, *n'est-ce pas?* And perhaps a ham, cooked in pastry?"

One of the guards threw an uneasy glance at his companion, who grinned openly at such audacity. Neither, it was obvious, had any certain idea how to treat these "guests." Handled carefully, Charles felt assured he could establish friendly relations.

From the depths of his pocket, he drew out a quizzing glass that he had not had cause to use in over three weeks. Idly, he swung it on the end of its black riband in perfect imitation of a bored dandy. Only his rugged, well-worn appearance belied the effect.

"If the kitchens are not up to our standards, I am sure we will overlook their failings." He waved an airy hand at the junior of the two guards, but his voice held a crisp command. "Be off, my good man. We await our meal."

The hapless guard reacted to his aura of authority and withdrew at once. The other, with no attempt to hide his grin, bowed deeply.

"Certainly, my lord, upon the instant." He followed his cohort from the room. The lock clicked softly into position.

Thérèse collapsed once again into a fit of giggles. "Will you next order Milord Wellington to be brought to you at your pleasure?"

Charles considered. "No, but I think I will call for a bath." He raised the glass and regarded his stained and ravaged buckskins with every appearance of horror. "Do you suppose there is a single batman here worthy of the name? I must ask our new friend. My leathers are in the most distressing state."

"But you must not permit anyone to touch your beautiful boots!" Thérèse, all mock concern, cried out in horror. Her eyes sparkled in amusement. It was the relief of tension, she knew, that made them joke like this. But after so much danger, so many, many days of strain and worry, the release was necessary! "They would blacken them, *sans doute*, with something most unsuitable," she continued. "Of a certainty they would be ruined."

Charles stuck out one booted foot and regarded the scratches and mud through his glass. With every appearance of anxiety, he asked, "Do you suppose they have a champagne blacking?"

Harding regarded his commander with attempted reproof. "This is all very well, sir, but what are we to do now?"

"Eat," Charles pronounced briskly, dropping his affectations. "And have a bath."

"You are the most provoking man!" Thérèse exclaimed. "You rush us across France, Spain, and Portugal, and then all you can think of is your dinner!"

"Well, the thought of a good meal, a hot bath, and clean clothes has been occupying my mind completely these last few days," he admitted, grinning.

"And mine as well." Margit cast a disapproving look over herself. "I did not know it was possible to be so dirty. We shall ruin this comfortable furniture!"

"We are very dirty, *du vrai*." Thérèse regarded the remnants of what had once been a quite presentable riding habit. "But as for a good meal! Margit, he insults us! You have taught me many excellent ways to prepare fish and fresh game!"

"And we salute you both." Charles gave them a teasing bow, though a note of sincerity underlay his tone. "Indeed, you two are the epitome of all the wifely virtues." He broke off suddenly, then smiled in an odd manner. "How wasted you both would be in society."

"They would be an asset in any company," Althorp asserted stoutly. He smiled at the ladies.

"Aye, you two can cook a dream." Bosworth nodded, apparently lost in the memories of many meals. "Pleasure to travel with you."

"We're avoiding the issue!" Harding, exasperated, came away from the window. "If I know you, sir, you already have a plan. Will you not tell the rest of us?"

Charles shook his head. "Not a plan, really. We have no idea how far ahead—or behind—that impostor is. But the stakes are high in this game, so we can be sure he's on the move. Wellington's withdrawal behind the fortifications must have been expected, yet the French could not prevent it. Hence the impostor plan."

He rubbed his chin, thoughtful. "First, we'd best find out what has been going on in Portugal. There was obviously a battle nearby, and only four or five days ago. And at a guess, I'd say it was a French defeat. That means they'll be all the more anxious to cut off the supply lines from Lisbon. I think we can expect our impostor to put in an appearance any time, now." He looked up, a broad grin lighting his weary countenance. "It looks like we'll just have to save the British in spite of themselves."

Thérèse stood, stretched her cramped and tired muscles, and went to the door and knocked. Their friendly guard answered, and she favored him with her most beguiling smile.

"S'il vous plaît, m'sieur, at what hour may we expect our baths to be brought up? Before or after we dine?"

Her heavy French accent brought a slight frown to his brow, but he bowed to her with every semblance of respect. "I will see to it at once, ma'mselle."

"And our luggage? I fear we brought very little with us on this difficult journey. Our clothing, *cela va sans dire*, it is so very dirty. Is there a laundry maid?"

The guard withdrew with promises to see what he could arrange, and Charles chuckled in deep appreciation.

"Do you think we should request a footman or a page to wait on us?"

Thérèse considered it. "A maid, or perhaps an abigail, would be most welcome. And, *du vrai*, I should like a fire. Margit, have you selected for us a bedchamber?"

They were distracted from their inspection of this by the arrival of their dinner. While not the elaborate meal of Charles's fanciful ordering, it proved both good and satisfying. All ate ravenously, though Charles loudly bewailed the absence of wine.

Their guard, who bore every appearance of enjoying his prisoners immensely, exclaimed in mock dismay, "An oversight, sir! A terrible mistake! I shall look into the matter at once." He bowed himself out of the room only to return a short while later with not one but two bottles. He uncorked these himself.

Charles beamed at him. "Admirable fellow!"

They had barely drunk a toast to the man's health when the door opened to admit several soldiers bearing two large, cumbersome tubs for bathing. Behind them came more soldiers carrying cans of hot water and wood to build the fires.

The senior guard bowed to Thérèse. "I trust everything is to your satisfaction, ma'mselle?"

"*Merci, m'sieur*. It is very good of you."

With no further ado, she followed the soldiers into the chamber Margit had selected and ordered the laying of the fire and the placement of the tub. When the soldiers withdrew, she and Margit engaged in a friendly squabble over who should bathe first. Margit won the coin toss and self-consciously prepared for her bath. Thérèse retired to the sitting room to sip her wine and contemplate the pleasure to come.

In a surprisingly short time, Margit called to her. Thérèse entered to find her already dried off and wrapped in her old gown. She knelt by the tub, scooping out the dirtied water so that they could replace it with fresh water from the canisters that stood warming by the fire. Thérèse went to her assistance.

With her bath ready, Thérèse dropped her worn garments on the floor, stepped into the tub, and settled back to relax in the steaming, inviting water. With a sigh of pure contentment, she found she could forgive the British Army a very great deal. As soon as the aches in her muscles eased, she set about washing her bedraggled hair. With this completed to her satisfaction, she dried herself off, wrapped up in one of the large, coarse towels, and turned her attention to the horrified Aimée.

It took Margit's assistance to get the little dog into the tub, but they succeeded at last to give the poor creature a thorough scrubbing. Their laughter brought a pounding on the door.

"What are you doing in there?" Charles demanded.

Thérèse rose to answer, but remembered her state of undress, and soft color warmed her cheeks. "Aimée also must be clean!" she called to cover her sudden confusion.

"Well, when you're ready, our favorite guard has managed to bring us our baggage. And it's only been mildly ransacked for weapons."

"Clean clothes!" Thérèse exclaimed.

The door opened a crack and Charles tossed in the only change of garments they possessed. These were relatively fresh, having been washed only two days before in a river. They hurried into them and emerged at last into the sitting room to find a cheerful fire crackling in the hearth.

Thérèse sank down on the floor before it and set to work combing out her long, fair curls. Aimée settled before her, as close to the flames as she dared. Dropping her head on her paws, the little dog let out a deep, contented sigh.

Thérèse tilted her head to look over her shoulder at Charles. "And what now?"

His eyes rested on her with a glowing light in their dark, compelling depths. She met that disturbing gaze and almost forgot to breathe as she sank beneath his unconscious spell. A strange tingling sensation danced across her skin, leaving her pulse light and rapid. Her lips parted as a wave of yearning swept over her.

His jaw tightened and she felt his tangible effort of self-control. He looked away, breaking the magnetic force that pulsed between them. Shaken, Thérèse looked down and stroked Aimée.

"Now we go to bed." In an oddly tight voice, Charles answered the question Thérèse had forgotten she asked. He continued in a lighter tone. "It's too late to do anything else tonight. Tomorrow, when I look a bit more respectable, I shall speak to Wellington."

But in the morning, the expected summons to the great man's presence did not come. After waiting with growing impatience, Charles called their guard and asked if a message could be taken to him. The man hesitated, looking uncertain.

"I'm sorry if this puts you in a difficult position," Charles said, torn between exasperation and amusement at the man's discomfort. "But our errand is rather urgent, or we would never have undertaken such a journey in the first place."

The guard took the message, but returned in less than a quarter-hour. "I thought it odd you weren't sent for at once," the man said, pleased to have his own curiosity settled. "It seems that Lord Wellington received an urgent message to go to Lisbon. He left at dawn. My orders, begging your pardon, are to keep you here until he returns."

"Damn!" Charles swore explosively. "This must be it! They must have lured him away so they can bring in Brienne!" Charles turned to their guard, regarding him through narrowed eyes. He read in the man's face a willingness to go along with their whims, but not for a moment did Charles fall into the error of thinking the guard would disobey orders for them—or anyone. Nor could Charles blame him. Common soldier or not, this man had the makings of an officer—or perhaps even something far more interesting.

Charles sank down onto the arm of a chair. "Tell me what has been going on. We passed a number of French troops as we crossed Portugal and they looked pretty battle-weary. And defeated, or so we hoped."

"No harm in telling you, I suppose," the guard decided. "There was a battle at Busaco less than a week ago. The French took heavy losses and retired, and Lord Wellington withdrew to the fortifications."

Charles nodded and his gaze met Harding's eyes. "And now Wellington has been summoned away from Torres Vedras." His voice held a wealth of significance.

Althorp jumped to his feet. "We've got to do something! We can't just sit here and allow this—this plot to succeed!"

Margit glanced at the guard, who eyed them with considerable suspicion. She leaned back in her chair, her eyes half-closed. "This may not be part of the plot," she pointed out, reasonably. "If we go around screaming for no reason, then no one is likely to listen to us. We must wait—and watch."

Harding stared hard at her, then nodded his approval of her good sense. "She's in the right of it, sir."

Charles turned back to the guard. "Watch for any unexpected actions today, by anyone. And if Wellington returns, kindly let me know upon the instant. There is a very great deal at stake."

The guard nodded. "Nothing in my orders against that," he assured them and took his leave.

"Do you really think Wellington's departure is pure coincidence?" Althorp turned on Margit as soon as the door closed behind the man.

"No," she admitted. "But now the guard, he will expect us to do nothing."

Thérèse walked in an uneasy circle about the room. "The imposture, it would not be meant to last for long. Half an hour with Wellington's papers, might that not be enough?" She raised anxious eyes to Charles.

He nodded, his expression grim. "Well, now that we have our guard convinced we're content to wait for Wellington's return, it's time we took matters into our own hands." He looked around, then hefted the tray on which their breakfast had been carried up. "Getting careless, isn't he?" Charles shook his head as if in sorrow. "Thérèse, I believe this is your forte, but if you do not mind, I think I'll do the honors this time. Can you provide a commotion for me?"

"But of course." She considered this for a moment. "Monsieur Harding, will you be so kind as to attack me?"

Charles stepped behind the door, the tray firmly in his hands, and Thérèse let out a terrified scream. Harding grabbed her shoulders and, as they pretended to struggle, the junior guard burst into the room. He hesitated, staring at them in consternation.

Charles swung and the tray connected neatly. The man dropped like a dead weight. Shaking his head, Charles picked up his rifle.

"Really, this was too easy," he complained. "I will have to talk with Wellington about his security." He rolled the guard over and looked at him. "Althorp, I think. You're about the same size." He glanced at the other man and nodded. "Yes. If the ladies will retire to the other room for a moment?"

When Thérèse and Margit rejoined the men, the guard was no longer in sight. Thérèse looked about, then turned an inquiring gaze upon Charles.

"Tied up on one of the beds." Althorp grinned at them. "Well, do I look all right?"

Thérèse regarded his scarlet-coated uniform critically. *"Eh, bien.* You make a very nice soldier. But what now?"

"We've got to get some more news." Charles handed the rifle to Althorp. "And make sure 'Wellington' does not return unexpectedly. A walk about the courtyard, perhaps?"

Althorp escorted them out of their suite and thoughtfully locked the door behind them. By trial and error, they found their way through the halls and down the stairs to the open yard they had glimpsed through their window. Even in the morning, the area seemed filled with soldiers. Aimée stuck close to Thérèse's ankles, almost invisible beneath the long bombazine skirt.

Althorp remained to the rear, his rifle raised as he marched them about the yard. Thérèse, walking next to Charles in the lead, took the opportunity to look about. A wide variety of uniforms were present, and a good number of men bore the effects of battle in the form of bloodstained bandages and slings.

As they completed the second circuit, an officer wearing the insignia of an aide de camp strolled into the yard from the street beyond. He stopped, looked them over with interest, and approached. Thérèse caught herself stiffening in fear and tried to relax. This was a British officer! They might have had to resort to unconventional methods in unusual circumstances, but they had never stood in danger of facing a firing squad!

Althorp came to attention as the man approached. "Sergeant Althorp, sir." He accompanied the words with a smart salute. "Just bringing Wellington's guests down for some fresh air."

The officer nodded. "Carry on, then."

To Thérèse's relief, he walked on, apparently paying them no further heed. With this worry behind her, she turned her attention to the windows that looked down onto their yard.

"Which do you think is Wellington's room?" she murmured to Charles.

He shook his head. "Could be any of them. I don't think this is getting us anywhere."

As he spoke, the sound of galloping hoofbeats reached them. Two riders drew up their blowing mounts just beyond the ironwork gate and a sentry ran to open it. Wellington, accompanied by a single officer, rode in and jumped down from his horse. He tossed the reins to a soldier who came running up and handed a parcel to another.

"Take it to my command center at once!"

The soldier hurried to comply and Wellington, with the officer at his heels, followed.

"Very clever. And so he is shown the way." Charles's voice sounded near her ear. "Thérèse?"

She stared very hard as Wellington marched past, perhaps twenty yards away. His head was bent, turned toward his companion as they engaged in a low-voiced conversation. The mongrel growled softly as she sensed Thérèse's nervousness.

"It is not Wellington." She let out her breath. "I have seen this man, this Brienne, at the chateau. But it is an imposture of the most perfect! He is the very image of the man we met last night. If I had not seen him before, I would never have guessed!"

"Well, anyone who knows Wellington won't be taken in for long. Which means this is where we step in! This is it!" he hissed to the others.

Thérèse stooped and picked up the little dog to hush its soft whining. The last thing they wanted was to attract any attention. Aimée whimpered, tried to lick her face, and let out a sharp yip.

Wellington—or rather, Brienne—turned and looked about the yard. Thérèse, hugging Aimée close in her arms, stepped back behind Charles. The impostor had seen her before; she did not want to be spotted now. Charles touched her arm and she peeked out. The man had entered the building.

"Shall we follow them?" Charles, his eys dancing with excitement, raised a questioning eyebrow at Althorp. Their supposed guard nodded and gestured for them to return inside.

As they entered the building, "Wellington" and his companion disappeared up the staircase. Charles followed at a leisurely pace, as if he weren't eager for the approaching confrontation. Thérèse was not deceived and her anxiety grew. Charles would positively enjoy a fight!

At the top of the steps, he signaled for the others to wait. With Althorp, whose uniform allowed him access to any part of this great house, he slipped along the hall.

Ahead of them, a guard stood on duty at a door. Charles assumed the mien of a prisoner, with his hands clasped behind his neck and his head lowered. He shuffled along, dragging his feet as if seeking to postpone the inevitable. Althorp, all bristling efficiency, shoved the barrel of the gun into his back and prodded him along.

The guard jumped to attention. "State your business!" he ordered.

"Prisoner to be questioned by Wellington."

The guard eyed them, skeptical. "I wasn't given no orders 'e was expectin' someone."

"He wanted him brought the moment he returned."

The guard shook his head. "Come back unexpected, 'e did, and just to fetch a paper and send a message. Won't 'ave time for your prisoner. You go away and bring 'im back tomorrow."

Althorp shook his head. "I'm not going against orders. You just let him know we're here."

The guard shook his head and a mulish expression settled over his florid countenance. "Don't you listen? Off with you! Gave orders as no one was to disturb 'im."

Althorp shrugged, started to turn, then swung back, delivering a punishing left to the guard's stomach. The man doubled up and dropped his pistol, but as Althorp closed for a finishing punch, the guard struck upward, delivering a telling blow to Althorp's chin. Althorp staggered backward and sprawled on the floor.

Charles closed his eyes and shook his head. Where did these men get their training? Never had he been privileged to view such a perfect display of inefficiency. He turned back to the guard just as the man came at him with fists raised and the light of battle in his eyes.

With one well-placed jab to the stomach and another to the face, Charles landed him neatly. He stood over the fallen man and shook his head again.

"Regrettable, but there it is. Harding!" He called his reserve forces to join him. Thérèse and Margit were left to revive the groggy Althorp with the help of Aimée, who enthusiastically licked his face. Charles consigned the fallen guard to Bosworth's care and picked up the man's pistol. He checked to make sure that Harding held Althorp's rifle and then, at Harding's nod that he was ready, they burst through the door.

Two men occupied the room. The officer who had ridden in with "Wellington" stood at a long table on which a number of maps were spread. The other man, seated at the desk, might in truth have been the great commander. Not a single flaw could Charles's searching gaze detect. A master of disguise himself, he knew how easy it was to make a mistake. This imposture seemed perfect.

Wellington looked up in frowning surprise. "What is

going on here? I told the guard I did not want to be disturbed." He gestured to the officer. "Show them out."

"Not just yet, if you don't mind." Charles motioned to Harding, who obligingly pointed his rifle at the officer. The man's eyes widened and he drew back a step. Charles barely spared him a glance. He focused his attention on the sheet of stationery on which Wellington had been writing an order. His tone, when he spoke, was purely conversational. "That piece of paper ought to prove rather interesting."

"Not really." Wellington casually laid his arm over the writing. "It is no more than a routine matter. But you will kindly explain the meaning of this intrusion!"

Charles shook his head. "Is there really any need? It is a shame to ruin your plans when you have gone to so much trouble, but so have I, to stop you. I really can't let this succeed."

"What the devil are you talking about?" Exasperated, the man rose, drew himself up to his full height, and glared down his nose at the intruder.

"I fear you were seen in Paris. At a certain chateau, to be exact." Charles spoke in perfect French.

Only by the slighest eye movement did the man betray any surprise. It might have been no more than a blink, for Charles could detect no sign of fear or even apprehension in his bearing.

"Is this some sort of jest? If so, it is in very poor taste. I am extremely busy at the moment." The man appeared no more than irritated, as if with any interruption.

"No jest, Monsieur Brienne." Charles still spoke French. "We are aware of the plot to impersonate Wellington."

"Then you know more than I do. Who is this Brienne? Are you trying to say you think I am impersonating myself?" A touch of amusement underlay his words.

"If you are not, then perhaps you will tell me on what

day I arrived." Charles raised his pistol.

"Now how should I remember that? This has gone far enough!"

"You are quite right, it has." Charles took a step closer and cocked the pistol.

The man hesitated. Before Charles could move, the man ducked under the desk and shouted "Guards!"

Charles jumped after him at the same time that a scrambling came not from the hall but from the next room. A door he'd barely noticed flew open wide and five soldiers rushed into the office, three brandishing rifles and two with pistols.

"They are French spies!" shouted the man beneath the desk.

"Harding!" Furious, Charles stopped his assistant, who swung his rifle toward the soldier bearing down on him. "Damn it, man, they're British! You can't shoot them!"

Chagrined, Harding allowed his weapon to drop. "Well, under the circumstances, sir, I feel pretty silly surrendering to my own side!"

Chapter Eighteen

Charles turned a reproving eye on his companion. "We're not surrendering, Harding. Captain!" He turned to address the officer who followed the guards into the room. "We have very good reason to believe that this fellow," he gestured to the man who emerged from beneath the desk, "is not Viscount Wellington."

Wellington straightened his coat and brushed the dust from his impeccable sleeve. He directed a scathing, head-to-toe glance at Charles. "He is either a French spy or an escaped Bedlamite!"

"Possibly the latter." A smile played about Charles's firm mouth. "But there is a very easy test. I am an agent, Captain, but for the British, not the French. My *nom de guerre*, as it were, is *Le Maniganceur*."

"Is it, indeed?" the Captain's eyes narrowed. "If you really are *Le Maniganceur*, I've heard of you. A master of disguise, or so it's been said."

Charles nodded. "In one of the packs in my room there is a small kit of theatrical makeup that includes glues and solvents for attaching false features . . . such as noses." His appraising gaze rested on Wellington, who stiffened. "Without one of these solvents, a false nose could not be removed. It would, in fact, give every appearance of being natural. But with it, I believe you will find your commander here will look quite different."

"You will not listen to this nonsense!" Wellington glared at the Captain. "Arrest him and get him out of my way. I don't have time to listen to the ravings of a lunatic." He sat down behind his desk once more and picked up his quill.

The hapless officer looked from one man to the other, his expression grim. "It's a pretty serious charge that has been made, sir." He addressed Wellington.

"I thought I asked you to arrest him. Do so, and at once! That is an order! Get him out of here and let me get on with my work."

The door from the hall burst open and Althorp staggered in, followed closely by Thérèse, Margit, and Aimée. The soldiers stared at them in surprise and, in the moment of ensuing confusion, the officer who had acompanied Wellington bolted for the door. Wellington shouted, but the man paid no heed. He charged toward Althorp, who jumped in his way. The officer thrust him aside and continued.

The little mongrel launched herself in vociferous pursuit. Thérèse grasped the back of a chair and half-shoved, half-hurled it at the man's legs. It caught him on the ankles and brought him down.

"Quite neat." Charles nodded his approval. "But will you kindly silence Aimée, Thérèse? Her yips can be ear-splitting. Captain, I would suggest you have a couple of your men take him into custody. And don't let his uniform put you off, He is no more a colonel in the British Army than I am!"

"You will do no such thing! The only person you will arrest is this—this maniac!" Wellington came to his feet and waved an angry hand toward Charles. "And those two, for assaulting an officer!"

"If you like." Charles perched on the edge of the desk

and swung one leg. "If you will not bring my kit, then I suppose we will just have to wait until the real Wellington returns. How long does it take to ride to Lisbon and back?"

"If you think I have nothing better to do this day than sit here and wait for something that is not going to happen, you are making a very great mistake!" Wellington's voice trembled in suppressed fury.

The captain's eyes narrowed. "That's as may be." He turned to Charles and his companions. "Could one of these ladies show my men where your things are?"

Charles nodded. "Margit, will you fetch a solvent?"

Over Wellington's furious protests, the captain ordered one of his men to escort Margit, and the two left the room. Charles remained where he was, idly swinging one leg. Wellington started to come around the desk, but Harding stepped in his way, blocking his escape.

"This entire business is absurd! What could an impostor hope to do?" Wellington demanded of the captain. "No one could expect to carry it off! I am too well known!"

The captain looked at Charles. "He has a point. I haven't the honor of knowing him except by sight, but there are others here that even the most perfect disguise could not fool."

"I don't think he meant to remain longer than twenty minutes. Less, probably. I believe that letter he has folded and placed inside his coat will explain a great deal."

The captain hesitated and his gaze flickered back and forth between Charles's calm face and the rigid, flushed countenance of the commander of all the British forces in the Peninsula. He swallowed hard. "I—I think perhaps it would be best if I take a look at that paper, sir." He held out his hand.

"If you think I will let you look at confidential orders, you are even more a fool than I thought—if that's possible! And if you try to take it, you had better be prepared to face

306

the consequences of a court-martial!"

Charles shrugged as the captain cast an uneasy glance at him. "It doesn't really matter. As long as his message isn't sent." He turned to see the fury in Wellington's face and knew he was correct.

They did not have long to wait. Less than fifteen minutes later, Margit and her guard returned, carrying with them Charles's disguise kit. This they handed to the captain who, after subjecting it to a brief but thorough examination, passed it on to Charles.

"If you will help me?" Charles drew a vial from the case and opened it. "We will apply this about his nose."

"You would not dare!" Wellington drew back, his eyes flashing as his jaw thrust out in defiance.

"It will be the fastest way to settle this business, sir." The captain came to stand beside Charles and peered at Wellington's face, trying to detect any flaw that might verify the accusation. "If there is nothing in any of this, no harm will have been done. And you, of all people, sir, wouldn't want me to be derelict in my duty."

"It is an insult! I will . . ."

But he got no further. Charles, tiring of talk, poured a generous amount of the solvent onto a handkerchief supplied by Thérèse. Before Wellington could finish his threat, Charles bore down on him and wiped the soaked linen across his face. Even as they watched, the solution went to work. The false skin about his cheekbones and nose began to curl as it came loose.

"Well, I'll be . . ." The captain stared, his eyes wide.

Wellington—or Brienne, as he was now revealed to be—straightened up, drew his own handkerchief from his pocket, and pulled at the remnants of the nose. Charles obligingly handed him the vial, and with the aid of its contents, the false skin came free. Brienne mopped at his chin and more of the disguise dissolved.

"It seems I have the honor of being defeated by no less an

adversary than *Le Maniganceur.*" The impostor handed back the bottle with a slight bow. "I congratulate you, *m'sieur*. But how . . . ? Ah, yes." His gaze came to rest on Thérèse. "I see. I thought the lady seemed somewhat familiar. A triumph for you, to bring her out of France."

A commotion at the hall door interrupted Charles's acnowledgment of the praise. The real Wellington, scowling in annoyance, stormed into the room and stopped dead. The two soldiers who hurried in his wake almost bumped into him. Aimée, too excited now to be discreet, set up a furious barking that she varied on occasion with a threatening growl. Thérèse hushed her by the simple expedient of clamping a hand over the dog's muzzle.

Wellington stared at each of the occupants of the room. He came forward, his frown deepening. "Would someone care to explain what is going on here?" He stopped before the captain of his guard.

In halting tones, the man complied. Wellington listened in silence, his eyes resting on his impostor's rigid face.

"And do you mean to tell me that not one of my men could tell this wasn't me?" he demanded at the end.

"It was very well done." Charles picked up the false nose and looked at it. "I don't think I could have created a more perfect disguise myself."

"Ah, yes. You. *Le Maniganceur*, I believe? I have learned a bit about you this morning. We have much to talk about. But first we must get to the bottom of this."

On Wellington's orders, the captain subjected Brienne to a rapid search. The orders he had been writing were discovered hidden inside his coat, and both Wellington and Charles read the page with intense interest.

"My God!" Wellington breathed as he finished.

Charles, his jaw tight, raised measuring eyes to the impostor. "An ingenious plan. And I believe it would have worked."

"What would?" Thérèse, who had been trying to peer over the men's shoulders, could wait no longer.

"It is a request, supposedly from Wellington, for the naval commander to bring as many ships as possible up the coast, as near to Torres Vedras as possible, to facilitate the removal of a great number of badly injured and sick men. I assume the French fleet is waiting to move in and take Lisbon as soon as the British numbers are reduced."

Wellington stared wtih unseeing eyes at the paper he held. "It might very well have worked." He raised his thoughtful gaze to Charles's grim face. "It seems we—all of us who serve in the Peninsula campaign—have a great deal to thank you for."

Charles dismissed the praise with a gesture. "I believe it is Mademoiselle de Bourgerre and the others to whom most of the credit is due."

"But of course." Thérèse smiled at the commander as he took her hand. "He came for his health, *enfin*. One cannot blame him, for it was a journey of the most delightful."

Wellington's singularly charming smile flashed. "I shall look forward to hearing your story in greater detail. But at the moment, I fear this little incident must be dealt with. Do you have everything you require for the moment? Then perhaps your entire party will honor me by dining with me this evening?"

He bowed over Thérèse's hand, and she knew herself dismissed. She murmured a polite response and he turned back to Charles.

"And now, *Le Maniganceur*—no, really, what do people call you?"

"Charles will do."

"Very well, Charles. Would you care to stay? I'd be interested in your opinion on a few matters."

Thérèse, followed by the others, slipped out of the room. There was no reason to stay. She wasn't needed, but

Charles was. Was this to be the story of her life? To play her role and then be dismissed, forgotten by those in authority? She did not feel hurt, precisely, just . . . unnecessary, as if she had been spare baggage that Charles had carted along on his mission.

"What now?" Harding stood beside her and she realized she'd stopped just outside the door.

Bosworth looked from one to the other, his expression one of hope. "Lunch?"

Thérèse bit her lip. Dear, practical Bosworth! How much she had come to care for each and every one of her companions on this mad adventure. But it was over now. It must be the aftermath of completing so difficult an undertaking that left her feeling so low. They had been successful against all odds!

"To our rooms? Oh!" Her hand came up to cover her mouth in dismay. "Our poor guard! He has been tied up all this time!"

Margit giggled at her expression. *Mais non.* We released him when we went for Charles's kit. And I apologized most sincerely. He was most generous in forgiving us."

Thérèse sighed. "The poor man. We treated him in the most shameful way!"

"We didn't have much choice." Harding, who led their procession down the long corridor, looked back, his eyes twinkling. "What stories we will all have to tell our children!"

"Children!" Margit almost hooted. "And you refused to play the role of my papa!"

Harding flushed to the roots of his sandy hair. "I had a different role in mind," he muttered, and marched ahead, leaving Margit to stare at Thérèse in bewilderment.

Back in their room, Harding went to stare out the window, his hands folded behind his back. Thérèse curled up on the sofa with Aimée in her lap. Margit hesitated,

310

then went to join Harding.

"Do you think they would permit me to ride? I would very much like to see more of these fortifications."

"I'll see what I can do." Without so much as a glance at her, Harding left their now unguarded suite.

"That might be what we all need." Althorp paced the length of the room with his long-legged stride. "Funny, isn't it? I never thought I'd want to ride for pleasure so soon."

"Me, I wish to ride for escape." Margit continued to stare out the window. *"Hélas,* I feel so very trapped in here!"

"If they do not let you ride, you can always walk." Thérèse hugged the little mongrel. She could well understand the other girl's restlessness. After so much excitement and fear, it seemed wrong to be idle. And matters that had long been pushed into the background now came to the fore to haunt her—with a vengeance.

They remained where they were in silence until Harding returned. He looked about the room, and suddenly his stern-featured face broke into a smile.

"You'd think we'd failed! We ought to be celebrating! Just think what we accomplished!"

Althorp eyed him without enthusiasm. "Hip, hip, hurrah."

"Well, I've accomplished something else. Margit, you can have your ride. But the guard suggested you might prefer to go toward the ocean."

"Anywhere, just to be outside! Thérèse, do you come?"

"I am going to await my lunch. Monsieur Harding, you will accompany her? It does not seem safe that she should ride alone."

"That it doesn't," he agreed. He met Thérèse's smiling glance and looked down at once.

Margit looked at her companions, startled. "But—none of you will go with me?"

"Perhaps this afternoon," Thérèse spoke up quickly. She turned and caught Althorp's puzzled gaze and directed a meaningful look at him. His eyes widened in sudden comprehension and he turned quickly away to hide his grin.

Harding glared at them. "Come along, then." He ushered Margit out of the room, turned to direct a quelling glance at Thérèse, and slammed the door behind him.

Margit looked over her shoulder at him in surprise. "You are not pleased? You do not have to come with me. I will not ride far."

"Glad to." His gruff tone did not encourage either argument or conversation.

Margit fell silent. At the foot of the stairs, a soldier met them and led the way to the stable. There they found their horses groomed, saddled, and apparently well rested. Margit stroked the neck of her mount and the animal nuzzled her hand.

"Well, my friend, today we ride at our ease." She took hold of her stirrup only to have Harding come up behind her. He cupped his hands for her, and helped to lift her lightly up into the saddle. He swung onto his own horse and led the way out of the yard.

"It seems odd to ride openly." She glanced at him, suddenly shy, as an unsettling flutter of nerves threw her off balance. She had not felt so confused since they'd left the tavern in Paris!

"No more danger." He was silent a moment, then added, "Situations change."

He was tense! That explained her own sense of everything being disturbed. Harding, who always seemed calm and in control of himself, was uneasy! It made him very human, almost approachable. But approaching him was something she did not dare to do.

They rode on without speaking. At the outskirts of the village they continued without a pause, on toward the forest of scattered evergreens that stretched beyond. Margit searched her mind for some topic of conversation, but found herself distressingly tongue-tied. She had absolutely no idea what to say! Here she was, alone with the kindest, most dependable and considerate man she had ever known, and she was frightened, of all things! If she spoke, would he scorn her words as being silly? She was nothing more than a tavern wench, when all was said and done. And he—he was everything she most admired.

Why could she not flirt with him, and be gay and charming? She wanted to fascinate him, to enthrall him with a beauty and wit she did not possess. If only she could borrow even a tiny portion of the unconscious charm that characterized Thérèse! Now there was a lady who would not be reduced to stammering incoherence in the presence of a man she adored.

But Margit was not Thérèse. She lacked any semblance of wiles, and she could think only of mundane things to say, things that would bore a man of Harding's vast experience!

She peered across at the firm line of his jaw, at the tense set of his broad shoulders, at the fixed gaze of his hazel eyes. He accompanied her out of duty, nothing more! He would probably rather be back in the suite, talking over everything they had done with Althorp and Bosworth, or perhaps drinking tea with the elegant Thérèse. He admired her! He thought Thérèse brave and beautiful, and found her fluttery, impetuous manner delightful . . . and well he should.

Margit swallowed in a vain attempt to force down the uncomfortable constriction in her throat. Anyone must admire Thérèse! But who would look twice at a short, stocky half-gypsy who knew little of life outside of a rough tavern? Her manners weren't delicate, they were direct, and she could fight as well as if she were indeed the boy she had been raised to imitate.

Dissatisfied, she urged her horse into a swift trot. Even after the past few weeks, it still irked her to ride in the sidesaddle. That was for ladies like Thérèse! She was accustomed to ride astride—though more commonly on a donkey than a horse. Wouldn't that shock the very proper and British Harding, if she were to throw her leg over the saddle as did he!

She threw a measuring glance at him. He kept pace with her, though his expression remained impenetrable, almost forbidding. It was as if he defied any attempt on her part to breach his own line of defense. And she had no idea how to begin such an assault. If only she didn't care!

She slowed back to a walk. "It is over, our adventure."

"Yes." The single syllable came out cold and uncompromising . . . almost a conversational dead end.

Why must he be so annoying? Could they not even be friends? Several times on the journey, she had thought he might almost like her. But now . . . Unhappy, she urged her horse into a canter up a hill.

As they reached the top, she caught her breath and reined her mount to a halt. Below them, beyond many miles of forested terrain, stretched the ocean. Large white clouds hung low, almost touching the horizon where the soft blue sky shaded into gray and blended with the sea. Margit stared at it, lost in thought, as the gentle breeze rustled through the pines, bringing a soft scent to them. Above her, hidden in the evergreen branches, birds sang to each other.

"It is very peaceful here."

"Aye." Harding swung down and walked forward to the edge of the hill, leading his horse behind him. He stood with arms folded across his chest, staring down over the rugged terrain.

She regarded him uncertainly. "And what do you do now? Return to England?"

He squatted down on the ground, picked up a small rock, and hurled it into the shrubs below. A shrill protest rose from the startled birds. "Maybe. My job's done."

"That was only to rescue Thérèse. Yet you came with her all the way to Portugal." Her throat felt oddly tight.

He shrugged. "The job wasn't done until we had her safe. She's that now, unless she takes some maggot into her head and goes rushing off again."

"And then you will follow her once more, *n'est-ce pas?*"

An odd smile touched his grim features. "Oh, Mr. Charles will do that, like as not. But I suppose I'll have to follow him."

"It is madness!" Margit jumped down, unable to contain any longer the seething emotions she did not fully understand. "You will dash off into danger again, just for the sake of a woman!"

"For a woman? What a hairbrained thing to say!"

"*Vraiment?*" She regarded him wide-eyed. "Then why will you do this so foolish thing, *enfin?*"

"Duty." He shook his head. "I go where I have to, even into danger. And you?"

"Me?" She held her breath. "Do—do I have something to do with this?"

"I suppose not, damn it!" He sent another rock hurtling down to follow the first.

She regarded his back, confused. She had said the wrong thing! But what was right? She was not even sure what they talked about! "My—my work in the tavern, it is not dangerous."

"No, it's just the right sort of thing for a kid."

"But me, I am not a child anymore."

His lips twisted into an odd, lopsided smile. "No, you're growing up, aren't you? So what will it be? Back to your tavern?"

"I do not know. I have not thought that far."

He turned to look fully at her. "Why did you come on this little excursion?"

Soft color warmed her cheeks and she avoided his gaze. His eyes narrowed, but when he spoke, his tone was gentle. "I thought at first it was to follow *Le Maniganceur*, but that wasn't it, was it?"

"*Le Maniganceur*? Charles? The idea, *c'est ridicule!*"

"Is it? Then why did you leave that comfortable little tavern of yours? Because you were tired of waiting on tables and scrubbing floors?"

"I—I wanted to see more of our work, but now that I have, I have had my fill of it! I want stability and security!"

He gave a short laugh. "Well, you won't find it in our way of life."

"This I know." Even to herself, her voice sounded bleak. "*Eh, bien.* I will now go back to the tavern."

He turned once again to stare out over the pines toward the sea. "You like it there?"

"It is all right. The work, it is hard, but I do not mind that. It is the only life I have known." She could sense the tenseness in his stance, but could not understand it.

"You're a worker, aren't you?"

She flushed with pleasure at what she took to be a compliment. "*Oui.*"

He concentrated on the trees just below them. "It might not be a bad life, running a tavern or a coaching inn. A busy one, maybe, on a post road."

"There is much excitement," she agreed. But any tavern he chose would be in England, many insurmountable miles from Paris. The idea left her strangely cold and empty.

"I've never done that sort of thing before. I'd have to have someone who knew the ropes to help me."

She studied her hands. "Me, I have worked in a tavern all my life."

"You must be tired of it."

"*Mais non!* It can be very satisfying."

"All that scrubbing and sweeping?" An odd light lurked in his eyes.

"And you meet people, *du vrai,* and hear all the news."

"Your tavern was special. It was a meeting place for the

British sympathizers. That alone made it exciting."

"*En avant*, you can operate a tavern for the agents in London."

An arrested look came into his hazel eyes. "I could at that."

A silence fell over them, but for once it was companionable, not fraught with tension. Margit took a deep breath, welcoming this change. Harding could be very easy to talk to, when he wished.

"It would be no good alone," he said suddenly. His gaze remained fixed on the trees below. "Will you come with me?"

She began to tremble with undefined emotion. "You—you need an experienced scullion?"

"No! A partner!"

The quivering within her became almost uncontrollable. "What—what type of partner? Me, I have no money."

"You don't need any." He turned to face her, his expression half-exasperated.

"But how then can I be a partner?"

He grasped her shoulders and pulled her gently, if somewhat clumsily, toward himself. His mouth sought hers and found first her nose, then a corner of her lips. On the third attempt, he succeeded in kissing her.

He released her almost at once, and his worried gaze sought hers. She stared back at him, her eyes round in shocked amazement.

He ran an agitated hand through his rumpled hair, shaking his head in disbelief at what he'd just done. "Margit. I—I'm sorry." He turned away. "I've been upset, worried, but that's no excuse for what I did. To kiss you like that . . . it was an insult! You have every right to be angry."

"*Vraiment?* This was an insult?" She touched his hand. "Please, Monsieur Harding, will you insult me again?"

An unsteady laugh set his shoulders shaking. He

reached out and just brushed her cheek with one finger. "Like this?" He cupped her chin and drew her face gently to his.

She went to him without protest, confused, yet reveling in the sensations of his lips on hers. When she at last sat back, she regarded him through wide, bemused eyes.

"You were right. I did come on this journey to follow a man. *You.*"

He smiled. "You lack any subterfuge. So straightforward, so very honest. There isn't an ounce of guile or deceit in you, is there?"

"*Non.*" Her reply was as honest as she. "Did you like kissing me?"

His smile deepened. "Very much." He rose and helped her to her feet. "Do you know, I never thought I'd want a woman cluttering up my life."

"But now you do? *Eh, bien,* I am glad." Without any trace of self-consciousness, she walked straight into his arms and lifted her face for another kiss.

It was late afternoon before they returned to the others. Thérèse, who stood staring out their window, did not even turn as the door opened. Her gaze remained focused beyond the confines of the village, toward the third line of fortifications.

"Did you see Charles?" Her voice, though carefully controlled, betrayed her concern.

"Did he ride out?" Harding threw his hat onto a table and cast a worried glance at Margit.

"With Milord Wellington."

"Well, that's nothing to be concerned about. I really can't see *Le Maniganceur* getting inside a fortification of this magitude without wanting to get a closer look. I'm sure he'll be back soon."

"That is true. *Le Maniganceur* would never let such an opportunity slip by." With a slight, almost fatalistic, shrug, she came away from the window. Here, at Torres Vedras, lay the greatest danger to Charles. How, in such a place and in the company of such a man as Wellington, could he resist the exciting lure of the old life he had renounced in a fit of depression? Nothing, not even those horrible injuries, could keep *Le Maniganceur* down for long.

The afternoon wore into evening, and still Charles did not reappear. They dined with the officers and those of their ladies who followed the drum, but Thérèse found little appetite for either the excellent meal or the polite company. Lord Wellington was also absent, and that could mean only one thing to Thérèse's heavy heart: they were together. But perhaps Charles would resist, perhaps he was only curious about the defenses, perhaps he was not lost to her yet. . . .

The ladies withdrew from the dining room, and Thérèse took the opportunity to escape and seek the solitude of their quarters. Margit, uncomfortable in what she termed "grand company," joined her. They would not have long to wait, they knew, for Harding, Althorp, and Bosworth. But what of Charles?

As the hour grew advanced, Thérèse yielded to Margit's entreaties and retired to bed. She lay awake long, listening to the deep, steady sounds of the other girl's breathing. Why did Charles not return? What did they speak of, the great *Le Maniganceur* and the commander of all the British forces in the Peninsula?

She must have been drifting off to sleep, for a soft click brought her fully awake. She listened, intent, and was rewarded by the sounds of stealthy movement in the sitting room beyond her door. She rose at once and pulled on a dressing gown loaned to her by one of the officer's wives. Without disturbing Margit, she slipped out of their chamber.

Charles looked up from where he bent over the sofa. His well-worn pack lay on the cushions before him, and his meager collection of belongings lay scattered about. A single candle illuminated the area. Thérèse hesitated in the doorway, her heart sinking.

"You're awake."

His comment seemed hopelessly inadequate, and Thérèse almost smiled. "So are you." She came farther into the room. "You have been very busy this day."

"I have."

He thrust his spare jacket, the one he wore when he left England, into the pack. It filled her with a sense of foreboding. "What—what did you learn from that man, that impostor Brienne?"

"Nothing." His expression was grim. "We have no idea when the attack is to take place."

"And now?"

"Oh, we'll have to see what we can find out." He sounded his usual cheerful self. "They'll have no idea yet that their plan has been ruined. It's not unreasonable that Brienne might have had to move carefully making his escape, so they won't be worried when he doesn't return."

"And what is it that you do?" Her throat felt dry, for she could hazard a pretty shrewd guess.

He laid down his disguise kit and went to her, placing his hands on her slender shoulders. "Only what I must."

She drew a deep, ragged breath. "You must go into danger once more." She made it a statement of fact, not a question.

"Oh, it won't be that bad." He tried to make his voice light, cheerful, but his dark eyes remained serious. "Wellington is sending a few capable lads along with me."

"Unlike Messieurs Althorp and Bosworth?"

His deep chuckle sounded, sending a shiver of longing —and misery—through her. Her hands crept up and closed about his arms, as if she sought to hold him with her.

"Those two have come a long way, don't you think?" His tone teased as he tried to rally her. "I'd like to see them

320

after they've had a few months of adequate training."

"I—I hope you may have that chance." The words were spoken more to herself than to him, but she regretted them at once. She had no right to try and influence him, to let him know how she hated the choice he made. She did not want his last memory of her, before he went into danger, to be of an argument.

His hands caressed her shoulders through the lace-covered muslin of the dressing gown. "It won't be for long, *ma Thérèse*. I should be back in a day or two."

She nodded, glad that the meager light of the candle would not let him see the tears that filled her eyes. "It—it must be you who goes?" She could not prevent herself from asking.

"For what must be done, yes. Wellington has no one else here with this sort of experience. And if we can just be ready for the French fleet and lay an effective trap for them, we can win a decisive victory here!"

She lowered her gaze and stared hard at the third button of his waistcoat. He looked forward to this! But she had already known he would. She had been deceiving herself, trying to pretend there was hope, that she might be able to find some semblance of a normal life with him.

He took her chin in one hand and raised her face to his. His solemn eyes gazed into her tear-filled ones. "There is still a job to be done, *ma Thérèse*. There can be no rest for anyone until this is finished." His voice held an apology mingled with a plea for understanding.

She did understand, and only too well. "There will always be work for *Le Maniganceur*." She whispered the words as she tried to disguise the unhappiness in her voice.

He released her. "There will come a day. . . ." He broke off as she raised a finger to his lips to silence him.

"You must do what you must, *mon cher* Charles," she whispered, and knew as she did so that she said good-bye, to her hopes, her dreams, her happiness—to him.

Chapter Nineteen

Predawn darkness engulfed the sitting room. Thérèse huddled into her borrowed dressing gown and peered out the window, down into the yard that blazed with torchlight. Seven men hurried back and forth, some saddling horses, some checking over the contents of their packs, all moving with the suppressed excitement of anticipated—and welcomed—danger.

Only one man seemed calm. Charles, his powerful, broad-shouldered figure unmistakable even in the wavering light, stood to one side in conversation with Harding. What they spoke about, Thérèse could only guess.

One of the other men approached Charles and saluted. Charles nodded, turned to Harding, and extended his hand. Harding gripped it, then stepped back to allow Charles to pass.

Her heart bleak, Thérèse watched as Charles and four other men mounted their horses and made final inspections of their packs. They started forward, but at the gate, Charles reined in and allowed the others to proceed. He turned in his saddle, looked up toward the window where she sat, and raised a hand in a gesture of farewell. Thérèse responded, though she knew he could not see her. Her eyes filled with tears. She blinked until her vision cleared, but by then he had gone.

She swallowed hard. Charles was gone. Fighting off the sense of inconsolable loss and emptiness, she turned back into the room.

Margit stood in the door of their bedchamber, her short curls tousled, the borrowed lacy dressing gown wrapped about her stocky figure. "I—I heard him leave." Hesitant, she went to Thérèse and held out her hands. "He will be all right. *Le Maniganceur* always succeeds."

Thérèse nodded and tried very hard not to sniff. "Oh, yes, *Le Maniganceur* will triumph. It—it is only Charles I worry for." Her voice broke on a sob.

Unable to think of anything adequate to say, Margit sank down onto a chair at her side. They sat together in silence until Harding returned to the suite. Margit sprang at once to her feet, ran to him, and threw her sturdy arms about his waist, holding him as if she feared that she, too, would lose the man she loved.

He gave her a quick, comforting hug. "Why are you two looking so down in the mouth?" He looked from one to the other and managed an almost convincing smile. "It's just a routine scouting mission. The sort of thing I should imagine he's done at least a hundred times."

"Oh, yes." Thérèse nodded. "And *voyons*, he will probably do it a hundred more."

"It won't be that bad. He says he shouldn't be gone more than a day or two."

Thérèse stared out the window with unseeing eyes. "When he gets back, I will not be here."

"What do you mean?" Harding came farther into the room, drawing Margit with him. His eyes narrowed. "Just what are you planning on doing?"

She shrugged her shoulders. "I am going back to England. I have had enough of adventuring, *enfin*. I want to live a normal life without thinking that everyone I meet might be a spy." That any life without Charles would be empty and purposeless, she forced herself not to consider.

"What will you do?" Harding still frowned.

"Go back on the stage. I am a singer, *hélas*. There will be more than enough excitement for me in such a life."

Harding glanced down at Margit and his arm tightened about her for a moment before he released her and went to stand before Thérèse. "Mr. Charle says as I'm to look after you while he's gone. He's not going to like your leaving like this, you know. Why don't you wait until he comes back?"

"You mean *if* he come back. *Non et non et non!* I cannot spend my life wondering when he will be killed. If he makes it this time, what about the next? Or the time after that?" She looked up at him and the tears she had fought to hold back slipped unheeded down her cheeks. "*Hélas*, he will never give up the danger. And me, I cannot live with it."

Harding shook his head, though he did not press her to delay her departure. "I suppose I'll go with you, then."

Margit looked up at him, her eyes gleaming. "*We* will go with her."

"There—there is no need." Thérèse looked away to dab at her eyes with her rumpled handkerchief. "You may escort me to Lisbon if you wish, but there you may turn me over to the Navy." She tried to smile. "They will prove an adequate guard, *bien sûr*."

Harding stood his ground, looking stubborn. "My orders from Lord Pembroke were to bring you back, if possible. It's my duty to be the one to take you to England."

"And what of Charles?"

Harding did not meet her gaze. "He's under orders to no one, is *Le Maniganceur*. He'll do as he wishes. But I've got to report back to Lord Pembroke. Even if Mr. Charles asked me to stay, I'd have to clear it with headquarters."

Margit raised dismayed eyes to his face. "You will

continue in this work? But I thought . . ."

"No, I'm done. I only meant—well, it doesn't matter. Just as soon as we have her safe back in England, I'll resign."

Thérèse looked from one to the other, at the joy and certainty that shone in both pairs of eyes. She fought back an unworthy pang of envy. They deserved it—and the happiness to be found with each other! "You will like England, Margit. It is the sort of land that makes one want to settle down and have a real home."

Harding smiled. "Aye, that it is."

Margit nodded. "Me, I want very much to settle down." She let out a long sigh. "How good it will be to have a home of my own, to live without fear—and to be happy."

Harding looked down into her upturned face. Their contentment filled Thérèse with such longing that she turned abruptly and went back into her room. Harding had made the decision to change his life. She could only be glad for his sake—and Margit's—though in truth, it surprised her somewhat. Harding had seemed as dedicated to the life of danger as was Charles! Yet he had chosen to give it up, to lay aside that driving sense of duty in exchange for love and the peace and serenity he had earned. If only Charles could do the same. But it was useless to torture herself like this! She had to think about something else!

Desperate to distract herself, she concentrated on Margit. Now *there* was someone who deserved her happiness after the difficult and risky life she had led. And the feisty, strong-willed girl was just the wife for a man like Harding. Her fierce loyalty, her toughness, her determination—she was so very like him in every way. They would never regret this decision.

If only . . . She cut off that recurring thought. Did she enjoy making herself miserable? After all, what did she have in common with Charles, aside from their work? And now she wanted to turn her back on the life that was so much a part of him that he had been dead without it.

True, she would miss the adventure. It was not the constant peril, the breathless danger that tore her apart, made her realize she could not continue in this existence. It was the knowledge that one day it would claim Charles. It was as if she mourned him already. And she would continue to do so, every day, until she could force her heart to forget him.

She pulled off her borrowed dressing gown and donned the freshly laundered riding habit of brown wool that had seen her through hundreds of miles of hard traveling. After that, she had very little to gather together. In a way, it all would be easier if she were kept busy folding garments and tucking things away in her pack.

As it was, she was finished and ready to leave in less than twenty minutes. It seemed hard to believe she had existed for several weeks with so few possessions. Perhaps she could busy herself with a shopping expedition in Lisbon. Anything would be better than sitting idly about, wondering how Charles's mission fared, whether he had been spotted by the French, perhaps injured. . . .

Evicting him forcibly from her mind, she tried to concentrate on the bright side of things. It would be nice to get back to her own house, her lovely gowns, and the competent ministrations of Symmons—except that both the house and her abigail had been loans from the government, hers for only two more months. Well, she would find herself a new home and a new maid, one who was familiar with the rigors of performing on stage. She had her whole life ahead of her! She could not allow thoughts of one reckless, foolhardy man to ruin her future!

When Margit entered the chamber a little while later, Thérèse sat on the edge of her bed, staring at her hands. Her much-worn pack sat on the floor at her feet. Aimée lay curled beside it, regarding her mistress through large, soulful eyes.

"The men, they are ready." Margit pulled her dress from the cupboard and began to untie her dressing gown. "I shall only be a moment."

Thérèse would have missed Margit had she stayed behind. They had become close friends over the past couple of weeks. A wave of warm emotion swept through her.

"I am glad you are coming. And for you and Harding. But I warn you, I shall come often to your tavern in London." Though that would keep her memories alive . . .

Thérèse rose abruptly and went out to the sitting room to find that two soldiers had brought up a substantial breakfast. The men sat at a makeshift table with generous portions before them. Althorp looked up and smiled as she entered.

"So, we're off again this morning, are we?"

Thérèse nodded. "*Oui.* If you do not mind."

Althorp just grinned. "It will be nice to laze about a ship for a few days."

Thérèse could almost smile. Did experience mellow his enthusiasm? "*Voyons,* you will not miss the activity?"

"Of course," he averred stoutly. "But we've earned a bit of a holiday, haven't we, Bosworth?"

That worthy regarded him with bovine stolidity. When he finished chewing his mouthful, he said, "It just don't make sense how anyone can enjoy being on a boat. But I'll be glad to get back to a Christian country."

"Very true," Althorp agreed. "It's been exciting and a lot of fun—that goes without saying. But it will be nice to see familiar places again."

Thérèse placed a few morsels of food on her plate, but found she had no appetite. She took a bite, then gave up the attempt. "When can we leave?"

Harding, who had been eating in silence, pushed his

plate aside and rose. "If go we must, it might as well be sooner as later. I'll be off to speak to Wellington, now."

His errand did not take long. He found the great man busy that morning, but was granted a brief audience. Far from being sorry to see his unexpected guests depart, Wellington offered Harding every assistance to speed him on his way. A soldier was assigned to accompany him and make sure he received everything he requested at the stables, and Wellington wrote a quick introduction to the naval commander in Lisbon, requesting his aid for the travelers. With this safely in his pocket, Harding received a firm handshake and somehow found himself back outside the commander's office.

"What will you be wanting, sir?" The soldier regarded him expectantly.

"Our horses saddled." In truth, he could think of nothing else. They were perhaps thirty miles from Lisbon, and the journey would take them no more than about four hours, even riding at a leisurely pace. With the vague feeling that everything suddenly proceeded too smoothly after so much trouble, he went to fetch the others.

He found Thérèse staring out the window with one of Charles's forgotten shirts clutched in her hands. As Harding entered the apartment, she set it aside and turned to face him, a false smile on her lips. Picking up her pack, she followed the others from the room without so much as another backward glance.

For the first time in a very long while, they had no need to rush. Still, Thérèse felt too restless to dawdle along the road. The others were eager to see Lisbon and the end of their adventure, so they pushed onward over the surprisingly rough countryside. But now they could ride openly on good roads that the army kept in excellent condition.

It was almost noon before they reached the outskirts of the city. They wended their way along narrow streets that wound through the oldest portion of the city, down toward the waterfront and the estuary, the *Mar de Palha*. Above them, the city climbed its wandering way up into the foothills, and from there looked down upon the widening Tagus.

Once they were near the waterfront, it proved a simple task to locate the temporary headquarters of the naval command. Messages had already passed back and forth to Torres Vedras during the night, so their arrival did not come as a complete surprise to the officer in charge. He welcomed them, examined Harding's letter of authorization, and asked what he could do to help.

"If you please, we wish to return to England as soon as possible." Thérèse stepped forward.

The man consulted a notebook. "We've got a boat sailing with the tide in the morning, if that would suit you. It's a supply ship, so it will only be carrying a few wounded."

"That—that would be excellent." It all went so smoothly . . . as if she were meant to be parted from Charles. She blinked rapidly and tried to smile.

"What of that French plot?" Harding frowned.

The officer's eyes narrowed and his smile appeared somewhat grim. "We don't know for sure when that will be, but you may be sure we'll be ready for them. And you should be well on your way to England by then."

Harding nodded. "Thank you, sir."

"I'll contact the captain and have your things taken aboard." Nodding his dismissal, the officer returned to his work.

Thérèse went outside into the sunlight and stared out over the estuary. In the morning . . . The sooner she left, the better! To remain would only be painful, for she would wait every moment for word of Charles. . . .

"William!" Margit tugged at Harding's sleeve. "There are things we must buy, Thérèse and I. Did you not say there was some money?"

"And when we are done, we shall explore the city, *n'est-ce pas?*" Thérèse looked from one to the other of her companions, hopeful. A day of enforced idleness would never be sufficient to keep her thoughts from Charles, who probably enjoyed this dangerous scouting mission immensely—insufferable, reckless man that he was!

In her estimation of how Charles regarded his assignment, she was almost right. There was nothing of leisure about the day for him, which suited him perfectly. As soon as his party left Torres Vedras, they rode hard, passing through Lisbon less than an hour after Thérèse left Wellington's camp. But rather than stay in the city, his party crossed the estuary at the narrowest point, procured fresh horses, and rode on in search of the French troops that must have accompanied the impostor Brienne on his journey from Paris.

They might have learned nothing of use from Brienne, but Charles had been involved in the work too long not to be able to make a few shrewd guesses. With the north closed to the French, they would be forced to cross the Tagus and move up from the south. And after considerable time spent with Wellington's maps, he had selected the Bay of Setubal, which lay just across a peninsula from the *Mar de Palha*, as the most likely spot for any number of troops or ships to wait.

He was not disappointed. In the late afternoon, as they crept up a hill that would provide a view of the bay below, the sounds of movement and voices reached him. Signaling his companions to hold back, Charles inched forward through the underbrush and out to a point where he could see without being seen.

A company of French infantry camped below on the edge of the bay. And everywhere were the signs of activity. Tents were being taken down, packs readied, and most interesting to Charles's searching gaze, three cannon were

330

being harnesssed to the teams of oxen that would pull them. Camp, he decided, would most likely be broken within the hour. That would give the lumbering cannon time to move up into position across from Lisbon during the night. And unless he missed his guess, which he very much doubted, they would lay siege to the harbor at dawn to clear the way for their ships.

Well, the British would be ready for them. And just to make sure . . . Keeping low, so that the straggly underbrush provided sufficient cover, he crawled forward, down the hill. There were officers in several different uniforms. Did that mean other troops lurked nearby? Or perhaps marched to their aid? It would never do for the British to repulse an initial attack and relax, believing themselves the victors, only to succumb to a second, unexpected onslaught.

Thirty minutes passed, and all below seemed in readiness for departure. Still, the officers made no move to leave and return to their own troops. That might mean they had none, that they had made up the guard for the impostor. As Charles watched, that suspicion took firmer root. The officers appeared to be in command of different bands within the company. It would seem that the French planned to take Lisbon with a naval battle and only a few supporting land troops. Reviewing what he knew—or could guess—of their plan, he decided they had every reason for anticipating success. Except that the British would be expecting them.

Satisfied, Charles started to inch his cautious way back to his companions. As he started to turn, he stiffened, every part of his being alert. A man not in uniform came out from behind the cannon. There was something more than a little bit familiar about the way he ran a hand through his rumpled, fair hair. Charles raised his field glasses and trained them on the man.

Armand, Chevalier de Lebouchon. He had not been

mistaken. A slow, grim smile just touched Charles's lips. So de Lebouchon *was* there. A few matters still lay between them, in particular this so-called gentleman's betrayal of Thérèse's impulsive and misguided friendship. Charles could not forgive that, knowing as he did what an innocent, loving creature the fool woman could be. The savage hope welled within him that he would meet up with de Lebouchon before the next day ended.

He returned to his men and told them briefly what he had seen, and they started back toward Lisbon. If the attack was slated for the morrow, which now seemed probable, then all must be prepared. They rode hard, but darkness closed about them as they boarded the tiny boats that would carry them across to the city.

Once they landed, Charles went directly to the naval command and made his report. With a flurry of activity, the officer in charge shouted for his captains, dispatched a messenger to Wellington, and placed every available soldier on alert to guard the waterfront. The real battle might take place in the sea, but there would be a skirmish here.

When he at last emerged from the meeting, the waxing moon rode high in the sky amid a dazzling array of stars. He stared up for a long moment, lost in thought. He had sent a note to Thérèse, assuring her that he was all right, but it had been brief and unsatisfying, even to him. But as soon as the French had been dealt with, he would return to Torres Vedras—and Thérèse.

The naval commander came out of the building and joined him. "There doesn't seem to be anything left to do."

Charles mentally reviewed the numerous details of their preparations and agreed. All had been done. Still, he could not rest easy. Lisbon—and the supply line for the entire British campaign in the Peninsula—lay at stake. He could not calmly seek a bed as if this were an ordinary night!

Instead, he followed the naval commander down to the wharves and with him paced between the various points where British soldiers were concealed. They exchanged tense jokes with the officers, peered across the narrow inlet seeking signs of enemy movement, and then were off again to the next post, always checking to make sure everything was in readiness.

An almost unseemly eagerness enveloped Charles. He could hardly wait for the coming battle! But it was not French troops, cannon, or ships that occupied his mind, but one man. He wanted to meet up with de Lebouchon, and this time, he vowed, nothing would prevent him from finishing his deadly work.

A smile crossed his face, relieving the grimness of his expression. It had been Thérèse who'd interfered with his last fight with de Lebouchon. Thérèse, with her ornamental shield—and the untimely arrival of the servants. He could not blame her for acting. In fact, he applauded her resourcefulness.

A soldier behind him coughed, recalling him to a sense of his surrounding. It would be a long night. . . .

After hours of tense waiting, the first dim rays of light lessened the darkness in the east behind them. Morning filled the sky with a gray haze that grew steadily brighter, though the sun still hid behind the hills. But across the estuary the countryside remained still, shrouded in shadows and silence.

The first of the British ships broke anchor, and still there were no sounds except for the clanking of chain, the lapping of the gentle waves against the wooden hulls, the flapping of canvas sails against the masts as they were dragged into position, and the occasional shout to heave harder. One by one, as ordered, the boats started down the narrow mouth of the river to the ocean.

They appeared to be no more than lightly armed supply vessels, bent on their errand to fetch the wounded from

Torres Vedras and return them to England, but Charles knew otherwise. Each had been prepared with a battery of artillery and bore a full complement of sailors and cannon, rather than medical supplies, as the French expected. And the guns were positioned forward, ready for defense—and attack—the moment the enemy ships hove into sight. There would be a battle the French would not soon forget.

The last of the vessels disappeared from sight. Only a few remained, rocking peacefully at anchor. Stillness enveloped the harbor, broken only by the shrill cry of a gull.

Charles leaned forward, peering into the lessening darkness across the estuary. Had he miscalculated? Was the trap planned solely for the ships? Did the French cannon line the river inlet leading to the sea? Would that be the target, instead of Lisbon?

The booming explosion of cannon shattered the stillness and answered his doubts. The opposite shore came alive with movement as a flotilla of tiny boats, carried across the Peninsula from the bay, now set forth across the estuary. The French had fallen for their subterfuge! They must be convinced that their plan worked, that the British expected nothing and the city of Lisbon was left almost defenseless.

Charles glanced at the British naval commander. The man waited, tense, watching, as he allowed the French to reach a position of no return. He raised his arm, noted that his officers did likewise, then let it fall. In unison, the answering British shots rang out.

Charles watched the resulting chaos with grim satisfaction. Unprepared for this onslaught, the French troops panicked, and their little boats turned every which way in an attempt to escape.

But it was too late for them to turn back. The officers were committed to this attack, to breaking the British control of Lisbon, and they would not give up. To the accompaniment of a fresh round of cannon fire, they rallied their troops and came on more determined than ever. Again the British returned the fire, and the battle was engaged.

The thundering explosion of cannon at close range brought Thérèse bolt upright in her bunk. The confusion of sleep fled as a volley of rifle shots answered. The French attacked the harbor, and she and her companions were in the middle of it! It hadn't occurred to her that it would happen so soon! But of course it would . . . once their man infiltrated Torres Vedras with his false orders, the French would waste no time, would give the British no opportunity to realize that phony orders had been issued.

Aimée whined and curled closer to Thérèse, who comforted the little dog as best she could. Propped on her elbow, Thérèse peered out the tiny porthole in her cabin. Diffused gray light blurred the view, hid the activity from her searching gaze. And where was Charles? Try as she might, she could not block the desperate question from her mind.

And she had to know! What a fool she had been to think she could leave Charles, abandon him to the dangers of his chosen life. She would share it with him—she must—if only she could convince him to let her! She had to find him, make sure he was all right! Life without him . . . the thought was unbearable!

She scrambled from her bunk just as another cannon boomed forth and the ship rocked crazily. The boat steadied, settled, but did not right itself. It leaned shockingly to starboard, so that Thérèse landed in a heap with Aimée on the floor. As she lay there recovering from the shock, the ship lurched and shifted farther.

They had been hit! Grabbing the edge of her bunk for support, Thérèse swung herself to her feet and pulled on the warm traveling gown she'd purchased the day before.

Sounds of scraping and movement reached her from the next cabin, followed by the slamming of a door. A frantic knock preceded Harding as he burst in on her.

"We're sinking!" He clutched at the perilously tilted doorjamb to stay upright.

"I know! Make sure the others are all right!"

While Harding rushed off, Thérèse grabbed up her reticule and pulled on her pelisse. With Aimée scurrying at her feet, she darted up the companionway and emerged onto the deck to see the gray sky filled with exploding lights as cannon and rifles fired. The air, so still and quiet except for the water noises such a short time before, vibrated with the volley of shots.

On the other side of the ship, she could just make out the figures of Margit, Harding, and Althorp. Bosworth ran a zigzag path amidst the scrambling sailors to join them. As Thérèse started in their direction, the ship gave a wild lurch that threw her to the deck. Aimée yipped in fear and began whining as she huddled so close to Thérèse that her mistress had difficulty in getting to her feet.

A running sailor stopped to help, then ran on. Thérèse clutched at the companionway wall, looking about, lost amid the frantic action. Her friends were no longer in sight! She started forward, uncertain, but another sailor grabbed her arm, shouted for her to keep her head low, and bustled her across to the railing. Rope ladders were flung over the sides, and down below, bobbing in the wavelets, floated dinghies.

Toward the stern of the ship, not too far away, she saw Margit scrambling down one of these ladders. Harding stood on the deck, looking about, his stance one of anxiety. Thérèse shouted and waved her arms, and she saw him relax as he waved back. He started toward her, but a sailor gestured for him to follow Margit into the lifeboat, where Althorp had already caught her and helped her to sit. Harding argued, but the situation was taken out of his hands. A sailor caught hold of Thérèse, and as Aimée yelped in protest, helped her onto the railing. All of Thérèse's attention became focused on finding and keeping her precarious footing on the swaying, knotted ropes.

As her slippered foot touched solid wood, another sailor already in the boat grasped her waist and steadied her, easing her down onto a seat. A man followed her down, holding the terrified Aimée under one arm. He handed the shivering mongrel over to Thérèse, and the little dog huddled against her mistress.

Thérèse craned her neck, peering about. In the growing light she saw Margit and Harding's boat pull away from the ship. At least they were safe! Althorp and Bosworth sat near them, gesturing frantically to her. She waved, signaling that she was all right.

And where was Charles in all of this? Was he here, in Lisbon, in the midst of the fighting? Or was he still out on his patrol? What if she were too late and he had already been killed by a French bullet . . . ? She could not bear to lose him! And if he didn't want her . . .

An eerie, sucking splash sounded close by, and Thérèse spun about. Her heart seemed to block her throat as the massive ship shifted and heaved farther so that it loomed over them at a precarious angle. The oarsmen, recognizing the inevitable, shoved off and drew with long strokes toward the shore. Sailors now jumped from the great boat's side to get as far from the ship as possible before it slipped beneath the water.

Chaos reigned. All across the estuary, little boats pulled toward the docks of Lisbon as the guns kept up their deafening barrage. The flotilla! Aghast, Thérèse recognized the French uniforms of soldiers crouching low in many of the rafts and dinghies that were frighteningly close. The wharves teemed with men hurrying back and forth, loading guns, fending off the attack. And all the while, the short, staccato rifle shots were punctuated by the explosion of cannon or large-bore guns.

Thérèse, cramped between two men, huddled down in her little boat, her eyes wide with the horror of battle. The rising sun made it easier to see, but the view that met her terrified gaze could not make her glad of that fact. How long had it been going on? It seemed like hours, though it could be no more than twenty, perhaps thirty, minutes.

"Head down, miss!" one of the oarsmen shouted, and she dropped low again. Where were Margit, Harding, and the others? Had they reached the safety of the shore? From a safer level, she scanned the turmoil that only hours before had been a peaceful harbor. There! She knew that green dress! Margit was safe on a dock, and that must be Harding, Althorp, and Bosworth scrambling out after her.

A sharp cry escaped one of her oarsmen. He came partway to his feet, his expression one of horror as he lurched forward with one hand groping ineffectually toward his shoulder. Blood seeped through his uniform from a bullet hole. He teetered and slumped toward the side of the little boat.

The other oarsman made a flying dive to catch him before he could go overboard, but the action proved too much for the overloaded craft. It tilted wildly, hung at a precarious angle as the churning wavelets beat it back, then flung over and capsized.

Icy cold water enveloped Thérèse as she was thrown clear of the overturning boat. She came to the surface, gasped for breath, and tried to shake the wet hair from her face so she could see. Which way . . . She floundered as she tried to find the shore. There! She started swimming, but it was so very hard to move, so hard to keep her head above water. . . . Something dragged her down—her heavy woolen skirts, soaking up water, pulling at her. . . . She gasped again, half a scream, half a desperate attempt to get air into her lungs as she slipped helplessly beneath the gray waves.

Chapter Twenty

Charles clutched the wooden railing of the dock as he stared across the estuary. The growing light revealed the fast-approaching flotilla, setting aglow the shiny buttons of the French uniforms. They made excellent targets, except the British soldiers were no longer able to shoot freely at anything that moved in the harbor. There were British sailors out there now, both sitting in dinghies and swimming in the dark waters, escaping from the supply ship that had been struck by enemy cannon fire. Even as he watched in concern, the boat heaved at an angle and began slipping beneath the surface.

The soldiers nearest Charles paused in their firing. The French flotilla came too close to the British dinghies! The waters of the harbor roiled with activity as the fleeing men struck out for safety.

The first of the enemy rafts touched the dock. French soldiers swarmed out onto the wooden platforms and up from the water's edge, launching themselves onto the hapless British, who surged down to stop them.

The naval commander, who stood at the rail beside Charles, shook his head. "I never thought they'd continue this assault!" His voice sounded grim. "They must know by now that their plot failed and that we're prepared for them!"

"Did you really think they'd give up?" Charles shot him a quick glance, his expression sardonic.

The commander nodded, for the moment bereft of words.

"Lisbon is too important to them . . . and to us. This is a battle to the death."

The commander's knuckles whitened as he gripped the rail. "May God help us all."

Charles, casting a quick look about, decided to offer his services to the Almighty and lend a helping hand. Signaling to a small group of soldiers nearby, he led them down to launch a counterattack.

How so many French soldiers could possibly have crossed the estuary was a mystery. Charles did not even spare a thought as to how the naval battle progressed in the sea beyond. He had his hands full enough of problems here. Reckless as ever, he dashed into the fray, his sword drawn, in time to prevent a Frenchman from stabbing a fallen British infantryman. Turning, he countered a parry from a French bayonet, lunged forward, and stopped short. Out of the corner of his eye he caught a glimpse of a blond man of medium height in civilian dress jumping from one of the French boats to the dock . . . *de Lebouchon.*

Suddenly the fight was no longer the French forces against the British. It was personal, a duel between just two men. It was Charles Marcombe, against Armand, Chevalier de Lebouchon.

A bayonet flashed and Charles swung to parry the thrust. He would have to finish up here before he got on with his own business. Grimly determined, he went to work clearing his path, until his small band earned a momentary respite.

Near him stood an officer leaning heavily on his sword as he breathed hard. Charles signaled his men, formally handed them over to the command of the officer, and looked about. Somewhere amidst the docks and wharves lurked de Lebouchon . . . and he was going to find him.

He took off, fighting as necessary, his rapid gaze searching the teeming waterfront. And there, less than twenty yards ahead on the dock, almost as if he waited, stood de Lebouchon. Charles cleared his path with a swipe of his sword and advanced. His aching shoulders heaved as his tired lungs sought more air.

De Lebouchon pulled back as if aware of the menace that approached. His gaze swept the dock and came to rest on Charles, who bore down on him, thrusting the fighting men from his path as if they were no more than inanimate objects. The puzzled expression in de Lebouchon's blue eyes cleared.

"Le Maniganceur?" He breathed the name as Charles came to a stop less than five feet away.

"The same. And this time without disguise."

Face-to-face at last, there was no doubt in either mind that this time one of them must die. De Lebouchon tossed aside his empty pistol and drew his sword. His cold eyes gleamed with murderous intent.

Charles gave a brief salute, which de Lebouchon copied sketchily. The Chevalier closed almost at once, pressing the already tired Charles, forcing the deadly battle. Thrusting hard, he drove his opponent back a pace.

Charles parried, countering the desperate attack that lacked any of the finesse of polite fencing. De Lebouchon was a formidable swordsman, but Charles knew himself to be one as well. He lunged, taking advantage of his greater height and longer reach.

But the Chevalier possessed a strength to match his compact build, and had the advantage of being fresh, while Charles had already fought hard that morning. De Lebouchon thrust again, advancing, and Charles found himself on the defensive.

He retreated a pace, holding the Chevalier off, searching for a weakness in his opponent's decisive attack. But inch by inch, de Lebouchon forced him backward along the dock. Perspiration dripped into Charles's eyes, blinding him, and his lungs fought for air.

A devilish smile lit de Lebouchon's countenance. The advantage was his, and he knew it. He could toy with *Le Maniganceur* as he pleased, for the man was tired at the start. Every succeeding thrust came with less precision, less speed, as the strain of the morning's work took its toll on Charles. De Lebouchon had only to wait, to bide his time.

Charles retreated another step, his muscles straining. His bad shoulder cramped, and a searing pain shot through the old wound, yet still he fought on. He took another step backward, only to find his foot in thin air. He wavered on the brink of a short flight of steps, lost his balance, and tumbled downward, rolling as he hit the splintered wooden planks below.

A soft, triumphant laugh escaped de Lebouchon. The man leaped down the four shallow steps, landing lightly beside the fallen Charles, and raised his arm for the thrust that would finish him off. Charles threw himself into another roll, came to his feet, and in one motion thrust with his sword and sent it flashing as he delivered a dangerous and deadly blow. De Lebouchon crumpled beside him, dead.

Charles came to his feet, breathing hard, staring down at the fallen man. A surging hatred filled him, for both the Chevalier and himself. Damn this war! And damn men like de Lebouchon! He backed away, repelled by the killing.

The noise and commotion he'd blocked from his mind during the duel penetrated his consciousness, dragging him back to a sense of the fighting that raged about him. Wiping the perspiration from his eyes, his grim, disgusted gaze swept across the chaos and carnage of battle. War was a bloody hell! How many widows and orphans would there be this night? And how many heartbroken girls, waiting for the eager young men who would never return to them . . . ?

He closed his eyes for a long, shuddering moment, then turned to gaze out over the harbor. Most of the boats were ashore now, except a little one that lay capsized not far from the damaged supply ship, whose prow sank lower in the water.

He stiffened, for someone clung to that dinghy, someone who stood in imminent danger of drowning! No one else seemed to have noticed. All at once, saving this one life became as important to him as killing de Lebouchon had been just a few minutes before.

Oblivious to the shots that rang out about him, Charles ran along the dock until he spied a fisherman's dory. Jumping into this, he cut it free with a swipe of his sword and rowed to the rescue, his head turned over his shoulder for guidance. It was a woman, and there was something beside her—an animal? He missed a stroke as he stared in disbelief. *Thérèse*. He could not be mistaken. *Thérèse and Aimée*.

Thérèse wiped a dripping strand of hair from her face, then grasped again at the overturned boat to keep her head from slipping beneath the surface. Charles . . . It was Charles, and he was safe, not killed or wounded! And he had come for her . . . ! She tried to call his name, but her mouth filled with the brackish water, choking her. Tears of exhaustion, relief, and joy mingled with the salty mire of the estuary on her cheeks.

"What the devil are you doing here?" He dropped the oars into their locks as he reached her.

How typical, that his first words should be sharp! She could almost laugh!

"What—what do you think?" She gasped for breath,

trying to keep the wavelets from splashing down her throat. *"Voyons,* I am trying not to drown!"

"Damn it, woman, I mean here in Lisbon! I left you at Torres Vedras!"

"I—I was going home!" With her elbow, she pushed at Aimée, trying to lift the little dog onto the hull of their boat.

"Unless you live under the harbor here, I'd say you took a wrong turning."

"How amusing."

He picked up an oar and sculled, turning the small dory so that he pulled up beside her. "Why didn't you wait for me? I told you I'd be back soon. Or couldn't you bear the prospect?" Hurt, chagrin, exhaustion all sounded in his voice.

"Can we not discuss this later?" She floundered toward him and half-lifted the shivering little Aimée from the water.

Charles grasped the dog and set her into the boat. She found her footing and indulged in a thorough shake, showering Charles with water from her shaggy coat. He threw her a glance of mild irritation, then returned his attention to Thérèse.

Reaching down, he caught her dripping hand and tried to pull her up. The boat tilted.

"Have you got weights tied to you?" he demanded. He pulled again, harder, which proved too much for the dory. The side dipped precariously low, hovered for a moment as water splashed over the side, then flipped upside down.

Thérèse pushed away, then grasped at her dinghy once again to keep from sinking. "Charles!" The scream tore from her throat and her frantic gaze searched the water.

He broke the surface, spluttering and gasping for breath. Thérèse reached out to him, but he was too far away. Aimée surfaced at her side, shook her dripping head, and yipped her protest at this turn of events. Charles stared at them and suddenly burst out laughing. For several moments he floundered in hilarity.

Thérèse regarded him with resignation, too exhausted to share in his amusement. "But of course, this is of all things the most delightful, to go swimming in the middle of a battle."

He nodded. "Of all the *ludicrous* . . ." he began, but could not continue, as another paroxysm of laughter got the better of him.

Thérèse felt her grasp on the dinghy slip. Her fingers clutched at the wooden spine as she managed to get her face above the water once more. "Charles!" she gasped. "You—you may think this is funny, but me, I am cold, and it is not easy to hold onto this boat!"

Still chuckling, he swam over and threw a supporting arm about her. Dragging her fully into his arms, he kissed her as thoroughly as possible, under the circumstances.

For one moment, the gunshots, the battle, even their precarious position faded from her mind as she clung to him, wanting never to let go. His hand crept around to the back of her neck and suddenly he pulled hard, tearing off the tiny buttons and separating the seam of the light wool gown. It came away with surprisingly little trouble.

"Charles!" She pushed away and stared at him, startled more by the insanity of his actions than by the laughter that still lurked in his dancing eyes.

"I am making you lighter, so you won't sink." He grinned at her, enjoying himself.

He finished the destruction of her gown and she felt the sodden material slip down, catch on her knees and feet, then fall away into the murky depths. At once, she rose higher in the water.

"Your shoes, next," Charles ordered, and she kicked these off. "Think you can swim to shore, now?"

They started off, and Aimée kept pace with them. Charles, in the lead, stopped abruptly and began to tread water. He brought his head up and looked about.

"The shooting's stopped!"

Thérèse caught up to him and gripped his shoulder for support. The sun shone down fully now, and she could see small groups of French soldiers standing with their hands on their heads, surrounded by the armed British troops. Across the estuary, the French cannon were silent. She could just glimpse the brilliant scarlet coats on that side as well.

They started swimming again, and in a few minutes they reached the dock. Charles boosted Aimée to safety and scrambled up after her. Turning back, he helped Thérèse up as well. She stood beside him, shivering, wearing only her thin muslin chemise, which clung revealingly to her shapely form. He could discover in himself not the least desire to look away.

She followed the direction of his gaze, and hot color flooded her cheeks. A quick glance about warned her that Charles was not the only man to regard her with interest. The dock seemed filled with soldiers, and their frankly admiring stares were mostly directed at her.

Charles, grinning broadly, looked about and spotted a stiff sailcloth. Grabbing this, he wrapped it over her shoulders. "I'd rather have no one look at you like that except me, if you don't mind."

Her color deepened even more. She looked down at the water that dripped into a large puddle at her feet.

He brought her chin up with his hand and his amusement faded. "Back to our discussion, if you don't mind. What were you doing on that boat? And don't bother telling me again you were going back to England. I want to know why!" Tension sounded in his voice.

She hesitated. Why did it matter so much to him? Was it his heart or his pride at stake? She couldn't tell! And she loved him so desperately. . . .

"I'm waiting."

"What did you expect?" she cried. To her consternation, her voice broke into a sob. "That I should sit there and wait for word to be brought to me that you'd been killed?"

"But I hadn't been."

"Not this time, but what of the next? Or the time after that?"

"Damn it, Thérèse, aren't you anticipating just a little? That has nothing to do with right now!"

"*Voyons,* you were nearly killed that last time, in Brighton!"

"Oh, my God . . ." He dragged her roughly into his arms and held her tight. "Did you think that by leaving, you could keep me alive?"

She buried her face in the shoulder of his coat. "I—I could not bear it any longer!" She gave up all pretenses as a racking sob set her shoulders quaking. "Oh, Charles! I want to be with you, but it is too terrible each time you take on a mission. To worry every moment, never knowing if this will be the time you will not return to me . . . !"

"Thérèse!" He ran a hand over her dripping golden curls, then gathered the sailcloth about him as well, joining her in the protective canvas cocoon. He pressed her shivering body closer against his own and held her as tightly as he could. "My poor darling . . ." he murmured against the soft hair behind her ear, then broke off with an irritated exclamation.

She heard her name called and with reluctance turned from the pungent but comforting aroma of his wet wool coat to see Margit and Harding running up to them. Margit's steps were almost dancing, and she held tightly to Harding's hand. Althorp and Bosworth followed more slowly.

"It is over, *voilà tout,* and we are all safe!" the girl exclaimed. Her eyes shone with excitement.

"I'm delighted to hear it." Charles's tone was short. "Harding, will you please . . ."

"Glad to see you made it back safely, sir," Harding interrupted. "Can't say as we haven't been worried about you." He reached for Charles's hand.

Charles disengaged one from the sailcloth, but kept the other firmly about Thérèse. "As you can see, I'm fine. Now, be a good fellow, please, and . . ."

"When we saw your boat go over like that, ma'mselle, I'll tell you . . ." Althorp broke off, grinning and shaking his head. "We didn't know what to do!"

"Someone might have gone back to help her." Charles wrapped his free arm around her on the outside of the cloth. His other hand, under the safe, concealing tent of fabric moved slowly over her still wet form, caressing gently.

A thrill raced through her and she risked the briefest of glances at his dark, glowing eyes, which danced with mischievous intent. Firmly she lowered her gaze and tried unsuccessfully to control the erratic leaping of her pulse.

"Bosworth," Charles said suddenly. "Take them off and see if you can get us all some breakfast. You'll need Harding for such a difficult task, I'm sure."

Harding turned his affronted gaze on Charles, caught his wink, and grinned suddenly. "Come on, Margit."

"But Thérèse, she is so very wet! She needs. . . ."

"She has all she needs. Come on."

Harding led the others off, leaving Thérèse staring in indignation after them. "What does he mean, I have all I need? I am cold and wet and hungry!"

"And nothing else?" Charles's wandering hand crept up her back, still caressing.

She turned toward him and subjected the top button of his coat to a thorough study. "These are all that I am able to take care of, *enfin.*"

"And what of me? Is there nothing I can give you?"

His voice, soft and enticing, tore at her heart. She swallowed hard, tried to keep her erratic senses and emotions under control, then abandoned the hopeless attempt.

"I knew on the boat, when those cannon began to fire, that I could not leave you!" She raised earnest eyes to meet his. "If only you will let me stay. I will not tie you down, *je vous assure*. I will not cling to you or make scenes of the most unpleasant whenever you must go!"

"Won't you? I'll be extremely disappointed if you don't." A soft laugh hovered in his voice.

"You will let me stay with you?" Pressed so close against him, her head somehow resting against his shoulder with the gentle touch of his lips on her hair, she could not withstand the desire that had radiated between them, like a palpable force, since the day they had met.

"Just try and leave me again!" His voice was hoarse with emotion and his arms held her so tightly she could scarcely breathe.

She rubbed her forehead against his squarecut jaw. "Only death . . ." She broke off, aghast at the appalling aptness of the traditional vow. "Oh, Charles!" she cried, and her shoulders trembled. "I—I don't . . ."

He set her slightly away so that he could stare down into her face. His own burned with intensity, almost anger. "Will you refuse me if I do not give up this life?"

"*Non.*" She whispered the word. "I am yours, whatever comes to us."

A smoldering fire danced in the depths of his dark eyes, together with something else, something that might have been humor. "And will you continue in the work with me?"

Her heart sank. It could only bring her unhappiness, but she never again could gather the strength to leave him. "*Oui.*"

He folded her against himself again and his lips brushed her hair. "Do you really love me that much?" Wonder filled his voice.

"More." Unheeded tears slipped down her cheeks.

"My beloved Thérèse!" His shoulders shook with the release of his tension and his deep chuckle sounded. "I am so sorry to disappoint you, but there will be no more missons for us. Could you bear to become a mere teacher?"

"A teacher?" Her brow creased in puzzlement.

"A teacher." He nodded, affirming his statement. "Wellington and I discussed the matter in great depth, and he agrees with me that our agents need much better training. And who is better qualified to provide it than two who have been serving in France for over five years?"

"You mean . . ." She choked out a sob of relief. "We will be training new agents? In England? Together?"

"If you do not mind." His voice barely disguised his soft laugh of enjoyment.

"We shall live where it is safe? We shall have no more adventures?" It seemed like the epitome of all her dreams.

"Well, not exactly." His tone held only apology.

Her expression sobered. "Tell me."

"I intend to enjoy a great deal of excitement and adventure." His soft breath stirred the hairs behind her ear. "The kind that only *you* can provide."

She gave herself over to the delicious sensations his words and actions roused in her. This was one adventure Charles would make sure she welcomed.

"But I fear you will not be Mrs. Marcombe."

She stiffened, but would not let him see how his words hurt, sending a stabbing pain through her. With difficulty, she controlled her voice. "I have said that I will not tie you down. You must be free, this I know."

His grip tightened about her until his shoulders trembled with the force. "Dear God, Thérèse, can you know me so little? Do you really think I would offer you *carte blanche?*"

"Then—then what is it that you want?" Uncertainty filled her with anguish and longing.

"You! As my wife! I love you too much for anything else!"

Laughter, happiness, joy surged through her to be replaced a moment later as her confusion resurfaced. "But if not Madame Marcombe . . ."

"I thought you'd help me decide. I hope you don't mind too much, but according to Wellington, there's some plan afoot by the government to ennoble me. Services to the crown, or some such nonsense. They intend to make me a viscount. Would you care to be *Lady* Marcombe? Or shall we select another title?"

Wasn't it like him to tease her so! Relief left her giddy, and her spirits soared to match his nonsensical mood. She tilted her head to one side and regarded those large brown eyes so filled with love and amusement. The last of her fears slipped away forever. Life with Charles Marcombe, Viscount Whoever, would never be dull.

"Marcombe?" He prodded her.

"Mais non." She shook her head. "You must be Lord Maniganceur."

"What?" He regarded her in mock reproof. "It lacks dignity. If we are to be viscount and viscountess, we must cultivate decorum!"

"Do you think we could?" She shook her head in dismay. "To me, it sounds of all things the most boring!"

"Life with you will never be that!" he declared with feeling, unconsciously echoing her thoughts. "How about Ranleigh? Or would you mind being named for the estate?"

"M'sieur le Vicomte de Ranleigh," she mused.

"No, it's a British title! I would be Viscount Ranleigh!"

She shook her head. "It is not *convenable*. Suggest to me something else."

The light that came into his eyes was her only warning. Before she could protest, he swept her up, sailcloth and all, into his arms. He silenced her objections by the simple expedient of kissing her until she was too breathless to speak.

"Do you intend to argue with every suggestion I make?" he demanded his eyes sparkling with enjoyment.

"Mais non, m'sieur," she responded meekly. She slid her arm about his neck and nestled her cheek against his still-wet shoulder. "You may make to me whatever suggestions you wish."

"May I, by God!" His deep laugh of triumph rumbled forth, sending a shiver of delighted anticipation through her. "We'll just see about that." Cradling her ever tighter in his strong arms, he strode off the now-crowded dock, oblivious of the appreciative stares of the onlookers.